c02750

CW01665982

'AC

COMPLY OR DIE

A DARK TIDES THRILLER

TONY HUTCHINSON

CHESHIRE CAT BOOKS LTD

Durham
County Council

7501087

Copyright © Tony Hutchinson 2018

Tony Hutchinson has asserted his right under the Copyright, Designs and Patents Act 1984 to be identified as the author this book.

All rights reserved. No part of this publication maybe reproduced, stored in a retrieval system or transmitted in any form or by any means, electronic, mechanical, photocopying, recording or otherwise without prior permission of the publisher.

This is a work of fiction and any resemblance to persons living or dead, or to actual events is purely coincidental.

Cover photograph copyright © Ben Hutchinson.

The book is published by Cheshire Cat Books Ltd
Suite 50-58 Low Friar Street, Newcastle upon Tyne, NE1 5UD.

ISBN 978-1-9164457-3-4

To Jean and Ken, Tanis and Tania.
Your lifetime of support makes everything possible.

CHAPTER ONE

Friday 13th December 2013

I LOVE FRIDAYS.

No lessons after 2.30pm, two-and-a-half hours in the town before catching the bus home.

My time.

Nobody at home knows I have those two-and-a-half hours.

My time.

CF. College Friday.

My time.

College is great; when I walk through those gates I can be whoever I want to be, talk to who I want, but like all 18-year-old girls, I love shopping. Well, window-shopping in my case, but hey, we can all dream.

I'm not allowed to go shopping with my college friends on a Saturday. Not allowed to go anywhere on a Saturday.

The only time I'm allowed to wear Western dress is when I go to college. Ridiculous. I was born in Seaton St George. I'm British.

I wear black trousers and white blouses for college, a black jumper in the winter. Whoppee-do. There's no uniform code, that's what I have to wear: uniform code according to dad. Somebody should remind him I'm British, but I wouldn't dare.

As soon as I get home it's the same routine... upstairs, changed, traditional dress, Western gear abandoned until I'm next at college.

I'd love a pair of jeans.

Love to go shopping with my mates.

I'm not even supposed to have white friends, but as long as I don't take them home, don't go out with them, don't go around their houses, it's okay. My parents accept I have to mix with them, for now.

I'm not allowed any of the things my friends take for granted. They go mental when their parents ask where they've been when they're coming home from clubs at five in the morning. 5am?! You must be joking. The milkman's started before they're home. I'm not allowed out after 10, if I'm allowed out at all, and even then only when I'm round one of my cousins.

I left secondary school with nine GCSE's and now I'm in my second year of A-levels. The college has better courses than the sixth form at school. I'm interested in philosophy and politics. I had hoped to do them at university.

'Had' being the operative word. That dream was crushed last week, crushed like a piece of Indian scrub under an elephant's foot. I've lost count of how many times I've relived the memory of it. What day it was. What time it was.

Apparently, old people remember where they were when Gazza cried and Diana died. Well I remember where

I was at 4.37pm on Friday 6th December 2013 – our kitchen.

I've got a mobile phone, but it's only so my parents and elder brother can keep in touch with me. Keep in touch? Stalk me more like. It's like my debit card. My dinner money and pocket money get put into my account but I wouldn't dare get cash from a machine. They'd demand to know why I needed the money, what I was buying. Drugs? Booze? So I use the card for everything and they check my account every day. Internet banking for them is spying without leaving the house.

But can you see how manipulative it all is? Aisha's parents must be very modern – she's got a phone and a debit card.

The phone? I'm not allowed to use it in the house. My father gives it to me before I leave for college. He's at work when I return, so my mother takes it off me and goes through all my messages, photos. Privacy settings? Don't make me laugh.

I'm a social amputee outside college, cut off from everything, and don't even ask about the college holidays. They're the worst, especially the summer; last year it was eight long weeks of traditional clothes and Bollywood movies. I once asked my white girlfriends, Gori they're called in Punjabi, have you any idea how long those films last? They're endless. My friends go bowling, walking in the park or by the sea, cinema, shopping. I'm a cross between a prisoner and a slave. I have to help my mother run around after my father and brother.

I wish I were a man. I'm a bloody servant to any men who visit, men in one room, women in the other. Can you believe that? In 21st-century Britain?

That's why I love College Friday.

Every night, when I'm in bed, before I go to sleep, I

dream of freedom. I can't imagine what it must be like to make your own choices. Some of my friends smoke. I know it's bad for you, but I'd love to try. I'd love a drink as well. My brother drinks. So does my father. All Sikh men drink. None of the women do. Not allowed, too shameful. If I could just drink one of their beers, or the whisky my father loves, just to say I tried.

If I wasn't talking in my head, I'd look around now, make sure nobody could hear; if I'm being totally honest, I did have a drink, and a smoke, the Tuesday after that Friday.

The heating broke in college so we all finished early, before lunch. I went round Bethany's, she's my bezzie, and had a can of lager and a cigarette. God, how do people smoke? It was disgusting, made me really dizzy. The lager was bitter and horrible but it was the fact I'd tried them, made my own decision that I didn't like them, that was the difference for me. Mind you, I've never chewed so much gum on the bus home.

I did get out once. It was amazing; at least it was at first.

Me and Bethany got invited to a party at a doctor's house. His daughter goes to college with us. She's Asian. My dad let me go, obviously because I was mixing with a doctor, but the GP is nothing like my dad and of course the three of us girls went out.

I wore some of Bethany's clothes. We're the same size. Size 8. She knew I'd be in a Sari. The only person at the doctor's to be wearing one; even his wife wore trousers and a jumper. I borrowed a short tartan skirt, more like a belt, and black leggings. I got to wear make-up. Bethany put that on for me. I wouldn't know where to start.

I was terrified that I'd bump into my brother, but the

girls talked me into taking the risk. Luckily I didn't see him or any of his friends.

The night didn't end well even though I was only drinking coke. I went all woozy and my legs wouldn't work. I've no idea why, but I was better after a lie down, although my head was banging for ages. I was okay the next day.

I was a bit panicky going home, but everything was sorted. The doctor dropped me off, told my parents I'd been very polite, had been no bother.

You see I can't do anything that might damage the precious family honour, the family Izzat. Girls carry the family honour. My brother will eventually have to marry a nice girl from India, but before that he can go out with English girls – "white trash" my mother calls them. He can go to pubs, clubs. Me? No chance. He could probably still go out with white girls after he's married the nice girl from India, as long as he keeps up appearances. Me? You must be joking.

He goes to university, but guess what? He still lives at home. Surprised? You shouldn't be. Do you seriously think he's going to move out? Who are you kidding? My mother, sister and me do everything for him. When he marries, his wife will do everything for him. Why would he move out?

Equal opportunities. No discrimination. Don't make me laugh.

Sons and daughters: same womb, different rules.

But going back to last Friday. The argument was massive, the biggest one we've ever had. We really went at it. I came home from college and straight upstairs to get changed. At 4.37pm (I feel my life will forever be determined by that moment, by those three numbers) my mother showed me a photograph of the man I am to marry. She deliberately told me on a Friday. All weekend to threaten me not to tell anybody when I went back to college.

I screamed at her: "I don't want to get married. I'm not some backward girl from an Indian village."

She slapped me across the face, screamed at me in Punjabi. I'm bilingual. I have to be. My mother can't speak a word of English. She doesn't have to. She doesn't know anyone white. All the years over here and she's never tried to integrate with anybody. Multi-culturalism? Not in my world.

My mother came from the Punjab to marry my father. It's somebody from her village who I have to marry. He's 31. He was 13 when I was promised to him. I was a baby. Apart from him being ugly, and I mean Quasimodo ugly, I don't want to get married. My parents want the wedding to take place next year. I want to finish college, go to university, and get a good job. My mother doesn't believe in education. Not for girls anyway. She says I know everything I need to know... how to wash, iron, clean, and make perfectly rounded Roti. What more could I need? Err hello – how about a life?

My father was born here. I wonder what it would have been like if he'd married someone from the UK, not necessarily white, but someone born here, like me, like my sister, who's 15 now.

We were making lentils last Sunday, mother and me. She was chopping fresh coriander. I was still in shock, still sulking. I asked her who would marry my sister, said no doubt it was already arranged. She started screaming at me, brandishing the knife in her hand. She called me a whore.

My mother, who came from a village outside Jalandhar, goes on about Izzat much more than my dad does.

We're going to India next year. We go every three

years. My mother wants to build a house there, a big house. You see plenty of them when you visit, all built by people living in England, all of them screaming "Hey, look at me, look how well I'm doing".

It's all about showing off. They have models on the roof, bigger than TV aerials. I've seen model planes on them. What's that all about?

We're Jats, you know, the top caste. Don't let people tell you it's irrelevant. My mother would go ballistic if I married someone from a lower caste. She constantly reminds people of our ranking down at the Gurdwara.

My brother's car registration number even ends in JAT; my mother bought it for her prodigal son.

It's about skin tone as well. I'm fairly light skinned. Chamars, the lowest caste, the lowest of the low who pick the shit up off the street in India according to my mother, are invariably dark skinned – a bad sign as far as my mother's concerned.

Next time you're out in an Asian area, keep an eye out for different skin tones, and check out how many JAT number plates you can spot.

I was looking forward to seeing my maternal grandparents next year. They have a farm – another thing my mother brags about – but now I'm worried that when I'm out there, my parents will force me to marry. You hear it happening to girls.

My friends at college said I should just say no to the marriage… yeah right, like it was that easy. They have no idea. Even saying no brings shame, *Behsti*, on the family. My friends have freedoms and choices I can only dream about.

They say if I'm out there and something bad happens, I should go the British Embassy. How? They have no idea how big the country is, and everybody would be out looking for me. Not just family, but the whole community.

They say I should run away and hide in the UK. I told my friends about the bounty hunters. They didn't believe me. Why would they? Who would believe that parents pay members of our community to hunt us down here in the UK? Read the papers, I tell them.

Everybody just open your eyes. Look around. It's not unusual for South Asian girls to be taken out of school, taken to India and Pakistan, forced to marry. It happened to Shazia down our street. She was left in Pakistan until she was pregnant. Came back with a kid. She was 16 when she came back. She was out there for over a year; only 14 when she went out. None of the authorities looked for her. She married a bloke who was 32. None of the authorities batted an eyelid when she turned up with a four-month-old baby. No one asked how old she was when it was conceived. All terrified of being called a racist so they look the other way. Racist? If I was white, they'd call it child abuse but I'm not, so they call it "cultural".

One girl was only 13 when she married. Thirteen! Married a man in his late 20s. Some of these girls are five. Yes, you heard me, five years old when they go out and get engaged. Some white people have an idea what goes on, but most haven't got a clue. As I said, those who have an idea don't want to get involved; hiding behind an "it's what they do" attitude. Think what would happen if white girls were taken out of school and married off... child protection and all that. Not us. We have to get on with it because "it's what they do".

I met Sukhvinder this afternoon. Sukhi to his friends. He's gorgeous. Drop dead. He's told me he loves me. His parents are dead. Killed in a car smash when he was 16. They were from the Punjab and they're Chamar. He lives in a rented flat. He's 22. I told him I love him, too. I think I do. He knows about my marriage. He says I should run away with him. Really? Where would we go?

He wants to hold my hand in town, but I always tell him no. Someone might see us. He wants to kiss, to kiss in public. I want to but I wouldn't dare.

Sukhi has a car so perhaps we could run but they would never stop hunting us down.

It's not like what Walter Cannon, that American physiologist I read about, said in the 1920s: fight or flight. We can try the flight, but we'd have no chance of winning the fight. I've come up with another phrase if I don't run: comply or die.

You probably think that sounds a bit over-dramatic. Check out the Internet. See how many honour killings there are.

Some people – politicians, women's groups, lawyers – don't like the 'honour crime' label. There's no honour in violence, no honour in murder, they say. Of course there's not, but they miss the point. What drives the violence is the honour code; how women are supposed to behave. They'd be better challenging the behaviour than arguing about what it should be called.

When we're told we have to marry, we have few choices. You heard me right the first time... run, comply or die. You don't believe me? As I said, read the papers.

Shopping was great this afternoon, walking around with Sukhi. I was just like the white girls at college. Well, for those two-and-a-half hours anyway. I didn't buy anything, any clothes or make-up. What would be the point? I'd never get to wear the clothes and, as I've already told you, I don't know how to put on make-up. Besides, taking things like that into the house would only lead to one thing.

My mother would go mental if I went home with a pair of jeans. Sukhi says if we were together, he would buy me jeans. I don't know how. He'd have to get a proper job first. He's got one here, part-time, but he'd have to give that up.

He walked me to the bus stop. It was cold and getting dark. As my bus came he bent down and kissed me on the lips. I forgot where I was. I stood on my tiptoes, put my hands around the back of his neck, pulled him into me, and pushed my tongue into his mouth. It was incredible but almost immediately I pushed him away.

Insanity. Absolute insanity. I had just snogged Sukhi at the bus stop!!

I giggled as I got on the bus and waved goodbye. I was grinning, blushing, giddy. It was true – I was floating on air. I dropped into the seat behind the driver.

Then I saw him standing under a lamp post staring at me. I locked my eyes on the floor. Shit shit shit!

My mum's brother. Uncle Gurmej.

He had followed my mother to the UK. One arranged marriage, in this case my mother's, and loads of family members end up coming. Control immigration? Dream on.

I took my phone out of my bag. My hands were shaking as I tapped out a text to Sukhi. If he wanted to run away with me, it had to be today. I would never be let out of the house again. Next week college finished for Christmas, but I wouldn't be there. They'd lock me in my room, keep me off college.

Then India and the wedding fast-forwarded.

I had to get home fast, had to pack. I didn't have much. Take a few clothes, a couple of photographs, one or two books, kiss my little sister one more time, get away before my dad came back, get away before my uncle got there and told them what he'd seen.

Run but run where? Other than going to India every three years I'd never left Seaton St George. I'd never been camping or in a caravan like the girls from school, never set foot in a hotel. I'd never even been in English restaurants. I had been to a few weddings: Sikh weddings, of course, with hundreds of people, but even then there was always the invisible code. Izzat. It dominates our lives.

Running away to a strange town with no money, no family or friends?

The fingers of my left hand had curled hard around the bright yellow pole below the red 'stop' button and squeezed until they went white.

Maybe I would be better off getting married.

I leaned forward and stared at the floor again.

Why couldn't I have the life other girls in this country have? I wouldn't go around getting drunk, being sick, that sort of thing. I'd be good, I told myself, like most of the English girls.

I am an English girl.

I just happen to be of Asian descent so I would never get the same freedom. I desperately wanted everything this country has to offer, but it would never happen.

I didn't want to run away from my family, but what choice did I have? I didn't want to marry Quasimodo. And my uncle had just seen me kissing a boy in the street.

This was going to be the longest bus ride of my life.

CHAPTER TWO

Saturday 12th April 2014

'We just want you to come home. Whatever it is, we still love you. Please, we are begging you, come home.'

Detective Chief Inspector Sam Parker and Detective Sergeant Ed Whelan were watching the TV in the corner of the Major Incident Room, a huge deep black TV, a throwback to an earlier time. Nobody could remember who brought it into the office.

The father, dressed in a black shirt and black turban, spoke to the camera. 'We are worried about you. There's nothing to be afraid of. Please get in touch, please come home.'

He wiped his tears with a blue handkerchief.

'How long she's been missing now?' Sam said, her eyes shifting from the TV, glancing at the detectives watching the screen, tin-foil containers on their desks, the remains of chicken fried rice, beef satay, beef curry, floating in a sea of reddish oil, the lingering aromatic smell a clue to what they'd eaten.

'Four months,' Ed said. 'Look at him. All tears, head down. And her, the wife, been in the UK what, 20 years, still doesn't speak English. Look at her dress, totally traditional. And they'd have you believe that all's well, the daughter's got nothing to be afraid of, that they've integrated, that she can have her own life. Bollocks.'

The top of Mrs Bhandal's head filled the screen, thick black hair with streaks of grey. Not once had she looked up since she sat on one of the three chairs behind the long table.

The family solicitor, Jill Carver, had organised the press conference in a small hotel on the sea front of Seaton St George. Starting the conference at 11am made sure it was featured on the lunchtime news, but more importantly, it gave Carver an element of control; the bar had to be vacated by 11.30am in preparation for the Saturday lunches.

'As usual Carver thinks she's pulling all the strings,' Sam said. 'Organising it for a Saturday, typical slow news day. Maximum coverage for her clients.'

They watched the husband again, listened to him as he read from a piece of paper, his index finger following the words like a small child learning to read.

'Some of the reports by the media, fuelled by the inept police investigation into our daughter's disappearance, have been hurtful. We would never harm our children and to say such things is terrible. I was born in this country. My wife came here when we married. We love our children dearly. We just want our daughter to come home, to enjoy all the things the UK has to offer.'

'Yeah right,' Ed said, rolling his eyes.

'What's up?' asked Sam.

'I'll tell you after this has finished.'

'Please, please, just come home.' The father buried his hands in his head. Cameras flashed.

Jill Carver spoke. 'This is a very emotional time for Mr and Mrs Bhandal, a very stressful time. You heard their appeal today.'

Flashlights bounced off her dark hair.

'All they want is for their daughter to return home. She has been missing for four months now. They cling to the hope that she is alive and well.'

She paused, looked around the room, picked up her Montblanc pen and pointed it at the assembled media. Aggressive authority replaced the tones of empathy.

'They have answered all questions asked by Eastern Police, but they feel that the police investigation is focussing on the family and not investigating Aisha's…'

'Finally somebody mentions her name,' Ed pushed his chair away from the desk.

'... disappearance,' Carver continued. 'My clients are peaceful, loving people who abhor the suggestion that has been played out in the media, fuelled, to use my client's phrase, by the inept police investigation, that this is an honour crime. This is a case of a young 18-year-old who has gone missing…'

'And was missing for three days before they reported it,' Ed shouted, jumping out of the chair.

'And my clients are as desperate as any other parents would be to have their daughter safely returned to the love and support of her family,' Carver finished.

The father spoke again.

'Please, please, Aisha, just come home.'

Jill Carver stood up.

'Thank you everybody. As you can see my clients are very distressed, and answering any questions that you may have would just add to that. Thank you once again for coming.'

Despite the barrage of questions that followed, she ushered the couple out of a side door.

'Well Carver wrote that speech for him,' Sam stood up.

'Absolutely every word,' Ed added, following her to her office.

'Go on then,' Sam said, sitting at her desk. 'Enlighten me.'

Ed pulled out a chair.

'He talks about Aisha being able to do what she wants. You saw them. They're traditional Sikhs. No way will she be able to do what she wants. Let's see if there's an arranged marriage in the background. He's obviously had one.'

'How do you know?'

'C'mon. He's born here. She's been here 20 years. They're in their 40s. Aisha's 18. Wife comes over from rural Punjab. Probably arranged when they were kids, maybe even when they were babies. Families like that stick to the traditional way. Arranged marriages. Bring someone over from India, guaranteed entry to the UK, the better life.'

'What's it like over there, over in India?'

'Where they come from? Rural Punjab. Best way to describe it is how I imagine England to have been in the days of Robin Hood, only less rain and more heat: oxen pulling ploughs, life very slow, water drawn from wells. It's different to the cities, different to Delhi, Mumbai, different to Goa. The wife's family, from what I remember, lived in a small village about an hour from Jalandhar. Next to the village where his family come from.'

'It's a place Tristram and I always fancied,' Sam said. 'Before…you know?'

'I know.' Ed paused, waiting for Sam's glassy eyes to lose the film of water. 'There's no doubt it's a fascinating place.'

He slowly shook his head from side to side as he recalled his visits to India. 'Delhi's packed. Every time you turn a corner it's like St James' Park emptying, people flashing their white teeth, brown eyes staring at you, curious about you. Then there are the smells... spices, curry… and the bright clothing, a Picasso on a canvas of thick, grey exhaust fumes.'

'Very poetic,' Sam smiled.

'But here's the thing Sam, Jalandhar is 11 hours by road from Delhi. Eleven hours on the same road, the GT road, a road running the length of the country built by the British during the days of the Raj. There are even bloody songs about it.'

'Like Chris Rea's 'Road to Hell'.'

'Trust me,' Ed said. 'No way does the M1 compare to that road. Any girl born in this country, sat in the back of a car, looking out of the window, driving up there with family for an arranged marriage, must be absolutely terrified.'

Ed looked away, picturing the scene: the three lane Grand Trunk road, cars overtaking, undertaking, braking for carts pulled by cows, scooters carrying father, wife, and as many kids as they had. The heat. The dust. The never-ending road bordered by fields and occasional petrol stations and food outlets, the sense of enormity. A British-born girl taken there for a forced marriage had no chance. Where would they go? He was a well-travelled middle-aged detective, not some girl shy of her 19th birthday, who'd never been out of her home town, other than to visit relatives in either England or India. These girls would be overwhelmed, helpless.

Sam leaned back in her chair and stretched her legs.

'Is that your opinion? Forced marriage?'

'Been at the back of mind since the day she went missing,' Ed told her. 'She's the eldest of two daughters. Mum and dad must have had arranged marriage. If people are happy with that arrangement, fine. Let's be right, it's no more of a lottery than meeting someone at work or in a pub.

'But when the girl doesn't want to go through with it, when she is forced, that's a different issue. There'll be so many pointers in the family. I wouldn't mind having a look at the file to be honest.'

Sam thrust herself upright, coming to 'attention' in the chair.

'Well that's good. We've been asked by Monica Teal, our new ACC, to have a look at it and I'm reckoning you can provide some investigative pointers. You've been on national working parties, plus there's your personal insight. Giving the investigation another coat of looking at is not going to hurt. And be honest, you love getting one over Jill Carver as much as I do.'

'Why do I think I've just walked into a big trap?' Ed said.

'And there's an 18-year-old who could do with your help right now. Nobody has a clue where she is.'

Ed shook his head. 'Unless she's got clean away, and I hope she has, she's dead'

'God I hope not. Look, I'll give you Bev Summers and Paul Adams. That should be enough to be going on with. We can look at staffing once we know where we are splodging. Just get a feel for what's been done up to now.'

'Honour crimes are a nightmare to investigate,' Ed said. 'Everybody'll just clam up. And if she's dead, here or in India...'

His words hung in the air, that time-standing-still moment between pulling the ripcord and the chute unfurling.

Sam rubbed her face and stood up.

'As JFK once said, we don't do these things because they're easy, and let's be right, if the job was easy, we wouldn't be getting it.'

'True enough," Ed nodded.

The meeting of the Mortimers was under way in the Jolly Roger. Steve Donnelly, the licensee, watched the group of five in matching blue T-shirts with their pathetic logos, sink another round of shots. Did this lot ever do any studying? Did they ever make it to a lecture? Forty grand's worth of debt just to learn how to be a piss-head. Christ, he had regulars who been on the dole for years who were piss-heads, but they'd never felt the need to undertake a three-year degree course to learn how to do it.

Mortimers might be good for trade, but shots at 2pm, the Newcastle game televised at 3pm thanks to some foreign channel and young girls piling in later was a Molotov cocktail on a smoking fuse; more Bloody Brawl than Bloody Mary. At least he'd had the foresight to put a couple of bouncers on. Pay weekend and 'The Toon' playing away guaranteed a till drawer like Tigger on crack cocaine.

This lot of juveniles would keep themselves in order while the match was on – too many hard lads who would sort them out if they stepped out of line – but later, once the football lot had gone, and the night crowd came out, it would be different. These gobshites had no manners around young women. If they spoke to his daughter like they spoke to some of the girls in here, he would happily lose his licence and his liberty.

The final whistle and the football crowd shuffled out, shoulders slouched in resignation at another away defeat.

The pub moved to the transitional stage between daytime and evening drinkers. Except for the group of five Mortimers in the corner. Their table was littered with pint glasses, shot glasses, empty crisp and salted nut packets, and they were getting louder. Steve Donnelly considered refusing to sell them any more drink, but they were filling his till with their student loans. Besides, when did the police ever do licensing checks these days? Not since the old days.

He remembered the dedicated police-licensing department checking up all the time in the 1980s. When that department closed down, a uniform Sergeant and the local PC carried out spot checks. Now? Nothing. Financial cuts. Government austerity. Whatever the cause, there were no visits these days. So he just kept taking their money and would sort any drink-fuelled trouble later.

The first group of girls came in about 7pm, five students dressed for a Saturday night out in their short shirts, skimpy tops and high heels, young girls out with their friends and not bothering anyone.

He watched three of the Mortimers swagger unsteadily over to the group. The lads said something. He couldn't hear what. The DJ was into his third track of the night, Pharrell Williams belting out Happy. He watched the tall redhead mouth 'Fuck Off'.

The boys walked away, exchanging the usual juvenile comments he'd heard all his life... 'dirty lesbos', 'dog rough anyway'. Fashions might change but whether it was the platforms and flares of the 70s or the jeans and T-shirts of today, the abuse was the same.

By 9pm the pub was bouncing, bass booming and bodies bumping. Strobe lighting completed the transformation, the pub morphing into a nightclub. The Mortimers had left their seats and were now staggering around, incoherently speaking to girls who weren't interested in listening. When a couple of the group, mouths open, tongues out, tried to pull two young women towards them, Steve decided enough was enough. He signalled to the doormen.

The bouncers approached and asked them to leave. One of the group, the biggest who obviously fancied himself with the ladies and in a fight, held his ground.

'Fucking make us.'

The odds were not good for the student. Billy, in his 50s with a black leather jacket, broad shoulders and huge arms, had worked the doors in most of the rough establishments in town. He remembered the old days before the advent of the Door Supervisors course and the three-year licence. He would have loved to smack the arrogant little prick on the spot. But there were too many cameras and the risk to his badge, and his employment, was too great.

'Come on then. Fucking make us,' the student repeated, his forearms flexing, fists clenching.

Customers moved away, an unspoken no-go circle of space between punters and antagonists appearing.

Donnelly shouted 'reinforcements on their way' as he put down the phone.

The younger bouncer moved in... 6ft 8in, slim, and 19 years old. He leaned in towards the group's apparent leader.

'We don't want to make you, we've asked you nicely. One way or the other you are leaving, whether that's you walking out, us throwing you out, or somebody bringing a stretcher to carry you out. I don't care. But you're leaving. I haven't had a drink, you have. I've had a good Thai kickboxing sparring session this afternoon. Warmed me up nicely.'

'Just leave it Jack,' one of the others in the group said.

'Yeah, let's just go,' another added.

'Listen to your mates,' the tall, young bouncer said.

'Fuck them.'

Three started to walk away; one remained with the aggressor in a show of solidarity.

Again the tall bouncer spoke.

'Just us now. Your mates are heading out.'

The aggressor turned away, picked up a half-drunk pint from one of the empty tables and threw the beer over the young bouncer.

Billy stepped in.

'You pompous little shit. You'll pay for that.'

He grabbed the beer thrower's arm.

'You'll not pay now. Too many cameras, arsehole, unless you swing for me, then the cameras will show self-defence. But you will pay.'

The young bouncer flicked beer from his face and smiled.

The last two blue shirts with the daft logos were escorted off the premises.

Outside as the group staggered away, the aggressor had to have the last word. 'I'll get you two later.'

Billy nodded and stretched his arms in a come-on-then stance.

'Yeah right, little boy. I'm bricking it.'

The young doorman just kept smiling.

CHAPTER THREE

'THERE's no money for overtime, you know that,' Sam told him, walking to her car.

'Yeah I know, but we may as well make a start tomorrow,' Ed said. 'I've had a word with Paul and Bev. We'll just take another day off later.'

'How many lieu days have you got now?' Sam asked.

'Forty-odd, just like everybody else. What do you do? Just because there's no money doesn't mean the job stops. We've got an 18-year-old missing here. I'll feel better myself knowing I tried. I just wish they'd involved us earlier... It'll only take a couple of hours tomorrow, then we'll hit the ground running on Monday.'

'Okay then,' Sam said, opening the door of her Audi. 'Anything you need, give me a shout. I'll look forward to a briefing on Monday.'

'Much planned for tomorrow?'

Sam shrugged. 'Nothing. Lazy day. Can't even go out for lunch with Bev now that you've talked her into coming in.'

'Sorry about that,' Ed said.

'Don't worry. Give me a day to catch up. I'm doing a short literature course at the uni. Discovering some of the literary greats... Hemingway, Dickens, George Orwell and... '

'All animals are equal, but some animals are more equal than others,' Ed quoted Orwell with a grin.

'You never cease to amaze me,' Sam said, closing the car door.

All animals are equal, Ed thought as he watched her drive out of the HQ car park, unless you happened to be a young girl growing up in a traditional Sikh family. Then you weren't equal. Then you were a second-class citizen.

He drove home, considering what indicators he would look out for tomorrow with regards to the missing girl. He'd sit down with Sue tonight, explain what was happening, perhaps get her input. Ellen was away for the weekend.

He had tried to spend more time with his wife, but whatever he did would never be enough. Truth of the matter, she had never wanted him to rejoin the police. If she'd had her way, he would still be in her family's business, and while they were financially comfortable, had he stuck with the firm, as she kept reminding him, they'd be millionaires.

Convincing Sue money wasn't everything, that sanity was more important, was an ongoing battle.

Sunday 13th April 2014

Ed was drinking tea and unwrapping a two-fingered Kit-Kat when the office phone rang. He was reading the Missing From Home file while he waited for Paul and Bev.

'Anything interesting overnight?' Sam's voice came down the line.

'Thought you were having a lazy day.'

'I always ring control room when I'm off just to see what's happening. Easier than trying to catch up when I come back in, and it gives me an early heads up if there's a potential job for us. I knew you were in, so I thought I'd ring you. I'm wandering around the garden centre at the minute.'

Ed swallowed a piece of biscuit.

'Never had you down as a Charlie Dimmock.'

He scrolled through last night's incidents.

'Quiet night by all accounts, certainly on the crime front. There was a fatal. Traffic dealing. Uniform in Seaton St George had a bit of a job. Student fell into the river. Pissed by all accounts.'

'Another one?' Sam said. 'How many's that? Five in six months? Will they ever learn?'

'Hey, it's always somebody else's fault,' Ed said. 'Council's for not building railings, pubs for doing 2-for-1 drinks, ours for not having foot patrols along the riverbank and cops in boats. Everybody's fault except the students for throwing more down their neck than they can handle.'

'Male or female?'

'Male. Not formally identified yet, well not according to the Control Room Incident Log. Has a driving licence in the name of Jack Goddard, student card in same name, University Seaton St. George.'

'Who's dealing?'

'The bold Inspector Wright.'

'Why need Britain tremble?'

'As much as I'd like to talk about Inspector Never, I've got to go, Bev and Paul have just walked in.'

Bev Summers and Paul Adams were both well-respected members of the Murder Investigation Team. Paul was a relatively new addition, a young ambitious officer. Bev joined the job at 18 in 1991 and wore her wrinkles with pride.

All three of them were casually dressed in jeans and shirt.

'I've got the Misper file,' Ed said. 'I suggest we get to know what's in that and go from there. Sam wants a full briefing in the morning. You both know my views. They haven't changed since she went missing. I've always had a bad feeling about this… so get the kettle on and let's make a start.'

'What we looking for?' Paul said.

'I'm interested in the family,' Ed told him. 'What are the dynamics? And I want to get the sequence of events clear in my mind. From there we can look at an investigative plan.'

The three of them were standing by the window, kettle on the windowsill, desks and computer terminals filling the long HOLMES room.

'See Newcastle managed to keep it down to one,' Bev said, like Ed, a life-long supporter.

'You know,' Ed said, 'Where are we now? 2014. Twelve years ago I was watching them in the Champions League. I went to Barcelona, Milan... '

Bev interrupted: 'You'll never see a Mackem in Milan.'

Ed smiled. 'Dead right. The nearest Sunderland ever get to Europe is Southampton away but that's the same for us these days. Beaten at Stoke. To think Bobby Robson got sacked for finishing just outside the top four.'

'Did you say you wanted another tea?' Paul asked, living proof not all North East men were football fanatics.

'Please.'

The door burst open.

'Tea on?' Sam Parker marched into the room.

'I thought you were having a lazy day?' Ed said.

'No plants took my fancy and I finished my Hemingway book last night, so I'm on track with my course work. Thought I may as well come in. You said it'll take a couple of hours, so here I am. Save you having to brief me in the morning. No sugar for me, thanks Paul.'

Paul nodded.

'Which Hemingway?' Ed asked.

'What? Oh. 'For Whom The Bell Tolls'.'

'You can't beat a bit of Spanish Civil War,' Ed said.

'Maybe I should take you along to my course, what with your knowledge of Orwell and Hemingway.'

'Don't you think I spend enough time with you here without spending more when I'm off?'

They both laughed.

Tea drunk, last night's TV discussed, the four of them sat around Sam Parker's desk.

'Okay,' she said, 'What have we got, Ed?'

'Aisha Bhandal. 18 years. Goes to college Friday 13th December 2013. Leaves college at 2.30pm... '

'Anyone superstitious?' Sam said.

All three shook their heads.

'Normally gets home at 5.30... '

'Sorry Ed.' Another interruption from Sam. 'As a matter of interest, do Sikh's celebrate Christmas?'

'Over here they do,' Ed said. 'They're not Muslims. Different religion all together. But, and this is the big but, don't go thinking it's just Muslims who have the culture of arranged, and as a consequence of that, forced marriages. It's not.'

Ed picked up his mug.

Sam looked at Bev and Paul.

'Do you both understand the difference between an arranged marriage and a forced marriage?'

'Think so,' Bev said. 'One's with consent, one's not.'

'That's about the size of it,' Ed said, 'in its most simplistic terms. In the main it's girls, although about 15% of reported cases are male.'

'Really?' Paul took a pen from his pocket.

Ed nodded. Most people coming at the issue for the first time never thought about it happening to men.

'Really,' Ed said. 'Think of homosexuals for starters. Homosexuality is frowned upon. That could be a trigger for a forced marriage, but there are others.'

Sam pulled her chair closer to the desk.

'You said in its most simplistic terms?'

Ed nodded. 'Bev's right, but the girl who agrees, who consents just to keep the family happy or consents through overt or covert pressure, is that arranged or forced?'

'Fair point,' Sam said.

'I've read Davinder's statement, the dad,' Ed said. 'He describes a happy family. Aisha goes to college on that Friday morning and is not seen again. The college confirm she was there that day and left after lessons finished. Like I said, 2.30pm.'

'Any comments on the family in the file?' asked Sam.

'Not really,' Ed told her. 'They haven't asked the right questions to be fair. A PC has asked about honour, but in a bull-in-a-china-shop way. That's what the family latched on to in the press conference.'

Ed paused. 'Look I'll formulate some questions. The father is saying they embrace the British way of life, but there are ways we can test that because I don't believe him.'

'Okay. Anything else?' asked Sam.

'Yes. Aisha's captured on CCTV walking around the

shopping centre. That footage was used in our TV appeals but it doesn't sit right with me.'

'Why?' Sam asked.

'I'm not sure. I'm wondering if her parents knew she finished early. Her friends from college say she was a nice girl, but never met them outside college. Is that Aisha's doing or her parents? I fancy the latter.'

'Who was the guy she was last seen with?' Sam asked.

'In the shopping centre? Believed to be Sukhvinder Sahota. He's not been seen since that day either.'

'Has he been reported missing?' Bev piped up.

Ed shook his head.

'He's a student too. No next of kin on his student file. He owns a Fiesta though, so we've flagged that up on the PNC.'

The Police National Computer would allow every force to know Eastern were interested in the car.

'So, is she last seen in the shopping centre?' Bev said.

'Yes. We don't know where she goes from there. The cameras outside the centre are pretty sporadic.'

'Have they all been checked though?' Sam demanded.

Ed's eyes were moving about like a spectator at a tennis match.

'Apparently.'

'There's the first line of enquiry,' Sam said. 'I want all the CCTV doing again.'

Paul grimaced. Someone was going to get that shit job, and around this table, as the youngest in service, he was odds-on favourite.

'Okay,' Ed said. 'One of her friends at college, Bethany...' Ed flicked through the few statements attached to the file. 'Bethany Stevens. She says Aisha had mentioned a marriage, and how she was worried about going to India, but of course the family denied that.'

'Let's revisit Bethany,' Sam said, 'and at some point, Ed, you and I are going to introduce ourselves to Mr and Mrs Bhandal.'

'If the answer does lie within the family, there are a couple of potential triggers here,' Ed said.

'Go on.' Sam stood and walked to the window.

'The boy she's with has not been found. The suggestion is that either they ran away together, or he has caused her harm. From the family point of view, walking in town with a boy is shameful behaviour, affects the family Izzat.'

'Sorry?' Paul looked up from his writing pad.

'Izzat. Honour. That could be a trigger for the family to cause her harm, or spirit her away. The other is the fact that she's even in the town. The question has never been asked, but I have a feeling her family thought she was at college. I suspect she never told them college finished early on a Friday.'

'Why would she do that?' Bev asked.

'Buys her some freedom. You have no idea the life some of these girls lead. They're exposed to Western society, Western freedoms, on a daily basis, when they go to school or college, but when they go home, it's like stepping back in time. They're back in rural India, back to being second-class citizens.'

'Poor kids,' Sam said, turning to look out of the window: bright blue sky, wispy cirrus clouds, and contrails from a commercial aeroplane. She hoped Aisha was looking up somewhere, enjoying the sunshine.

'What a life. What was the reason the family waited until Monday before reporting her missing?'

'This is a huge indicator that something's not right,' Ed said. 'Her father told the police the family thought she must have gone to stay with friends for the weekend. Without them knowing about it? Not a cat in hell's chance would they allow that to happen. Not look for her? She was allowed to stay out all night? Without her telling them? No chance. Families like that control their daughters. She wouldn't be allowed out for the weekend even if she asked their permission. They would fear being talked about in the Gurdwara.'

Ed saw the puzzled look on Paul's face.

'Sikh temple…the boy, the shopping centre, the deceit about college finishing early on a Friday, any one of those is enough for them to kill her.'

'Seriously?' Paul said.

'Girls have been killed for wearing jeans, make-up, becoming too westernised, having a mobile. Izzat is more important to these people than their own kids. Unless Aisha managed to make a run for it, we're looking for a body.'

CHAPTER FOUR

Inspector Mick Wright was determined to use the death of Jack Goddard to improve his reputation.

He'd already organised a 'Special' – a post-mortem conducted by a Home Office Forensic Pathologist. It would take place later that morning. Forget the cost. It would come out of the Major Incident budget, out of Sam Parker's budget, but she couldn't argue. A young man dead in the river. A fall or something more sinister? He was just being thorough. Never again was Parker going to criticise him.

He hated the CID, a bunch of poseurs and piss-heads. Uniform did the real work, around-the-clock policing, not just cherry-picking jobs. CID got everything they wanted – staff, equipment, the lot. On Jack Goddard's death it was him and two PC's. If Parker were doing it, she'd have a full team.

It was the same when he'd been on the Accident Unit as a PC. He'd deal with a fatal collision alone. They'd have an army on a murder. Why did society treat road death victims as the poor relation to murder victims? Try explaining that to the family of a teenager killed in his mate's car while the driver walked away.

Jack Goddard was the same age as his son, went to the same university. He'd ask his son tonight whether he knew him. West Midlands Police delivered the death message in the early hours to Jack's parents. Fortunately Jack had not changed the address on his driving licence.

Mick had spoken to Clive Goddard on the telephone, a short, difficult conversation. Weren't they always? His parents were already discussing emptying his digs. Distraught, they were en route from Birmingham. They had provided Jack's student address. He must remember to update the message, certainly before the likes of Nosey Parker got wind of it.

He read the statement from Alex O'Connell again. He didn't want to miss anything.

At 4.05am I was walking along the south-side tow path by the river after a night out with my friends.

He skim read the friends' names. It never ceased to amaze him why young girls walked home in the early hours along a river tow path. Alcohol usually had something to do with it, although the officer who took the statement had said Alex wasn't too drunk.

I was walking in a westerly direction towards Stanhope Road. I was texting my friends Charlotte Swains and Tracey Davies who had 'pulled' in The Jolly Roger. I wanted to make sure they were safe.

I looked up from my phone and my attention was drawn to something in the river. It was floating, but had got snagged in the weeds on the opposite bank to where I was stood.

I immediately knew it was a body. It was approximately six metres away. There is street lighting, and my view was unobstructed. The body was floating face down in the river. It appeared fully clothed, but the T-shirt had ridden up at the back. I couldn't tell whether it was male or female, although by the size I suspected it was a male.

Mick Wright shook his head. What a waste.

At no time while I was on the tow path did I see anyone else until the arrival of the police. I did not hear anything untoward.

At the time I was wearing a red sleeveless silk top, black shorts, and silver thigh-high boots.

At least she would be easy to eliminate if anybody else on the tow path mentioned seeing her.

Mick Wright scribbled in his book: no follow-up witnesses as a result of Alex's statement, no CCTV on the tow path. His phone rang. The pathologist was at the mortuary.

'Do you know Mick Wright's doing a Special?' Sam asked, returning from the toilets. 'He's just rang me.'

'Know nothing about it,' Ed said.

'It would have been nice if he'd ran it past me before he spent a few grand of my budget. I'd have said yes. Can't be too careful, especially with all the attention these student deaths are getting in the Post.'

The Seaton Post had until quite recently been an evening paper, but like so many provincials it was now on the streets in the morning. Cost savings no doubt.

'At least Darius hasn't gone along with the serial killer theory bandied about by a lot of the students,' Sam said.

'Darius Simpson,' Ed grinned. 'The Seaton Post's intrepid sleuth who swoons at the mere mention of your name.'

'Behave yourself.'

'Anyway, he knows better than to print garbage.

Students trying to get police patrols on the tow path. We all know why they fall in.'

Sam's mobile rang.

'Hi Julie… yeah that's fine. Thanks for the call… yeah keep them right.'

She ended the call and looked at Ed.

'Julie Trescothick's the Senior SOCO doing the PM. She just wanted to make sure we knew about it.'

'Good girl is Julie,' Ed said. 'Right, back to Aisha… I think we should also re-interview her friends at college.'

'Agreed,' Sam said. 'Bev, can you start that off. Get their names. Let's start revisits first thing. Paul, grab the CCTV.'

Paul raised his eyebrows and nodded. He knew he'd cop for that job.

'Ed, let's go into my office.'

Sam sat on her chair. 'Still think she's dead?'

Ed spoke as he pulled out a chair.

'The more I read, the more I find out about it, yes, unless she got away. If she got away, she might be okay. Whether they'd send bounty hunters after her, who knows.'

'Bounty…would they? Send bounty hunters?'

'People in that community get paid to track missing girls down. It's not unheard of.'

'Jesus, it's a different world.'

'It is,' Ed said. 'I see from the Misper file her phone's not been used since she went missing, and what little money she had in her account's not been touched. Her debit card's not been used. Not good signs with normal Missing from Homes, but in Aisha's case potentially the opposite. She'd be too scared to leave any sort of trail. She'd know they'd be coming after her.'

'Hospitals?'

'All checks negative according to the file.'

Sam dug her cigarettes out of her handbag.

'Jesus, Ed, what sort of parent even contemplates hurting their own child?'

'Not one you'd relate to. None that most people in this country would relate to. But we're not talking about most people.'

'Pass me her photograph please.'

Sam looked at Aisha, a young girl sat on the sofa in her living room, wearing what looked like college uniform.

'She looks like every other young girl in the country, happy, a zest for life, looking forward to the future.'

'Notice how the family provide a picture of her wearing school uniform?' Ed said.

'It's not so unusual,' Sam told him. 'Some parents, it's the only photograph they have of their kids.'

'Agreed, but in this case, bet your bottom dollar, it's the only photograph they have of her in Western dress,' Ed said. 'Giving us a photograph of her in a sari doesn't back up their claim of her being integrated, able to go to her mates for the weekend without telling them.'

'But they all wear saris and traditional dress.'

'Of course they do, at weddings, special occasions, family gatherings, but not every day. Walk the streets. See how many young Sikh girls are wearing jeans, tracksuits, whatever. I can guarantee that didn't happen with Aisha. Just look at the way her parents were dressed on the TV.'

Sam's mobile rang again.

'Hi Julie…shit… okay…thanks… yeah. Twenty minutes. Cheers.'

'Julie Trescothick,' Sam said. 'Jack Goddard may have been pissed, we'll get toxicology on that, but his death's not a case of a drunk stumbling into a river.'

Ed looked at Sam. Many cops got over-excited when

something out of the norm occurred. Not Sam. In the main she was unflappable.

‘He’s got a depressed fracture at the back of his skull, caused by something like a ball hammer. Easily missed at the scene under his thick hair.’

‘Could he have hit something in the river?’ Ed asked.

‘Always a possibility, but he hasn’t drowned. He’s been asphyxiated.’

‘Really?’

‘There’s a tiny piece of plastic in his mouth. It’ll need more tests but it looks like a bit of a carrier bag.’

CHAPTER FIVE

Sam was already getting her coat. She looked at the as-yet-unopened copy of Yachting Monthly on her desk. Maybe she should get out on the water again. 'I'll go to the mortuary. Speak with Mick Wright.'

'Who's doing the PM?' Ed asked.

'Jim Melia.'

'Good old Jim.'

Sam was at the door.

'They've got an address for Jack Goddard. Lives with his student mates. Take Paul. See what they can tell you. I'll get Bev to call out some more staff. She can also sort out the press office.'

'You doing a press conference today?'

'Not on a Sunday. They've all got skeleton crews. We'll get minimum coverage. We need impact. We'll arrange it for first thing in the morning. Then we'll have a shit storm.'

'The students?'

'Yep,' Sam shouted, already striding down the corridor. 'Adds credence to their theory of the serial killer.'

The terrace house had been built in the early 1900s. Like many period town centre houses it had gone from middle-class family home to landlord-owned student let. Not all students wanted to live in new apartment blocks.

Five students lived in this particular house, but those inside were about to be told that, as of the early hours, they were now a four.

A dishevelled male, early 20s, short and plump with ginger hair and a face full of freckles, answered the door. Ed and Paul stood on the stone steps, the black paint flaking, scrubbing them daily a thing of the past.

'CID,' Ed said. 'Can we come in? We need to speak about Jack.'

Elliott Prince turned, sprinted into the house.

'Lads, lads,' he shouted. 'Get down here...get down here now...it's Jack. The police are here.'

Elliott ran upstairs leaving the front door open. The detectives stepped inside, stood in the hallway and listened to the raised voices.

Three others, looking as hung-over as Elliott, followed him downstairs. Only Elliott had a tracksuit on, the rest were in their boxer shorts.

'What's happened?' one of the three asked, peering over the banister, the last in the line.

'Is there somewhere we can all sit down?' Paul said.

Elliott led everybody into the living room. The stench from stale cigarettes, cheap lager and body odour hit the detectives like the clapper striking Big Ben. Overflowing ashtrays were on the floor, discarded beer cans and pizza boxes were everywhere.

Ed brushed crumbs and whatever else off the armchair and sat down. Paul remained standing, not wanting to risk the other armchair. The four students squashed on to the three-seat settee.

'What's happened?' one of them asked again, rubbing his eyes.

'I'm sorry to tell you that Jack's dead?'

The young man covered his face with the palms of his hands. Elliott and the other two sat in silence.

'How? What happened?'

'He was found in the river in the early hours of the morning,' Ed said. 'When did you last see him?'

The talker stood up and walked to a small dining table buried under a mound of clothes, rummaged around, and found a packet of cigarettes.

'Last night we were all out together.' He lit up. 'What do you mean in the river? Another one drowned?'

'All of you were out together? All of you in this room?' Ed said.

'Yes,' the young man said as he exhaled smoke.

The others nodded slowly.

'Where were you all?'

'The Jolly Roger until we got thrown out,' Elliott said.

Ed didn't miss the glare the smoker flashed at Elliott.

'Okay, I need you all to come to the police station right now. Get some clothes on. I'll sort out some transport.'

Mick Wright waved when Sam walked into the morgue. Sam smiled. *Wait until I tell Ed you were in the viewing room, up a height behind a glass screen, with your handkerchief over your nose.*

She and Ed always stood close to the pathologist, close to the body, close enough to smell it, but more importantly close enough to see first hand the injuries.

'Hi Sam,' Jim Melia said. 'I'll show you the depressed fracture.'

Sam walked across to the metal table. Jack Goddard was laid on his stomach, his broad shoulders squeezed in between the raised sides of the steel table.

Sam went up close, bent forward, face inches from the deceased's head. Jim had neatly trimmed the hair around the fracture.

'See what you mean. Almost perfectly round. A ball hammer is a good bet. What do you think?'

'Approached from behind.' Jim stepped away from the body, took off his gloves, and washed his hands in the sink. 'Whacked. If it didn't render him unconscious, it would certainly temporarily incapacitate him, knock him off his feet. Then asphyxiated, possibly with a carrier bag over his head. Julie's got the fragment for testing.'

Julie Trescothick held up a small, clear bag containing the piece of plastic. 'Then dumped in the river once dead,' Jim continued. 'Obviously don't go public with any of that just yet. Let me do some more tests.'

'Sure. Murder then?'

'If not, it's one hell of a way to commit suicide.' Jim smiled.

'Jim, you're getting as bad as Ed.'

'I know, but it's Sunday. I was hoping to be carving a joint of beef not this young lad. Anyway, I'll tell you more when everything's done and dusted. I haven't started anything yet other than the external examination, but I wanted you to see the fracture.'

'Thanks, Jim, you're a star.' She looked across to the viewing room. 'For continuity, you okay to stay Mick. We'll pick up the investigation.'

He nodded.

Sam strode out, lines of enquiry flying around her

head: tomorrow's press conference, appealing for witnesses and information, down-playing the serial killer angle that would no doubt be raised, fingertip search of the area near where the body was found, a walking search across a broader area – she would set the parameters with the Police Search Adviser or POLSA for short – looking for discarded weapons, CCTV examination of the town centre looking for Jack, who he was with and whether he was he followed, examining his sodden mobile for incoming and outgoing calls, texts, social media, checking his background, his associates and lifestyle and enemies, probing the accounts and potential alibis of the friends he was out with.

Her brain felt like Vesuvius; if the molten ash was the lines of enquiry pouring out of her head, Ed and the rest of the team were Pompeii, about to be engulfed in a shed-load of work.

She took out a Marlboro and lit up, remembering again how the death of a colleague in February last year had sent her back to the bosom of her nicotine mistress, her long smoke free sabbatical gone in a moment. She inhaled deeply. Her feet were tapping.

God, I love this job!

By the time he got to the police station Ed Whelan had made a snap judgement on the dynamics of the group he was about to interview: Elliott appeared the weak link, Glen the strongest. Elliott had been taken straight into an interview room. The door was closed and he was sat alone.

A uniform officer was sitting with the other three, his orders simple... don't let them talk to each other, watch them like a hawk and report their NVC's, the non-verbal communications that could sometimes speak louder than words.

Ed stood outside the interview room, ear pressed against the door, and listened. He heard the chair scrape along the floor, then footsteps, light-footed; Elliott was pacing about. Ed stepped back from the door and nodded at a passing uniform but didn't speak.

He stood for another five minutes. The footsteps stopped, the resulting silence only broken by the sound of Elliott's breathing, deep breathing bordering on hyperventilating. He could picture him, his back to the door where Ed had deliberately positioned him.

Too many young cops gave no thought to the seating arrangements in an interview room. It was the first opportunity to try to secure a small advantage, like keeping suspects out of eye line of solicitors. When they're under pressure they'll forget to turn around, forcing the lawyer to either say instructions out loud, not just shake their head, or say nothing at all. By sitting them in a corner you can give the impression you're encroaching on their personal space. The tactics had to be subtle, not overtly oppressive or intimidating.

Elliott was a witness, for the time being at least, but Ed didn't want to waste time getting to the truth.

Back in the late 70s when he'd joined the police for the first time, his old Detective Inspector was always telling him: 'Crack the witnesses son and after that the suspects will be easy.'

It was a lesson Ed had never forgotten... get every last piece of information from the witness in the first interview, make sure there were no holes in what they were saying, no details omitted, and your case would improve in strength.

Conversely, witnesses who were forever altering their story were weakening your case. Taking three or four witness statements from the same individual because they forgot to mention something – either through a genuine failure to remember, selective memory, or worse, the cop forgot to ask - gave the impression the investigators were trying to strengthen their case, when in reality the information was there from the outset.

Ed burst through the door. The table jumped as Elliott's thighs hit its underside.

'You alright?' Ed said, walking around him and sitting opposite.

'Yeah… No. Not really… I can't believe Jack's dead. Another one in the river.'

'You okay to talk to me? I just want to ask some questions about your movements yesterday?'

Elliott pulled his chair closer to the table and sat upright, looking like a young graduate going for an interview. 'Yeah.'

'Just talk me through yesterday then, from when you went out. I'm not interested in what you did from when you got up.'

'Simple really,' Elliott said. 'We all went out together. Jack and the lads you've brought down here. We just went to the Jolly Roger. Got there just after 12. Watched the match. Stayed there until after nine. We all left together... well, Glen and Jack followed a couple of minutes after we left. They said they were going for another drink. The rest of us got a kebab and shared a taxi home. That was it until you came.'

Ed watched his tongue circle the walls of his mouth.

'What were you drinking?'

He looked away from Ed and stared at the wall.

'Lager. We were taking it steady. Probably had about four pints all day.'

'Now answer that question while you're looking at me.'

'Four pints... '

'Elliott, the Jolly Roger's got more cameras than you can shake a stick at. Right now you're not in any trouble, but if you lie to me then I begin to think maybe you have something to hide.'

He leaned across the desk.

'If you want, I can pop along to the Jolly Roger and watch their CCTV while you sit here. Your choice. Now, what were you drinking?'

Elliott took a deep breath.

'Lager and shot chasers all day. By half nine I was wrecked. We all were, but as I said, Glen and Jack stayed out.'

'Talking of out, in the house you said you were in the Jolly Roger until you were thrown out. What did you mean?'

Elliott looked away again and stared in silence at the wall.

'Elliott, I'll just go and see Steve Donnelly, the boss. He'll tell me because he won't have been anywhere near as pissed as you lot were.'

'The bouncers told us we had to leave,' Elliott said quietly. 'I don't know why. Maybe because we were pissed. I can't really remember. I know they wanted us out though.'

He looked away.

Ed said: 'Go on.'

'Jack told them to make him. He was being a bit of an arse.'

Elliott told Ed, to the best of his recollection, what happened in the Jolly Roger with the door supervisors.

'Did he just fall in then?' he asked.

'Don't know yet,' Ed said.

'What then? Murdered?'

Ed pushed his chair backwards, stood up, placed his hands on the desk and leaned in towards Elliott, who shrank in his seat, pushing himself against the wall. Ed closed the gap between them until he could feel Elliott's breath on his chin.

'Let's not go jumping to conclusions, Elliott. I don't want to see any ridiculous theories appearing on social media. Catch my drift?'

CHAPTER SIX

Ed was back at Headquarters. The students all gave the same version... Jack having an argument with the two doormen, picking up a pint glass and throwing the remnants of a drink over the taller one. Two went home with Elliott. Glen said he had another drink with Jack. He couldn't remember where, and he couldn't remember getting home.

Ed rang the Jolly Roger.

'Steve… Ed Whelan. Sorry to bother you. I know you'll be busy with the football being on the box. Keep this to yourself for now but a student was found dead in the river in the early hours.'

'Another one? I don't think I've ever fallen when I've been lashed.'

'Looks like he was one of a group of five,' Ed said. 'Spent a lot of time in your place yesterday. Ended up getting thrown out.'

'Could be anyone Ed. Saturday night, students and ejections. Goes hand in hand.'

'One of this lot threw a drink over your youngest bouncer.'

'Dickheads,' Steve said. 'I remember them. All had the same T-shirts on.'

'What do you mean?'

'You know when you see lads and lasses on stag and hen weekends, all wearing the same T-shirts. That's what this lot were wearing. I've seen them wearing the shirts before. Yesterday was pale blue but I've seen them wearing red ones, yellow, green. Same logo though.'

'Which is?'

'They call themselves Mortimers. There's a big cartoon of a mouse on their shirts.'

'Mortimer? Mouse? What, like Mickey Mouse?'

'It's a cartoon mouse, but it's not Mickey,' Steve told him. 'Mortimer is printed above the mouse. Underneath, in copperplate writing, it says, 'If you love the mouse, chase the pussy'. They're a bunch of knobs, Ed, but there's thousands like them.'

'Can I pop round?' Ed asked. 'Look at the CCTV?'

'Yeah, come whenever you like. At least today it's just the football. You'll not be deafened by the music like last time.'

'True. Cheers Steve.'

'Steve who?' Sam said, walking into the HOLMES room, the smell of a freshly smoked cigarette on her breath.

'Donnelly. Licensee of the Jolly Roger. Jack Goddard and his mates were in there last night. Got asked to leave by the doormen. Jack refused. Threw a drink over one of bouncers. I'm going to have a look at CCTV.'

'Might be interesting,' Sam said. 'I'll come with you. If nothing else I get to meet another licensee.'

'He's alright…I've told Bev to get the files on the other students who fell into the river. We need them sharpish. You're going to get asked about them tomorrow at the press conference.'

'Tell me about it,' Sam said. 'Make sure Bev gets the names of Aisha's friends as well. I'm still keen to revisit them. I've just had 20 minutes with Jack's parents and the Family Liaison Officer.'

Ed nodded. Nothing needed to be said.

Sam sat down. 'Never gets any easier does it? I get sick of meeting nice, decent people in tragic circumstances, people just going about their daily lives, not bothering anyone. Then they get dropped the worst bombshell. Lives turned upside down in an instant. They've got a thousand questions and I don't even have a dozen answers.'

Ed watched her and listened. He knew when she needed to ventilate. All Senior Investigating Officers did. She pushed herself hard, always insisting on meeting the grieving family members.

'You know,' she said. 'I look at them and I know life will never be the same for them. They'll never get over it. They may learn to live with it. I've seen too many of them over the years. They're shells, existing in the same world but not living the same life. Last night it changed forever for them.'

She spun the chair and looked away.

Ed needed a distraction.

'Did you happen to look at Jack Goddard's T-shirt?'

Sam tilted her head backwards and pushed her fingers through her hair. 'No…Should I have done?' she asked, slowly turning to face him.

Ed told her about the shirts the group apparently wore.

'Okay. A few early decisions for the Policy File,' she said.

Sam, like all SIOs, documented every decision she made in relation to the investigation in a bound book called a Policy File. She would record the time and date of the decision and her reasons for making it. More importantly, she would record what other options she'd considered and why those options were dismissed.

'Firstly, let's put it on HOLMES,' she said. 'No need to call everybody out now. Sort it tomorrow.'

Sam was acutely aware that HOLMES, the Home Office Large Major Enquiry System, was labour intensive, which was why the decision to utilise it was never taken lightly.

'The so-called police intelligence system?'

They both laughed; contrary to many police dramas, HOLMES is not a police intelligence system. Once a major investigation is completed, the system is mothballed until its use is again authorised.

Sam rattled off the lines of inquiry she'd identified outside the mortuary, Ed scribbling them down in an A4 pad.

'Finally,' Sam said. 'Ian Robinson, the POLSA, is calling out a search team. He'll arrange the search along the tow path.'

The Jolly Roger was full... Sunday-morning footballers together with lunchtime drinkers, all watching the match on Sky Sports. A couple of groups of young women stood chatting, not interested in the latest offering from the Premier League.

Steve Donnelly rushed across the room to meet them,

or to be precise, waddled as fast as his splayed feet and huge beer belly would allow him.

'Ed,' he said.

Ed shook his hand, and then turned to Sam.

'This is DCI Sam Parker,' Ed said.

'Hello,' Steve said, offering a sweaty palm to Sam. 'DCI eh?'

He turned to Ed.

'They're getting younger by the day. And more attractive.'

'And more aware of sexual harassment,' Sam said evenly.

Steve looked at the floor, his face red.

'You want to look at the CCTV?' he muttered.

Ed smiled at Steve's embarrassment and Sam's quick put-down.

'Yes please,' Ed said.

Sam shook her head as she followed them – the Elvis hair, the black shirt and black trousers, the huge silver buckle on the belt, a 50s throwback and a ridiculous look for a town-centre licensee.

The only part of the Jolly Roger that was not covered by CCTV was the toilets. Other than that, the system had 100% coverage, which from an investigative point of view was fantastic. Whether the civil liberties brigade and the left-wing students agreed was highly doubtful, although the Mortimers were so hammered they probably never noticed the little infra-red lights.

They all concentrated on the images. Identifying Jack Goddard and his group was easy as they were in the pub so early.

'I see what you mean about their shirts,' Sam said.

'Pathetic,' Steve scowled.

He fast-forwarded the machines until it was almost

9pm. Jack, Elliott, Glen and the other two, could be seen staggering around, chatting to girls who weren't interested.

None of the watching trio needed to be lip-readers to understand the redhead's simple dismissal.

'Stop the tape,' Sam said, pointing at the screen. 'Look at that group, those five girls with the redhead in it.'

She moved towards the screen.

'That girl with her back to the camera.' She pointed her out. 'Red top, black shorts, silver boots. Wasn't that what Alex O'Connell was wearing?'

Ed nodded. 'The girl who found Jack's body.'

'I knew getting around the shifts, reminding uniform what we needed in statements would pay off.'

'Always get them to describe their own clothing,' Ed said.

'Exactly.' Sam looked at Steve. 'Thanks. Can we continue?'

They watched the two doormen approach the Mortimers, watched Jack adopt an aggressive stance, and watched the tall young bouncer lean in and speak to him. Glen Jones remained with Jack while Elliott and the other two backed off. Jack picked up a pint glass and threw half a pint of beer over the tall bouncer.

'He's very calm, the young one,' Ed said.

'Cool as a cucumber,' Steve said. 'Thirty-odd years in this game and he's the most frightening I've seen. Not massive, certainly not aggressive, just controlled. Frightens the shit,' he glanced at Sam, 'sorry, life, out of me. He can apparently handle himself, not that I've seen him. It's what you hear, some sort of martial arts champion.'

'We'll need names and addresses,' Ed said. 'I'll need to speak to them both. Replay that bit Steve.'

He moved closer to the screen and watched the confrontation again.

'The older bouncer? Is that Billy Wilson?'

'Yeah. Been at it for almost as long as I have.'

'Well I am impressed. Back in the day the Billy I knew would have levelled Jack for that performance. Is he going soft?'

'Times change Ed,' Steve said. 'They're licensed now. Cameras everywhere. Not as easy to give someone a kicking as it was years ago. Give them a kicking these days and it's on somebody's mobile, Fight Night on YouTube starring a doorman near you.'

'Times might change but the Billy Wilsons of this world don't,' Ed said, standing straight. 'They just become more careful.'

'So who's Billy Wilson?' Sam asked, settling herself into the passenger seat of the unmarked Ford Focus.

'He's been around for years. Father did the doors. The whole family are fighters... him, his dad, and his six brothers. None of them have convictions for dishonesty, just violence. The plastic gangsters have hired them as enforcers over the years.'

'Capable of attacking someone with a hammer?'

'Absolutely,' Ed said. 'Especially if he's dwelt on it, had a drink, popped a couple of pills. He'd see it as an affront, a liberty, someone challenging the Wilsons. Forget the fact the beer was thrown over the younger one, Wilson was there. He'd see it as an attack on him.'

'What about the younger one, this Tom King?' Sam said.

'Never heard of him,' Ed shrugged. 'Steve sounded impressed.'

'That'll be Steve the overweight-Elvis-impersonating-misogynist?'

Sam put a cigarette between her lips, searched her

trouser pockets for her lighter, and spoke through the corner of her mouth.

'Terrified more like,' she inhaled. 'Let's do some background checks on the pair of them. And let's call on Alex O'Connell. Tell her it's a follow-up visit, we're just checking if she's alright.'

Ed turned his head, eyes off the road and glanced at Sam.

'Her statement's all about finding Jack Goddard's body,' Sam said. 'It starts about five minutes before the discovery. We never asked her where she was before. In fairness, I didn't expect the young cop who took the statement to do that. But if it is her in that group in the Jolly Roger, her mate is telling the lads to do one.'

'The issue being, did anything else happen between them?' Ed asked.

'Exactly. Elliott and two of his mates went home in a taxi after getting their kebabs. Jack and Glen didn't. It opens up all sorts of scenarios. Potentially we have a witness who is involved in an argument with Jack and then contacts us saying she's found a body.'

CHAPTER SEVEN

'I'LL JUST GIVE Monica Teal a quick call before we go in, bring her up to speed,' Sam said, as Ed pulled up outside Alex O'Connell's apartment block.

Ed got out of the car, arched his back, stretched, and waited for Sam to update the Assistant Chief Constable.

The apartment block was modern: communal glass entrance leading to a terracotta-tile floor and a concierge desk, two large pots containing green ferns either side of the glass doors.

'Jesus, I didn't live like this at Durham when I was at university,' Sam said, getting out of the car. 'Concierge on the desk, secure underground car park, balconies.'

'Can't see you in a hovel.'

They walked across the visitors' car park.

'It was clean enough but nothing like this,' Sam said. 'This isn't normal student accommodation I can assure you.'

Ed pulled a face. 'Student loans, live the high life, live for the day.'

Alex O'Connell buzzed them in and they took the lift to the 14th floor. There wasn't a 15th.

'Penthouse,' Ed said.

'Told you this wasn't a typical student.'

'Hi, come in.' Alex was a 22-year-old second-year student. She was tall, elegant, and graceful with long ink-black hair that had a hint of blue swaying in unison with her slender hips.

The focal point of the room was a huge abstract painting, the eggshell pastel-coloured walls and cream, linen sofas the perfect foil for its vibrant colours and broad-brush strokes.

Three sofas, each capable of seating three people, were placed around a large black marble-topped coffee table, each affording a panoramic view of the sea. Every external wall had a floor-to-ceiling window. On the balcony, a table and four chairs with enough space for a marquee.

Books filled the shelves and an iPad sat on the coffee table next to a Mac Air laptop.

'Nice place,' Ed said.

'I like it.' Her diction and Home Counties accent suggested a life of privilege. 'Please, take a seat.'

'Great views,' Ed said, looking at the North Sea.

Sam was trying to rekindle her love of the water. A lifetime ago she felt bonded to the sea, but that was when Tristram was alive, before the accident. In February last year she'd jumped into a fisherman's coble in a vain effort to rescue someone from the sea. That had been the first time she'd set foot on a boat in years. She wondered if she would ever sail the seas again. She loved it once. Maybe she could grow to love it again.

'Why Seaton St George?' Sam said.

'It was the closest daddy would let me get to Newcastle,' Alex said. 'He reasoned that if I was miles away and had to travel, I wouldn't be in the big city, partying every night.' She laughed. 'If only he knew. It's no different here. It's the North East. Everybody parties.'

Ed smiled. 'My wife once said the CID would throw a leaving party if someone was moving desks.'

Alex laughed again. 'Yeah I can imagine. Detectives seem fun but with that air of arrogance. Us girlies like that, real men. Military, police, fire. We've been chatted up by detectives before.'

'Not as old as this one I hope,' Sam said, jerking her thumb towards Ed.

Alex smiled.

Sam continued. 'As we mentioned on the phone, we just want to ask a couple of questions if that's alright?'

'Yes,' she hesitated. 'Only, will it take long? I'm supposed to be meeting some friends later for a drink, then dinner.'

Ed smiled again. Call him old school but in the North East, dinnertime was around noon, tea was the evening meal, and supper was eaten in your dressing gown, usually consisting of a couple of Jacob's cream crackers.

'Not long at all,' Sam said. 'I'm just trying to get everything in chronological order. Get things right in my own mind. What are you studying?'

'English.'

'Nice subject. I did psychology. Anyway... Saturday. Were you at anytime in the Jolly Roger?'

'Yes,' Alex said. 'We were in there from about 7.30 until, let me think...until about 10. The music's decent and the drink's cheap.'

'Who were you with?'

'Friends. Let's see. There was Juliette, Charlotte, Tracey, Anastasia and myself.'

Sam saw a photograph of a group of five girls on the TV stand.

'Is that them by any chance?' She pointed at the photograph.

'That's them.' Alex got out of her seat and passed the framed photograph to Sam.

'Who's the redhead?'

'That's Tracey. She's from the North East. Everybody else is from Cirencester. I've known the other girls for like, forever, but I met Tracey on the course. She's great.'

'Did she have an argument with any boys on Saturday?' Sam said.

'Tracey? Every week. Look at her, gorgeous. Six foot. And that hair. There's always somebody hitting on her. We girls have a code. If we like someone, we'll say to the group 'is that assignment due in next week?' If we don't like them, we'll say 'what time does your mother arrive?' That way everybody in the group knows whether to stay for another drink or move on.'

'And Tracey does this, does she?' Sam asked.

'Tracey?' Alex laughed. 'No. If she likes somebody, she'll just say Julian, Conner... whatever, is going to buy me a drink. If she doesn't like them, she'll just tell them to eff off.'

'Are you out with Tracey today?' Sam said.

'No. She and Charlotte had a late one. They both went to a party with some guys they met. I was texting Charlotte to make sure she was okay, you know, before I saw the…'

Her head dropped forward.

'That's why I said I'm supposed to be meeting someone. I'm not sure I can face going out. Juliette and Anastasia will want to know all the details.'

'It's a natural human tendency,' Sam said. 'You're in the limelight. How long have you lived here?'

'Not long. I was pleased to get out of the halls. Daddy looked at some rentals but didn't like them. He bought this place so I didn't have to share.'

Sam passed Alex her card.

'If you need anything, or just want a chat, give me a call. What you saw in the early hours is not something people normally see. If you want to talk to someone about it, there are organisations I can recommend.'

'Thanks,' Alex said.

All three stood up and walked to the door. Sam looked at the spiral wooden staircase with brushed metal banister going to the upstairs of the apartment. *Penthouse by the sea. Daddy's got some cash.*

'May as well do Tracey while we're out,' Sam said, speed-marching to the car.

'No problem,' Ed said. 'Nice flat.'

'Very, and all because daddy doesn't want her sharing. Must be nice.'

Tracey Davies's flat was on the Conifers, an estate built in the 80s; two-storey buildings, each flat with its own ground-floor door.

Sam stared out of the passenger window.

'I can't drive past this place now without thinking of Danielle Banks and that masked bastard.'

It wasn't a bad area per se. Dealers and low-lifes hadn't infested it, but it was no penthouse by the sea.

Tracey answered the door and invited them in. Still in her dressing gown, she looked like she'd spent the night in a wind tunnel, hair wild and her naturally pale skin, a sign-post to her Scottish heritage, so white she could have had an appointment with an embalmer.

'Sorry about the state of the place, but it was a heavy night.'

Sam saw the wet patch on the carpet, her nose

twitching at the lingering smell of vomit. A half-eaten pitta, red-stained doner, and a wilting salad lay in a Styrofoam container on the floor; even the pirate-eye-patched Jack Russell snoozing by the window had been blessed with sufficient canine common sense to leave the food well alone.

Tracy flicked the top of a gold Zippo and lit a cigarette.

'You're aware that Alex found a body in the river last night,' Sam said.

'God I know. How awful for her. I saw it on her Facebook, not the body, the notification… I think I'd have thrown up… I did that anyway.'

A short burst of laughter was followed by a long bout of smoker's cough. Tracey shot up, raced into the kitchen and the detectives heard her clear her throat then spit. Sam hoped it was into the sink.

'Sorry about that,' Tracey said, dropping on to the armchair and putting three pieces of sugar-coated chewing gum in her mouth, the cigarette no longer in her hand.

She confirmed that she'd been in the Jolly Roger with her friends.

'Yeah, a group of lads came over. Pissed and wearing the same T-shirts. Juveniles. Anyway they were drooling all over us. I told them to fuck off. You know what it's like.'

She looked at Sam.

Sam shook her head. Yes, she'd been chatted up, had her share of wolf whistles and the like, but there seemed no barriers now. Somehow it seemed much worse. The number of schoolgirls and students suffering indecent assaults their attackers passed off as 'banter' was frightening. Social media had sparked an explosion in cyber bullying, trolls threatening rape and worse from the safety of a laptop screen and anonymity.

'Had you ever seen these men before?' Sam asked.

'Not that I remember. Was it one of them in the river?'

'We're following a number of lines of inquiry,' Sam said. 'Have you seen them around the campus?'

'I don't think so.'

She popped more chewing gum in her mouth.

'As a matter of interest, Tracey, what are you studying at university?' Ed asked.

Tracey flashed a big smile, looked Ed up and down, and fixed her eyes on his. 'English Lit.'

Sam stood up. 'Thanks for your time. Somebody will take a statement from you tomorrow.'

Tracey shook Sam's hand then Ed's, her hand lingering on his just a little longer than needed.

Walking down the path, Ed's stride was longer than normal as he rushed to the car. He bleeped it open, pushed the key in the ignition, and had the engine running before Sam sat next to him.

She pulled her seat belt towards her and looked at him.

'Well how much was she flirting?'

'Don't be daft. She's the same age as my daughter.'

Sam patted his thigh. 'Her eyes were devouring you.'

Ed's face flushed. He shoved the gear stick into first and hit the accelerator harder than necessary. The car shot forward, the engine whining, demanding second gear.

'Oh Ed,' she cooed. 'You're embarrassed!'

'Look, over the years it's happened, women coming on to you, thinking you have an exciting life. But when it's young lasses like that, well, it makes me uncomfortable.'

'She's very confident alright.'

'Maybe, but there was something about her,' Ed said. 'The way she spoke about what happened in the pub, really spat the words out. Her eyes gave nothing away but she's one aggressive young lady. Almost regressed back into that situation, a cognitive interview without any prompting from us.'

At the turn of the millennium more and more academics became involved with police interview techniques. Ed had undertaken the nationally recognised witness interviewing training that cascaded out of the academic research.

The cognitive interview revolved around getting the witness to describe sounds and smells, in an effort to put them back in the moment, the theory being it would maximise the information.

'So what's your point?'

Ed said: 'Not sure there is one, except there's more to her than meets the eye.'

CHAPTER EIGHT

'SORRY I'M LATE,' Ed said, removing his jacket, pulling out a chair from underneath the table in the kitchen, his stomach reminding his twitching nostrils how hungry he was. The two guests nodded. His wife glared.

'We're used to it,' Sue said, in a monotone voice without a hint of humour.

Roast beef and Yorkshire puddings were off the menu; today it was chicken curry, lamb curry, dhal, and roti.

Surinder, or Sue to almost everyone, was a wonderful cook and over the years all of Ed's friends and colleagues had jockeyed for invites to his famous home curry nights. Indian restaurants were fine, Punjabi restaurants better, but nothing beat the curries Asians made at home.

Sue, like Aisha, was of Punjabi Sikh heritage, but while Sue had been able to choose her own husband, Ed doubted the same would apply to Aisha.

Ed spooned chicken curry on to his plate and tore his roti.

'Do you know this family, the Bhandals?'

'Not personally,' Sue said. 'But Leela and Eric do.'

Sue glanced at her lifelong friend. They'd met on the first day of infants, two Sikh girls in a predominantly white school.

'You still think she ran away?' Ed asked.

'Not unheard of and there's nothing to say otherwise,' Sue said. 'Why you asking?'

Ed picked up the ice-cold Kingfisher, the condensation wetting his fingers. 'We're doing a review of the initial investigation,' he told her. 'Nothing unusual in that, but that press conference yesterday... '

'Yeah, I saw that,' Ekbir, Eric to his friends, said. 'The CCTV with the boyfriend. I thought that was a bit iffy at the time.'

'How?' Ed asked, picking up some chicken with a piece of roti. There were no knives and forks when they were eating curry.

'The father's at the Gurdwara nearly every day. Then his daughter's on the TV walking around a shopping centre with a boy.'

Leela nodded.

'Nobody around this table is a practising Sikh,' Eric said. 'I don't wear a turban, but even I might find it difficult if my daughter is supposed to be at college and then she's seen walking around the shops with a boy. It's deceitful, disrespectful.'

'Multiply that by a hundred, a thousand if they're strict,' Leela said, dabbing her napkin around the corner of her mouth.

Ed raised the bottle to his lips and drank a little. This was a social occasion but he couldn't let it drop.

'You obviously know him, know the family. What are they like?'

'He's a bit of a leader in the community,' Eric said. 'Not the go-to guy, but a respected member. Had an arranged marriage, wife came from the Punjab. Her brother followed her. He's anti-Western everything where Sikh women are concerned. Like the mother, thinks all white women are trash.'

'How do you know?'

'You don't need to scream your views from the rooftops,' Eric said. 'You know that. Body language, throw-away sentences... it's hard to hide your attitudes and beliefs.'

'Another bottle, Eric?' Sue said, her chair scraping across the tiles as she pushed it away from the table. At the fridge, out of sight of Leela and Eric, Sue raised her eyebrows, the non-verbal communication for 'Back off Ed'.

Ed nodded.

'So do you think she ran away?'

He would just have to deal with the domestic argument that would follow.

'Everything's possible,' Eric said, nodding his appreciation at the lamb curry. 'I've no doubt she's not at home but whether she removed herself or was removed, I don't know. That's your job, Ed, not mine, but after the TV today, I did hear that she was promised.'

'Where did you hear that?' Ed said, trying to stop his voice rising.

'Ed, we have been friends for many years and I respect you. Our wives went to school together but there are some things you cannot ask me because I will offend you when I refuse to answer, and I have no desire to offend you.'

'The arranged marriage. Aisha's. Was he in India?'

'Yes,' Eric said. 'Same village as her mother. There was an engagement party when Aisha was four, although I suspect if she remembers it, she'll just remember a party.'

'In India?'

'Of course.'

'What do you think happened?'

'Ed!' Sue exclaimed.

'It's okay,' Eric said. 'As I see it, she either ran away, was shipped off to India, or was… you know, look, well I don't want to make wild accusations.'

Sue's voice was just loud enough to be above conversational, it's tone slightly aggressive.

'And you weren't invited round to do anything of the sort. That's quite enough, Ed. Our friends have come around for a pleasant evening, not to be given the third degree like one of your police interviews.'

'What the bloody hell were you thinking about,' Sue shouted as soon as she slammed the front door, goodbyes exchanged. 'It was bad enough being an hour late but then you start interviewing them about that poor girl.'

She followed Ed into the sitting room where he flopped into an armchair. 'You're always at work,' Sue raged. 'You were there yesterday, today, all weekend you've been there.'

Her hands were on her hips, voice getting louder. Ed stared at one particular spot on the wall.

'Today was meant to be a couple of hours and you were there all day. You see more of Sam Parker than you do of me.'

Ed jumped up and side-stepped around Sue.

'It's my job,' he shouted, walking to the door.

'That's right. It's always the job.'

Ed climbed the stairs as Sue rushed into the hallway.

'Go on,' she shouted. 'Go to bed. Half 10 and you're off to bed. Funny how you can stay out all hours when you're working or down the bloody pub but when you're here with me, you're straight to bed.'

Ed slammed the bedroom door.

'I'll sleep down here tonight.' He heard Sue's parting shot.

Ed undressed, slipped into bed. *Another day in paradise.*

Ed was under the duvet before Sam left the office.

Her whiteboard was full. She had split the board in five columns, each column representing a student who had died in the river. The columns covered the usual: name, date of birth, date of death, where discovered, who by, where they'd been on the night of their death, toxicology results, visible injuries, physical characteristics.

Once she had gleaned that information from the respective files, she had sat for about 30 minutes on the edge of her desk trying to establish if there was a connection.

Were they known to each other? Nothing in the files to answer that question either way. Had they come into contact with the same people when they were out? Another unknown. All had drunk to excess. All were male. Was there something in that? Physically, none were as big and muscular as Jack Goddard.

There was no apparent pattern regarding the days of their deaths – they didn't all happen on a Saturday night, Sunday morning.

Only Jack Goddard had injuries inconsistent with falling into the river and drowning. He was the only one not to have drowned.

She stood up. It was late and on a Sunday this corridor in Headquarters was deserted. The Force Control room was on the other side of the building. She opened the window, lit a Marlboro Gold, and inhaled deeply before walking back to the board. She drew a line underneath the last of the entries and wrote MOTIVE. She stared at the board. Nothing. She couldn't think of one. Sexual? No evidence. Theft? Nothing stolen. A random need to throw people in river? Why? Nothing linking the victims.

The serial killer theory might gain some momentum in tomorrow's press conference, but here, in her office, it was slowing quicker than a bobsleigh with the brakeman doing his job.

The first four deaths, while tragic and avoidable, appeared to be down to drink.

Sam re-read the names on her white board, thought of the devastation to the families; without any evidence she would never publicly agree to even the remotest possibility of a serial killer. Doing that would cause a media storm, and heap more suffering on to the deceased's loved ones, more unanswered questions. Here in private?

Jack Goddard was a big physical specimen. But what if the others had been pushed in?

CHAPTER NINE

Friday 13th December 2013

SUKHI SENT ME A TEXT. Told me not to worry. Told me to meet him at the end of my street. He'd be in his car. We'd go wherever I wanted. Where would that be? London? Plenty of jobs and miles away from here.

It's always the same when you're in a rush, more people than usual getting on and off at every stop, people without the right money waiting for change, old people taking ages. I thought about getting off, running, but I forced myself to stay where I was. Even with the stopping and starting, the bus would still get me there quicker.

Gurmej, my uncle, had a mobile but my mother, who would be down the Gurdwara, didn't and dad would be at the factory until six. The best my uncle could do was an answer-phone message for dad. Gurmej didn't have a car. The next bus wasn't for half an hour and the journey itself was 25 minutes. He couldn't get to me before 5.55 and my dad would still be at work at that time.

I turned my wrist. 5.15. I opened my purse: a couple of £2 coins. That wouldn't get me very far.

I stared out of the window, the familiar sights rolling past... the shops, banks, the streets of my childhood, of my teenage years. People shuffled past the brightly lit shop windows, heads deep in collars, the flashing lights hypnotising them. The Christmas decorations, stretching between the lampposts, twinkled above the cars.

Christmas? I hadn't even given it a thought, not since those numbers, not since 4 3 7.

I was born here, know nowhere else. Now I was about to leave it all behind, not a student on a gap-year adventure, but a shameful whore on a lifetime of family exclusion. I'd never return. Never see these landmarks again, never see my friends again, never see Bethany…Bethany, a true friend, the type who is bridesmaid at your wedding. I rubbed my eyes. The type of wedding where you chose your husband. I was leaving everything.

I pressed my nose against the cool glass and saw Christmas trees blinking brightly in windows.

I loved Christmas. Would I be able to buy a tree wherever we ended up? Presents?

I pressed the bell and stood as the bus slowed. Time seemed to be going faster. I checked my watch. 5.29pm. Today of all days it had to be four minutes late. It was never late. I couldn't rely on the next one being late.

I stepped down off the bus, clutched my bag into my side, and ran.

Monday 14th April 2014

Sam walked into the HOLMES room at 7am and said: 'You're early.'

Ed looked up from the computer.

'Yeah, sometimes it's easier to jump in the shower and skip breakfast. Saves all the post-argument analysis.'

'Oh, I see,' Sam said, flicking the switch on the kettle. 'Tea?'

'Please. Bit of intell on Aisha.' Ed said, getting out of his chair.

'Go on,' Sam said, sniffing the milk.

'Nothing we can use at the minute. Strict father. Big in the community. Suggestion that she was to have an arranged marriage.'

'Really?'

'Yeah, and the CCTV of her with a boy, as I said, a potential trigger for honour-based violence. If it's okay with you, I'd like to go and see this Bethany Stevens. She mentioned a marriage in her statement. I'll sort the bouncers out with Bev when I get back. I'll get Paul Adams to draw up an interview plan for them.'

'That's fine,' Sam said. 'I've got the press conference at 9.30. I stared at the whiteboard in my office for ages last night. Five columns, one for each of the lads that drowned in the river.' She poured the hot water into the mugs.

'Anything?'

'Nothing. Jack Goddard's the only one with unexplained injuries. He was attacked. The others. Nothing. Drowned. All drunk.'

'As we thought then,' Ed said.

'But what if we're wrong? What if the students are right? What if they didn't fall in? What if they were pushed?'

Ed used the dirty teaspoon to press the tea-bag against the inside of the mug. 'And your evidence of that comes from where?'

'Nowhere,' Sam said. 'I'm just posing the question. Jack's too big to be pushed but I've looked at photographs of the others and full of drink, they could definitely be shoved into the river.'

'And you are posing this question because?' Ed leaned back against the windowsill and drank from the mug.

'Five in six months,' Sam said. 'Do you know how many people, students or otherwise, fell into that river and died in the last year, last two years, last three years?'

'I do now. Obviously none.'

'Correct. So are we saying that students have suddenly started getting drunker? I just think we need to keep an open mind.'

'Have there been any inquests?' Ed asked.

'Not yet. First one shouldn't be long though. What are your thoughts on Jack Goddard?'

'Argumentative. Aggressive. That's clear on the CCTV from the Jolly Roger… A misogynist? Probably. Certainly no charmer around the women. Look at the T-shirts.'

'Get his phone examined asap,' Sam said.

Bethany Stevens lived at home with one parent. Her mother, a woman in her early 40s, opened the door. Ed followed her rounded shoulders down a long narrow hall, his enforced short steps making him focus on her bowed head, her chin obviously tucked into her chest. The printed skirt looked washed out; the mules barely had a sole.

'I've heard of this girl, Aisha,' she said in a voice so quiet Ed was straining to hear. 'But of course I've never met her. I do hope she's alright? Would you like a cup of tea?'

The kitchen was plain shabby, not shabby chic. The dark brown units belonged to the 60s, the free-standing cooker with its solid door, was probably new in the 70s, and Ed hadn't seen a twin-tub washer since he was a kid.

'Yes please. No sugar, and with help from people like Bethany, we'll find out if Aisha's okay.'

He sat at the table, the strip of veneer peeling away from the side, and glanced at the brown carpet with its frayed edges. 'Have you lived here long?' When had he last seen a carpet in a kitchen?

'Bethany and myself moved in here about two years ago. My grandparents bought this house when it was first built. My nana's death coincided with my divorce, so we moved in.'

She placed a mug of tea in front of Ed. The mug was chipped, her hand shaking.

'Of course we need to spend some money on it, but it's a solid house.'

'It's very nice,' Ed said. 'Beautiful.' He looked over his shoulder. 'You must be Bethany.' He stood up.

'I am and you must be Sgt Whelan.'

Bethany extended her arm, shook his hand. 'I see you've got tea.'

She smiled at her mother. 'You can go now, mam. I'll be fine. I'll shout if I need you.'

'Okay pumpkin.' She rubbed her hand on her pink Paisley apron, nodded at Ed, and walked out.

What a contrast, Ed thought. Introvert mother, confident daughter.

'Always been a stay-at-home mam, but bad with her nerves now.' Bethany sat next to Ed. 'Devastated when that bastard of a father of mine shacked up with another woman. Much younger of course. My mam should have left him years ago. I told her to leave when I was 15. Anyway, how can I help? I've already made a statement.'

'As I explained on the phone we are going right back to the beginning, make sure we haven't missed anything,' Ed said. 'In your statement you mentioned a marriage.'

Bethany nodded. 'Yeah. I thought she was joking at first: 18 and getting married off. It was only when I saw how upset she was, I realised she meant it. I couldn't believe it. And did you see her dad on the TV, crying buckets? It's his fault she's run away.'

Ed looked at her over the rim of his mug; self assured, shiny brown hair, subtle make-up. He sipped his tea. 'Is that what you think happened?'

'Don't you?' Bethany said. 'I just thought she ran away with Sukhi. He was nice. She'd meet him on a Friday. We used to go to the shops together. It was the only day she could get out. I couldn't even ring her at home.'

'Why not?' Ed asked. 'She had a mobile, access to social media.'

'Yeah right. Is that what they told you, her family? She had a mobile at school. That was just so they could all check up on her. That phone was taken from her as soon as she got home and given back to her on a morning.'

Ed said: 'She tell you that?'

'She did. Again I didn't believe her. I rang the phone one Saturday. Her brother answered and went mental with me. Told me his sister didn't associate with white slags.'

Ed sat there, impassive. There was no mention of any of this in Bethany's first statement. The bright-red warning indicators of an honour-based system began flashing in his head.

'I told the police about the phone, her not having it after college, but they didn't write it down, said it wasn't relevant,' Bethany said. 'They were just interested in whether Aisha had a boyfriend, whether I knew the lad on the CCTV.'

'And did you?'

'Of course I knew him, but I didn't tell them that.'

'Why?'

'After Aisha told me about the marriage I read an article in a magazine about honour crime. Funny how one minute you know nothing, the next you're seeing and hearing about it everywhere. I knew what honour meant in Aisha's world. She told me. The police never mentioned that to me. They told me Aisha ran away with a boy. If that was true, there was no way I was going to help them find her, send my mate into a marriage with some old bloke from India.'

Ed smiled and shook his head at the same time; smiled because this young woman had grasped the concept of honour, shook his head because his uniform colleagues had not.

'The boy, Sukhvinder, he's never been seen since.'

'I know, so they got away,' Bethany said. 'I knew he'd take care of her. They were in love. I just hoped she'd call me.'

'You told the police officers that you'd last seen Aisha at college. Your last lesson finished at 2.30pm and then you had gone your separate ways. Is that right?'

Bethany stared into Ed's eyes.

'Can I ask you something? Do you believe this honour thing exists? Do you believe she could have been forced to marry? That was what she was worried about, worried that they'd take her to India and leave her there.'

Ed leaned in towards her. 'I do. And I'll tell you why. I've spent most of my adult life married to a Sikh.'

Her eyes widened faster than a child's kaleidoscope. 'Really? Wow…so you know what I'm talking about.'

'I do,' Ed said. 'So if there is anything you haven't told us, now's the time. I won't necessarily tell Aisha's parents, and you won't be in any trouble.'

Bethany stood up and walked to the Formica workbench, took her phone off charge, tapped in her password, and clicked on an icon.

'Here,' she said, bending down next to him, showing him her phone. 'I took this on the afternoon she went missing. I was going to show it to her the following Monday, tease her, you know, pretend I would show her parents, her brother.'

Ed looked at the picture. 'Will you email this to me, and any others you've got?'

A series of rapid nods.

Ed focussed on the photograph. Aisha at the bus stop stood on her tiptoes, hands clasped around Sukhvinder's neck, kissing him. What horrified him was the Asian man, traditional dress, standing on the other side of the road. A sense of foreboding overwhelmed him. Aisha's dash for freedom needed to have succeeded. That man would undoubtedly know her parents. Ed shivered. Had he just seen The Kiss Of Death?

CHAPTER TEN

Sam was sitting at a table on the stage in the media briefing room, half-way through her prepared statement. The usual suspects from local TV, radio, and of course, Darius Simpson from the Seaton Post, were assembled, a couple of agency photographers walking around, flashes lighting up the room. There was also a regionally based reporter from one of the 'redtop' nationals.

'We are keen to trace Jack's movements between 9pm on Saturday and 4.05am on Sunday, and would like to hear from anybody who was in the town centre, or on the tow path, or who may have spoken to Jack between those times, to contact us. Viewing the town-centre CCTV is an obvious line of inquiry for us.'

Sam believed in avoiding jargon. Nothing turned viewers off more than cops talking in language that the average man in the street didn't understand; if members of the public switched off, her appeal was in vain, potential witnesses lost.

Redtop got in first. They always did. 'This is the fifth young person to die in the river in the last six months.

Some students are saying their deaths are not accidents. Five young men: five deaths. Is Eastern Police considering a possible link, that they may have all been murdered?'

Sam looked directly at him. She'd anticipated this.

'As I have already pointed out, Jack was assaulted before he went into the river. He did not drown. The other tragic losses of lives were the result of drowning. We will always keep an open mind, but the evidence at this stage is that only Jack was assaulted.'

'But of course the others might just have been pushed in?' Redtop said.

'Anything is possible, but there is no evidence to back that up, and without evidence all we have is speculation,' Sam smoothly held her ground.

In a room full of journalists and media, Sam was now in a one-to-one with the Redtop... and Redtop wasn't stopping.

'The council have announced this morning they have no plans to put up fencing along the tow path, but might erect large gates to block entry to it after a certain time. Any views, Chief Inspector?'

'That is a matter for the council,' Sam said. 'While there maybe some input from Eastern Police, it is not something I will be involved in.'

'Are you going to increase patrols along the river?'

'There will undoubtedly be a greater police presence over the next couple of days as we search for witnesses and evidence,' Sam said. 'If you are asking me will there be a long-term increased police presence, then I'm sorry, but you'll need to ask the Divisional Superintendent with policing responsibility for that area.'

'In light of the five deaths in six months, do you think he should have been present today?'

Sam had to admit Redtop was quite the operator.

'The purpose of today is to seek information and search for witnesses into the tragic death of Jack Goddard,' she said evenly. 'It is not to discuss policing arrangements, or council policy, with regards to the tow path.

Redtop nodded. He'd made his point.

The background questions followed: what type of person was Jack, how was his family coping, could they have a picture?

Sam left the stage, ready to do one-to-ones with local TV and radio.

'Can I have a quick word Sam?' Darius said.

'Of course. You were quiet in there. Post not interested?'

'All the questions I had were asked; the angle about the deaths being linked. Some of the students are up in arms. You know, serial killer on the loose.'

Sam sighed. 'I know.'

'Look, the activists among them are organising a demo.'

'You're joking?'

'No. They've tipped me off because they want coverage. 5pm tonight. Outside the Town Hall.'

'Town Hall?'

'Yeah, one of the things they're protesting about is the council's announcement this morning that they're considering alley gates at the entrance to the tow path.'

He ran his hands through his mop of blond hair. 'They're saying it's a breach of their human rights, that closing the tow path would mean they'd have to walk the long way round, which for a lot of them would add an extra half-hour to their walk home?'

Sam didn't try to hide her contempt.

'Pleeease! Have they got nothing better to think about?'

'Sam, they've thought this through,' Darius said. 'This

way they'll get the anti-police students who think the cops are ignoring a serial killer and won't spend money on an extra patrols, the human rights activists who think the gates are an interference with their liberty, and the environmentalists who'll say putting up the gates will destroy the plants and wildlife in the hedgerows the council will have to dig up. They've got all the anti-establishment bases covered.'

'Jesus,' Sam sighed. 'Any idea of numbers?'

Darius shook his head.

'No. But this will spread like wildfire on social media. Nearly every student will fit into at least one of the protest categories.'

'Okay, cheers Darius,' Sam said. 'I'll need to make these one-to-ones as quick as possible, warn uniform. We don't want to get caught with our pants down.'

She smiled inside as a red surge spread from Darius' neck.

Once all the interviews were finished, Sam went to ACC Teal's office and updated her on Aisha, Jack Goddard, and the demo.

Sam was comfortable with her. Teal had come on promotion from Northumbria Police, which she'd joined as a PC before climbing to the rank of Chief Superintendent. She had replaced Trevor Stewart, who had moved to another force on another promotion taking his sexual innuendos with him. 'That's great Sam,' ACC Teal said. 'Thanks. You concentrate on Goddard and Aisha, although give more resources to Goddard. Aisha's been missing since December. Leave the demo to me.'

'Thank you Ma'am.'

'Sam, in here, Monica does fine.'

She checked her ringing mobile.

'It can wait,' she said. 'When we've more time I'd like to discuss your plans for the future. Where do you see yourself? How far up the ladder do you want to climb? That sort of thing. I'd like to help you. I believe in looking after our good people, irrespective of gender, and all I hear is that you're one of the good ones.'

'Thank you… Monica.'

Sam left the office feeling elated. When Trevor Stewart had occupied it, she invariably left full of fuck.

Her phone vibrated in her trouser pocket. She answered it. 'Hi Ed…I'll be in my office in two minutes.'

'Billy Wilson's popped in to see us,' Ed said. He had been sitting in her office, waiting for her.

'What, here? Headquarters?' Sam put her phone on the desk.

'It'll be okay. He's a witness at the minute. There's an empty office at the end. He's already in it. Paul brought him up.'

'Bloody hell, Ed,' Sam said. 'We shouldn't be doing it at HQ. This place is non-operational.'

'He's here now. Let's just crack on.'

'Go on then, but don't make a habit of it,' Sam told him. 'Just this once.'

'And I'll fill you in on Aisha later. I've seen a camera photo of her kissing her boyfriend at the bus stop.'

Billy didn't move when Ed walked into the room.

'Don't stand up on my account,' Ed said.

'You what?'

'Never mind. This is Detective Chief Inspector Parker.'

'Alright,' he said.

Ask a hundred people to describe a bare-knuckle fighter and Ed was convinced they'd describe Billy Wilson: fingers like bananas, 'love' inked crudely on one set of knuckles, 'hate' on the other, and a nose that had been broken more times than a teenager's heart.

'I understand you've popped in to see us about the young lad found in the river,' Ed said, sitting down.

Sam leaned against the wall, arms crossed.

'Thought I'd come and see you, Ed,' Billy said. 'Save you the trouble of coming to find me. That's why I came here. No point in going to the nick in Seaton. They'd have rung you. I'd have to wait. Quicker to come here.'

'Why did you think we wanted to see you?'

Wilson held both palms up. 'Come on, Ed. I know the pompous little pricks. They're in regular. We threw them...' He corrected himself, 'escorted them out on Saturday. One of them threw beer over Tom. I'm sure Steve'll tell you that. It'll be on the cameras. So I came to see you. Alibi's watertight. I never did anything to any of them.'

'Time was you'd have decked the one with the beer on the spot,' Ed said.

'Times change,' Billy answered. 'You know that, Ed. I can't hit them any more than you can. CCTV. Mobile phones with cameras and videos. Everything you do's recorded these days. So everything's by the book, meaning everybody gets away with being a twat.'

'The young lad didn't deserve to die,' Ed said.

'Ed, I agree. If they were taught to be more respectful, they wouldn't get into trouble. They'd have some manners. That's the problem these days - no manners, no respect.'

Sam unfolded her arms, stood straight.

'Save us the lecture on respect and society's ails,' she said. 'Sgt Whelan will take a statement from you. If everything you say checks out, we'll not need to see you again. If it doesn't, we'll see you at a time and place of our choosing, not yours.'

Sam slammed the door behind her.

'Who rattled her cage?'

Ed smiled. 'Don't cross her, Billy. She's good, takes no prisoners, if you catch my drift.'

'Doesn't look like she does.'

Billy Wilson relayed the events of Saturday night. Ed wrote his statement.

'What's Tom King like then?'

'Quiet. Confident. Good lad, good craic. Very polite. Likes his footie. Not a big drinker though, too much into his martial arts. Local champion. Drinks Cranberry juice and eats those avocado things like they're going out of fashion.'

'Is he any good? At martial arts, not eating avocados?'

Billy, oblivious to Ed's wise-crack, leaned across the desk and spoke as if he was divulging a secret.

'Ed, I went to one of his fights a few months back. He's so fast, and his reach.' He stretched out his arms. 'He's like a bloody albatross.'

He dragged the chair closer to the desk with his backside. 'But it's not just his speed.' He tapped his temples. 'It's his focus. Concentration. He's fearless. He just waits and waits, and then, bam!' Billy punched the palm of his hand. 'Fists, kicks, he's got it all. I wouldn't tackle him, neither would most of the doormen round here. He's that good Ed, and he's just a kid.'

Ed thought about Tom King. Would a trained fighter need a weapon?

'What about the group of lads?'

'Gobshites. Always wearing them daft T-shirts. Think they're it. Call themselves Mortimers.'

'So I've heard.'

'Never had to throw them out before, but they're

pricks, Ed. Think they're God's gift. I could imagine them upsetting all sorts.'

'Enough to kill one of them?'

Billy pushed his chair backwards. 'Doesn't seem to take much these days, Ed. Like I said, no respect.'

'When you next see Tom, tell him to give me a ring.' Ed passed him his business card.

'I will, but I don't know he'll call. Hates your lot.'

'Why's that?'

'His mother suffered years of good hidings from his old man,' Billy said. 'Tom saw it all, but was too young to stop it. Used to get a few bats himself. Police would to go to the house but did nothing. One day, after she'd had a good kicking the night before, she snuck up on hubbie when he was having his breakfast and brayed him over the head with a shovel. Brains and blood all over the ceiling.'

Ed raised his eyebrow. 'Really? When was this? Where did it happen?'

'Tom went into care,' Billy said. 'Blames the police. Reckons if they'd done their job, the old fella would have been banged up and his mother wouldn't be in jail. It happened here, Ed, in Seaton.

'King?' Ed stared at the wall. 'Name means nothing.'

'That's because he changed it. Tom Cotton.'

'Pat Cotton! Gordon. Tom was... '

'Twelve,' Billy jumped in. 'Twelve years old and his mother, who he idolised, still idolises, locked up for killing one of the nastiest bastards ever to walk. He was a pussy among men was Gordon Cotton, but a big man around Pat. That kid visits her every fortnight, and I'll tell you this much, Ed, he can't stand blokes being disrespectful to women.'

CHAPTER ELEVEN

'No more killings,' the speaker shouted into his megaphone, his lisp very pronounced. Sam was in the Command Room adjacent to Control Room, watching the live stream from the CCTV. All those people and they'd chosen the guy with the lisp as their head chanter; talk of politically correct gone mad. She could only imagine what Ed would make of it.

Six screens, same protest, different viewpoints. The students had left the Town Hall and marched on the police station.

Sam reckoned there were about 150 people; Darius was right, every type had been attracted, and they weren't all students at the university. She recognised a couple of activists who'd never finished school never mind gone into Higher Education. Only social media could have produced a crowd this large in such a short period of time.

Monica Teal had been true to her word and had acted swiftly. There was a serial of one inspector, a sergeant, and eight constables deployed, keeping a watching brief on the demo. Ten cops in total, all dressed in normal uniform, low-key, their objective to ensure that everything passed peacefully.

Sam knew in the underground car park at Seaton St George police station were two, long-wheel-based Ford Transits, each with a Public Order Serial inside them, kitted out in riot gear. If it kicked off, the police were prepared.

Banners were held aloft:

'Police Cover-Up'

'Justice for the Five'

'No to Alley-Gates, No Restriction of Movement'

'Save the Riverside Wildlife and Fauna'

And Sam's particular favourite... 'Student Debts, Students Deaths, Society in Denial.'

The gathering was noisy but peaceful. Traffic and pedestrians had been diverted away from the area, as a precaution.

Sam stood there, concentrating on the screens. One small incident was all it took, one idiot, and the crowd dynamics would change.

And bang on cue, that idiot appeared, running out of the crowd to hurl an open tin of gloss paint at one of the police stations windows. As the window shattered and white paint flew from the tin, a young cop ran and rugby tackled the paint thrower to the ground.

Cue mayhem.

Two students, now with chequered scarves covering their faces, ran and pulled the uniform cop off the paint thrower. Police officers sprinted forward, barging into a slender young woman, sending her crashing to the floor. Scuffles were breaking out as the mood turned.

Two police vans hurtled around the corner with blue lights flashing and sirens blaring. Cops in full riot gear jumped out and quickly formed a well-drilled three-sided formation, using their reinforced plastic shields to push the crowd back. Three mounted officers joined them, horses a brilliant asset at crowd control.

A student threw a stick from one of the banners, spearing a cop in the cheek, blood flowing instantly following impact. Banners were dropped as the students were forced backwards, the cops kicking the sticks behind them as they advanced.

A 'snatch squad' of three riot police broke through the shields, grabbed the spear thrower, spun him round and dragged him backwards, the wall of shields opening up and letting them back through to the police side of the cordon.

Students banged their fists on the shields as they were pushed backwards towards a high wall. Pandemonium. Some shouted abuse, most screamed to be let out of the crowd. The majority, as was usually the case, hadn't come for aggravation.

The shields formed three sides of a square; the wall formed the fourth.

The students were penned in, corralled.

The riot cops were now able to step backwards, extend the perimeter of the square, but the students were going nowhere.

Their dispersal was now a matter for the Public Order Commander.

Sam left the Command Room. The on-duty uniform Inspector would be inundated with complaints of heavy-handed policing, police brutality, false imprisonment; just another day at the office.

Ed walked into Sam's office and told her about the interview with Billy Wilson.

'We'll see Tom King tomorrow then,' she said. 'Get a witness statement off him, even if it's lies. Gives us something to have a go with later if he comes into the frame.'

'Much happen at the demo? I heard it moved to Seaton nick.' He sat down opposite her.

'Everything was fine and dandy until some half-wit threw a tin of paint through one of the windows. Gloss all over one of the locker rooms but luckily no one was in there. He got locked up. Debbie Strong got hit in the face by a flying stick. That one got locked up as well.'

'Good,' Ed said. 'We had plenty there, didn't we?'

'Yeah. I think some are still penned in. They're only letting a few go at a time.'

'Fair enough.'

'I'm going for a drink with Bev if you fancy a quick one,' Sam offered.

Ed scowled. 'I promised Sue a while back I would stop drinking on a school night. She'll not be happy if I can't even get past Monday.'

Sam stood up and took her jacket from the peg.

'I thought you were in the bad books?

'I am.' He looked at the wall clock. 7.50pm. He'd been there since 6.35am. 'Bollocks,' he said flatly. 'Hung as a sheep and all that.'

'Hey, don't let me stop you getting house points.'

'See you in the Golden Eagle.'

An hour later, Bev Summers was on a high stool in Sam's kitchen. Both had limited themselves to one drink in the pub – driving. They weren't driving now.

'You sure it's okay to stay?'

'I've got four bedrooms. Course it is. Now…' Sam bent down, opened the door of her wine cooler.

'Hey, nothing too expensive, it's a Monday. Okay to smoke?'

'Carry on,' Sam said. 'I'll be joining you. Just open the door.'

Sam poured the wine into two large Riedel glasses, sat on a stool opposite Bev and put the bottle into a silver wine bucket full of ice.

'Seems ages since we had a girlie chat,' Bev said. 'I know Christmas was tough.' Her voice trailed away.

Sam held the glass to her lips, but didn't tip it far enough for any of the wine to slide towards her mouth.

Bev waited. She and Sam had known each other years, known each other since Sam was a young PC. Sam had been promoted three times but it hadn't affected their friendship. Sam had insisted on it.

'I just wonder if I'll ever move on from Tristram?' she said quietly. 'It's been… God I lose track of time.' She took a large glug from the glass, swirled the wine in her mouth, and swallowed. 'I still don't sleep brilliantly. Every dream I recall, he's in it. One day I want a new relationship; the next I can't even bear the thought of starting again. And where would I start?'

'I'm not going to say give it time, because you already have,' Bev told her. 'I never wanted a long-term relationship, not where they moved in anyway. I'm not having some bloke moving in, then taking me to the cleaners when we split up.'

'God I never thought about that.'

'Hey, we're both good catches,' Bev smiled. 'Decent jobs, nice cars, houses paid for... and not forgetting bodies!

They might be ageing a bit, especially mine, but nothing's dropped through childbirth.'

Sam pointed at her thighs. 'We'll both still be tight down there.'

The bout of laughter began.

'Maybe you should let Darius Simpson and his blond mop find out,' Bev said.

Sam tried to speak through the giggles, glassy eyes focussed on Bev.

'Can't imagine him doing that,' she said. 'Looks too innocent. Probably thinks oral sex is when you talk about it.'

They threw their heads back, laughing like horses neighing.

'I can't breathe,' Sam said through the laughter.

Bev shrieked, her voice much higher than normal.

'He's so posh he probably thinks fellatio is a character from a Shakespeare play.'

Sam banged the black granite top, bent forward, and tried to inhale.

'Stop it…Oh my God, I've got a mental picture now.'

'He'll be here like a shot if I ring him.'

'Don't you dare!' Sam waved her hand in front of her face, composed herself. 'He's a decent bloke, but… you know.'

'I know… he's not Ed.'

Sam lifted her head. 'God, is it that obvious?'

'I'm one of your oldest friends,' Bev said. 'It's obvious to me, probably not to anyone else. Does he know how you feel?'

'No,' Sam shook her head slowly. 'I've never said anything. He's married. He wouldn't do anything. He's not that type.'

She took the bottle out of the ice bucket, poured a little

into each glass. 'And I wouldn't want him to. It would just cause too much shit; too much shit for him at home, too much shit for us both at work.'

'But?'

'There's a chemistry,' she said. 'I can feel it. I think he does, but it'll never happen.' She glanced at the microwave. 10.10pm.

'What do you think about Aisha then?'

'Not sure,' Sam said. 'I hope Ed's wrong. I hope she's not dead. We're going to see her parents tomorrow. Introduce ourselves. We're here to help find your daughter... the usual, but it'll give us a feel for them.'

'And Jack?'

'You know as well as I do how tough it is to sort when they're found in the open.'

She sipped the wine.

'A missing Asian girl and a body in a river,' Sam said. 'Two of the hardest type of jobs to box off and we've got them both together.'

'Nightmare,' Bev agreed. 'Did you hear how Debbie Strong's doing?'

'She's fine,' Sam told her. 'Strong by name and all that. Couple of stitches.'

'Stitches?' Bev said, a smile breaking out. 'Well I bet her new girlfriend will be impressed... the butch touch.'

She took a slow drink from her glass.

'Oh by the way, I was in custody when they brought them in,' she said. 'Elliott Prince threw the paint.'

CHAPTER TWELVE

Tuesday 15th April 2014

SAM RUBBED her bloodshot eyes as Ed walked into her office.

'Good night then?'

'God Bev can still drink.' She massaged her temples. 'My head's busting and she looks like she's gone to bed with a cup of cocoa and a book and slept for 12 hours.'

'You're obviously out of practice, not match fit,' Ed said, sitting down.

'Something like that… What about you? Everything alright when you got home?'

'She went ballistic,' Ed said. 'I had one more pint after you and Bev left. Two pints and you'd think I'd been out all night. I should have just come round yours and got pissed. Wouldn't have been any worse. Anyway…'

Sam looked at the sadness in his eyes, swallowed hard before she spoke. 'Elliott Prince was locked up yesterday.'

'Really? What for?'

'He threw the paint through the window.'

'Elliott Prince?' Ed said. 'You sure? He's the last kid I'd expect to do that.'

'Why?'

'You haven't seen him,' Ed told her. 'He's the kid you knew from day one at senior school would get bullied. Little, fat, freckles, and ginger. If he turned out to be a geek, he'd have a full house.'

'Well it was definitely him,' Sam said. 'Get down and see him. He's at court this morning. Do an intelligence interview with him…tell you what, we'll both go. I could do with the fresh air and I can't be bothered with these emails at the minute. Then we can go and see Aisha's parents. I've got their phone number from the file.'

The prisoner was brought into an interview room.

'Elliot, this is Detective Chief Inspector Parker,' Ed said. 'Sit down. We want to conduct an intelligence interview. We don't want to ask you about the paint. Do you understand?'

A nod.

'The T-shirts you were all wearing. What's their significance?'

'They're just a laugh?' Elliot said.

Sam leaned in close. 'As a woman I find them highly offensive. I find you highly offensive.'

She allowed her words to linger in the confined room. 'How many are in your pathetic little club?'

His eyes stared at the grey linoleum, his speech unsteady and slurred like a Saturday night drunk. 'About 12 of us.'

'And if I was a pathetic little boy wanting to join, how do I do that?' Sam asked.

'There was just the five of us originally, the ones who live together,' Elliot said. 'Well that's not strictly true. There were four. I joined when I went to live with them. I was last there. It's why I've got that tiny room. It's not even a room really, there's not even a window.'

'What you live in a cupboard?' asked Ed. 'Like Harry Potter?'

Elliot raised his head. 'I suppose so, but I just wanted to live with them. Sound lads. So I was the fifth member, Glen and Jack then let others join, if they thought they were sound.'

He stared at Ed, the words leaving his mouth faster than a swarm of flies fleeing a chemical spray.

'Look, it was just a laugh, just banter,' he gabbled. 'They wore pink 'Pussy Patrol' T-shirts in 'The Inbetweeners' movie. No harm in it.'

'Tell that to the DCI,' Ed said, indicating Sam.

Prince's eyes dropped as Sam leaned in again.

'You approached a group of girls in the Jolly Roger. One of them told you to fuck off. Seen them before?'

He looked at her. 'Think so. About town... campus. Never spoke to them though. Glen and Jack always fancied themselves around the girls.'

'Did you argue with anyone that night?' Sam asked.

'Jack argued with the doormen,' Elliot answered. 'Threw the dregs of a pint over one of them but I left. I didn't want to get beat up.'

'Have any of your group, what's it called… Mortimers. Any of that group been beaten up before?' Sam pushed.

'No, not to my knowledge.'

'Do you do anything other than walk around in your stupid T-shirts sexually harassing women?' Sam said evenly.

'We don't sexually harass anyone.' Elliot looked offended.

Sam shot forward, her face inches from his as he squirmed backwards, trying to increase the distance.

'What, so saying 'I suppose a fuck's out of the question' is not sexual harassment?'

'I never said it.'

Sam moved away from the table.

Elliott sighed heavily.

Ed handed him his business card. 'Think of anything else Elliott, anything, like why would someone want to kill Jack, let us know. Okay?'

Another nod.

Friday 13th December 2013

I burst through the door. Mam was at the Gurdwara, Mia was in the sitting room.

'Only me.' No response; just voices from the TV.

I sprinted upstairs. The house was boiling. Mother never acclimatised to England.

I yanked open the bedroom door I shared with Mia. Baljit, being the only son, had his own room, bigger than ours, of course. My pink suitcase was under the bunk bed. I had the top one, privilege of rank I used to say to Mia; heard that once in a military drama.

I grabbed a couple of dresses from the drawers. Some underwear. Stuffed them into the case. The 'uniform' I was wearing was the only western dress I had.

I took a pen and an A4 pad out of my school bag, sat on the bottom bunk and started to write. More like scribble really, balancing the book on my knees.

Dear Mammy-ji and Daddy-ji
I am sorry but I cannot stay. I cannot marry that man. I want my

own life, on my own terms. I want to go to university. I want to meet a man and fall in love with him.
I was born here, in England. I have British values. I don't want to marry a stranger who is way much older than me.
I hope you understand.
I love you all, but cannot stay.
Sat-sri-akaal
Aisha

I tore the page out of the book and left it on top of the drawers. They would find it, but not straight away. Mia wouldn't come up here until bedtime. She would probably be the one to find it.

I glanced at my watch. 5.50pm. Sukhi should be at the end of the street now. I stopped at the door then turned. One last look. *I've slept my whole life in this little room.*

Shit. The bathroom.

I dropped my suitcase and ran on my tiptoes. I grabbed my hairbrush, toothbrush, and deodorant, ran back to the bedroom, bent down, and stuffed them in my case. I turned around again at the door. Justin! Can't leave Justin. I shuffled under the bed, rummaged amongst the old toys and got the signed photo Bethany had found on eBay. 'Put it on your wall,' she'd said when she gave it to me. No chance. A white pop star? Just watching him on the TV would mean trouble if I was caught.

Run. Get out of here.

I dropped my case in the hallway, dashed into the sitting room and gave Mia a kiss on the top of her head.

'Get off,' she shouted, as she pushed me away.

I've no idea when I'll next see her and she's pushing me away. She doesn't know what's happening. Fifteen and she thinks she knows everything. I silently promised to come back for her. She's not being told who to marry.

Tuesday 15th April 2014

Sam knocked on the black door of the terraced house. Davinder Bhandal opened it, stepped aside, and beckoned them in. Crossing the threshold reminded Sam of emerging from an aircraft when it landed somewhere hot. The white paint on the woodchip wallpaper had long since faded to yellow, but the dark wood frame surrounding the picture of Guru Nanak was gleaming.

Sam caught a glimpse of Mrs Bhandal in the kitchen.

Ed and Sam were ushered into the front room and sat on the sofa. Davinder sat on an armchair. 'My wife does not speak English. I will tell her what was said after you leave. First, some tea.' He shouted in what Sam presumed was Punjabi. Almost immediately Parkash Bhandal appeared carrying a gold-coloured tray with upturned sides.

Head down, she placed the tray on the large mahogany coffee table and without speaking a word, left the room. Her face had been as expressionless as a Victorian servant waiting on her master.

Davinder passed Sam and Ed a plate, invited them to a vegetable samosa and a cup of milky tea.

Sam spoke. 'Mr Bhandal, as I explained on the phone, the purpose of our visit is to introduce ourselves. Myself and Sergeant Whelan are now leading the investigation into Aisha's disappearance.'

'I understand,' he said. 'My solicitor is not impressed with the police action. Everything's been done from the view of Izzat. It is ridiculous. Aisha had a good life. We were perhaps too soft with her. I blame myself. I should have been firmer.'

'So would you describe her as being happy in the lead up to her disappearance?' Sam asked.

'She was happy all the time. Not just in the lead up, as you put it.'

'I know how difficult it must be Mr Bhandal,' Sam said. 'I cannot begin to imagine how you must be feeling. A missing child. It must be heartbreaking. We will do everything we can to find her.'

He bowed his head, an almost undetectable couple of nods, and wiped his eyes. He didn't look up.

'Thank you. We just want her back home. To see her again.'

Sam couldn't see Ed's right hand, it was out of her line of sight, tucked under his leg, but she saw his forearm tighten.

'We will go back to the start. Review everything,' she said.

Davinder's head jerked up. 'Why? She's with that boy. The one she was in the town with. He's vanished. He took Aisha, kidnapped her. I wanted to say she'd been kidnapped on the TV but Ms Carver didn't think it was a good idea.'

Sam knew that Jill Carver wasn't foolish enough to allow allegations to be broadcast without some substance. Better to concentrate on the lack of progress rather than throwing in spurious, unsubstantiated claims.

Sam said: 'We will look at everything. Start again. Make sure we have missed nothing. Everybody wants the same result, Mr Bhandal, the safe return of Aisha.'

He held her gaze.

'My wife cannot sleep. Our other daughter won't sleep in the bedroom she shared with Aisha. Baljit wishes he'd done more to protect his sister. All because of some boy she'd met. This is what happens.'

Ed sat forward. 'In the press conference on Saturday you said you wanted Aisha to enjoy everything the UK had to offer.'

'I am sorry,' Davinder said. 'I don't understand.'

'If you wanted her to enjoy everything the UK had to offer, surely that would include allowing her to walk around the town with a friend, boy or not.'

Davinder stood up. 'Mr…'

'Whelan,' Ed said.

'Mr Whelan.' His shoulders were stiff, chest inflated, hands in his pockets, the *I'm-the-master-in-this-house* stance. 'By that I meant education, better standard of living, good place to raise a family, but we still believe in certain traditions, certain behaviours that perhaps white people don't. There are certain standards expected from our daughters.'

'Izzat,' Ed said.

Davinder's hands shot out of his pockets. The heel of his hand hit his forehead. His words were quick, accusatory. 'Yes of course. Is it such a bad thing? Everybody should have honour.'

He sat down and shook his head, his words measured. 'There are so many temptations today.'

Sam stood up. 'Thank you for your time, Mr Bhandal.'

In the hallway she stopped at the photograph on the tall, narrowed-legged table. A family photograph: mother, father, Baljit and Mia sat on the sofa in the living room, a Christmas tree the background. Where was Aisha?

'Last Christmas?' Sam asked.

'Yes, although a far from normal one, as you can imagine,' Davinder said. 'My brother-in-law took it before Mia went to stay with him. She was too upset to stay in her own bedroom with Aisha going missing.'

'Thank you for your time,' she said.

Sam and Ed walked back to the car, feeling Davinder's eyes on their backs before he closed the front door.

'What do you make of him, then?' Sam asked as she slid into the passenger seat.

Ed depressed the clutch and started the engine. 'Same as I did when I saw him on TV. You saw his reaction to Izzat. To them, it's the most important thing in their lives. More important than everything, including their own kids.'

Ed turned left into another terraced street, glanced at a group of youngsters bouncing a football towards each other, and saw the women talking by front doors, heads covered with scarves.

'Every one of these people is a potential gatekeeper.'

'Meaning?'

'East Germans grassed on their neighbours to the Stasi. Same principle here, everybody spying on everybody else. Anybody causing shame, report back to the family. Gatekeepers of Honour, Sam.' He accelerated. 'They're all self-appointed Gatekeepers of Honour.'

CHAPTER THIRTEEN

JAMIE TELFORD OPENED the fridge door and took out a can of Fosters. The fridge was packed with lager. If they weren't eating take-away food, they ate tins which allowed the fridge to be the alcohol cupboard.

He pulled the ring. Lager fizzed, shot out of the can on to his hand. 'Bollocks.' He rubbed his hand against the pink cotton of his Mortimer T-shirt, gulped the lager, and flicked through the letters on the kitchen table. There were two for him. One from the bank. That could wait. He didn't need to read a statement to know he was skint. The other was handwritten, addressed to 'Mr. J Telford'.

He put the can on the wooden table, opened the envelope, and pulled out the folded piece of paper.

The wind wouldn't have flown out of his body any quicker if a boxer had punched him in the gut.

He jumped up, knees ramming into the underside of the table. The can flew through the air, its contents exploding across the floor as it hit the washing machine. The envelope's contents, in contrast, fluttered like a stalling paper aeroplane on to the table.

When had that photo been taken?

He ran to the can, kicked it hard against the wall, and then slumped into a chair. Taking hold of the paper, he stared at the photograph and handwritten words, the writing like a child's, undoubtedly disguised by the author. This wasn't the work of a child.

TOMORROW THIS WILL APPEAR EVERYWHERE. SEE HOW YOU LIKE IT.

He stared again at the photograph but didn't recognise the room or remember the night... just another party, only this time his drink, or at least one of them, must have been spiked. He had no recollection, his memory a blank.

His hands were shaking as they repeatedly ran through his tight, curly hair. *Rohypnol*, Jamie's panicked mind was shouting. No other explanation. He fumbled in his pocket for his smartphone, jabbed the call register, and hit the entry for Elliott Prince.

Bev Summers walked into Sam's office.

Yeah, Sam was right. Ed thought. *Fresh as a daisy.*

'Got the info from Jack Goddard's phone. Right charmer.' She sat down, passing a folder to both Sam and Ed.

Sam flicked through the pile of sheets, about 20 in total: lists of calls, texts, and photographs.

The printing department had quartered the pages, each segment showing a photograph of a young woman in bed, alone, the bed covers pulled back. Most of them were topless.

'Who do we think they are?' Sam said.

'University students,' Bev said. 'Those rooms are in the Halls of Residence. The students are asleep, unaware the photo's being taken. Look at page 5. Look at how many followers he's got on Instagram. More than 200.'

Horrifying. Sam thought. *Thank God social media wasn't around when I was at uni.*

Ed stiffened in his chair. 'The most well-connected generation in history and the loneliest. Don't know how to converse outside their Facebook groups. They'll get a hell of a shock when they have to step into the real world.'

Ed had seen two pictures just the other day. One showed a young soldier on a landing craft approaching Normandy with the caption 'A 19-year-old in 1944. High chance of certain death.' The next showed a lad of this generation sitting alone, knees tucked under his chin, arms wrapped around his legs. The caption read 'Because words hurt'.

To Ed, it confirmed what he had long thought. Moral cowards who leave university with bags of debt and a Mickey-mouse degree that would get them a job behind a bar or a shop counter.

'The arseholes taking the photos want stringing up,' he said quietly.

Sam stood up and stretched, her headache not as fierce but the furry carpet on her tongue a lingering reminder of the hangover.

'That's what's worrying me,' she said. 'What if there's a link between the deaths of these students. We may have just found a connection. Check if any of the deceased were following Goddard on Instagram. Check his Facebook account as well. What's this then?'

Sam had turned to a photograph of nine clearly drunk young men. Ed turned to the same page. Students, all holding cans, arms around each other, all wearing the same blue T-shirts. The printed logo, a play on Facebook and in the same font, said 'Freshers' and in the rectangular search bar 'hashtag slags and beer'.

'Are they all like that?' Bev asked, shaking her head. 'The so-called educated generation?'

'I'm sure they're not,' Sam said. 'But unis seem to get their fair share these days.'

'Half of them just want a good bat,' Ed scowled. 'Look at this lot. Arrogance personified. We can do what we want, sod the rest of society. To think my family fought in two world wars to give these tossers their freedom. Why did they bother? They'll all run home crying to mummy when the nasty policeman asks them questions.'

Sam and Bev smiled.

Bev pointed at the picture in Ed's bundle. 'We've identified Goddard, Elliott Prince, and the others who live in the house with them. There are a couple of unknowns.'

'I'll go and see the bold Elliott Prince tomorrow,' Ed said. 'He'll name them for me.'

Sam looked at Bev. 'Nothing from Tom King?'

'Not yet.'

'Another thing on the list for tomorrow,' said Sam. 'But I'm not being late tonight. It's my course.'

'Can't tempt you for one then?' Bev said.

'No. Take Ed.'

'I'm in enough shit,' Ed shook his head. 'Straight home for me. I need some brownie points.'

Sam strolled through the campus, all Tarmac, concrete and gleaming new buildings. The University of Seaton St George, USG, with the inclusive motto 'Generation Us', had been a polytechnic until 1992.

The rise in tuition fees had seen it grow almost as quickly as the vice-chancellor's salary. Almost.

Tonight's two-hour session would involve a discussion about Hemingway's 'For Whom the Bell Tolls', in particular whether Pablo was a coward because he didn't want to blow up the bridge.

Sam walked down the sterile corridor; plain cream walls without pictures or posters, light grey floor covering, and the sound of her heels echoing. She'd been home, changed into jeans and a light blue cashmere V-necked sweater.

She stepped into the classroom, desks arranged in a U shape and chairs facing the white board.

'Well you're a dark-horse.' Liz Jacobs's personality matched her size – huge.

'What do you mean?' Sam asked, pulling out a chair, knowing exactly what Liz meant.

The eyes of the other five classmates were on Sam.

'Working for the Local Authority indeed,' Liz said. 'We all saw you on the TV last night. Detective Chief Inspector. Same rank as Morse, higher than Rebus.'

Sam smiled as she sat down. 'I just wanted to keep a low profile, enjoy the course without being asked about whatever murder or high-profile crime story was in the papers. And I'm impressed you know so much about the ranks of the fictional detectives.'

'Well done you,' said Jean Stones, the grey-haired self-appointed grandmother of the group. 'I think it's wonderful that a young girl can climb the ladder in a man's world. It would never have happened in my day.'

She pulled herself closer to the desk and turned down the volume of her voice. 'I wanted to burn my bra in the early 70s but by then I'd breast-fed three kids and believe me, I needed the support.'

The women in the group laughed. Steve Jenkins, a thirty-something IT worker went crimson.

Stella Burton burst through the door. 'Evening class,' she boomed.

Sam shook her head in wonderment; what God-like mix-up had happened that bestowed such a petite young woman with a Brian Blessed voice?

Stella's eyes settled on Sam. 'Ah, our very own under-cover agent. Our very own Robert Jordan.'

'Not quite,' Sam said. 'Robert Jordan's identity was known to the group. Pablo, Maria, Anselmo etcetera.'

'Well, it seems our very own Jane Tennison, our Prime Suspect, has read Hemingway's book.' Stella grinned as she walked into the middle of the horseshoe. 'Good for you, Sam.'

The booming voice filled the room.

'Let's make a start.'

She turned and walked towards her desk, speaking with her back to the students.

'You were asked to consider whether Pablo was a coward.'

Sam was so absorbed in the session, so entranced by Stella's passion and skill, she felt a sinking feeling in her stomach when Stella called time.

Two hours had passed. She would soon be back in her car and her thoughts would turn from Hemingway's characters to the reality of Aisha and Jack Goddard. It had been good while it lasted.

'Anyone up for a drink,' Liz asked.

A few murmured yes.

'Sam?' Liz's eyes were almost pleading.

'Sorry. I need to get an early night.'

Sam saw the disappointment on Liz's face but couldn't

be bothered with the 'what's-the-worst-case-you-ever-dealt-with?' scenario tonight.

'Maybe next week,' she said

Sam rushed out and almost knocked the coffee out of the hand of a passing student. 'My God, I'm so sorry. Are you alright?'

'Yes, I'm fine. Don't worry about it.'

'Tracey?' Sam said.

Sam watched Tracey Davies's eyes glaze, knew her brain was frantically searching through the filing cabinets of her short-term memory bank.

Sam had the advantage; she didn't have a massive hangover when they last met, wasn't the one running to the bathroom.

'Sam Parker. Detective... '

'Oh hi. Sorry for not recognising you. I was a bit, you know, worse for wear the last time.'

Sam glanced at the three women grouped around Tracey. It was her turn to search her memory.

'Amber?' she said, staring at one of the girls.

'Hello Sam.' She turned to the others. 'I'll catch up, girlfriends.'

Tracey and the girls headed towards the doors.

'What are you doing here then Amber?'

'I could ask you the same.'

'I'm doing a literature course. What about you?'

'I'm a facilitator with an unofficial self-help group... girls, students, who've been subject to sexual harassment, indecent assaults, rape.'

Amber Dalton had been one of the victims of a serial rapist last year, attacked in her own bed. After her ordeal she had told Sam she wanted to help other victims.

'That's great,' Sam said. 'But why is the group unofficial?'

'I'm not sure the university would approve,' Amber told her. 'They should be doing more, Sam.' She glanced around. 'Let's talk outside.'

The cool April evening made them both shudder.

'After the attack, I had a choice... go back to Bristol or stay here,' Amber said. 'I decided to stay but I couldn't face going back to work at the council. That's when I decided to do another degree.'

'Good for you, Amber.'

'It wasn't much of a choice really,' Amber said. 'Waste my life thinking about him and asking myself 'why me?' or move on. I've moved on. Then I heard stories about girls suffering harassment and set up the group. It's a word-of-mouth thing. Like I said, the university probably wouldn't approve. Most of the time they're in denial about what goes on.'

They stopped by Sam's car.

'What sort of harassments, Amber?'

'Sam, I tell the group they can report to the police, report to you. I tell them my experience with the police was nothing but positive. But you know what it's like. I can't breach confidences.'

Sam nodded.

'These girls don't want to report because they don't want it going public. They feel they'll be judged. Got drunk so it's their fault, they asked for it. Look at the way the Press gets mileage out of students on a session... Friday nights or bank-holiday weekends. Most of the photographs they use are of girls pissed, lying on pavements, showing their knickers or flashing their boobs. Just as many lads are pissed but the girls make a better story. Drunken girls equals fair game and it doesn't matter what sex offence laws the Government brings in. It's all about perception.'

Sam could see the fire in Amber's eyes.

'So is it as big a problem?'

'Bigger than I thought. Over 50% of female students say they've been touched up when they're out or had to put up with vile comments. It's outrageous, Sam, an absolute disgrace.'

Sam knew decades of violence against women strategies and zero tolerance towards domestic abuse had failed to hold back the tide.

Social media had only made things worse.

'How did it ever get to this?' Sam said, shaking her head. 'Changing the subject, did you know Jack Goddard?'

'The guy in the river?' Amber asked. 'No. I knew of him. Part of some sick misogynist group. What did they call themselves?'

'Mortimers.'

'Yeah that's it,' Amber said. 'Sick bastards. Got what he deserves.'

'Did he?'

'Too right,' Amber said, full of defiance. 'When he got pissed and drowned in that river, if there's a God, he did his job.'

'And if he didn't fall?' Sam asked.

'Someone did God's job for him,' Amber said. 'Either way it's a win-win. I'll see you later Sam.'

Sam got into her car, watched Amber catch up to the others, and saw Tracey look over her shoulder. The group were obviously discussing her.

CHAPTER FOURTEEN

Wednesday 16th April 2014

'Morning,' Sam said, popping her head around the HOLMES room door. 'Got a minute, Ed?'

Ed followed her into her office, mug of tea in hand.

'Driving in this morning I couldn't get that Christmas photo out of my head.' She took off her blue Mac and gave it a shake, the light spray of water flying into the air before vanishing like the vapour of an e-cigarette.

'Why's that?'

Sam opened her drawer, took out a brush, and ran it through her hair.

'There just seemed something wrong. Not only that they were smiling just after Aisha had gone missing, but something else. Then I realised.'

She sat down and switched on her computer.

'Realised what?'

'They were on a different sofa to the one we were sat on,' Sam said.

Ed tried to picture the Bhandals' living room.

'People do change settees,' he said.

'I know,' Sam told him. 'The one in the photo seemed fairly new. It's probably nothing. Liked you said, make a change. Anything new?'

Ed took a drink from his still steaming mug.

'Search team's finished at the riverbank. Nothing.'

'I wasn't holding out much hope. Anything else?'

'Thirteen calls saying there's a serial killer on the loose,' Ed said. 'All anonymous. Seven males, six females. Three made from phones in the university, the rest from public phone boxes.'

'Anything we can do with the university phones?' Sam asked.

Ed shook his head.

'Could be any internal phone. A few girls from the university have called to say Goddard was a sexual predator who didn't like being turned down. They've been actioned out. Bev's going to see them and we're going to see Tom King, the doorman, in 30 minutes.'

'What?' Sam demanded. 'How did that come about?'

'A mutual acquaintance set it up for me.'

'I won't ask.'

'He'll meet us by the pier,' Ed told her.

'In this weather?' Sam said.

'Better that than chase our tails looking for him. Apparently if he doesn't want finding, he can be very elusive.'

Sam was surprised.

'What, a 19-year-old with no previous and we couldn't find him?'

'We've not managed up to now.' Ed was already at the door. 'We'll get a coffee down there. He's not a suspect. We can bring him if we want the interview on tape but I'm not sure it'll be necessary.'

Sam stood up and put her wet Mac back on. 'Why?'

'From what I've heard he's not the type to hit someone from behind and especially not with a hammer,' Ed said. 'Everyone says he's good enough to take people on face to face, and certainly someone like Jack Goddard.'

The rain was fine, persistent and penetrating and the mist patchy, swirling around like the set of a B-movie horror. Wet trousers as tight as Lycra clung to their thighs and strands of Sam's hair were plastered to her head. Ed's bald scalp was a wet sheen.

In the 10 minutes they'd stood on the esplanade, backs to the pier, they had seen only a middle-aged woman jog past with her black Labrador, his pads splashing water as he ran. The promenade coffee shop was empty. No one had gone in since they'd bought a flat white and a cappuccino.

'Looks like a no-show,' Sam said, hands wrapped around the paper cup, the dregs of the cappuccino failing miserably to warm them.

Ed squinted, eyes searching for a silhouette appearing out of the grey, dreich shadows. 'Give him another five.'

'Ed Whelan?' Two quiet words conveyed politeness and confidence.

Ed and Sam spun around. Neither expected him to emerge from the unprotected pier, not in this weather. He must have been on there before they arrived.

Ed wasn't used to looking up at people. 'Yeah, that's me. You must be Tom.'

Tom King, all 6'8" of him, wore a blue-and-yellow Berghaus jacket and black waterproof Berghaus trousers. He kept his hands in his pockets and nodded. 'I hear you want to speak to me about Saturday night?'

'You heard right. Coffee?'

'No thanks.'

'This is Detective Chief Inspector Parker. She's in charge.'

'Hi Tom, thanks for coming.'

'No problem. What do you want to know?'

'You had an argument with a man on Saturday night... ' Ed said.

'I'll stop you there,' Tom King interrupted. 'I argued with nobody. A group of lads who were being dicks needed to leave. One of them squared up then threw beer over me. I just smiled at him. I've seen him before. He's the original King Dick. He left with his mates and I've not seen him since. He was pissed. If he fell in the river, tough shit.'

Sam spoke. 'So you know he's dead?'

'It's obvious,' Tom said calmly. 'Why else do you want to see me?'

'You don't feel any sympathy for him?' Sam said.

Tom's eyes were steady, his tone neutral.

'You wouldn't feel any sympathy for him if you knew him,' he said. 'Treats women like dirt. Don't get me wrong, I'd have loved to give him a good kicking. His sort deserves it. Arrogant and no manners, especially around women. No loss to society as far as I'm concerned.'

'Did you not fancy university?' Sam said, trying to read him.

'No. I work the doors to pay my way. I do landscape photography, a bit of sport photography. Best way to learn is by getting out there, not sitting in some class. Those who can, do, those who can't, teach. You know the saying.'

'What did you do when you finished work Saturday?' Sam asked.

'Straight home,' Tom told them. 'Taxi. Ate some chicken and beans then went to bed. I was at the gym for about 10 on Sunday.'

'Anybody verify that?' Sam said.

He stiffened and the veins on his neck stuck out. Politeness was suddenly replaced with aggression.

'What, like my mother?' Tom said. 'Locked away because the system failed her.'

He looked over his shoulder, towards the invisible sea, now covered in a blanket of fog. When he next spoke, his voice was again quiet and controlled.

'I live by myself. The taxi driver, Eddie, I think he's called, should remember dropping me at home. We use the same firm all the time from work.'

'But nobody can verify you stayed at home all night,' Sam said.

'No they can't.'

'We'll need to get a witness statement,' Sam told him. 'When's a good time?'

'Today, I suppose.'

'I'll send someone round to your house if that's okay?' Sam said.

'Yeah, no problem. That it then?'

'That's it,' Sam said. 'Thanks for coming to meet us.'

Tom was already walking away.

'Coffee?' Ed asked.

'Definitely. I'm damp to my bones… polite lad.'

She made no attempt to move. 'But the way he turned when I asked about verifying his alibi… the aggression in his voice… and we know he can handle himself.'

'Which is why I tend to believe him,' Ed said. 'He doesn't need a weapon, and we're never going to be flavour of the month in his world. His mother's beaten almost daily and ends up in prison because every time we go round it was just another domestic and we did nothing.'

'Things are different now, thankfully,' Sam said.

'Are they? Do you believe that Sam? Everybody might say the right things at your level in morning prayers when the previous night's jobs are being discussed but are you convinced the rank and file on the streets are dealing with domestic violence, sorry domestic abuse, any better than we were years ago? I'm not.'

Ed started walking.

'Well I hope so,' Sam said, bending down, pulling at her trousers, trying to get them to part from her thighs.

'You have more faith than me,' Ed told her. 'There are plenty of solid, hard-working cops, the ones who stay dedicated to the job, but there's still a smattering of lazy bastards who'll do anything to do nothing.'

'Flat white?' Sam asked.

'Go on then.' Ed answered his mobile. 'Alright?'

He stood away from the counter. 'Make it half an hour…okay, I'll see you there.'

He took the coffee off Sam, who had opted for proper cups, and walked to the table furthest away from the counter. The shop was still empty.

He waited until they were both sitting.

'That was Elliott Prince,' Ed said. 'Wants a meet. Says it's urgent.'

'Did he say what about?' Sam asked.

'He didn't want to talk on the phone,' Ed told her. 'He was bricking it, though. We're meeting in 30 minutes in the last lay-by before the Golden Eagle.'

Sam sipped her coffee. 'All a bit clandestine.'

'Like I said, he was bricking it.'

Elliott Prince stepped out of his battered Vauxhall Corsa as soon as Ed pulled into the lay-by and was in the back of the police Ford Mondeo before Ed switched off the ignition.

Ed looked over his shoulder. 'You remember Detective Chief Inspector Parker.'

Elliott blushed and nodded. 'I thought it was just going to be you.'

'Sorry to disappoint, but I was already out with the DCI,' Ed said.

Using someone's rank, especially a rank above Sergeant, normally unnerved people who had something to worry about in the first place.

'Now what was so urgent?'

Elliott reached into his inner coat pocket and handed Ed a piece of A4 paper.

Ed looked at it before passing it to Sam.

'Who's the lad?' she asked.

'Jamie Telford.'

Jamie Telford was on all fours, naked from the waist down, trousers and underpants around his ankles. A sex toy was inserted in his backside.

CHAPTER FIFTEEN

SAM TWISTED in her seat and looked at Prince.

'And has it?' she said, referring to the written message on the piece of paper.

'What?' Prince looked non-plussed.

'Appeared everywhere today?'

He nodded quickly.

'I've had calls to say that there are loads going around the university. Jamie's nowhere to be found now. Not surprising, I suppose.'

Elliott Prince explained how Jamie had contacted him after receiving the photograph and then brought it to him. Since then Elliott hadn't been able to contact him.

'The message is signed by the Sisters of Macavity,' Sam said. 'Any idea what that's about?'

'No.'

'What's going on, Elliott?' Ed pushed. 'Is this something to do with your little group?'

'I don't know,' Elliot Prince said slowly. 'Maybe. Jack dead. Jamie getting this.'

'So Jamie was in your Mortimer group?' Ed asked.

'Yes,' Elliot answered. 'He doesn't live with us, but he's in the group.'

'The note says, 'see how you like it'. What's Jamie done?' Ed went on.

Elliot looked at the carpet.

'Some of the lads take pictures. You know, of the girls when they're asleep, pissed up.'

'And then you circulate them on social media,' Sam said. 'We've seen some of them.'

Her voice was cold with contempt and disgust.

Elliot didn't look up. 'We never harmed anybody.'

'Are you kidding me?' Ed shouted. 'Circulating pictures of girls? Pictures you had no right to take let alone spread around. Some might say this Jamie Telford character is getting what he deserved.'

Elliot's shoulders shook and his breathing resembled an asthmatic reaching for their inhaler.

'There's a difference between taking photographs of them sleeping and what they've done to Jamie.'

The condensation on the windows was hiding everything outside. Ed turned the ignition key, depressed the switch for the windows, and opened them all a crack. 'Tell that to the girls.'

Sam spoke. 'Elliott, do you think there are photos of you?'

'I don't know,' he said. 'There could be. Jamie couldn't remember anything about that photo. He says he must have been drugged. He's convinced of that.'

'So what do you think then Elliott?' Sam said.

His jaw tensed and his eyes grew dark.

'People are after us,' he said. 'I can't get hold of Jamie. Glen's not answering his phone. Jack's dead.'

'Elliott, I want you to drive Ed to the police station,' Sam told him. 'He'll take a statement from you. I want to know the name of every girl you photographed... '

'There are loads,' he said in a whisper.

'Well you better start racking your brains then, and I want the name of every member of this pathetic group of yours. Is that understood?'

He nodded, rubbed his eyes and sniffed.

'Good,' Sam said. 'And Ed will show you a photograph of a group of you wearing T-shirts with the hashtag 'slags and beer' written on them. I want the name of everybody in that group.'

'I don't know which photo you're talking about,' Elliot told them.

'Ed will show it to you,' Sam said. 'I'm sure it will jog your memory.'

Elliott Prince had given Ed the names of 14 girls before they reached the police station. In the interview room he identified every lad in the hashtag photograph.

'Glen will give the names of any girls I've forgotten or didn't know about,' he said. 'Glen was there every time with Jack.'

Ed wrote the girls' names on a piece of paper, the boys' names he wrote on the photograph.

'Do you think any of them had anything to do with Jack ending up in the river?' Elliott said.

'Do you?'

'I don't know. It was only supposed to be banter. It wasn't about killing people.'

Ed finished with Elliott and found himself walking along Aisha's terraced street. He walked past her house, got to the junction, turned around and watched. He had no idea what he was looking for. Inspiration?

Friday 13th December

He was at the end of the street. I was worried he wouldn't be there. What if he hadn't come? Then what? I didn't know whether to walk or run. Running would attract attention. My bag felt heavy, but that was more to do with my heart than its actual weight.

I'd lived in this street all my life: played hopscotch, hide-and-seek, street games. It was great until I reached puberty, then wallop. Everything changed. I'd known about Izzat since I was about seven, but by the time I entered my teenage years, the levels of expectation around my behaviour increased massively.

And the thing was, you had absolutely no idea who was watching you and reporting back. The only way to stay out of trouble was to conform. But how many teenage girls brought up in England want to do that? Have a guess. Exactly. Zero.

So you ended up in No Man's Land. We did the First World War at school, so I understand the concept. That's where I was; caught between the land where I'd been born, and the land that was dictating my behaviour. My No Man's Land might have been invisible but it was no less real.

The car lights were off but I could make out Sukhi behind the wheel. The car was parked directly under a lamppost.

I had no idea where we'd go. South, I supposed. Not

Birmingham or Leicester, way too many Asians. As soon as you turned up they'd be asking where are you from, who are your parents, what village are they from? That's what it's like. Everybody is linked, everybody knows someone in your family. Not London either. Too big and I like being by the sea.

I remembered watching holiday programmes on the TV. Cornwall always looked nice. Bethany's been there, said she had a great time. The sea is warmer than it is up here. And that Rick Stein's from there, you know, the chef on the TV who cooks fish.

I liked the sound of Cornwall. Suggest it to Sukhi. It'd take a few hours to drive there, maybe three? I was just guessing. I'd got no idea. Hey, we might be there in time for fish and chips. That'd be good, especially if Rick cooked them.

And it'd be worth the journey because I'd never heard my family talk of any Sikhs living there. No Asians, no questions. And if people were looking for us, we'd be miles away.

Sukhi would have to get rid of his car. They'd be able to trace us through that. I saw a programme once. It might have been on the news, or was it a short documentary? Anyway, a girl like me had run away. The family didn't report her missing. They reported a theft, said she ran off with a load of money. Police saw her car, arrested her. Family dropped the charges saying they would take her back, forgive her. What happened? You guessed it. She was never seen again.

Sukhi was out of the car now, stood by the passenger door. I was memorising as much as I could, even the colours of the doors. It'd be a long time before I was back in this street. Probably never.

Cornwall. We might need to buy a map.

Wednesday 16th April 2014

Sam's intention was to drive straight back to HQ, not park up, but she was distracted, fishing the rivers of her memory, trying to catch Macavity.

The Sisters of Macavity? The answer was swimming in there somewhere.

She found Classic FM, turned the blown air to high and pulled out of the lay-by. Johan Strauss seeped from the speakers, emptying her head of everything except a school trip to Vienna, a life of first dates and friendships, dead boys and missing girls not on her teenage radar.

She headed out of town, concentrating on the music, trying to forget about Aisha and Jack Goddard.

Her fingers tapped the wheel. Strauss and Vienna... theatres, costumes, darkened auditoriums. Her mind lingered – theatres, costumes, dark auditoriums.

Strauss was still playing when her left palm slammed the wheel, a bite on her metaphorical rod. Eliot, not Elliott. She dropped into third gear, sped towards the university, and called Stella Burton en route.

Stella, in the corner of the canteen, stood up when Sam walked in.

'Sam. Good to see you.'

They air kissed each other's cheek. 'Coffee?'

'That'll be great. White. No sugar. Thanks.'

Sam sat on the metal chair and took in the soft yellows and earthy browns on the walls, glancing at academics huddled in twos and threes and talking in whispers. Stella was standing perfectly still in the queue, a 50-year-old spinster with frizzy, mousey hair, thick-framed black glasses, and a heavy-duty, ankle-length, olive-green, knitted skirt that probably weighed more than she did.

She walked back towards Sam, greeting a couple of people as she negotiated the tables.

'So, you're interested in Macavity.'

'I am,' Sam said, pulling the coffee towards her.

'Thomas Stearns Eliot. T.S.Eliot. Genius of a man. Macavity was the only villain in Eliot's Cats. You know, the mystery cat, the flying paw, the master criminal, baffling Scotland Yard, driving the Flying Squad to despair.'

Again Sam was entranced, lost in Stella's almost musical voice. She might consider a degree in English Literature.

'So if I aligned myself to Macavity, am I saying I'm a criminal, albeit an educated one?'

Stella said: 'I think it's more subtle than that. Educated to the extent that the individual knows about T.S.Eliot's Cats. Macavity was outwardly respectable.' Stella leaned across the table and whispered.

'Although they say he cheats at cards.'

She laughed and rocked back in her chair.

'When the police arrive at the crime scene, he's not there. So it's more than just being a criminal. It's about a criminal who never gets caught.'

Worrying, Sam thought.

'The cats had colours, didn't they? What colour was Macavity?'

'Tall, thin, and ginger,' Stella said.

An image appeared... a tall, redheaded English Literature student Sam had recently met.

CHAPTER SIXTEEN

THE MIDDLE-AGED SIKH man ignored Ed as he walked past. Ed didn't ignore him. He stared long and hard: grey stubble, thin lips, maroon turban. His heart rate increased. It always did when he made his own luck.

He'd seen that combination of stubble, thin lips and maroon turban before.

His eyes never left the short man with the un-pressed black trousers and scuffed dark brown shoes, willing him to knock on Aisha's door.

Ed held his breath. The Sikh was about three doors away, four, tops. If he walked past, Ed would follow him.

The Sikh didn't walk past. He didn't knock. He walked straight in.

Jackpot. He's family.

The man in the background of the photograph Bethany Stevens had taken as a joke, the photograph showing Aisha kissing Sukhi, is family. The Kiss of Death scenario had just seen its odds slashed.

Ed walked slowly towards the house. It would be considered incredibly rude not to introduce everyone inside if you were the head of a Sikh household. Get inside and he would know who was in Bethany's photograph.

He knocked. Davinder Bhandal answered.

'Sergeant, come in please.'

Ed looked at the photograph on the table. Sam was right. The settee Mia and Baljit were sitting on did look new.

In the living room, thin lips was on his feet. It was a different sofa to the one in the picture.

'Gurmej, this is Sergeant Whelan. Sergeant Whelan, this is my brother-in-law Gurmej.'

Ed held out his hand. Gurmej shook it, albeit with some reticence.

'Tea, Sergeant?' Davinder asked. 'Or perhaps something a little stronger?'

'No thanks. I won't take up much of your time.' Ed sat down, the others followed. He looked at the father. 'In the initial report you said Aisha had her mobile with her when she went missing.'

'That's correct.'

'Had you ever considered she had more than one?'

'I'd never thought of that, Sergeant. I don't think she'd have had any money for phones, but I'll ask my wife.'

'It's just with her not using the number you have for her, I wondered if anybody ever suggested she may have had another one.'

'Not to my knowledge Sergeant, but I will ask the family, see if it could be a possibility.'

'Thank you.' Ed stood up. 'I'll not keep you any longer.'

Ed was shown to the door. Pleasant good-byes followed.

Ed grabbed his mobile. He needed a lift back to HQ. His face was gleaming, his body glowing. It was always like this when a plan came together. Whether Aisha was alive or not, and he still hoped she was, the family were of the belief Ed thought she was. That's exactly what he wanted them to think.

He burst into Sam's office.

'The guy in the background of the photo, the one Bethany took, it's Aisha's uncle.'

'Really? Oh my God.'

Ed filled Sam in with the details of his visit.

She stood up and walked to the window. It was still one of those miserable days you get in April, although this April had been warmer than most, but at least it had stopped raining a couple of hours ago.

'Macavity was the bad guy in T.S.Eliot's Cats,' Sam said. 'The criminal who never got caught.'

Ed sat down. 'Very clever. Goddard's group's called Mortimers. A play on Mickey Mouse? I'm shooting from the hip here.'

Sam nodded. 'Feel free.'

'Motto – if you love the mouse, chase the pussy. One of the Mortimers gets a compromising photo, sent by the Sisters of Macavity. Sisters, suggesting women, and Macavity's a cat. Cats chase mice. Is this making sense?'

Sam turned around and leaned against the window.

'Absolutely. Plus Macavity suggests a decent standard of education. And Macavity was a skinny, tall, ginger cat. Not unlike... '

Ed smiled. 'Our very own feline Tracey Davies.'

'Well you certainly made her purr,' Sam teased.

'Ha ha, very funny, but seriously, it's all a bit far-fetched, tenuous bordering on the ridiculous.'

'I agree.' Sam sat down.

'That said, I did say that there was more to Tracey than meets the eye, and she was aggressive, but murder?

Sam was lost in thought.

'And she was with Amber Dalton at the university last night.'

'Really?'

'Did I not tell you?' Sam said. 'Sorry. I'll fill you in on that later. Okay, let's check out Tracey's movements for Saturday night after Goddard was thrown out of the Jolly Roger. And the girl who got tapped up…Charlotte. What was her name?'

'Swains, plural of the guy who played for Villa years ago – Kenny Swain. That's how I remembered it.'

'And Alex O'Connell,' Sam continued. 'She found the body. Get their phones done. I know Alex said she was checking up on Charlotte, so no doubt she did text her. Question is, was Alex's phone in close vicinity to Charlotte's when the text was sent?'

'Will do,' Ed said. 'We need to know where we stand with these girls.'

'And we need to check out Aisha's uncle,' Sam added.

Ed was at the doorway.

'By the way, you were right,' he said. 'The settee in the photograph does look new.'

Tracey Davies opened her front door. The look of disappointment on her face was instant and obvious.

'Can I see some ID please?'

Bev Summers showed Tracey her warrant card.

'Sorry about that, but I was expecting Ed.'

Obviously, Bev thought.

Tracey's eye shadow was subtle, the pale red lipstick accentuated her plump lips, the swirl of perfume just a little heavy for 2pm.

'He sends his apologies,' Bev said.

She followed Tracey into the living room, watched her short red skirt ride up her long thighs as she sat down.

'I just need to ask a few questions about Saturday,' Bev said as she sat in an armchair. The room was a lot tidier than Sam had described, probably down to 'The Ed Factor'.

'Sure, fire away. I was expecting to do this on Monday.'

'Sometimes things happen in an investigation that take priority,' Bev told her. 'After you spoke to Jack Goddard in the Jolly... '

'Hardly spoke. He came up to us.'

'My apologies. After Jack Goddard left your company, what happened during the rest of your night?'

'We saw him get thrown out by the doormen,' Tracey said. 'We stayed a bit longer, probably until about 10. Charlotte and me got talking to a couple of lads in there. We arranged to meet up with them later and go to a party. We went to Rendezvous club about 11. Left there with Charlotte and the lads about half three then went to the party. It was crap.'

She reached across the floor and picked up her cigarettes and disposable lighter. 'You don't mind, do you?'

'Not as long as you don't.' Bev said, reaching into her handbag.

They both lit up.

Tracey blew smoke and spoke again.

'Left the party about half four, got a kebab from the all-night takeaway and came home. Knew no more until I saw Alex's post on social media and then when Ed and the woman came round. I saw her last night at the uni.'

Bev took a piece of folded A4 from her bag and rummaged for a pen.

'Okay. The lads first. What were their names?'

'No idea,' Tracey said behind more smoke. 'I mean, I

knew at the time, but not now. I couldn't remember the next day. Charlotte might know.'

'Had you met them before?'

'Seen them around,' Tracey said. 'But never spoke to them.'

'Can you describe them?'

'I'll try.'

'Did you see Jack Goddard or Glen Jones again that night?'

'No,' Tracey said, tapping her cigarette on a clean tin ashtray.

'Okay, I'll just get a quick statement,' Bev told her. 'It won't take long.'

She stubbed her cigarette and began to write.

Charlotte Swains was shorter than Tracey but no less attractive. They were making Bev feel old. Where did the time go? It only seemed like yesterday when she was their age. It was as if she'd closed her eyes for a moment and shot forward 20 years or more in a time machine. Now standing in the small kitchen, watching Charlotte make the coffees, she felt like a granny, more years behind her than in front. Maybe it really was time to start planning retirement.

'So, Saturday,' Bev said. 'Tell me about your night.'

'We all went to the Jolly Roger at eightish. Me, Alex, Tracey, Anastasia and Juliette. Left there about 10 and went to Rendezvous.'

She handed the mug of instant to Bev.

'We left with a couple of lads about half three,' Charlotte went on. 'Went to a party with them, left there half four or so and came home.'

Charlotte reached for her cigarettes. She offered one to Bev, who accepted.

'Do you remember the lads' names?'

Charlotte smiled. 'It wasn't that kind of night. We were just having a laugh. Nothing serious. I couldn't tell you their names.'

She agreed she had seen them around town and would be able to provide a rough description.

'Where did you meet these lads?' Bev asked. 'Rendezvous?'

'No. The Jolly Roger.'

'Jack Goddard.'

'Who?'

'The drunks in the Jolly Roger.'

'Oh, them,' Charlotte said, studying the glowing tip of her cigarette.

'Did you see them again that night?'

'I didn't,' Charlotte answered. 'Poor Alex obviously did.'

'So did you meet the lads before or after the drunks?'

Charlotte gave that some thought.

'After,' she said.

'There's something not right about them,' Bev said, standing by the kettle in the HOLMES room.

'In what way?' Sam asked.

'It's just a feeling in my water,' Bev shrugged. 'Mind you, you were right about Tracey. Dolled up to the nines. You should have seen her face when she saw me. Even told me she was expecting Ed.'

Sam rolled her eyes.

Bev smiled and whispered: 'Walls have ears.'

Ed walked in. 'What did you make of those two then?'

'I was just saying there's something not right about them.' She poured the hot water into two mugs. 'Want one, Ed?'

'Cheers.'

'Their stories were too similar, the times too precise, the vague descriptions of the two lads could have fitted half the under 25s of the UK.'

'When was the last time they said they saw Jack Goddard?' Ed asked.

'In the Jolly Roger.'

He took the mug from the windowsill. 'You best follow me.'

The three of them stood around a TV monitor in a small adjoining office. Paul Adams was sitting in front of it.

'Show them, Paul.'

He pressed play and the screen flickered into life. Seaton St George town centre.

'Look at the time,' Ed said. '11.30.'

The picture quality wasn't great, but it was good enough.

'The time is about five minutes out,' Ed said. 'The tower clock is showing 11.30 when the timer shows 11.35. Look,' Ed said, pointing at the screen. 'Here's Tracey and Charlotte.'

Sam and Bev stood either side of Paul and leaned closer to the screen.

'Keep watching,' Ed said. When he next spoke, his voice was louder. 'There.'

Paul froze the screen.

'Well, well,' Sam said.

'I knew they were lying,' Bev said.

Both girls looked at ease with Jack Goddard and Glen Jones.

CHAPTER SEVENTEEN

Ed unwrapped a Twix.

'The best lies are always the ones closest to the truth.' He turned the confectionery in his hand. 'Jesus, if these shrink any more The Borrowers will be able to eat them… Tracey and Charlotte say they went clubbing with two guys they met in the Jolly Roger.'

'Goddard and Jones?' Sam said.

'Exactly.'

'Paul.' Sam was on her feet. 'Sort out the CCTV from the front door of Rendezvous. See if we can get Tracey and Charlotte going in and more importantly, coming out.'

'Will do.'

'Start with them coming out,' Sam told him. 'Look after three. Maybe Jack Goddard was in there…Christ, wouldn't you think someone would have a conscience and tell us? The calls from the public are a joke. I've seen more calls on prostitute murders.'

It was well known within murder teams that the type of victim often dictated the amount of help coming in from the public. A child abduction and the phones were melting but with prostitutes, the attitude often seemed to be 'so-what', despite the best efforts of SIOs to humanise their victim.

'They either despised Jack Goddard and don't want to get involved, or they were so pissed they genuinely can't remember seeing him,' Ed said.

'Or high on whatever and don't want us poking around in their business?' Bev ventured.

'Nonetheless, a young man is dead... murdered,' Sam said. 'I want Jamie Telford and Glen Jones locating. Bring Jones in. Can we have a have quick heads-up?'

Nods all round.

'My office in 10.'

Sam threw the Manila folder into the centre of the table. A4 paper with four photos to a sheet slid out. Each photo a different girl, all taken from Goddard's phone.

'I don't want these photos being shown to all and sundry, but we need to identify these girls,' Sam said. 'Some will be too embarrassed to want anything doing but some might.'

Bev thumbed through them and stopped on the third sheet. She pointed at the girl in the bottom left corner. 'That's Charlotte Swains.'

Sam held out her hand, took the sheet from Bev, and studied the picture.

'She was with Tracey Davies and Amber Dalton when I saw them in the university on Tuesday night.'

Paul looked at the photograph.

Ed looked at Sam. 'You got on well with Amber, didn't you?'

'I did.'

Paul Adams's only involvement in that rape and murder investigation was as a Family Liaison Officer. He put the paper on the desk.

'Amber reported to me,' Sam said. 'She was the rabbit in the surveillance and I kept in touch with her up to trial.'

'Perhaps you should pay her a visit,' Ed said. 'Could the group she's involved with be Macavity?'

'Possibly.'

'One thing's for certain,' Ed continued. 'Elliott Prince never mentioned Charlotte Swains when he gave me the list of girls they'd photographed.'

Bev jumped in, her words rapid.

'Another two of these photographs,' she said, 'They're women I visited who'd rang in to say Goddard was a predator.'

'But,' Sam said. 'They never mentioned the photographs.'

Paul spoke. 'As we've all said, maybe they were embarrassed, and if they thought we didn't know about them, they may have just chosen to not tell us.'

Sam moved that slice of the investigation to one side and turned the attention back to Aisha.

'Tomorrow I want samples of Aisha's handwriting,' she said. 'Get them from college or even better from friends but not from her home. I don't want the parents antagonising. Not yet anyway. If something has happened to Aisha, I want them to think we're on their side, that we believe them. If something has happened to her, we're not going to sort it overnight, but just in case she writes to us, or anybody else, I want to be ahead of the game.'

Ed walked along to the small office where the Intelligence

Cell was located. It wasn't the biggest intelligence set-up, but it was, for now at least, dedicated to both investigations.

Two detectives, late 40s, were sat behind desks, writing in the A4 books next to their computers.

'Stand by your beds,' Ed said, closing the door behind him.

The two greeted him with the look of tired, hungry men.

How's it going guys?'

'I'm just about finished with Aisha's uncle,' one answered.

Ed wheeled the spare chair alongside the detective, sat down and looked at the screen.

In the centre was the name Gurmej, a spider's web of lines spreading out from it.

The strands showed his address, properties and vehicles he had access to, and his associates. He hadn't come to the attention of the police, but some of those associates were already known. He was unemployed and moonlighted as a taxi driver, but as the Licensing Authority had no record of him, he was probably driving someone else's car and using their hackney carriage licence.

'So, bogus taxi driver,' Ed said.

'Yes.'

'You know what, Asian taxi drivers have a better intelligence set-up than we do.' Ed rubbed his eyes. 'Families use them to spy on their daughters. Any shameful behaviour is then reported back to the family. Can I get a printout of that?'

A key depressed and the printer whirred into life.

'Cheers,' Ed said, standing up, pushing the chair and letting it slide towards the wall. 'Did I ever tell about the time when I was a young PC, a superintendent came into panda control, handed me an envelope and told me to fax it to a superintendent in a neighbouring police station?'

Both detectives shook their heads.

'I started to open the envelope and he went ballistic,' Ed told them. 'Called me a moron and said 'can't you read?', it says private and confidential, you imbecile'.

'But... ' I said. 'Don't you 'but' me, just fax it, or you'll find yourself on point duty for the next month. I didn't fancy directing traffic so I just faxed the envelope.'

The two detectives started laughing.

'The daft bugger thought he was Doctor Who, fax the envelope and the Super at the other end would open it. He never came back when the other Super no doubt ripped the piss out of him. How would the likes of him manage now?'

He took the paper out of the printer and walked out, the detectives still having a chuckle. They were in a windowless office, more like a cupboard, and did a great job. It was Ed's responsibility to make sure they kept it up. A little humour went a long way.

Ed's smiles didn't last long. He'd barely walked 10 metres along the corridor when he answered his mobile and spoke to a Detective Inspector from Devon and Cornwall Constabulary.

Introductions over, the DI outlined the reason for his call.

'It was found in a disused lock-up on the outskirts of Plymouth,' he told Ed. 'On bricks, stripped. No interior, engine gone, but the VIN plate was still on it. That's how we identified it.'

Ed terminated the call. Why was Sukhi's car in a lock-up in Plymouth?

CHAPTER EIGHTEEN

Ed walked into Sam's office. His nostrils twitched at the smell of a recently smoked cigarette. Since people had to actually walk off-site to smoke, she'd probably had two.

'Enjoy them?' Ed said.

'I need to quit again,' Sam sounded like she was trying to convince herself. 'I hate standing out there, smoking on the roadside.'

The lunatics had finally taken over the asylum. Headquarters was set in acres of its own grounds but people had to walk on to the main road and smoke in front of passing motorists – a great image for the police.

'Still beyond me why people can't smoke in the grounds,' Ed said. 'You know when I joined for the first time back in 1978, the only non-cops were the cleaners, the typists, and the cooks. That was it. Everybody else was a cop. Chief Inspector in charge of admin and finance at each nick, overseen by one of the ACCs. Now support staff, an oxymoron if ever was there was one, make up a huge proportion of our numbers and complain about everything.'

Familiar rant over, Ed sat down. It was just after 6pm.

'Sukhi's car's been found in a lock-up in Plymouth.'

'What?' Sam looked up.

Ed told her the gist of his conversation with the DI.

'Plymouth?' Sam repeated. 'So what does that mean? They drove as far away from the North East as possible? That would make sense.'

Ed wasn't convinced.

'Or somebody drove the car there so if it was found, it would throw us off the scent, focus all our enquiries down there.'

Sam was silent, running possibilities through her mind.

'I can understand why they'd get rid of the car,' she said at last. 'It could be used to trace them. Aisha's family would only need someone working in the DVLA. The car's got to be taxed and tested.'

Both Sam and Ed knew there had been cases around the country of runaway girls being tracked down by distant relatives with jobs working in housing departments, benefits offices, even the police.

'They couldn't sell it, not legally,' Ed was saying now. 'But it could be moved on for parts to someone who wouldn't ask questions.'

'Car ringers?' Sam suggested.

'Possible.'

Sam stood up. 'You know, the romantic in me hopes they've got to Devon and are living happily ever after in a little white cottage overlooking the sea.'

'And the realist?' Ed asked.

'Just keeps hoping they're alive.'

Jamie Telford and Glen Jones had spent the day holed up

in one of the sea-front beach huts, their phones off. The huts, run during the summer by the local authority, were locked out of season. Glen had forced the padlock from the end hut months ago and put his own padlock in its place. He knew he'd have the hut until the end of May when the council prepared them for hire.

'Why did you tell Elliott?' Glen said, sitting on an old beer crate. 'You know he'll only feel more important.'

Jamie lit another cigarette.

'I couldn't get hold of you and I was panicking.'

The inside of the hut was like the worst inner-city smog or the infamous smoking rooms in Schiphol airport, fresh air as scarce as rocking-horse dung.

Glen opened the door, the rush of salty sea air a relief even to a devoted smoker like him.

'Does he know about your letter?' Jamie said.

'Nobody knew about it until I told you an hour ago,' Glen answered. 'Nobody alive anyway. Jack knew.'

Jamie picked up the piece of paper from the wooden table.

'And you've no idea when this was taken?'

'None,' Glen said. 'How many parties have we been to in the last two years? How many times have we woken up with hardly a clue what happened the night before?'

Jamie looked again the paper. 'Yeah, but on this one you and Jack are together.'

'We were always together,' Glen said. 'Besides, the pictures could have been taken separately and messed with on Photoshop. There's no such thing as 'the camera never lies' anymore.'

Jamie was still looking at the paper and the photograph it held, Glen and Jack on their hands and knees, a vibrator inserted into each of their backsides. 'What did Jack say about it?'

'To ignore them,' Glen said. 'Ours never came with a threat to distribute. Never came with a threat, full stop. Just said Sisters of Macavity.'

'Have you no idea who's doing it?'

Glen shook his head once. 'Perm any one from dozens.'

Jamie stubbed his cigarette into a glass ashtray.

'Are you going to the police?'

Glen laughed with zero humour. 'And say what? We've taken pictures of loads of girls asleep in their beds and sent them out on Instagram and now this has happened? Don't think so.'

'But what if these Sisters of Macavity killed Jack?' Jamie said.

'I think they did,' Glen hesitated. 'When we find out who they are, we might tell the police... or we might solve the problem ourselves.'

Jamie looked hard at his friend.

'Don't be daft, Glen,' Jamie said. 'What can we sort? We don't even know who we'd be looking for.'

'Not every girl on campus hates us, Jamie,' Glen told him, then fell silent.

Jamie Telford reached for the half bottle of whisky. Maybe he should go to the police himself.

Ed turned into his street and immediately saw the E-Class Mercedes parked on the road outside his house. Eric's car.

Shit, have I forgotten another night?

He was pulling on to the driveway as Sue rushed out and opened the driver's door almost before he had stopped.

'Eric and Leela have popped round,' she said quickly.

Thank God I haven't forgotten anything

'Is everything okay?' Ed asked her.

Sue was almost whispering. 'They have some information about Gurmej – Aisha's uncle.'

'What information?' Ed shut the car door.

'I don't know,' Sue said. 'They want to tell you. They want certain assurances, Ed. They're scared.'

They walked towards the front door.

'Have they had a drink?' Ed asked.

'Leela's driving but Eric's on the whisky.'

Ed looked at his watch. 'In that case, I'll have a beer, pet.'

He chanced his arm and playfully smacked her on the bum as she crossed the threshold. Her little shriek and jump meant he was out of the dog house, for now at least.

'How's it going, Eric? Leela?' Ed said in greeting.

They were both sitting around the large farmhouse table.

'Could be better,' Eric said, eyes fixed on the whisky in the tumbler he held in his hand.

Sue passed Ed a chilled bottle of Newcastle Brown.

'We'll leave you to it,' Sue said, leading Leela into the living room.

'What's up, Eric?' Ed asked when the two men were alone.

'Ed, I need certain guarantees,' Eric told him. 'What I'm about to say has to be between you and me.'

His hand shook as he raised the crystal tumbler.

'I won't make any statements and I certainly won't go to court. I can't let it get out that I've told you.'

He gulped the whisky and wiped his chin.

'You know that not everybody in my community approves of your relationship with Sue, or my friendship with you.'

Ed poured his beer into a Wellington glass.

'You know my thoughts on some of the so-called leaders in that community,' he said. 'Self-elected and bigoted misogynists.'

Eric was looking at his whisky again.

'I know, but Ed, I cannot let them know that my relationship is anything but one of friendship with you. If they thought I passed on information, that I was a police informant... '

His voice trailed off, his eyes full of doubt and fear.

'Hang on,' Ed said. 'You're hardly a paid informant and what information you give me is tittle-tattle. Do you want a snack?'

Eric shook his head and swallowed more Scotch.

'No thank you,' He said. 'What I'm about to tell you is not tittle-tattle.'

His shaking hand went to the bottle. Another top-up. Beads of sweat formed on his forehead.

'Okay,' Ed said. 'I won't say anything. Whatever you tell me is between you and me.'

'Can you guarantee that?' Another gulp. 'I'm trusting you here.'

Ed nodded.

'I can Eric. One hundred per cent.'

Eric closed his eyes and took a breath, galvanising himself to overcome his fear.

When he spoke his words were firm.

'It's about Aisha's uncle,' Eric began. 'Many years ago, when he still lived in the Punjab, he killed one of the girls in his village for bringing shame on the family. Killed her at the father's behest... an honour killing. She was 16.'

Ed stepped into the pause. 'What had she done?'

'Kissed a boy,' Eric went on. 'They dragged her into a field, raped her to rid her of the devil, strangled her and buried her in a shallow grave.'

CHAPTER NINETEEN

Sam adjusted her dressing gown, tightened the belt and pressed the button on the microwave, the kitchen floor cool on her bare feet: another night, another push-button Marks and Spencer special.

Is this it for me now? Ready meals for one?

She'd never cooked a meal from scratch since Tristram died, almost forgotten what it was like to peel vegetables, cook fish, eat a rare steak.

Bending down, she reached for the black plastic container, tonight's offering a Cumberland pie.

'Jesus!'

She dropped the food on the granite work top, rushed to the tap, and held her scorched hand under the flow of cold water for the third time in a week. Fingers still red and stinging, she took a knife and rammed it through the plastic film. A cloud of steam billowed around her as traces of mince seeped on to the bench through the pierced hole in the bottom of the container.

Shit!

She put the container on a plate, sat down and gingerly peeled off the rest of the film. Her fork broke through the mash, releasing the smell of the mince and hitting the small piece of metal that seconds ago was the tip of the knife.

She was determined to take her time, determined to spend longer eating than the microwave did cooking. As usual she failed, but at least a glass of wine had been resisted.

Tea brewed, she took her mobile off the bench, scrolled through the contacts, and hit a number. The call was answered on the second ring.

'Amber, it's Sam Parker. Sorry to bother you. I hope you don't mind me ringing. I know it's late.'

'Hi Sam.' Amber's voice sound friendly. 'No trouble at all, and as for late, well you know me. I don't sleep much at night these days. I still sit in the armchair; go to bed through the day if I have time.'

'How are you managing?' Sam asked.

There was a short silence.

'I'm okay,' Amber told her. 'It's a cliché but it really is a day at a time. How are you?'

'Fine,' Sam said. 'Busy.'

'Yeah, I saw you on the TV.'

'That's what I'm ringing about,' Sam said. 'Your self-help group.'

She listened for any change in Amber's tone but heard none.

'Just a bunch of young women who've suffered abuse of varying kinds from men,' Amber told her.

'Do you have many members?'

'About 20.'

'And the abuse. Is it specifics or general?'

'General mostly.'

'And the girls I saw you with,' Sam said. 'I know a couple of them.'

'Yeah, they said.'

'Have any of them been targets for any abuse?'

Amber took a moment before she spoke again.

'Sam, we talk about the overt inappropriate sexual behaviour of men in the round and how we can influence change, how we make sure our sisters in the future don't have to put up with what we did.'

Sam made her move.

'It's just that we've heard some of the male students were taking photos of girls when they were asleep.'

Amber's answer was instant.

'Not heard that Sam,' she said.

Sam was about to ask if she was sure when her house phone began to ring.

'Sorry Amber, I've got to answer another call,' she said quickly. 'I'll speak to you later. Take care.'

She darted into the living room. 'Hello.'

'It's me,' Ed said.

'Hi. Nicely timed.'

'Sorry?'

'I was just talking to Amber,' Sam said. 'Asking about her group.'

'And?' Ed asked.

'I felt she was being evasive in the beginning, lying at the end,' Sam told him. 'She denied knowing anything about the photos of the girls but Charlotte's in her group and so is Tracey. I just can't see it.'

'Me neither,' Ed agreed.

'And she referred to womanhood in general as 'sisters'. Now I know that's not an unusual term these days, but... '

'Tracey and Alex would know enough to call themselves Sisters of Macavity,' Ed finished for her. 'They study English.'

Sam broke the short silence that followed.

'Anyway, were you just ringing for a chat? I only left you an hour and a half ago. Missing my velvet tones already?'

'No,' Ed said. 'It's Aisha's uncle.'

He relayed his conversation with Eric.

Sam shivered. 'This just keeps getting worse.'

Sam tossed and turned. Every time she closed her eyes, the images alternated between Jack being hit over the head, a carrier bag drawn over his face before he was pushed into the river and Aisha in the front seat of a car fleeing to Plymouth. She turned on the light. Trying to sleep when she was like this was futile. Years of experience had taught her if her mind was on the job not to fight it.

She sat up, picked up the glass on the bedside unit, and drank. Why she never took an orange cordial to bed when she'd had too much to drink was a question she felt weekend drinkers everywhere would share.

The revelation about Aisha's uncle was more than troubling. Ed was considered a 'Subject Matter Expert' around honour-based violence, even if he played it down. He always believed if Aisha hadn't got away, she was dead. There was no halfway alternative.

Would Aisha, following the publicity, have come to the police or would she have been too scared? Would she have called her parents after their TV appeal or would she have seen only crocodile tears?

Sam needed to make something happen. Should she seek authority to get a listening device in Davinder Bhandal's house? Could she do something to spark a conversation? Arrest them perhaps?

Their solicitor, Jill Carver, would love that. At the slightest opportunity she would publicly slag off any investigation if she thought procedures were not being followed. The Butcher, as Ed and many others called her, had built her career on carving up police officers.

And these jobs always had the potential to increase racial tensions, spark disorder, something the Superintendent in charge of Seaton St George would be anxious to avoid.

Jack Goddard was different, but no less difficult. She had one body but there were four more the students and the media wanted to link together as the work of a serial killer. She could only kick that theory into the long grass once Jack's killer was arrested. There was talk of another student demo and that was making the Superintendent at Seaton twitchy.

'Can't you get this sorted Sam? We need it boxed off, pronto.'

She got up, went downstairs, and poured hot water over a teabag. A cat screeched loudly outside. Bloody cats, she couldn't get away from them. Sisters of Macavity. What was that all about? And Amber? Why was she so evasive?

Sam opened the fridge door, blinking as the bright light flooded her eyes, then poured milk into the mug and unwrapped a mint Club biscuit.

Back upstairs 20 minutes later, she slid under the duvet and closed her eyes.

Thursday 17th April 2014

Sam stared at the bright red eyes looking back at her from the wall mirror above the sink. Three hours sleep, tops. She'd read once that Paul Newman used to submerge his head in a bowl of cold water every morning to fight facial ageing. She ran the cold tap, filled the sink, and dunked her face. Brain freeze. She spluttered, dried herself, and looked again in the mirror. The puffiness around her eyes was still there. *Cheers Paul.*

Thirty-five minutes after a hot shower she was in her office, speed reading her emails. Most of them could be deleted without a response. Those that needed one would have to wait. She was way too busy to provide statistics to the bean counters.

Ed walked into her office, face ashen. With a little eyeliner he could have been an extra in Michael Jackson's Thriller video. Suddenly she felt 100 % better. 'Rough night?'

'Yeah, ended up on the whisky.' He sat down. 'Rough as a badger's now but I'll be sorted in an hour. Bev's gone out for bacon sarnies. Want one?'

'Go on then.'

Sam answered her phone. The deep Cornish accent should have been advertising clotted cream or starring in Jamaica Inn.

She listened then spoke. 'I'll get DC Bev Summers to liaise with your DC Welch, sort some photos out. Cheers.'

Ed was putting his mobile back in his pocket. 'Sarnie's sorted.'

'That was the DI from Devon and Cornwall,' Sam told him. 'They've got a witness who saw a young Asian man drive the car into a lock-up and walk away. Could be Sukhi.'

Ed said that sounded promising.

'I hope it is,' Sam went on. 'I've said we'll get Bev to liaise. She can email them a photo, one of the ones we took off Bethany's phone.'

Their noses twitched, nasal partners in a synchronised dance of hunger pangs, the smell of cooked food alerting their stomachs before their eyes saw Bev.

'Two bacon with brown.'

'You're a lifesaver,' Sam said.

'Suppose you want a cup of tea as well?'

'Only if you're offering.'

'Make that two,' Ed said.

'I've got the CCTV from Rendezvous,' Bev told them. 'I'll start on that this morning.'

'And Bev,' Sam said. 'Can you liaise with a DC Welch from Devon and Cornwall? He needs one of the photos of Sukhi. They've got a witness down there who saw a young Asian male driving the car into the lock-up.'

'Yeah, no problem.'

Sam bit into the bun, a dollop of brown sauce dropping on to her finger.

Ed wiped his mouth as his mobile rang.

'Any idea what it's about, Charlie? Okay, give me half an hour.'

Bev walked in with two mugs of tea.

'I'll have to pass,' Ed said. 'Fatty Sanderson's in the cells and wants a favour. Says he got something for us.'

'And he is?' Sam asked.

'Joey Sanderson, Handler of this parish, too fat to do burglaries. Been around the block a few times. We go way back but he's never given information before, not to my knowledge anyway.'

'How old is he?' asked Sam.

'Fifty-odd,' Ed said, as he stood up, reaching for the

mug on the desk. 'Convictions going back to when he was a juvenile: theft, burglary, handling stolen goods, deception. No violence, but a full house for dishonesty. Even got one for 'removal of an article from a public place'.'

'Not often you hear of that,' Sam said.

'I'll let you know the sketch if it's anything worth knowing.'

Joey Sanderson waddled. Like a giant penguin, he came up the corridor from the cell block, his black Fila trainers squeaking on the glistening, recently mopped linoleum, three yellow 'caution, wet floor' signs stating the obvious.

Ed closed the interview door.

'Long time no see, Joey.'

'Yeah. How you been?'

'Champion,' Ed said. 'You still getting around the pubs and clubs with stolen gear?'

Sanderson smile was almost shy. 'You've got to earn a crust, Ed. You know what it's like, grab it while you can.'

'What you in here for?'

'Handling. They come round with a warrant.'

'What did they get?' Ed asked.

Sanderson looked ridiculous as he shuffled, trying to get comfortable in the tiny seat. Ed estimated his six-foot frame now weighed about 30 stone.

'Clothes and food.'

'Food?'

'Big business now, Ed,' Sanderson told him. 'People are skint. Not everybody wants to go to food banks, so I provide an alternative.'

'How much food did they recover?'

'About 500 quid's worth. Forty-odd carrier bags.'

Ed shook his head. 'Five hundred pounds worth of food.'

'Ed, it's done to order,' Sanderson said. 'People bring their shopping lists to me. I've got a team of young lads and lasses that go out for the stuff. I pay them, then dish it out at 40% of the marked price.'

'So what went wrong?'

Sanderson's fleshy face looked sad. 'Got this morning's deliveries and as the last arrived your lot burst in.'

Ed nodded. Sanderson had obviously been grassed up. 'So what do you want me to do?'

'Ed, I'm on a bender. I don't want to go down for this. I'm too old for bird.'

The 'bender' – slang for a suspended prison sentence – explained Sanderson's eagerness to do a deal.

Ed was thinking fast. The police had gone into his house after the last bag drop. They were either lucky or had the place under surveillance. He favoured the latter. An informant had to be involved, and if that were the case, the handler would want payment for his snout.

'So what do you want me to do?'

'Help me out Ed. I scratch your back.'

'What you got then?'

'I need some insurances, Ed.'

'I think you mean assurances, and I can't give you any, not until I know what it is you're giving me.'

Sanderson paused, weighing up his options, and then spoke.

'The Asian guy,' he said. 'The one on the TV on Saturday whose daughter's gone missing.'

Ed concentrated on keeping his face neutral, concentrated on breathing slowly and quietly. 'What about him?'

'What about me?'

'No promises,' Ed said. 'But if it's good, I may be able to help, and that's better than you've got now.'

'They call you a twat in my world, but it's a mark of respect,' Sanderson sighed. 'Everybody says you're good, fair, and a man of your word. The Last Mohican, Ed, that's what the older villains call you. Old school. The young cops haven't got a clue. You're different. You promise you'll help?'

'If what you tell me is good, I'll do my best.'

'It is.' Sanderson took a noisy, deep breath. 'A couple of weeks before Christmas I saw Dav Bhandal in a pub. I won't say which one. He knows I do a bit. Told me he wanted me to burn a settee. Would give me a ton, and whoever helped me carry it, he would give them a Commodore.'

'Commodore?'

Sanderson looked surprised.

'Fifteen quid. You know... fiver's a Lady Godiva, that Commodore's song, 'once, twice, three times a lady'... three Lady Godiva's is 15 quid.'

'What and he said Commodore?' Ed said, surprised.

'Don't be daft. I'm telling you that. He said 15 quid.'

Ed shook his head. *Who thinks these up?*

'So you burnt the settee?'

'I told him I would burn it, but when I went to get it, it was brand new,' Sanderson said. 'Bit of a smell of pee about it, but that soon washed off. No way was I burning it. He gave me £115 to get shot of it, and I sold it for another £50.'

'Who's got it now?' Ed asked, doing well to hide the adrenaline rush.

Sanderson grinned and laced his fingers over his huge stomach.

'Not so fast, Ed,' he said.

CHAPTER TWENTY

Two hours after delivering bacon sandwiches, Bev was back in Sam's office.

'Photo sent to the Devon and Cornwall Dee?' Sam asked.

Dee, slang for detective constable.

'Yeah, that's sorted,' Bev told her. 'You might want to view the CCTV from Rendezvous. Tracey Davies and Charlotte Swains coming out at 3.25am, each with an arm around... '

Sam slapped the table as if it were the buzzer on a quiz show. 'Jack Goddard!'

Bev nodded. 'Bingo.'

'Are we sure about the time on the cameras,' Sam asked. 'I always get a bit paranoid with times when the clocks go forward.'

'The times are right,' Bev told her.

'So, out at 3.25am. What, a 10-minute walk to the tow path? Ten minutes when you're sober anyway. So, that's at least 3.35am. Alex O'Connell finds him dead at 4.05am.

Where had she been? Check to see if she's in Rendezvous. Do you see them going in?'

'We'll check that now,' Bev said. 'You wanted the later time doing first.'

Sam nodded: 'I did, but let's see if Alex O'Connell's in there. And find them all going in. See if Glen Jones went in with them.'

Sam got into her car and drove to a local park. She needed to think without interruption, think with a cigarette in her hand, in a place devoid of diesel fumes. She ordered a coffee from the travelling barista, his glistening chrome machine attached to the back of a tiny French Citroen, a vehicle so small Sam couldn't decide whether he got into it or put it on.

The wooden bench under the willow tree, a small plaque confirming it had been a much-missed grandfather's favourite spot, was speckled with green, decades of waxy foliage leaving its mark. Sam sat down, lit up, and inhaled as she watched a distant dog chase a tennis ball. She sipped the double espresso and began to process.

Goddard dead... Davies and Swain lying... O'Connell probably lying about her movements prior to finding the body... Amber evasive... the photographs sent by the Sisters of Macavity – or someone pretending to be the Sisters.

The ABC of investigations... accept nothing, believe nothing, challenge everything.

She looked up and saw a mouse form in the wispy cirrus clouds. Mortimer. Her brain was in full race mode, mice scurrying everywhere.

The bouncers, King and Wilson. Ed didn't think the likes of Wilson ever changed, and young King? Why was everybody wary of him? Not forgetting, he despised men bullying women.

Sukhi's car in the garage in Plymouth. Had they got away? Perhaps caught a train to somewhere like Falmouth, took the water taxi from there to St Mawes? Could they be living in that white cottage overlooking the harbour and a sea that didn't judge them?

And the demos? Would there be another? Was there a serial killer on the loose? Were the dead students all Mortimers? Could Elliott Prince be believed?

What had Ed once said? 'Crack the witnesses…'

Jill Carver... Aisha's parents... The uncle.

Her head churned like a food mixer fighting a thickening mass of information, but the faster it spun, the more solid it became, impossible to separate, impossible to interpret.

Sam chain-smoked another cigarette.

She didn't believe all the ingredients were in her mental mixing bowl. There was more to come.

Smoke left her lungs and forced its way out of her pursed lips like the barista's pressurised steam. She dropped the disposal cup into a bin, bought another coffee. The ringtone broke the silence but not her concentration. She ignored the phone, ignored the subsequent text or voicemail alert.

Paul Adams was sitting with Bethany Stevens. While Ed had noticed the ageing kitchen and the fraying brown carpet, Paul had eyes only for the young woman in front of him.

'I'm a bit of a hoarder,' she said. 'Here are as many notes as I could find.'

She handed him eight handwritten notes.

'Most were written in classes when you couldn't talk. I hope it helps. She was a writer, so it's entirely in keeping that she could write to someone.'

Paul examined each in turn.

'Like I said on the phone, we're just pre-empting things really, you know, just in case Aisha gets in touch by writing.'

'Is there any news?' Bethany locked her green eyes on to his.

'Did she ever talk about going to Cornwall?' Paul asked, ignoring the question.

'Cornwall?' Bethany looked puzzled. 'No. She'd never been out of Seaton St George, unless it was to go to India or visit family. She said she'd never been on holiday. But I told her about Cornwall. When I was little, Mam and Dad took me there most summer holidays. Newquay. All the fun of the surf, as my father used to say.'

Paul held her gaze. She was beautiful. Nine years younger than him but if she hadn't been a potential witness, he would have asked her out. Now if he did anything to compromise the investigation, Sam Parker would crucify him. He'd replaced Jason Stroud on the team. Jason had left under a cloud after playing out a sinister rape fantasy with his now ex-wife. That was enough for Sam to get rid, and that didn't happen at work. If he screwed the inquiry into Aisha, Sam Parker would finish him. He needed to stay professional.

'Any reason you're asking about Cornwall?' Bethany asked him.

'I'm sorry, I can't say at the moment.'

'I think about her every night.' Bethany's eyes clouded. 'I just hope she's happy. I can't imagine what she was going through. None of us at college could. But if she got somewhere like Cornwall, somewhere miles away, I'd have thought she'd have rung me.'

Paul pushed back the urge to hug her.

'Maybe she lost her phone, couldn't remember your number. Maybe she didn't want to compromise you.'

Or maybe the unthinkable happened.

Bethany didn't look convinced.

'Sukhi could have called… I don't know. Would you like a tea? Or are you too busy?'

'I think I can manage a cup, thanks.'

Stay professional, Paul. Stay professional.

Sam closed the Audi door and saw Bev marching across the car park.

'Something urgent?'

'I tried calling,' Bev said quickly. 'I left a voicemail.'

'I was tied up. What is it?'

'Alex O'Connell leaves Rendezvous at 3.34am, nine minutes after Jack Goddard, Tracey and Charlotte.'

'Really?'

'Now I'm trying to establish what time they enter,' Bev went on. 'I've started after 10pm, because that's when they say they left the Jolly Roger.'

Sam nodded her approval.

'You can always view the earlier CCTV if they're lying, which they seem to be doing a lot. Is that why you rang?'

'No,' Bev said. 'Inspector Wright was looking for you.'

Sam felt a small wave of dismay wash through her.

'Any idea what Never was after?'

'He *never* said.'

The word play left them both laughing.

Ed considered Joey Sanderson's information. 'The best I can do, providing it's good, is get a letter to the judge, telling him you've provided important information. But remember, Joey, I can't lie. He's going to know you gave this information while you were already banged up.'

Sanderson mouth dropped into a frown.

'Can't you just make it all go away?'

'Probably not,' Ed told him. 'A letter's better than what you've got now.'

Sanderson slid down the chair and looked up at the ceiling. 'Will you get me some fags at least?'

'I think I can run to a packet of smokes,' Ed said. 'Now, I haven't got all day. The settee?'

Sanderson was staring at the ceiling again, considering his final decision.

'Cigarettes and a letter,' he said, almost to himself. 'Jesus, I'm trusting you here, and it goes without saying you can't tell anybody what I'm going to tell you.'

Ed knew Sanderson was coming on board.

'How long have we known each other?' Ed said. 'Years, right? Have I ever told you anything others have told me?'

Sanderson's eyes darkened.

'No, and by the way, I'm not one of your grasses. Grasses are scum. This is a one off.'

Ed nodded. Sanderson would be an informant; he just didn't know it yet. Once you had them, you rarely let them go.

'The settee was brand new,' Sanderson began. 'You could tell by the cushions. That lot don't go to posh furniture shops, they go to their own. I went to Singh's, the little furniture shop not far from their house. Owned by Karan Singh. He gives me a few quid to keep an eye on his shop.'

'Protection money?' Ed said.

'Ed, please,' Sanderson looked hurt. 'Private security. Ask him. They pay their money and they feel better protected than they do with your lot.'

Ed hid his contempt and let that go. He'd agreed to put a letter in to the judge about the handling offence. He'd not agreed to give Sanderson immunity from prosecution for other offences.

'I don't recall seeing people in uniform with your logo on their jackets.'

'We're more effective,' Sanderson told him. 'Undercover, my lads.'

Protection rackets had a simple USP – pay up or your business will be burgled or burnt down.

'Was it one of your lads who helped you move it?' Ed asked.

'Come on, Ed. I'm not grassing on my own.'

'And did Bhandal buy it from Karan Singh.'

'He did, and here's the thing,' Sanderson said, moving his vast bulk forward. 'He got the one he wanted me to burn delivered on the 14th December. Saturday. He didn't know I knew that. He asked me to get rid of it when I saw him in the pub on the 15th, the Sunday. I took it out of his house on the Monday... put it on a big trailer.'

'How do you know when he bought it?' Ed asked.

'Singh's is a little furniture shop,' Sanderson told him. 'No computers, so everything's written down. He's got a little book with all sales written in it. When I asked how much it was worth, he showed me that he'd sold it to Dav for £120.'

The dates were running like a sequence in Ed's head.

'What did it look like?' Ed asked now.

'Semi-circular, brown, and so low you almost laid down on it.'

The one Aisha's brother and sister were sitting on in the photograph.

'And your point is?' Ed pushed, already knowing the answer.

Sanderson sat up straight and leaned across the desk.

'Why would somebody want to burn a settee that's days old? No better way to get rid of evidence.'

He leaned back, stretched out his legs and put his hands behind his head.

Ed gave it a moment before he jumped up and pushed his chair against the wall.

'You've wasted enough of my fucking time here,' he said. 'I'm impressed you know the date someone bought a new settee. Now, I've got work to do.'

He opened the interview room door.

'Alright, alright keep your hair on.' Sanderson sat up and Ed sat back down.

'At one end of the settee, right in the corner, there was blood,' Sanderson said. 'They'd tried to wash it, you could tell, but there was blood. I know the difference between brown material and brown blood.'

'Much blood?'

Sanderson smiled: 'Enough to see. Look, something happened on that settee, otherwise why ask me to get rid, to burn it.'

Ed said: 'Where is it now?'

Sanderson paused again.

'I sold it to Billy Wilson.'

'The doorman?' Ed said.

'Yeah.'

Ed raised his eyebrows and held Sanderson's gaze.

'He's going to love you.'

CHAPTER TWENTY-ONE

DRIVING BACK TO HQ, Ed considered their next move. Recovering the settee from Billy Wilson was important. It wasn't stolen but it was potentially evidential. Billy would just have to get over it. Of course he would go straight to Fatty Sanderson's unless Ed warned him off.

Visiting the furniture shop was crucial if they were to prove continuity through Karan Singh's records but as soon as that was done, Singh would probably notify Bhandal.

Ed would suggest to Sam they stall going to the shop until they had been able to confirm whether it was blood and if it was Aisha's. A 'yes' and a 'yes' would see the investigation take a dramatic turn. They were told Aisha went missing on the Friday 13th, albeit she wasn't reported missing to police until the Monday, the 16th. The settee, according to Sanderson, wasn't delivered until Saturday 14th.

Friday December 13th 2013

I was close now, so close I could see Sukhi's beautiful white teeth flashing me that massive smile. I always said he could advertise toothpaste. His teeth are that good.

I ran around the car to the open passenger door where he was standing. I was breathless, excited. 'How does Cornwall sound?' I threw my arms around him. This was it. I kissed him.

He eased me away. 'Nearest town?'

I couldn't remember. 'Head south, set the satnav for Plymouth.' I opened the back door; my pink suitcase could sit on the back seat for now.

'We should get going,' he said.

I don't know what I saw first, the arm or the metal bar. I certainly didn't see who the arm belonged to. The arm and the bar were a blur, swinging in tandem along a shoulder height arc parallel to the ground. I tried to shout, scream, but nothing came out. It was as if my vocal chords had been cut. I realised somebody's forearm was around my neck, dragging me backwards towards the boot.

Sukhi's head twisted, whiplash-like to the side, the sickening crack sounding like a gunshot, blood spraying from his mouth, white teeth bouncing off the bonnet.

I was choking out, darkness close, the pressure on my windpipe like nothing I'd felt before. My eyes wanted to pop out of my face.

I couldn't breathe.

My arms were listless. I dropped my bag, saw boots swing into Sukhi's face and stomach, then a boot stamp repeatedly on his head.

Tears streamed down my face. I was helpless, lightheaded. The arm squeezed my neck, the pressure relentless, the forearm digging into my throat while another arm pushed against the back of my neck. Sukhi was lying motionless in the road, by the side of the car. The last bit of consciousness was calling his name. Then blackness.

When I opened my eyes, I saw the walls of the room, the floor where Justin had been hiding under the bed. The note was gone. My throat was raw. I stroked it. It was tender, swollen.

What time was it? Where was Sukhi? I got off the bed, crept to the window, and pulled the curtains back the tiniest amount. Pitch black.

Voices downstairs... my mother, father, uncle and brother. Mia must have been in the house somewhere.

I tiptoed to the bedroom door, took hold of the handle as if it were a bomb, slowly applied downward pressure and pulled. Nothing. It was stuck. I grabbed it, tighter this time, pushed down and pulled again. Nothing. I yanked the handle, pulled it back and forth. The door groaned but didn't budge.

Now footsteps running up the stairs. 'Whore,' my mother screamed in Punjabi. 'You little slut,' shouted my father. 'You dare to shame this family.'

'Let me out,' I screamed. Only I couldn't scream. It was more like a whimper. 'Let me out,' I croaked, my voice hoarse, every syllable feeling as if Mr Geppetto was sanding my throat instead of Pinocchio's body.

'Stay there,' my father yelled. 'We'll deal with you later.'

I banged on the door with my fists. No response. They'd gone back down. They must have put a lock on the outside of the door. How had they done that so quickly?

I walked away from the door. Then I saw them. The blister-pack on the chest of drawers. Sleeping tablets. My mother's sleeping tablets. How long had I been asleep?

Where was Sukhi? What had they done to him? Had

they left him or had he escaped? Had they done something really bad to him?

I went back to the window, pulled back the curtains. I opened the side window and peered up the street. Nothing. It looked like it always did. Deathly quiet.

No sign of Sukhi's car.

I stared at the ground below. How far? There were no trees I could reach, no climbing plants snaking up the wall to my window. A straight drop. How many metres? Too many.

I walked on my toes to the wardrobe. The clean bedding was always on the bottom shelf. I opened the dark wooden door. Nothing. Empty. Everything was gone.

I looked around again. This time I saw the bedding had been removed from the beds.

I walked to the drawers where the sleeping tablets were. Why was there so many? Why was there a bottle of 'Whyte and Mackay' whisky there?

Realisation hit me.

I ran to the open window and tried to shout for help, but nothing escaped from my mouth. I remembered the old school books under my bed. Was there a pen with them?

I could still hear the voices downstairs.

I crawled under the bed, reached for the books and felt my fingers curl around a biro. Sellotape. I needed Sellotape.

I opened one the books and took a deep breath. I'd covered them with wallpaper and drawn doodles on the woodchip. I checked. Recycle the Sellotape.

I sat on the bed, ripped the front and back covers off the books, and in block capitals began writing 'HELP ME'. Once I'd written each message I began colouring in the blocks. Any passer-by would see them. On one I even wrote 'PLEASE CALL THE POLICE'.

I began unpicking Sellotape from the first book. I replayed finding them under the bed, how they might just help rescue me.

Then I remembered.

I slithered back under the bed. I was right. Top corner. I stretched and pulled out the old clothes. I threw the sleeveless dresses back into the darkness against the wall, but the jumpers, the trousers, anything with arms and legs I kept.

Back on the bed I stared at my treasure. It wasn't a big pile, but it might just be big enough.

I started to tie them together, listening for footsteps coming up the stairs. If anybody came up, I'd throw them back under the bed. They wouldn't be looking for them; they'd forgotten they were there.

I tied them as tight as I could. Would they hold my weight? What was the worst thing that could happen if they didn't? Break my legs? Break my neck? So what? They'd left tablets and whisky for me.

It must have only taken me 10 minutes. Funny how quickly you can do things.

I crept back to the door and listened. It sounded like they were in the kitchen. I could hear cups rattling on saucers. That was good. The kitchen was at the back of the house; my bedroom was at the front.

The 'Help Me' signs were scattered across the floor. I didn't care. I needed something to tie to the end of my clothes. I couldn't afford for that something to drag across the floor as soon as it started to take my weight and crash into something, and besides I needed to keep my makeshift line as long as possible.

The bunk beds. I inched them across the carpet. A

noise now and it was all over. Not just escape but me. No way would I get the beds back in time if they came upstairs.

Each drag brought it closer to the window. Finally I tied one end of my clothes rope around the leg of the top bunk.

I threw the knotted clothes out of the window, gave it one last pull to check for tightness, and climbed out.

Once I hit the ground, I was just going to run. Run as fast as I could. Run to the nearest police station. They'd know what to do.

CHAPTER TWENTY-TWO

Thursday 17th April 2014

'OKAY.' Sam was sitting behind her desk, everyone waiting for instructions. 'Ed, Bev... go and see Billy Wilson and recover the settee. Tell him if he goes near the person who sold it to him or the owner of the shop it came from, he'll be locked up for perverting the course of justice.'

Ed raised his eyes.

'He doesn't know what offence he's committed,' Sam answered his unspoken question. 'If he believes it, it might stop him going after them. The 'Ways and Means Act'. Isn't that what you called it in the old days?'

Ed smiled.

'I want that settee testing for blood and I want it fast-tracking at the lab to see if it's Aisha's blood. Remember, if it is her blood, that settee was delivered the day after her parents said she went missing and removed from their house on the Monday before they reported her missing. By the time we've got round there, a new settee's in place.'

Ed looked up from his pad. 'Good chance he'll kick off when we tell him he's losing the settee.'

'That's why I'm sending you,' Sam said. 'He knows you. Tell him if he buys dodgy gear he runs the risk of us taking it away.'

She stood up. It was time to pace the room.

'Paul, I want interview strategies drawing up for Charlotte, Alex and Tracey. I want them bringing down to Seaton nick. Their lies point to them being involved in Goddard's death. Frighten them. I need to know if any or all of them are in this Sisters of Macavity.'

'What does your instinct tell you?' Ed asked her.

Sam kept moving.

'Maybe they were taking him somewhere to get his photograph taken.'

'Did Never throw any light on anything?' Bev asked her.

'Bloody hell, I'd forgotten about him!' Sam said.

'Mick, it's Sam Parker.' The ivory handset was sticky, needed a good clean, or was it Mick 'Never' Wright who made her feel dirty? 'You wanted to speak to me?'

'I did.' Wright's voice was cool, unfriendly. 'One of my son's mates goes to Seaton Uni. He was beaten up on the riverbank after a night out a few weeks ago.'

'Did he report it? Did he know his assailant?'

'No to the first,' Wright told her. 'Maybe to the second.'

'Go on.' Sam picked up her pen.

'He'd been out and was a bit of an arse around a couple of young girls. You know the type of thing.'

She could almost hear him shuffling on his seat, his deep breath a spotlight on his stress. She smiled.

'I gather he'd gone up to them in a pub. The Jolly Roger. He'd had a drink. I know him. He's not a bad lad. His dad was captain of the golf club last year.'

She didn't disguise the irritation in her voice.

'That makes it okay then,' she said. 'What happened?'

'I gather he's asked them, his words not mine, for 'a shag'.'

'Golf expression, is it, like shouting four when the ball's flying towards someone?'

Wright didn't take the bait.

'One of them threw a drink over him and a bouncer threw him out. It was near closing time. He staggered home, walked along the tow path and got jumped. He thinks it was the bouncer.'

'I need his name and address, Mick,' Sam said. 'You know as well as I do it could be linked, otherwise you wouldn't be telling me.'

'I know but I don't think he wants to get involved. He certainly doesn't want to make an assault complaint.'

Sam could feel herself getting hot with irritation.

'We'll find him, Mick,' she said sharply. 'Somebody will say something. Maybe not this week, but we'll find him, and it might have an adverse effect on him if he failed to come forward with what might be material evidence.'

'I understand.' Wright's voice was monotone, quiet.

'Was your son with him on the night?'

Silence.

'Mick?'

'Yes, he was, but he didn't see his mate get kicked out. They got separated. Someone told my lad that Luke had been ejected. He went outside but Luke had gone.'

Sam forced herself to soften.

'Tell you what, Mick, instead of us going in heavy handed, and Luke thinking he can't trust your son, why don't you have a word with him? Explain the importance and get him to give me a call. Tell him he might be able to help catch Jack Goddard's killer. Does he know Jack?'

'Think so… I'll have a word.'

An estate agent might describe the terraced house as being in need of slight modernisation. Ed knocked on the ill-fitting wooden door, varnish peeling, the brass letterbox mottled with green mould. He looked to his right. He could probably get his little finger between the blackened wooden window frame and the glass. Forget the spin. He'd call it a shit-hole.

Billy Wilson opened the door, barefooted in shiny tracksuit bottoms and a grubby white vest. 'Alright Ed?'

'Got a minute, Billy?'

'Yeah, come in.'

Ed stepped over the plastic tractor, his foot just missing the child's dummy on the chipped tiles. Ed knew this could go one of two ways – mild disagreement or open hostility.

He stepped into the living room. Wilson was throwing coats and clothes off the settee on to the floor where they joined the discarded shoes and socks and last night's take-away food cartons.

One look at the settee confirmed Sanderson's story. It was identical to the one in the photo.

'Have a seat,' Wilson said, flopping into the only armchair.

'It's the settee I've come about.'

Wilson leapt up.

'I paid a fair price for it,' he bristled. 'It's not nicked, it's second hand. If you're here about it, you must know that.'

'I do, but... '

'No buts, it's mine.'

Ed heard the front door.

'Why's the fucking CID outside?' a woman shouted. 'That dyke detective's sat in a car right outside the house.'

She was in her late 20s, tall with short blonde hair like straw, not in colour but consistency. 'What do you want?'

Ed said nothing, although he couldn't wait to tell Bev she had been called a dyke, and let Wilson speak to who he presumed was the bouncer's most recent girlfriend.

'It's nothing, Charlene. Stick the kettle on.'

She glared at him, gave Ed the finger, and stormed out.

Wilson watched her go.

'That's the problem with younger women,' he said. 'No respect. No respect for me, no respect for you. Imagine my first wife bursting in like that? Never happen.'

Respect seems to be a recurring theme in Wilson's world, Ed thought.

'Half her family's banged up so you can't expect her to welcome you with open arms,' Wilson said. 'She's a Jenkins. Harry Jenkins's grand-daughter.'

'Explains a lot,' Ed said. 'I've got to take this settee away with me Billy.'

'Why?'

'I can't tell you. I need to do some tests. If it's nothing, you can have it back.'

'And if it's something?' Wilson asked.

'I'll have to keep it.'

'What if I refuse?'

'I know you won't,' Ed said. 'I'll end up taking it anyway. And don't go around seeing whoever sold it to you. They didn't know it could be dodgy.'

Wilson nodded towards the kitchen. 'She'll go mental.'

'Has she got a bairn?' Ed asked him.

'Yeah, mine.'

Ed raised his eyebrows.

'I know,' Wilson said sourly. 'Goes with the territory if you chase younger women.'

'Tell her the police are working with the manufacturers, recalling all the ones that weren't treated with the right fire safety treatment. Tell her it's an accident waiting to happen with the kid.'

Wilson looked at the settee. 'And we're supposed to be the liars.'

'Mine are only little ones,' Ed clapped his hands. 'Right, I've got a van around the corner. They'll take it away. Do you need five minutes to tell the charming Charlene what's happening?'

'Any problems?' Bev said, as Ed got back into the car.

'Good as gold. I'll give him a couple of minutes to break the bad news to Charlene.'

'Was that the blonde who glared at me?'

Ed couldn't kill the smile: 'Yeah, she thinks you bat for the other side.'

'Cheeky cow.' Bev glared at the house.

Billy Wilson appeared at the door and nodded. Ed called Julie Trescothick's mobile and within a couple of minutes a white Transit pulled up behind Ed.

Ed opened his car door, but didn't get out.

He spoke to Julie. 'Can you just take it straight down to the lab?'

'No problem.'

Ed drove away, his thoughts on an 18-year-old girl he hoped had escaped to a new life.

Bev answered her phone.

'Hi Tony… really? Is he sure? If he only got a glimpse, he could be mistaken…100 per cent. Okay. Thanks then… Yeah, I'll get back in touch. Cheers.'

Bev turned to look at Ed. 'Tony Welch. Plymouth CID.'

'Oh yeah.'

'The guy driving the car into the garage?' Bev said. 'The witness is adamant. It wasn't Sukhi.'

CHAPTER TWENTY-THREE

'One hundred per cent certain,' Bev said, sitting in a chair next to Ed, facing Sam.

Sam had been hoping it was Sukhi but now she wondered if he was going to sell the car, the buyer would more likely be another Asian.

She told Bev and Ed what she was thinking.

'It's possible,' Ed said. 'But bearing in mind they're running, I reckon they'll be avoiding the Asian community. They'd have too many questions to answer.'

'Like what?' Sam asked.

'Like where are you from, where are your parents from, what village are your parents from? What are you doing here? They'll be terrified someone will know their parents. They might want to avoid any contact. How new is his car?'

'Fifty-nine plate,' Bev said.

'Why not just go to an Internet café and sell it on one of those 'we'll buy anything' sites?' Ed went on. 'What if they didn't drive it to Plymouth? What if someone just wants us think they did?'

'Family?' Sam asked.

'Could be anybody,' Ed said. 'Let's say they didn't get away. There might be a circumstance when Aisha's family need to get shot of the car. Burning it out up here would be too suspicious. But what if they drove it to a place where they found out the couple might go? We know Beth told Aisha about Cornwall. I don't think the immediate family would drive the car but they could get anybody to do it. And I mean anybody. A lot of people would be sympathetic and on their side.'

Sam was shaking her head, struggling to understand how a parent could hurt their own.

Ed was reading her mind.

'It happens,' he said simply.

Sam told them she wanted door-to-door teams knocking on houses in Aisha's street the following evening.

'As opposed to house to house?' Bev asked, the difference important.

'Absolutely,' Sam said. 'There's no need to speak to every member of the household just yet. Let's do door to door. It'll be much quicker. If we need to opt for house to house, that's an option further down the line. If Aisha went home after she got off the bus, she can't have had much time. Her mother was home just after six. It is a small time window. Let's see if anyone saw anything.'

'Uniform did that at the time,' Ed said.

'I know, and I don't expect to get anything this time, but you never know. We just need someone who's fallen out with the Bhandals since. It's also an opportunity to see what reaction we get from the family. Tell them and everybody in the street it's the so-many-weeks anniversary of her going missing. I'll get the Post on board, give Darius a call.'

The onions were huge and the curry sauce was so thick Sam imagined it sticking to her ribs. She had been about to go the canteen and get a sandwich when Bev said she was doing the Chinese run.

In the HOLMES room, the Scottish voice of a 'Yes' campaigner was coming from the television. Sam swore to herself as the plastic fork snapped, a fine spray of curry sauce splattering her white shirt. Thankfully there was always a collection of metal forks in the office, forks that never found their way back to the canteen. Her white blouse could wait. The curry was delicious.

The office manager, a Detective Sergeant, answered his desk phone, his fork stirring his curry as he listened. He put the phone down.

'That was the lab. There's blood on the settee. Human blood.'

Sam wiped her mouth: 'Keep that to yourselves. I don't want it leaving this room.'

Heads nodded. Everyone knew the importance of keeping quiet and the penalty for a loose tongue.

'We sit tight on the settee... '

Spontaneous laughter rumbled through the room.

'Very funny,' Sam shouted. 'You know what I mean. Let's see if we can identify who the blood belongs to.'

Everyone finished eating in silence. Sam knew they were all hoping the same thing; the blood wasn't Aisha's.

Luke Wylam contacted Sam just after 3pm and suggested they meet at the sea-front car park in an hour.

There was a salty crispness to the air, the best efforts of

the sun losing its battle against the chilled breeze sweeping from the sea. Sam stood by her car, watching the seagulls following a trawler coming into port, the birds' equivalent of a fast food outlet.

Was this Wylam heading slowly towards her? Head down, rounded shoulders, hands in pocket, probably walking at half his normal pace, walking to a meeting he didn't want to attend.

'Luke?'

'Yeah.'

'Thanks for coming,' Sam said.

'Did I have a choice?'

He was surly, unshaven, and anxious, perhaps even frightened.

'Let's cut to the chase then,' Sam told him. 'You said on the phone you wanted to talk about an assault but don't want to make a complaint. Believe me when I say, young man, it's years since I took a report of an assault. I'm here because you said you were attacked on the tow path when you were drunk. Correct?'

'Yeah.' His eyes bored as deep into the ground as his hands did in his pockets.

'Well I haven't time to mess about. Tell me what happened and don't leave anything out.'

She reached into her coat pocket, flipped open a packet of cigarettes, and offered him one.

He shook his head.

'It was a Saturday night,' he began. 'Well, Sunday morning, a few weeks ago. I'd been thrown out of the Jolly Roger. The doorman said I was being an arse. He's younger than me, cocky bastard.'

'Do me a favour, Luke. Look at me when you're talking,' Sam said.

'Why?'

'Gives me more of a clue whether or not you're lying.'

'I'm not.' He shifted his weight, just once, from side to side.

'Then you won't mind looking at me,' Sam insisted. 'Why did you get thrown out? Be specific. What did you do?'

He looked up.

'I slapped this girl's arse, tried to get a kiss off her,' Wylam said. 'I pulled her, she pushed me and I went backwards. Her and her mates laughed. I went to go back to her – I was angry – but before I knew it, the young doorman's got hold of me. Took me outside.'

An image of Tom King flashed through Sam's mind. He seemed to have a knack of being in the right place at the right time. Or maybe he kept an eye on particular individuals.

'Are you a member of any silly boys' groups wearing T-shirts that some may find demeaning to women?' Sam asked.

Wylam's eyes dropped again.

'Mortimers. There's a few of us in it. It's just a bit of a laugh, you know.'

'I know some of the people I work with take a slightly different view.' Sam's voiced was loaded with disdain. 'What happened on the tow path?'

'Somebody grabbed me from behind,' Wylam said. 'I didn't hear them coming. Punched me on the back of the head, just once. I stumbled forward. Then he kicked me in the stomach. I went down, puked up. He whispered 'prick' and jogged off. It looked like the young bouncer but I only saw him from behind and I don't want this going any further. If you arrest him, I'll say I can't describe him?'

'I understand,' Sam said.

'It was him though,' Wylam went on. 'He's so tall, and

no way could an ordinary lad kick that hard. It was like a proper UFC job.'

'A what?' Sam was thrown.

'Ultimate Fighting Championship,' Wylam said, a look of 'what planet have you been on?' crossing his face. 'Cage fighting. You know, martial arts. It was ages before I got up. I couldn't breathe.'

Wylam touched his head and told Sam he had been left with a lump behind his ear and a large bruise across his stomach.

'Do you know Jack Goddard?' Sam asked.

'Yeah.'

'The leader of Mortimers?'

Wylam scowled. 'Liked to think he was. He set it up but most of us knew who the real leader was.'

'And that is?' Sam pressed.

'Elliott Prince.'

Ed walked into Sam's office. Bev Summers was already there.

'Guess who comes out of Rendezvous at about 2.45am on the morning Jack Goddard's killed?' Sam said.

Ed felt tired. He hadn't been right since the curry and couldn't be bothered with the guess-who game.

He lowered himself into a chair, his forehead suddenly clammy.

'You alright?' Sam said. 'You're white as a ghost.'

Paul Adams walked past the office.

'Paul, any chance of a cuppa?' Sam called out. 'Do one for Ed, plenty of sugar.'

Ed loosened his tie. 'So who is coming out of the club?'

'Tom King,' Sam said. 'So much for him going home after work.'

'He must have gone home and come back out,' Ed told her. 'He was too sure the taxi driver would alibi him.'

Paul appeared with the tea. 'The kettle had just boiled.'

Ed had just put shaking fingers around the mug when he fell from his chair, the steaming tea hitting the floor a fraction before he did.

Paul dropped to his knees and was rolling Ed away from the tea before Sam and Bev were out of their seats. Ed was out cold as Paul struggled to move him into the recovery position.

Bev ran to the toilets, returning with dampened toilet paper she used to mop Ed's brow and face.

Slowly he began to come round and Sam helped Paul lift him so he was sitting with his back against the wall.

'Take it easy, Ed,' Sam said. 'You passed out.'

Ed's speech was slurred, his eyes fighting to focus.

'No idea what happened there. Sorry…Thanks,' he mumbled.

'You need a doctor,' Sam told him. 'Bev, can you call?'

Ed slowly shook his head and began to clamber to his feet.

'No need for that,' he said. 'I'll be fine. Maybe something I've eaten. More embarrassed than anything.'

Sam pressed him but Ed, sounding more like himself as the minutes passed, was adamant.

The compromise was Paul driving him home.

'I'll ring you later,' Sam said, still shaken. 'And don't worry about coming in tomorrow. Get some rest. Play it by ear. And I still think you need a doctor.'

Ed managed a weak smile. 'I'll be okay.'

When Paul and Ed, still unsteady, had left, Bev shook her head.

'None of us are getting any younger, and we still push ourselves,' she said. 'This is a young person's game, Sam. Me and Ed, we're not in our 30s any more. Long hours. Constant pressure. It's no wonder he flaked out.'

Sam nodded, wondering if she was pushing her team too hard.

'Let's see how he is tomorrow,' she said. 'Tell everybody to knock off early tonight, get a flyer. Paul's done the interview strategies for Tracey, Alex and Charlotte. We'll get them in tomorrow, and I want Tom King bringing in as well. That should do for tomorrow. Hopefully by Saturday tea-time the lab will have the DNA results on the blood.'

'Okay,' Bev said, 'And Sam, don't just preach to us. Look after yourself. How your brain doesn't go pop... '

Sam's eyes were dull with fatigue but she couldn't switch off.

'You know the most interesting thing I learnt today, Bev?' Sam said. 'The real leader of the Mortimers is Elliott Prince.'

CHAPTER TWENTY-FOUR

Sam eyed the microwave glumly and searched the freezer. There was a pasta dish she might eat later but for now, the lunchtime curry would do. She went to the wine chiller, selected a 2010 Albert Grivault, and popped the cork on the bottle of white burgundy.

She had spoken to Sue Whelan before she left the office. Ed was sleeping.

She kicked off her shoes, walked into the sitting room and sat down.

Elliott Prince was a conundrum, identified by Ed as the weak link but who had nonetheless thrown paint through a police station window. He was a frightened young man when he brought them the picture of Jamie Telford, then played down taking photographs of sleeping girls. He was also the student who named all the dead in the river as wearing the 'slags and beer' T-shirts.

Sam tilted her glass, looked at the clarity of the wine, took a long sniff, swirled her glass, and sniffed again. Elliott Prince was bothering her. What was that film? The weak member of the gang, a man with a limp, turned out to be the leader... convincingly lied his way through a police interview. What was it called?

'The Usual Suspects', Sam said aloud, remembering Kevin Spacey's turn as the bad guy, Keyser Söze.

Sam leaned back, closed her eyes. Was Elliott Prince their own Keyser Söze? She laughed. Bev was right. They were all in danger of cracking up. She took a sip of burgundy.

Friday 18th April 2014

As soon as she walked into the building, one of the detectives from the Intelligence Cell appeared behind her.

'Boss, I've got the text traffic between Tracey Davies, Charlotte Swains, and Alex O'Connell.'

Sam stopped. 'Anything useful?'

'Plenty.'

'Bring your stuff up to my office.'

Sitting at the desk, she laid out the analytical chart. A series of boxes contained a typed message then the name of the sender.

'This lot is just for the night of Jack Goddard's murder, the Saturday through until Sunday,' the detective told her.

Sam read the messages, most of them none evidential but short snaps of conversations giving a glimpse into the lives of young female students. The messages after 9pm caused Sam to sit up.

9.16pm. Tracey Davies. To Amber University. Some cheeky twat wearing those T-shirts walked up to me in the pub and asked for a shag

9.30pm. Tracey Davies. To Amber University. Bouncer threw him out after he threw pint over him I hope he beats the shit out of him

9.50pm. Amber University. To Tracey Davies. See where he goes. Might be able to get something later.

'Do we know who this Amber University is?' Sam asked.

The detective shook his head: 'No. She's listed in all three phones as Amber University, same number. We're getting a subscriber check done.'

Sam already knew exactly who she was.

10.20pm. Alex O'Connell. To Tracey Davies. Are you two in Rendezvous

10.20pm. Alex O'Connell. To Charlotte Swains. Are you two in Rendezvous

10.35pm. Tracey Davies. To Alexander O'Connell. Yes and so are the wankers.

'No messages from Charlotte?' Sam asked

'Not yet,' the detective told her. 'Later though.'

12.33am. Tracey Davies. To Amber University. Tossers in Rendezvous.

12.38am. Amber University. To Tracey Davies. Do what you can

03.35am. Tracey Davies. To Amber University. Me and Charlotte just left. Not alone.

03.36am. Amber University. To Tracey Davies. Where's Alex.

03.37am. Tracey Davies. To Amber University. Still in club.

03.37am. Amber University. To Tracey Davies. Are they pissed?

03.38am. Tracey Davies. To Amber University. Mortal
03.44am. Alex O'Connell. To Charlotte Swains. You ok.

03.44am. Alex O'Connell. To Tracey Davies. You ok.

03.46am. Tracey Davies. To Alex O'Connell. Yes.

'Is that the lot?' said Sam, looking up.

'Yes.'

'Any pictures?'

'Just the usual rubbish they all seem to take,' the detective said. 'Nothing of interest to us.'

Sam was disappointed. Those conversations could be about anyone, anywhere. They could deny all the messages were about Jack Goddard.

The detective spoke again. 'We've also triangulated the phones. Tracey's and Charlotte's are by the tow path. Alex O'Connell's phone's in the town centre.'

Sam stood up, slowly. 'Wow. Good work.'

'Cheers Boss.'

Ed called Sam as he left the house and she told him about yesterday's conversation with Luke Wylam.

He felt better after a decent night's sleep, but passing out for the first time in his life worried him. Why had that happened? Sue told him to take things easy, have a few days off, make an appointment with the doctor. She wasn't happy he was going into work on Good Friday but he had too much on his plate. He'd get around to the doctor eventually.

Ed knocked on Tom King's door. All the curtains were closed but as he knocked louder, he heard the footsteps thud down the stairs.

'Can I come in, Tom?'

His white boxers looked new, the green T-shirt creased.

'What now? I was working late last night. I should still be in bed. It's Friday, a bank holiday, and I've got a busy night ahead in case you hadn't noticed.'

Ed slapped down the attitude.

'If you prefer, we can do this down the nick and you won't be anywhere near work tonight,' he said. 'You can have bed and breakfast on the Queen and catch up on your beauty sleep. Now, can I come in?'

Tom King turned around, leaving the door to the bungalow open. Ed followed and sat down in the large lounge.

'Nice place.'

'It's mum's,' Tom told him. 'Once I got out of care, we used the money from the house, our house, you know, the house where it happened. It was sold when I was a kid. Mum wanted a bungalow for when she gets out. I printed the photos off for her. She liked it and I bought it. But I'm sure you're not here to talk about my mum's bungalow.'

He sat down.

'Tom, look, if it's any consolation I... '

'It's not,' Tom stopped him.

He was sitting on the edge of the settee, back straight, his muscular defined arms flexing slightly.

Ed stretched his legs and leaned back into the armchair.

'What I mean is I knew your mother, and... '

Tom jumped in again. 'It doesn't matter. Forget it. He beat us up all the time. You'd know that if you knew my mum. I was 12 when she killed him. But we used to talk, me and mum. We couldn't understand how he never got charged. He'd get arrested sometimes, but not often. Even then he'd be out next morning.'

Ed sat up. Domestic violence had always been difficult for the police. There always seemed to be a new initiative... zero tolerance... changing the name to domestic abuse… a recognition women didn't need to be physically beaten to suffer. Women's groups were quick to point the finger and Ed felt the police could do better.

'I've been to too many so-called domestic murders over the years,' he told Tom. 'We should be more proactive when women tell us they don't want to continue proceedings.'

Tom's face flushed.

'My mother never asked to drop the charges and she ended up with a simple choice – kill or be killed. My father once said he had immunity. If she didn't behave herself, he'd beat her to a pulp and nothing would happen to him.'

Ed stared at the young man. Tom King was getting ready to deliver some sort of punch-line.

'My father was a police informant and it didn't matter how much he beat me and mum, he was looked after. Well, whoever was looking after him didn't count on my mother crushing his fucking head with a spade.'

Ed didn't move, watching Tom's eyes mist.

'Their precious information was more important than my mother's health.'

His shoulders suddenly heaved and his voice, fighting to keep the sobs in the pit of his stomach, sounded like it was at the end of a bad mobile phone connection. 'Never mind her happiness.'

Ed stayed silent and motionless. He would wait, let the young man compose himself.

Tom lifted his T-shirt and rubbed his eyes and nose.

'Sorry. You still haven't said why you're here.'

'I want your work shoes.'

'You what?'

'I want your shoes,' Ed told him. 'Take them away for tests. If there's nothing on them, you can have them back.'

'And if there is something on them?'

Ed's voice was calm. 'You might be in the shit.'

Tom sat back and looked around the room.

'Well you can't have them then.'

'Then I'll arrest you on suspicion of assault, search your house under Section 18 of the Police and Criminal Evidence Act and take your shoes,' Ed said. 'If you've done nothing wrong, you've got nothing to worry about. Either way, I'm not walking out of this bungalow without checking every pair of shoes here.'

'What, so you just took his shoes?' Sam said.

Ed was in her office, washing down two paracetamol with a mouthful of lukewarm tea.

'Luke Wylam doesn't want to make a complaint, according to you,' he said. 'Besides, he wasn't bleeding. All we've got on Tom up to now is the fact that on the night Jack Goddard was killed he lied about being at home. Let's see if Jack's blood's on his shoes.'

Sam nodded. They'd both worked on investigations where offenders had burned their clothing. Those who were clever, who knew they may have been captured on CCTV, even bought identical clothes to those that they'd burned so they could give the new ones to the police. But many criminals forgot about burning their shoes – thought a polish, or a wash in the case of trainers, would do. Sam and Ed had come through with some great results where tiny amounts of blood had been trapped behind the eyelets.

'Didn't he ask why you wanted them?'

'I told him it was about an assault,' Ed said. 'He didn't bat an eyelid. If I'm honest, I don't think it's anything to do with him.'

'Why?'

'He thinks the world of his mother,' Ed said. 'He's sorted the purchase of a really nice bungalow. Well kept. The lawn was immaculate. She's serving time for murder, but she'll be out in a couple of years. Would he really risk serious time because some arsehole was rude to women? He might not like bad manners... who does? But would he sacrifice his liberty for some shit-bag? I don't think he would. If we find Goddard's blood on his shoes, we can go and get him and we'll have a bit more to talk about than the fact he was seen coming out of a club when he said he was tucked up.'

Two hours later, Sam picked up the office phone and punched the numbers.

'Darius, it's Sam…'

Christ, I must get this phone cleaned before I catch something.

'Fine thanks. Tonight, from about 5.30pm, we'll be in Aisha's street, doing door to door… Yeah, we want to do it again to see if anyone remembers anything… I'm just trying to jog people's memory.'

She waved Ed into her office, jammed the phone

between her ear and shoulder, held her arms out in front of her and rotated her hands as if she was steering a car.

Ed nodded.

'I'm going to put a Fiesta, identical colour to Sukhvinder's, at the top of the street. It's just been confirmed we've borrowed one. If Aisha did run away with Sukhi, then it's inconceivable he didn't use his car. He might not have driven to her door, but he must have driven where she would at least have seen him.' Sam paused then spoke again.

'Course you can take photographs,' she said. 'We want maximum publicity. It's all about trying to find Aisha… you're right, I don't know which end of the street he would have parked, so every 20 minutes I'll have a police officer drive it to the opposite end.'

Ed smiled. *Genius*. Much better than leaving it parked up. If Aisha's family had anything to do with her disappearance, if they knew Sukhi had a car, this would make them very uncomfortable. Every resident in that street would grasp Sam's tenacity; every resident would see that car.

'Yeah,' Sam continued. 'Peter Hunt from the press office is chasing up the local TV. I think they'll send a crew... good visuals, a car like the boyfriend's and a dozen uniforms knocking on doors... that'll be great, see you there…I'll be there, of course, and so will Ed.'

She replaced the receiver.

'Wouldn't miss it for the world,' Ed said.

'Sure you're okay?'

'Don't worry about me.'

One of the detectives from the Intelligence Cell appeared at the door.

'Boss, we've got the subscriber check through.' He said.

'Amber University is Amber Dalton. We're just waiting to see what we can get from her phone.'

Sam closed her eyes for a moment before she spoke again.

'While you're on, check the Facebook accounts of all the girls,' she said. 'Any joy with Mortimers and their accounts?"

'Still ongoing,' the detective told her. 'Open source Internet examinations can take a bit of time boss.'

Once the detective had left, Sam brought Ed up to speed.

'So the big news of the morning,' she said. 'Tracey and Charlotte's phones are on the tow path, Alex's is in the town and also out and about is Amber's.'

CHAPTER TWENTY-FIVE

'I'M sick of chasing these two,' Bev said, as she drove out of HQ. 'All day yesterday on and off looking for them and back out this morning. It's not as if we've got nothing better to do. It's their mate who's been killed, Telford who had his picture taken.'

Paul Adams was trying to turn Bev's rant into white noise when he suddenly sat bolt upright.

'Quick, pull into the bus lane,' he shouted. 'There's Jones!'

Glen Jones was walking among the few pedestrians.

Paul flung the door open and was running before the car stopped.

'Glen.' Paul had his hand on Jones's shoulder before the student had turned around. 'We need a word. You've been telling porkies and we're not happy about it.'

'What are you on about?' Jones spluttered, taking half a step away.

'Get in the car,' Paul ordered. 'We'll sort this out it in private, away from the street and law-abiding citizens' phone cameras.'

He ushered Jones towards the kerb, pushed down on his shoulder and shoved him into the back seat. Bev activated the child locks and pulled swiftly away when Paul jumped in.

Jones was agitated, squirming around on the back seat and trying to maintain an air of aggression. The timidity in his shaky voice showed he was failing miserably.

'What do you want?' he said.

'The truth,' Paul demanded. 'We know about you going into Rendezvous with Tracey and Charlotte, after you were seen being very luvvie-duvvie with them in the town centre. Marvellous thing close-circuit-television. So cut the bullshit.'

Jones' hands shot up to his face and he began to cry.

'Save it, Glen,' Paul said. 'Your mate's dead and you can't even tell the truth.'

Jones was shaking and hitching sobs from his throat.

'Okay, okay,' He croaked. 'Me and Jack got a letter... a picture more like. No threat but it wasn't nice.'

'Where's the picture?' Paul demanded

'In the flat.'

'Let's go and get it,' Paul told him. 'Let's get it now.'

Amber Dalton had moved since Sam had last visited her in February of last year. No longer renting, she had bought her own house after deciding against a return to Bristol. She had resigned from the planning office at the local council, immersed herself in various part-time counselling courses as well as her degree and was now helping victims of abuse.

Sam and Ed were on their way to Amber's new home.

'I just feel we're not getting anywhere fast enough,'

Sam said, staring out of the side window as Ed negotiated yet another town centre contra-flow system.

'Always the same,' he said testily. 'No repairs done all year, come March the council miraculously finds some money they need to spend before the financial year ends and bang – roadworks everywhere …sorry, what did you say?'

Sam wearily shook her head.

'I said, Mr Angry of Tunbridge Wells, I feel like I'm running through treacle. We're getting nowhere fast. Bloody hell, we can't even find Glen Jones and Jamie Telford.'

Ed scowled as he joined a queue at temporary traffic lights.

'I've sent Paul and Bev out looking for them. It's only 11 o'clock. Plenty of time. We'll get the girls in after we've seen Amber. They've got a lot to answer now. I'll knock up a quick questionnaire later for the door-to-door teams. Now wind down the window, light a cigarette and chill!'

Sam had chain-smoked two by the time they pulled up outside Amber's home.

Walking up the driveway, Sam noticed Amber still kept the garden beautiful. The same pale blue bench was underneath the front window, although she had taken the precaution of setting it into concrete.

'Morning Amber,' Sam said, when the door opened. 'You remember Ed.'

'Oh, hi Sam. To what do I owe this pleasure? I was expecting a parcel, not you…sorry, that sounded rude! Come in, come in.'

She led them into the kitchen and pointed at the glass-topped table, and the four moulded plastic chairs, each a different vibrant colour. Sam took the lime green one, Ed the purple.

'Tea?' Amber said.

'We're fine. Look, we'll not keep you. It's just a quick one.'

Amber sat at the table.

'I felt our conversation was a little rushed the other night when we talked about the girls being photographed,' Sam said. 'Do you know personally of it happening to anyone?'

'Lots, but I've told you Sam, it's not my place to report,' Amber said. 'I would have been devastated if a third party had reported my rape. The girls have got to report it themselves.'

Sam said she understood and moved on.

'Do you socialise with any of the girls.'

Amber moved her eyes from Sam to Ed and back again.

'Not really,' she told them. 'We might go for a drink after a group session but that's it. I never see them at any other time.'

'And your group,' Sam asked. 'Does it have a name?'

'Nothing as formal as that Sam,' Amber smiled.

'Okay, thanks for your time,' Sam said, standing to leave, Ed rising too. 'Please stress to your members – do you call them that? – we'll deal sensitively with any allegations they make.'

Sam pushed her chair under the table and pointed to a book on the kitchen bench, a book she'd seen as she walked in.

'Good read that,' she said lightly. 'My favourite character was always Macavity.'

Glen Jones sat, head bowed, looking at the black lino on the interview room floor.

'So you lied about meeting up with Charlotte and Tracey,' Bev said.

'I panicked.' He was sniffling. 'Jack was dead. I didn't kill him. I had no idea who did, so I just said I went home. I'm sorry, but that's why I did it.'

'And what do you think now?' Bev asked him. 'About his death?'

'Sisters of Macavity,' Jones answered quietly. 'I can't get their name out of my head. What does it even mean?'

Bev ignored the question. 'When did you first hear about them?'

'When I got that photograph,' Jones told her. 'I've tried to find out about them. I've asked girls I know but no one had heard of them. They're like a secret society. I think they did it though... killed Jack. What if I'm next? At least with Jamie they sent the photos out. They didn't do that with Jack's, and they haven't done it with mine.'

He reached for a plastic cup of water and drank slowly.

'Mortimers,' Bev said. 'Your little group. Who was the leader?'

'No one. We're all the same.'

Bev leaned towards him and lowered her voice. 'Every group that ever existed had a leader. Who's yours?'

Jones rubbed moisture from under his nose, stared at her through glassy eyes, and inhaled deeply.

'Elliott,' he said after a long pause. 'Jack wanted to be, but it was Elliott. He just had the way about him. He got people to do what he wanted without ever forcing them. Half the time he didn't even ask them outright. He just nudged them along with his smooth words.'

Bev glanced at the two photographs laid side by side on

the wooden table framed by desk-top graffiti; previous prisoners writing obscene messages about the cops who'd arrested them. Who had been stupid enough to leave prisoners alone in the interview room, and who the hell gave them a pen?

The first photograph showed Glen Jones and Jack Goddard naked on all fours. Jones had told the truth. There was no threat to make the picture public.

'And you have no idea where these were taken, what night?'

'No. It could be anywhere, any night.'

'Can you give us a list of the parties you've been to in the last two months?'

He raised his head, eyes wide open and still red.

'I couldn't tell you which parties I've been to in the last two weeks. We probably go to about three a week, maybe four. It's not like you get a written invitation.'

'So you've no recollection of the, how shall I say it, pose?' Bev asked him.

'No, but looking at it, I think somebody's put something in our drink,' Jones said. 'I would never do that, no matter how pissed I got.'

He looked at the floor again.

'What would they put in your drink?'

'You know... roofies.'

Bev tapped her biro against her upper teeth. Rohypnol – roofies – the date-rape drug.

'Many roofies knocking around the university?' she asked.

Jones looked up. 'I've never bought them so I wouldn't know. I suppose you can get them. You can get most drugs.'

'This picture here,' Bev pushed it across the desk. 'The charming image of you all wearing matching 'hashtag slags and beer' T-shirts. Write the names across each body.'

She slid him a pen and sat in silence as Jones printed each name. Nine in total.

When he'd finished, Bev took the photograph, removed a piece of paper from her jacket, and compared it to Jamie Telford's list.

'This lad here,' Bev pointed to a hairy arm on the edge of the group. 'You can only see this guy's arm. You've written down a different name to Jamie.'

'Who did he say it was?'

'Jonny White.'

'No, no way.' Jones sounded sure. 'I think Jonny might have been in hospital that night. He did his leg playing football. He wasn't out that night. It can only be Aaron Leech. He was definitely out with us that night and he's the only face you can't see on the photo.'

Bev studied the picture again, 'Was Aaron a member of your silly little group?'

'No, he wasn't,' Jones answered. 'I don't know why.'

Bev already knew which group Aaron had joined.

He was a member of 'The Drowners'.

CHAPTER TWENTY-SIX

'DO YOU THINK AMBER'S LYING?' Sam's brow was furrowed, elbows on her desk, hands cupping her chin.

'I don't know,' Ed's answer was honest. 'Maybe the group doesn't have a name, maybe she doesn't normally socialise with them. I suppose they'd have her number in case they wanted to talk to her. She's putting herself about as a counsellor. Maybe going to meet them is business, not pleasure. Maybe she just happened to be reading Cats. Maybe it's coincidental that all their phones are out and about when Jack Goddard dies.'

'All ifs, buts and maybes.'

'But more than enough to lock them all up.'

Bev poked her head around the door. 'Got a minute?'

'Course,' Sam said.

'Aaron Leech.'

'One of the ones who drowned?' Sam said.

'Yes. He's in the Hashtag photo.'

'What?'

'Yeah, Jamie Telford identified him, wrongly according

to Glen Jones. You can only see the person's arm. Jones says it's Leech. He remembers drinking with him that night. He told me Jonny White was in hospital. I've checked. He was.'

'Why?' Sam asked.

'Injured his leg playing football,' Bev said. 'They kept him in.'

'Get a crew checking on the known associates of the five who drowned,' Sam said quickly. 'I know it's been done but let's redo it. There's now a connection between Goddard and Leech we didn't know about, even if it is nothing more than they were photographed together. The bigger connection is that they were wearing the same T-shirts.'

Ed clasped his hands around his neck, stretched and looked upwards.

'Could we really have a bunch of vigilante women killing men who have wronged them on social media? Women serial killers are rarer than rocking horse shit, and we're contemplating a group of them.'

'We'll follow the evidence, but at the minute…I want to delay everything with them,' Sam said. 'When we go for them, I want as much evidence as we can get, but I don't want any more students dying on that tow path. Tonight, and tomorrow I want as many uniforms as they can spare us along that tow path.'

Ed knew the likely reaction.

'Bloody hell, Sam, the uniform Superintendent's going to have to open a new box. We already want a presence in Aisha's street tonight.'

'Well he'll have to borrow a box of uniforms from another policing area if necessary, but he won't need to. We can use the same crew. We want them in Aisha's street from 5.30pm. We can be done there by 11, give them an hour's break, then they can do midnight until daylight on the tow path.'

'I'll sort a couple of mounties out for the tow path,' Ed told her. 'Just in case there's a chase.'

Sam nodded once. 'Job's jobbed then. Let's have a cig, Bev.'

Admin, the unseen and often boring part of police work, filled the afternoon. Year on year, it increased, more forms to be completed, successive governments wanting ever more data and statistics on every conceivable facet of the job.

Then there was the change in status. When police officers stopped being Servants of the Crown and became employees, Health and Safety legislation kicked in. Risk assessments had to be carried out for every policing activity.

Ed sat at a desk completing the Operational Order for the door to door. In the old days it was done under the initials IIMAC – Information, Intention, Method, Admin and Communication. Now he had to add R – IIMARC – for a Risk Assessment.

He shook his head. *All this to knock on a few doors*. When he joined for the first time back in 1978, they just got on with it. Now, a minority of cops wouldn't move until a job had been risk assessed. How some of the recruits joining in the new millennium would have managed with just a radio and a wooden truncheon was beyond him. Now it was stab-proof vests, batons, quick-cuffs, CS gas, tasers, and more firearms officers than ever yet still everything had to be assessed. There comes a time when a police officer just has to get on with it, Ed firmly believed.

Thankfully, most still fell into the 'getting on with it' camp.

Ed also needed to liaise with the Neighbourhood Inspector and discuss a Community Impact Assessment.

All part of the fun in the modern day police force. No, police *service*, he reminded himself.

In another office, at another desk, Sam sat writing reams about the investigations, recording every decision made in relation to each major inquiry, her reasons for making that decision, what other options she had considered and why she had dismissed them in favour of her chosen one. Her Policy File was her shield against hindsight, and hindsight was a stick that could be used to beat her in any judicial proceedings or internal investigation.

If an army marched on its stomach, the police service was mobilised by keyboards and ink.

Both front windows were fully open as Ed drove to Aisha's street, the fresh air a natural coolant to the stuffy offices they'd left.

'Do you think we'll get a reaction here tonight?' Sam said.

'Guarantee it.' Ed applied a little pressure to the brakes, hoping to avoid coming to a complete standstill as he approached the red light. The lights changed and he gently accelerated. 'But just before we came out I sat down with the Inspector handling Neighbourhood Policing and did a Community Impact Assessment. He doesn't expect trouble on the streets. Like me, he thinks any reaction will come from Aisha's family, especially if they've got something to do with her disappearance.'

Copies of both the operational order and impact assessment were with the control room Inspector, giving the early heads up in case trouble broke out.

In the street, seven uniformed officers were knocking on doors, clipboard in hand, Ed's prepared questionnaire on top.

The borrowed Fiesta was slowly driving up and down.

Sam opened her door and hadn't even started to get out when Darius Simpson appeared. He bent down. 'The family are kicking up a shit storm Sam.'

'Good evening to you too,' Sam said tightly. 'What's up?'

Putting her left leg out of the car forced Darius to step back. She knew he'd love to get close to her.

'Mr Bhandal's been outside, demanding to know what's going on, who's responsible,' Darius said. 'He's going to make a complaint about us being here taking photos, says he's writing to the Chief Constable and the local MP, plus he's knocking on neighbours' doors after your lot have left.'

'Pity he wasn't so proactive when his daughter went missing,' Sam said. 'Leave him to me.' She stepped away from the car and walked towards Bhandal. He was closing the gap between them much quicker than she was.

'What is the meaning of this, Sergeant Parker? It's an outrage.'

She ignored the demotion, an old tactic employed by people trying to get the upper hand and rile the officer concerned.

'We are simply revisiting everything we have done in relation to Aisha's disappearance,' Sam told him, holding his angry eyes. 'It's been over four months now and what better place to start than where she went missing.'

Bhandal was shaking with rage.

'Nobody round here knows anything,' he said, his voice rising. 'Find her boyfriend then you'll find her. He's a kidnapper. You won't find her knocking on the doors here, bringing shame upon my family because we cannot control who our daughter sees.'

Sam's calm was the ice to Bhandal's heat.

'Shame, Mr Bhandal? We're not trying to shame you. We are trying to find your daughter.'

'My wife is very upset,' Bhandal went on. 'This is reminding her of what has happened.'

Suddenly his son, Baljit, quick-marched across the road, fists clenched. The shouting started before he was halfway across.

'What the fuck are you lot doing? Call this lot off.'

Sam waited until he was standing by his father.

'I'm not calling anybody off,' she told him. 'Now I suggest you go back in the house before you overstep the line and force me to consider arresting you for obstructing a police officer in the execution of their duty.'

'Execution?' Baljit shouted. 'The only execution likely around here is yours.'

Ed glided up behind him, gripped his arm, and whispered in his ear.

'Listen, sonny, go back inside before you're arrested for threats to kill, there's a good boy.'

Baljit pulled away.

'Keep your hands off me,' he hissed. 'I'll do you for assault.'

Ed smiled as Baljit slinked off.

Bhandal pointed his finger at Sam. 'I will be contacting my solicitor.'

'You do what you feel you must,' Sam said, smiling at him as the Fiesta drove slowly past.

He stormed off after his son. A third man, the uncle, Gurmej, was standing on the footpath directly outside the house, watching everything. The three of them went inside, Bhandal slamming the door.

'Told you there was going to be a shit storm.' Darius and the photographer were next to them now.

'Did you get any photos of that little interaction?' Sam said.

'Plenty,' the photographer grinned.

'Any chance of getting copies?'

'No problem, Sam,' Darius jumped in.

Ed smiled. *Put your tongue back in son!*

The Asian woman, a few streaks of black in her predominantly grey hair, was about 50 metres away when Ed saw her. He counted seven bulging carrier bags in her hands. He stepped away and walked towards her.

'Sat-sri-akaal, Mrs Maan.'

'Sat-sri-akaal, Ed.'

He had known her almost as long as he'd known his wife. 'Let me help you.' He reached towards her bags but she took a step backwards. 'I can manage.'

The sudden movement caused the aromatic smell of fresh coriander to envelop Ed and his stomach rumbled. Mrs Maan's curries were legendary.

He put his hands in his pockets and walked alongside her as she continued her way home.

The Fiesta drove past.

'Still looking for that girl, Aisha?' she asked.

Ed told her they were.

'Lovely girl,' Mrs Maan said quietly. 'Known her since she was a baby.'

With each step, Ed's foot paused mid-air, trying to match his strides with her shuffle.

'Terrible what has happened, Ed,' she said. 'Her

running away like that. The girls are Westernised these days, don't want to carry on the traditions. You should know that better than most… I remember the day Sue's mother told me she was seeing a white boy.'

She giggled, an old woman suddenly a schoolgirl again.

'Lucky for you her family were forward thinking. Not everybody was. Not everybody is.'

The Fiesta drove past again.

'Why is that car driving up and down?'

'It's the same make as the one Aisha's boyfriend had,' Ed answered. 'Have you seen it in the street before?'

Mrs Maan looked around, checking for twitching curtains.

'Maybe,' she said in a whisper. 'But I cannot talk here. Get Sue to meet me in the Gurdwara tomorrow morning, about 10. I'll talk to her.'

She reached her red door, opened it.

'What can you tell Sue?' Ed asked.

Mrs Maan nervously scanned the street again.

'The weekend Aisha went missing I did see a car like that,' she said. 'People were fighting, shouting.'

She stepped inside and turned to Ed. She was already closing the door when she said: 'I know who was fighting.'

CHAPTER TWENTY-SEVEN

'It's full of risks and ethical issues.'

Sam was staring out of the office window over the rim of her mug of coffee, the car parks of Headquarters almost empty.

'What have we got to lose?' Ed said. 'Mrs Maan will never make a statement. It's a piece of intelligence, a potential pointer in the right direction, something we might never get otherwise.'

Sam nodded. She couldn't argue with Ed's logic. Nothing had come from the door to door. That's not to say nobody would contact the police on another day. There were times when people didn't want to be seen talking on their doorsteps but would later get in touch.

Mrs Maan only talked because she knew Ed. Had she not seen him, it was doubtful she would have said a word.

'At least speaking to her might give us a steer,' Ed went on. 'That's more than we've got now, more than we've got in four months.'

Sam knew he was right.

'Don't mention it to anybody,' Ed said. 'The only

people who know are you, me, Mrs Maan and Sue when I tell her. If she has information and it has to go in the system, I'll put in an Officers Report, something to the effect I've been told by a source. Not a proper CHIS, just a source in the community.'

Covert Human Intelligence Sources were still informants, snitches, snouts, grasses and narks to Ed. He was using the term 'source' in its literal sense... where something began.

Sam sipped the coffee.

'Look,' Ed said, 'let's just see what she has to tell us. Nobody up to now has even mentioned seeing the car in the street, never mind a fight. If there was a fight, I'd rather know about it. Then at least we can start to look for some corroboration.'

'What about Sue?' Sam asked him, still uneasy.

Ed smiled. 'She'll love the opportunity to catch up with Mrs Maan.'

'Tell me you're joking,' Sue said, eyes wide. 'Tell me you don't want me acting as your Special Constable.'

She was standing by the cooker, stirring a big pan of chicken curry, Ed's stomach grumbling more now than when he smelled Mrs Maan's coriander.

'All I'm asking is for you to have little chat with her,' he said. 'There's nothing wrong with that, nothing unusual.'

Sue glared at him, spoon frozen in mid-stir. 'Except I'm reporting back to you.'

'Mrs Maan knows that,' Ed said. 'It was her suggestion. She wants to tell us something but can't be seen talking to police. We both know what the community's like.'

Sue had her back to him, the wooden spoon again going around in slow circles.

'What if I miss something out? I'm not trained to remember things like you are.'

'We're not trained to remember,' Ed said, sensing success.

'You could have fooled me.' Sue's tone had lightened. 'You still remind me of the night me and Leela came home drunk and that was five years ago.'

Ed came up behind her, put his arms around her waist, and whispered into her ear.

'It could go a long way to finding out what's happened to Aisha,' he said. 'And at least it'll stop you moaning at me for going into work on another Saturday.'

She spun around and pointed the spoon at his face. 'In with your girlfriend again are you?'

Ed didn't respond. Sometimes it was best just to stay quiet.

'Okay, I'll do it, but only because it might help Aisha, and I know Mrs Maan,' Sue said. 'Not because it'll get you in Sam bloody Parker's good books.'

Sam was walking along the tow path. It was 11.30pm but she had no desire to rush home. She wasn't tired and she had declined Bev's suggestion to go to the pub... too much going on for her mind to be dulled by alcohol.

She wanted to speak to the cops who were down on the tow path at her behest, thank them for their time and effort. Sometimes she did ask people to do pretty joyless tasks.

She had a quick word with the two mounted officers. As always, she admired the size and beauty of the two massive horses – one black, the other grey. If she remembered correctly, a primary school pupil had named the grey horse in a competition organised with Darius and the Seaton Post. She couldn't remember the horse's name.

She wondered how Ed was getting on with Sue and began wrestling with her decision to allow her to become part of the investigation. But what choice did she have? The fight might have involved Aisha, her boyfriend or both of them.

The blood results from the settee were due tomorrow.

Then there was Sukhi's car. Who had driven it into the garage? What if Sukhi wasn't capable of driving?

Sam stopped and leaned her shoulder against a tree, its bark rough, and examined the river, the grass bank sloping towards its edge. At this point, and for a half-mile in either direction, there was a drop of about four feet into the water. Had the students just fallen in drunk and been unable to get back out? There was no safety equipment as such, no red life-saving belts, but even if there were, they'd be no good to a lone student. Who'd throw the rings in to them?

But what if they hadn't fallen? What if they'd been pushed? And if they had, who'd done the pushing?

Tracey, Charlotte, Alex and Amber had all been in the vicinity the night Jack Goddard died. *Correction*, Sam told herself. *Their phones had been there*. Was she really looking for a group of female vigilante serial killers?

She started to walk again, getting further away from her car.

Was Amber's group called the Sisters of Macavity? Had they sent the photographs? If so, how had they taken them? How had anybody got the boys to pose? Drugs? Rohypnol? Payback time was one thing, but killing?

And Aaron Leech, the arm in the Hashtag photograph.

He had drowned. But was he pushed? Even the slightest suggestion of that and the media circus would come to town. Was it just a coincidence? No Senior Investigating Officer in the country believed in them. Coincidences happened but only after SIOs had exhausted every other hypothesis.

And Elliott Prince? The leader? She still couldn't get her head around that, even if it had no bearing on the investigation. Sometimes human nature just surprised her, the Keyser Söze syndrome.

Sam stopped again. The flame from the lighter illuminated her face. She drew deep on the Marlboro Gold, allowing the smoke to fill her expanding lungs, imagined the nicotine rushing around her veins, held her breath, then slowly let the smoke escape in swirls through her mouth and nose. She knew neither investigation was going to be brought to a swift conclusion.

'All quiet?' she said to a passing Community Support Officer astride a bike.

'Yes ma'am.'

She hated being called ma'am. It made her sound like some old woman from a bygone age. She was much happier with boss, even happier with Sam.

Saturday 19th April 2014

Ed dropped Sue at the Gurdwara at 9.45am. The morning had been a two-fold rarity... a leisurely breakfast and the enjoyment of her company.

While she'd had fresh berries and muesli, he'd devoured the kind of 'Full English' that had fuelled the working men in his family for generations: miners, shipyard welders and riveters, sent out with a belly full of bacon, fried eggs, fried potatoes and strong tea.

He parked in the town centre and went for a coffee. No point in going into the office. As soon as Sue had finished at the Gurdwara, he needed to pick her up and hear what Mrs Maan had to say.

He avoided the mass-market coffee shops and went into the Italian, run by the same family for decades. He opened the dark brown door and stepped into the small, cool, dark interior, all deep brown tables and chairs, brown paint on the walls, Antonio had his arms folded on the deep brown counter, back bent, smiling at the customers, a scene unchanged since the first time Ed had gone in more than 30 years ago. Antonio's white shirt and black apron were as immaculate as always.

'Ed, how are you today?' Antonio's sons had been schooled here, but he still had the accent he arrived with from Sicily a lifetime ago.

'Good. How are you, Don?'

The nickname, hardly original, had been bestowed in the early 70s, a throwback to the release of The Godfather movie. The affectionate moniker had stuck and now the majority of people didn't know Antonio's real name. Before the decade of Slade, Wizard and British Leyland strikes had finished, he'd even changed the name of the café from Antonio's to Corleone's.

'I'm fine, Ed. The usual?'

'Please,' Ed said, sitting on one of the tall stools at the counter, feet perched on its crossbar and buttocks planted on the hard, unforgiving wood.

'One double espresso coming up,' Antonio told him.

Here the choice was simple... espresso with or without milk, a short drink or a long one. And unlike the endless choices you got at the chains, in Corleone's it was either pastries or amaretto biscuits.

They discussed football. Antonio was devoted to the national team of his homeland but shared Ed's passion for Newcastle United.

Ed's phone vibrated and danced across the counter, the screen telling him the text was from Sue. She was finished.

'Have to dash, Don.' The coffee was like a shot of adrenalin.

'Slow down, Ed,' Antonio said reaching for the tiny cup. 'Enjoy the little things. Before you know it the big thing, death, will find you.'

Ed ran a hand over his smooth head and took in Antonio's jet-black wavy hair, still full and thick at 70 years old. *Slow down?* Perhaps he had a point. What had his dad once said to him? *Nobody lying on their deathbed ever wished they'd spent more time in the office.*

Sue was waiting for him on the corner of the street and jumped in the car as soon as he stopped in the middle of the road.

'How did you get on?' Ed asked as he pulled away.

'Hang on, let me get my seat belt on.'

He tried to hide his frustration. He was desperate to discover what Mrs Maan had said and whether it was worth knowing.

'I'd forgotten how many people go to that place on a morning,' Sue told him. 'Anyway, I made an excuse, felt guilty about not being there for a while. Luckily Leela was there so it looked normal. Me and Mrs Maan chatting was just two old neighbours from different generations catching up.'

Ed glanced across at her.

'Alright, alright, I know,' Sue sighed. 'Firstly, she won't repeat this to anybody and just deny ever saying it if necessary. She saw a car like the one driving up the street yesterday but didn't say anything because... well you know why.'

'Community,' Ed said.

Sue nodded then went on.

'She didn't know the driver, a young boy, but she saw Aisha talking to him. It looked like she was putting a bag on to the back seat. Aisha got grabbed from behind, two men attacked the boy and... '

'Does she know who they are?' Ed stopped her.

'God, are you this impatient at work?'

His head jerked around to face her. 'I am when people are going round the houses.'

She screamed his name.

He slammed the brakes; rubber screeched against Tarmac, his bumper stopping inches from the rear end of the stationary car in front.

He took a deep breath, told himself to calm down.

Sue pressed her nose against the side window. 'Watch what you're doing.'

Ed moved off with the traffic.

The 20 seconds she took before speaking gave Ed enough time to curse his impatience.

'Yes, she does know them,' Sue said. 'Aisha's brother grabbed her. Her father and the uncle from India, the one who took part in the honour killing... '

'She knew about that?' Ed broke in again.

Sue gave him a look.

'Come on, Ed, just because the police don't know... anyway, she says they beat up the young boy. Then the father and brother dragged Aisha home. The boy, who looked unconscious, was thrown on to the back seat and driven away by the uncle.'

CHAPTER TWENTY-EIGHT

SAM RUBBED eyes that stung through lack of sleep and blinked as the email forwarded by Bev Summers from DC Welch at Devon and Cornwall Constabulary came into focus.

DC Summers.
Re Ford Fiesta, registered to Sukhvinder Sahota

Sam skimmed over the details of the vehicle's VIN plate and which body parts were missing.

The car was discovered yesterday in a lock-up garage near Plymouth Hoe. This garage was subject of an ongoing operation into organised car theft.

Many parts of the car are missing – this garage is believed to be a chop-shop.

The front windscreen and interior rear-view mirror are still on the car. There are a number of fingerprints on the inside of the wind-

screen and two partial prints on the mirror. All prints are unidentified.

A witness did see a young Asian male drive the vehicle into the garage. This witness is confident of identifying the male. For the time being, Devon and Cornwall Police do not wish to reveal the identity of this witness.

Obviously a CHIS, Sam guessed.

I will forward a statement covering the recovery of the vehicle.

She answered the desk phone.

'It's Jill Carver.'

Brusque as ever, Sam thought.

'What was going on last night? My clients are extremely concerned about the impact a street full of police officers had on their family life, their private life. You do remember the Human Rights Act, Chief Inspector, Article 8, Right to a Private and Family Life?'

Sam took a silent breath.

'I'd have thought they would be pleased we're still putting resources into their daughter's disappearance,' she said. 'It seems strange to me that your client and his son last night expressed their anger personally and clearly they've expressed it to you. Why don't they want us to do our jobs? Is there something they're not telling us?'

Jill Carver's voice was sharp and clipped.

'You know as well as I do there have been suggestions of honour killing in the media,' she said. 'The police have done nothing to stop them.'

Sam reminded Carver the police had no part in censuring the Press.

'It's called freedom of speech, the freedom of the

Press... you know, free from state intrusion, which includes the police,' she said. 'I think you'll find that's Article 10.'

The silence was loaded, the voice that broke it crypt cold.

'You're skating on thin ice, Inspector.'

Another one wanting to demote me. Do they think I'm that hung up on rank that I'm bothered by their games?

Sam didn't respond. This time it was Jill Carver faced with silence.

'My clients feel that they are being harassed, which in turn is causing them distress,' she said finally. 'They are respected members of their community and these suggestions around honour crimes are ill-informed and without a shred of substance or foundation.'

Sam let that hang for long seconds before she spoke again.

'Neither I, nor any other police officer, has publicly said this is an honour crime. Nobody from Eastern Police has referred to it as anything other than a missing-from-home inquiry. Now is there anything I can help you with?'

Carver switched tack.

'Has your investigation discovered anything new?'

'We are following a number of lines of enquiry,' Sam trotted out the time-honoured answer. 'When we have any news, your clients will be the first to know.'

Sam could almost feel Carver's anger seep like sea fret from the receiver.

'You are creating smoke screens, Inspector, smoke screens behind which you are trying to hide your own inadequacies. You have not heard the last of this.'

Sam kept the receiver in her hand after Carver disconnected, dialled the HOLMES room and asked for Bev to come into her office.

'I've read your email,' she told her. 'Do you think they're protecting a CHIS?'

Bev closed the door and sat down.

'He was very cagey when I spoke to him on the phone,' she told Sam. 'He wouldn't confirm it was an informant. I wouldn't expect him to confirm in an email but on the phone?'

'What do you think then?'

'I got the feeling it was an undercover cop,' Bev said.

Sam gave that some thought. It would explain why Devon and Cornwall were keeping the identity secret. She doubted even DC Welch would know.

'Okay, it changes nothing,' she said. 'We've still got somebody who could identify who drove the car into the garage and the good thing, if it is a UC, I'm a lot happier with the 'it's not Sukhi' identification. I'll get our Director of Intelligence to call theirs… so, Jack Goddard.'

'And perhaps Aaron Leech,' Bev said.

'I know,' Sam told her. 'I want victimologies doing for every drowner. The usual... associates, habits, places they visit, social media. Get the information on an analytical chart. Let's see if there are any common denominators. We already know Jack and Aaron were on the 'hashtag' photograph. See if the others are somehow linked.'

'Will do,' Bev said, scribbling in a notebook. 'Did anything come out last night on the tow path?'

Sam shook her head. 'Too much police activity so just a few drunken arseholes staggering along at about 4am. All the publicity about students going into the river and still they walk home lashed.'

'What are we doing about the girls?' Bev asked her.

'Nothing yet,' Sam said. 'I want Amber's phone sorting before we go for them.'

Twenty minutes later, Ed walked into Sam's office. She looked up from her emails.

'How did it go?' she asked.

He relayed Sue's conversation with Mrs Maan.

'I wasn't keen Ed, but good call,' Sam said. 'It's given us a steer. Give me a minute.'

Ed sat down.

Sam picked up her mobile and called Darius Simpson. His phone rang and eventually went to voicemail. 'Darius, when you get this give me a ring. It's Sam Parker.'

She had barely put the phone back on her desk when it rang, Darius's name in the caller display. She put her phone on speaker.

'That was quick.'

His voice was groggy. 'Sorry, I couldn't get to the phone quick enough. I saw it was you on the missed call.'

'Hope I haven't woke you.'

'No, I'm up,' Darius said unconvincingly.

Liar. Sam smiled.

'I'm after a favour,' she said. 'Can you email some of those photos from last night across to me? The dad, brother and the guy outside the house?'

'Yeah, no problem but who was he by the way?' Darius asked her. 'He never got involved but was watching everything. We got a few of him anyway. Why the rush?'

'Just something I'm following up.'

'Sam, if it's anything, you will let me know?' Darius said.

'Of course.'

'They'll be with you in 10 minutes,' he told her.

'That's great Darius but send them to my personal email,' Sam said. 'They'll not get through the firewall.'

She hung up and looked at Ed.

'Interesting development down in Plymouth.'

Ed waited.

'Bev was right. There's a UC on the job. He or she is providing the ID evidence on the driver of Sukhi's car. I got our Director of Intelligence to ring theirs. Obviously they'll not let us use the UC for identifying the driver. Not yet anyway. Not until their own job's sorted. But I want Bev to send the photos from last night down to them. Maybe one of them was the driver.'

'What about prints on the car?' Ed said.

'Some,' Sam answered. 'The rear-view mirror has a couple and there's some on the inside of the windscreen. Rest are on the outside bodywork, which as you well know, are useless.'

Ed scowled. 'I know... '*My client must have touched it when it was parked in the street, your honour. Doesn't prove he stole it'*. Ever wondered what life would be like without lawyers?'

'Easy,' Sam said.

'They're like bloody wasps,' Ed ranted. 'Serve no real purpose other than irritate everybody.'

Sam's laptop pinged.

'Darius… good as gold.'

A number of JPEG images were attached to the email.

'Problem at the minute with this lot is that we only have Baljit's prints on file,' Sam said. 'Have a word with Bev. Get these sent down to DC Welch.'

'I was thinking... '

'Don't make a habit of it.' She smiled, flashing her white teeth.

'Ha ha.' Ed pulled a face. 'If what Mrs Maan says is right, and why would she lie, Aisha and Sukhi are split up. Aisha's dragged back to her house. He looks unconscious. We know where his car ends up but where is he? And if

Aisha escapes again, does she contact him again? How would she? No way she's got a phone and even if she could use someone else's, people don't remember numbers these days.'

'Thoughts?' Sam asked and waited.

Ed took a deep breath.

'I always said if she didn't escape, she was dead. Do I believe she escaped a second time?' He paused. 'No, I don't.'

'We could have a potential double homicide here, with the family right in the thick of it,' Sam said.

'That's what worries me. I'll sort the photos.'

'Make sure they do it right, Ed. Get other photos off the system.'

The detective constable from the Intelligence Cell walked in as Ed walked out.

'Just a quick one, boss.'

Sam waited.

'Somebody has just tried to use Aisha's mini-bank card.'

Sam was out of her seat. 'What? Where?'

'Embankment tube station at Westminster,' the detective told her. 'About an hour ago – 10.17 to be precise.'

London! Bloody hell.

In all the time she had been missing there had been no activity on Aisha's bank account and her phone had never been switched on. All the checks with hospitals drew a blank and now out of nowhere her card was being used in London.

'Feed that into Ed,' Sam told the detective. 'Tell him to get on to the Met. I want CCTV around that tube station. Villiers Street, Thames Embankment.'

The detective raised his eyebrows.

'I used to go there quite a lot, years ago,' she answered the unspoken question. 'Great wine bar in Villiers Street.'

Sam wandered into the finance offices and checked with the department head, Linda Foxton, how much money she was spending on each of the investigations. Each had a separate code: overtime, forensics, and all other costs billed to the respective inquiries. The budget was always in a perilous state.

'There you are,' Ed said, as she walked back into the corridor. 'Hot off the press, Devon and Cornwall. The driver? It's Baljit, Aisha's brother.'

CHAPTER TWENTY-NINE

'We'll hang fire,' Sam said. 'He's now linked to a disappearance. Get his prints checked against the ones they got off the mirror. I want that doing pronto, even if we have to pay to call somebody out at the Fingerprint Bureau.'

More money.

Sam stood by her office window, looking across the deserted car parks. Headquarters was populated with nine-to five-weekends-off workers... admin, finance, IT, training, and some centralised CID functions. Only those in the control room worked 24/7, and they parked on a different side of the site.

Today the Murder Team car park was full and yet Sam was still worried she wouldn't have enough staff.

'The cost of these jobs is spiralling,' she told Ed. 'Last night's operation at Aisha's street and then on the tow path was a fortune, everybody working a 12-hour shift. I saw Linda just to tot everything up.'

'She's top drawer,' Ed said. 'Coming in on a bank-holiday weekend. Not many civvies would do that.'

But even she can't magic money out of thin air, Sam thought.

'So Baljit's driving Sukhi's car in Plymouth,' she was saying now. 'That suggests they found out where Aisha planned to go. If the car was ever found we were just meant to assume Sukhi dumped it.'

The simple plan could have worked and probably would have save for the undercover cop being embedded at the chop-shop.

Sometimes you needed a bit of luck.

Sam sat down. 'I don't want to make a move on him until we find out about the settee.'

Then she told Ed about the bank card.

'All a bit of a coincidence,' he said. 'Nothing on her bank or phone since she went missing, and then after we're in the street... '

'Exactly.'

Bev Summers appeared at the door and passed a photograph to Sam. 'You might want to see this.'

Sam looked at it then passed it to Ed.

A small hammer with a metal head and a yellow handle was laid on a desk. The ball part of the head had traces of what was clearly blood, and a few hairs were stuck in the brown stains.

'Found by one of the crew in undergrowth by the tow path,' Bev said. 'About 200 metres from where Jack Goddard was found.'

'They did well to find that,' Sam said, impressed and surprised in equal measure.

'I think he went for a pee and stumbled across it,' Bev said, a 'go figure' look on her face.

More good luck.

'Get it off to the lab on Monday,' Sam told her. 'Pay the extra money for a quick turnaround. Let's find out if it's Jack Goddard's blood and or hair, and if it's not too much to hope for, let's see if we can find the killer's prints or DNA on the handle.'

'You do want it with a cherry on the top,' Ed grinned.

'I know... look, I need some fresh air. Let's go for a walk.'

The daffodils around the perimeter road swayed in the breeze, a gentle balletic movement that was almost hypnotic, and a soothing contrast to the investigative maelstrom thrashing around inside Sam's head.

'Funny fresh air that,' Ed said, watching Sam light a cig. 'And you're not supposed to smoke in the grounds, you naughty girl.'

Sam blew out smoke. 'Let them discipline me… If you wanted to get to London quickly, how would you travel?'

'Train.'

'Why not go to Plymouth?'

Ed thought for a moment.

'Too far,' he said. 'From here you'd have to get to London, then get a train to Plymouth from, I think, Paddington, or you get on that Cross-Country train at Newcastle or Darlington, but that feels like a two-day camel ride, takes about eight hours.'

Not for the first time, Sam was amazed at the things Ed had stored away in his head.

'I know it's bad practice, but let's assume Aisha is dead and her family still have her bank card,' she said. 'If they don't want to drive, they get the train or fly but last minute, train is easier. I know we're running out of staff but let's have somebody looking at the CCTV at Newcastle and then Darlington train stations. Find the time of the trains after we left the street last night. Let's see if anybody from Aisha's family got the train to London. We know what time the card was used. The station CCTV up here might be an easier spot than the Saturday cameras in London.'

Ed said he would get Paul Adams straight on it.

'I'm getting ahead of myself here, Ed, but if we can find someone and they've gone there with the intention of coming back today, we might get them coming cff a train still carrying Aisha's card.'

Ed called Paul Adams.

'Sorted,' he said, catching up with Sam, who had walked ahead. 'The uniform who took the initial missing-from-home report is now on the search teams. He remembers the mother, father and brother. He doesn't know the uncle but he's on the way to the station now and he'll get stills of any Asian men.'

He noticed Sam was on to her second cigarette.

'I want the girls getting in tomorrow,' Sam said, stopping suddenly. 'I can't keep paying for cops to walk the tow path, plus politically I don't want to give the 'we need more police patrols' camp any indication I agree with them. We had cops there last night and we'll have them there tonight, so tomorrow we get the girls. I don't want to put it off any longer. Amber's phone exam will be finished today, so tomorrow well go with what we've got.'

'We arresting them?' Ed said.

'Yes,' Sam replied with zero hesitation. 'I don't want them getting the opportunity of refusing to attend voluntarily. They're all on or near the tow path but only Alex O'Connell said she was there. They all know Goddard, at least with the possible exception of Amber Dalton. They had an altercation with Goddard. They're members of a group. Whether that's Sisters Of Macavity, time will tell. As they say on the TV, they've got motive and opportunity. Lock them up on suspicion of murder.'

She put the cigarette to her lips and inhaled.

'I've told the CPS the way I'm thinking, just to keep them in the loop,' Sam continued, smoke swirling around her face. 'I don't want them buried under a mass of paperwork they've no idea about if I'm looking for a charging decision sometime tomorrow.'

Ed answered his phone, listened, thanked the caller and turned to Sam.

'Paul Adams. The lab's been on. The blood on the settee…'

CHAPTER THIRTY

Saturday 14th December 2013

NOTHING IN THE STREET MOVED. Nothing except me, swinging from side-to-side, dangling from a line of clothes. I thought I'd be able to abseil down, like I'd seen on the TV, like how the girls from school told me they'd done it when they went on a trip to an outward bound place – not that I'd been allowed to go.

School? Why had they even bothered sending me? If it hadn't been against the law, I don't think they would have.

As soon as I got out of the window, any thoughts I had of abseiling vanished. The rope was swinging; my legs were hanging in mid-air, my weight taken by my arms and shoulders. This must be what the college gym rats mean when they go for the burn.

I tried to gauge where my legs were in relation to the living room window. I knew I had to be quick. If someone went into the front room and saw my legs I was finished.

I loosened my grip, slipped down a few centimetres then gripped the rope tight. My palms hurt, burning. I couldn't breathe. My legs were about two metres from the ground.

My heart was pounding.

I was swinging again.

I looked down. My feet were near the top of the window.

I didn't want to be swinging in full view of anyone who went into the front room.

The next time I would slide down to the ground. I could live with rope burns. They wanted me to kill myself.

I slid down. My hands were on fire. I was passing the window. The room was in darkness. Come on, Aisha! Be quick! I was at a point where I could just about jump.

Then it happened.

The ceiling light went on.

I froze, like a rabbit in a beam, staring at my mother. She stared back. Two motionless rabbits. I even stopped swinging.

Nothing. Just silence and empty time.

Then she screamed.

I let go, stumbled, jarred my ankle on the concrete and jumped over the little wall that runs around our tiny patch of front garden, if you can call a lump of concrete a garden. My ankle was on fire, but I had to run. I knew they'd come after me, and while I could probably outrun my father and uncle, there was no way I could outrun my brother.

I sprinted, arms pumping, trying to ignore the pain. I needed to get out of sight, hide somewhere, anywhere. I was already gasping for breath. I'd never won a race at school but I needed to be faster than I'd ever been before. I could see the end of the street.

Which way?

They'd expect me to go right so I'd go left, away from

the town centre. Right would take me towards the police station but it was too far. I'd never make it. I was too slow.

Behind me I could hear shouting.

Don't look back.

My ankle was getting hotter. Every time it hit the pavement I winced, but I couldn't stop. I knew they were after me. I turned left, half-dashed and half-limped across the road, my eyes darting everywhere, looking for somewhere to hide, to hide from my own family.

Find somewhere Aisha! Anywhere!

The parked cars were no good. The builder's skip, a big one, would do. It would have to. I couldn't run much further. If I could get there, hide there, I might be safe.

Please God let me be safe.

Why were there no white neighbours? The area was full of Asians. I wished I could knock on somebody's door but I couldn't. They'd side with my parents. Someone must have seen Sukhi getting beaten up, me being dragged home, but nobody would have reported it, or at least if they had, the police hadn't come around. The skip was close. I glanced over my shoulder. Nothing. I put on a burst of speed and dived into the skip. My torso cleared it but my legs didn't. I was half-in, half-out. I heaved myself downwards and my legs followed, falling over my head, forcing me to roll down to the bottom of the skip, my shoulders bashing into some broken bricks. I knew without looking that I'd taken the skin off my shins. I pushed myself up and got myself into a sitting position.

I was covered in brick dust.

Please don't let there be a cloud of dust above me.

Tears ran down my cheeks. I was playing hide-and-seek but if I lost this game, I would lose my life. I listened, tried to stop my teeth chattering. All I could hear was heavy breathing. My breathing. No footsteps. No cars. Silence.

Maybe they'd gone right.

Please let them go away.

My body was shaking like an old man I'd once seen outside the mini-market having a fit.

I listened. Nothing.

I couldn't see what was happening on the street. All I could see was the inside of the red skip. Should I risk a look over the top?

Don't Aisha. They'll see you.

I lay down, covered my legs and body with cardboard, and kept the last two pieces for my head. I tried to breathe slowly, tried to stop my body shaking. If I could stay there until morning, another four hours probably, I would get help even if it I had to run through the streets screaming.

I just had to hide.

The rubble dug into me but it was safer than lying in my bed.

I had to be still, couldn't move. The cardboard mustn't move. I eased myself on to my side, checked the cardboard on my legs and body, lay down and covered my head.

I closed my eyes, thought of 4.36pm, Friday, 6th December, one minute before my mother changed my life. A week later there I was lying under cardboard in a skip, hiding from my family. Why had they not accepted British values?

Suddenly I heard voices. Were they far away or just talking quietly?

I knew who they were. Who else was out at this time of night in an Asian area? A couple of sons perhaps, but they'd be really quiet if they were sneaking in so late.

It was my family.

Why hadn't they turned right?

Maybe they had and were doubling back on themselves. I hoped so. That would have meant they had no idea where I was.

I had to lie still. If they looked in here, they'd see rubble and cardboard.

Would they hear my breathing?

I shut my eyes. If I couldn't see them, they couldn't see me.

You're not four years old, Aisha.

My lips were moving really fast, like when I did my times tables at school, only now they were repeating 'I'll be okay' over and over again.

I couldn't relax. My body was stiffer than the cardboard.

Four hours. That's all. Then help.

I saw Sukhi's smile.

BANG!

The first punch had sent blood spurting from my mouth. The second made me dizzy. Hands clawed at me, dragged me by the hair, by the arms.

My uncle had jumped into the skip, punched me in the stomach. I couldn't breathe.

A hand covered my mouth and I was dragged backwards over the top of the skip. I could feel the skin peeling away from my back. My head was tilted backwards. I was looking at the ground. I recognised my father's shoes.

He punched me in the mouth.

Is this what it's like before you pass out?

The metallic taste of blood filled my mouth.

My ankles were grabbed, gripped tight. It must have been my uncle. Between him and my father they hauled me out of the skip. When my legs were clear, they dropped me. I crashed on to the pavement, landing on my shoulder. I cried out, but nobody heard. There was nothing to hear.

My father's black shoe booted me in the ribs. What air was left in my body flew out without carrying a sound.

What were they shouting?

My father grabbed me under my arms. My uncle grabbed my ankles. They started walking, carrying me like a rolled up carpet. They flicked me on to my side. Through my tears, through my terror, I saw my brother.

Will someone, anyone, help me?

Nobody did.

As they carried me up our path, I twisted my head and saw my mother open the front door. I tried to speak but couldn't. She must have seen the fear in my eyes.

As my father stepped over the threshold with his human roll of carpet, she punched me in the head. No words, just a punch.

They carried me to my room. I didn't speak, didn't scream. What was the point? Even my family weren't speaking. My mother ripped my clothes off and threw them on to the landing. The last thing I saw before the door was slammed shut and I heard the bolts being rammed in place was my uncle, my mother's brother, staring at my naked body.

I sat on the bed, legs tucked under my chin, back pushing against the corner of the two walls. My shins were red raw. The tops of my arms had finger bruises where they grabbed me, my face was swollen and my back felt like it had been skinned. But the one thing that bothered me the most? I honestly thought my uncle was coming back.

I sat like that for hours. Cold, alone, frightened.

Morning came. I heard knocking at the front door. The bolts moved on my bedroom door. My uncle walked in. I pushed back against the wall.

'Say one word and I have your mother's permission to rape you.'

He stood there, the door open, leaning against the door frame, his black eyes locked on me, his tongue sliding around his lips.

I bowed my head, closed my eyes.

Please just go away.

I heard my mother speak in Punjabi. It was the young Singh brothers. I'd forgotten about the new settee, but my mother and the shop owner hadn't.

My mother was polite, made small talk, no indication that her daughter was upstairs, naked, being guarded by her uncle.

Mia came into our bedroom. She didn't look at me but I knew she was scared. She pulled her big case from under the bed, rummaged through it and took out a scarf. She looked at me. Can eyes plead? She never spoke. What could she say?

It must have taken about 20 minutes to take out the old settee and bring the new one in.

My uncle just stood there. I didn't say a word.

I heard the van driving off. The bedroom door was slammed shut.

I got off the bed, walked to the chest of drawers and picked up the bottle. I sat back on the bed, unscrewed the top, sniffed, raised the bottle to my lips and took a mouthful.

It burned. I coughed, took another mouthful. I wasn't going to touch the tablets, but I was going to get drunk.

CHAPTER THIRTY-ONE

Saturday 19th April 2014

'It's Aisha's,' Ed said.

Sam dropped her head.

'Primary or secondary transfer?' She asked after a moment. 'Not that it matters at the minute. We need to prove the settee was delivered after they reported Aisha missing and then they've got some explaining to do.'

Primary meant Aisha had bled on to the settee; secondary, somebody had Aisha's blood on them and came into contact with the settee.

'It's a primary transfer,' Ed said. 'There's too much blood for it to be anything else. It's seeped into the cushion.'

She lit another cigarette, her third on their short walk.

'It won't be enough to charge them, unless they cough of course, but it'll be enough to arrest the parents. We've got plenty already to arrest the son for vehicle theft without the fingerprint results, but we'll wait for those anyway. So that means all three adults in that house arrested.'

Ed had been watching her closely. Now he smiled.

'You've got that glint in your eye.'

'Get them all in,' Sam told him. 'Get the youngest daughter looked after by Social Services and then the house is empty.'

'I see where you're going. It could work. Very resource intensive though,' Ed said.

'There's no rush to jump yet,' Sam went on. 'Aisha's been missing for months. Let's get the girls in tomorrow and see where we stand. If we can get that investigation boxed off, it'll allow us to divert some staff on to Aisha's... I don't know about you, but I'm starving.'

'Somebody will be going out for food.'

They walked back towards the building.

All that was left in Sam's office to indicate she and Ed had eaten was the empty polystyrene trays and the pungent smell of sweet-and-sour pork balls, beef foo yung, curry sauce and chips.

'I needed that,' Ed said, his hands around the cold can of Pepsi Max.

His phone rang.

Sam sighed. 'Can't you change that gangster song?'

'Coolio? It's quality. Ed Whelan... Hi Paul... Good shout. We'll meet you there... Cheers.'

He ended the call.

'Six-ten this morning Mrs Bhandal is in Newcastle station. There was a train to Kings Cross at 6.20.'

'I knew it,' Sam said, slapping the desk.

'I told him we'll get up there,' Ed said. 'We don't want him arresting her by himself and be wide open to false allegations.'

'And they'll definitely go on the attack,' Sam agreed. 'What times are the trains coming in?'

'There was a train out at 11.35 that gets in just before three,' Ed answered. 'After that they're about every hour.'

Sam looked at the wall clock – 1.30pm. 'Plenty of time. Interpreter?'

'We'll set that in motion as soon as we get her,' Ed said.

Sam was playing out the arrest sequence in her mind.

'Everything changes now,' she said. 'If we arrest mother, we have to get father and son. That means we need to see the guy who sold them the settee.'

Sam knew it wasn't ideal. She hated being rushed. Now there was no choice if they wanted to get Aisha's mother in possession of the bank card.

'What about Darlington station?' Ed asked.

Sam shook her head.

'We haven't got the staff to cover that. She got on at Newcastle, so it's a fair bet she'll get off there… hopefully.'

Newcastle railway station – all Victorian arches and amber stonework – has a dozen platforms and two footbridges crossing multiple sets of track, but the London trains invariably stop at the platforms nearest the entrance, platforms directly underneath the first of the bridges.

Sam and Ed were on the bridge with a good view of the main entrance, watching for any family coming to meet Mrs Bhandal, but the next London train came and went without her or anyone else showing up.

'Coffee?' Sam said. 'We've got an hour to kill.'

Sam bought Americanos from one of the platform cafes.

'Jesus,' Ed said, shaking his head and smacking his lips. 'Do you think they just let the water sniff the coffee beans?'

'Stop moaning. You didn't pay for it.'

'Just as well at the price,' Ed moaned. 'At least Dick Turpin wore a mask.'

Sam was fishing for her cigarettes. 'Let's get outside. I need a smoke.'

The road in front of the station was busy with stags and hens arriving for the weekend; some would get no nearer to their hotel than the Irish bar directly opposite.

Ed walked away when his phone rang.

Sam inhaled on the cigarette and watched a group of young men with strong Yorkshire accents walk past, all wearing American Indian costumes, all drinking cans of cheap lager, and with the groom-to-be in the middle dressed as a squaw.

She blew smoke and smiled as the squaw started talking to a group of unlikely ballerinas, all in pink tutus, the bride-to-be sporting L-plates and her bridesmaids, mother and future mother-in-law, wearing pink sashes identifying them as such.

All fun for now but for some, she knew, the long weekend would no doubt end in tears.

'The prints are Baljit's,' Ed said, back at her side.

'Get in!' Sam did a solo fist-pump. 'Come on then. Let's get back on the bridge. I don't want to be spotted. The family sees us here and they'll ring her and tell her to stop on the train. Next stop Berwick, then Edinburgh Waverley.'

Joey 'Fatty' Sanderson was deep in conversation with the man Bev presumed was the proprietor when she walked into the back-street furniture shop. Sanderson turned around when he heard the bell above the door tinkle.

'They're popping up everywhere this week,' he said with eyebrow's rising.

'Alright Fatty?' Bev nodded.

'Not really. You still working with Whelan?'

Bev nodded some more as he walked towards her.

'Give him my best, won't you,' Sanderson grumbled. 'Thanks to him I'm in here buying a new sofa for that psycho Wilson.'

He looked over his shoulder.

'See you later, Karan.' Sanderson's pronunciation made the man's name sound like a girl's. 'Watch this one... CID.'

He yanked open the door and strode out, the bell rattling behind him.

'Mr Singh, my name is Bev Summers. I'm from the CID. I need to speak to you about a sofa you sold.'

His English was good but still heavily accented.

'In 30 years in this business, never has one item of furniture caused me so much trouble.'

He reminded Bev of a serene religious figure; white turban, resplendent white beard, the type of man everybody wanted for a grandfather.

'How can I help you?' he asked now, arms out wide.

'I need to ask you about two sofas Davinder Bhandal bought from you in December,' Bev told him. 'And it's me who might be able to help you.'

'Help me?'

Bev smiled. 'I know the man who just left charges you for security.'

The train was due in 15 minutes. They were back on the footbridge, one eye on the passengers milling about on the platform, one eye on the main entrance. If she wasn't on this train, they were stuck another hour.

Sam gently tapped Ed's leg with her foot. 'She's on this one.'

Ed looked at the entrance, understood immediately. 'Jackpot.'

Standing by the ticket barriers, looking up at the arrivals and departure boards, he could have been just another husband picking up his wife.

CHAPTER THIRTY-TWO

'Mr Singh... '

'Please, call me Karan. I was just about to have some tea before Mr Sanderson came in. Would you like some?'

'That would be very nice,' Bev said.

She followed him into the storeroom at the back of the shop.

He flicked on the kettle, spooned loose-leaf Assam tea into the blue patterned Royal Doulton teapot, watched the kettle vibrate as steam came out of the neck, and poured boiling water into the pot.

He still had his back to Bev as he added milk from a glass bottle.

'Sugar?'

'No thank you.'

He handed a cup to Bev.

'Please take a seat.' Karan extended his right arm, the cuff of his shirt sliding up towards his elbow, a thin wrist and forearm visible. 'There's plenty to choose from.'

Bev smiled and sat down on a green velour sofa.

'As I said earlier, I'm here to talk about Davinder

Bhandal and two sofas he bought from you in quick succession.'

'Yes,' Karan said. 'Very strange.'

He sat on an armchair opposite. 'Mr Bhandal bought a sofa which my grandsons delivered on the Saturday morning. Then on the Monday morning, first thing, he was waiting outside the shop. He said his wife didn't like it, she had given it to some relative, and he needed another sofa. He needed it that day because the other one had already been collected the day before, the Sunday. He chose one and my grandsons delivered it about an hour later.'

'Do you have records showing the transactions?' Bev asked him.

'Yes, of course. I have a book of receipts. Self-carbonating. I'm too old for computers.'

Karan placed his cup and saucer on the floor and stood up.

'I've used the same system since I opened this shop in 1974. The year I started supporting Newcastle.'

'Malcolm Macdonald era.' Bev smiled.

'Supermac... Kevin Keegan... Shearer,' Karam rattled off the names. 'Great players.'

He walked across to the writing desk and took out a couple of well-used receipt books together with a hard-backed A4 book.

'They got to the Cup Final that year. I thought it would be a good idea to support a team from the region, one that looked destined for years of success. Oh well…'

Bev puffed out her cheeks. 'Tell me about it.'

'Closed the shop on Saturday afternoons so I could go the match,' Karan said, the past flooding the present. 'My wife hated me being at football when I could have been making money.'

He paused. 'I don't go now. Too old and I can't sit in those seats. I get stiff.'

He flicked through the books, found two receipts separated by one other, and handed them over.

'There you are officer.'

'Please, call me Bev.'

Karan dipped his head and tapped the pieces of paper in Bev's hand.

'As you can see, Bev, the receipts are dated and timed with a description of the sofa and the name and address of the purchaser.'

She nodded.

He sat down, turned the pages of the A4 book.

'And here is the record of the two deliveries, one on the Saturday, one on the Monday.'

'Can I take copies of these please,' Bev asked. 'I won't take the documents themselves as I know you'll need them for your business, but I would ask that you don't destroy them in case they are ever needed for court.'

Karan laughed, his dark eyes sparkling.

'My dear, had you wanted a receipt from 1974, I could have given you it. I'm a hoarder. Nothing gets thrown away… am I allowed to ask why the police are so interested in two sofas? Has it something to do with their daughter?'

Bev looked at Karan's enquiring eyes, curious and alive.

'Sorry, Karan, but I can't say. Now... about Mr Sanderson.'

She stepped off the train, walked slowly towards the ticket barrier, exited and met up with her husband. Sam and Ed hurried off the bridge. The Bhandals had taken less than five steps when they caught up with them. The couple turned around before a word was said, bottom jaws dropping and their mouths wide open. He clamped his shut very quickly but she collapsed on to all fours, her large bag sliding across the floor and coming to rest next to one of the coffee stall's three metal tables.

'Police brutality!' Bhandal shouted. 'My wife has a heart condition. A shock could kill her.'

People looked but kept on walking as he helped her to her feet, retrieved the bag, and handed it to his shaking wife.

'What do you want?'

'Would you mind stepping into that office over there,' Sam said.

She pointed to a glass window on the platform. She had walked into the British Transport Police base as soon as they'd arrived at the station and asked for an office in the event Mrs Bhandal got off a train.

'Why?' Bhandal demanded, taking his wife's arm and supporting her.

'We want to ask you some questions.'

'Can't it wait? My wife's had a busy day and you've just caused her to fall to the ground.'

'We want to ask her about her day,' Sam said. 'Specifically, we want to ask her where she's been and what's she's been doing?"

Bhandal's face twisted with rage.

'This is outrageous! Harassment, that's what it is. Harassment. We are peace-loving people.'

Sam held his glare. 'Mr Bhandal, can we go into that office please?'

'Racists!' he shouted, and spat at Sam's feet.

Sam leaned in close, bent down a little, and whispered into his ear.

'I've asked you nicely, now if you want to make a scene and get arrested for a public order offence, be my guest. Your wife can either come voluntarily, or she can be arrested.'

He stepped backwards and spoke with aggression, but there was fear drifting like smoke in his voice. 'On what charge?'

'Suspicion of theft.'

Mrs Bhandal had not moved or even looked up when her husband shouted. Her head was still bowed and she was still staring at the ground.

'Let's go,' Sam said. She took a step forward and everyone followed.

Bhandal began talking in Punjabi. Under normal circumstances Sam would tell him to use English but knew his wife didn't speak any. More importantly, she knew Ed spoke enough Punjabi to understand them.

'What did he say?' Sam whispered, standing in the corridor next to the open door of the office where Aisha's parents were sitting.

'Told her to say nothing,' Ed said. 'He asked her where the card was but she never answered.'

Sam's phone rang, a call from Bev. She listened then put the mobile back in her coat pocket.

'Everything Sanderson said about the sofa is true,' she told Ed. 'Bhandal bought one on Saturday and another on Monday morning, which he insisted was delivered straight away. Right, let's arrest him on suspicion of assaulting Aisha and her for theft of the bank card.'

'Do you want another car to take them back separately?'

'Let's keep them together,' Sam said after a moment's

thought. 'If they talk, you'll know what they're saying. I'll drive, you concentrate on them.'

Sam walked into the room. Both of them had ignored the wooden chairs. 'Would Mrs Bhandal like a glass of water?' Sam asked.

'She's fine.'

'Mr Bhandal, I am arresting you on suspicion of assault.'

'What?' His speech was measured. He was back in control of his emotions. 'How dare you.'

'I dare,' Sam told him. 'Interestingly, you never asked who you allegedly assaulted.'

Bhandal stared at her, lips clenched, his eyes burning into hers. If a portrait artist had wanted to paint raw hostility, Bhandal, in that electric moment, would have been the perfect muse.

Sam was speaking again.

'I am arresting you on suspicion of assault on Aisha Bhandal. You do not have to say anything but it may harm your defence if you do not mention when questioned something which you later rely on in court. Anything you do say may be given in evidence.'

Bhandal's hands were by his side, fists clenched tight, upper body stiff, the veins running like power lines down his neck.

'Outrageous,' he said, voice thick with venom. 'What is the nature of your evidence? Racist, that's all you are, that's what your organisation is... honour crimes indeed. We are grief-stricken parents, nothing more. Your actions today will haunt you for the rest of your career.'

'Is your car in a car park?' Sam asked him, calm and unmoved.

'What? No.' Bhandal's voice had dropped in volume.

'My son brought me. We were going to get the train home.'

Sam nodded once.

'Tell your wife she is arrested on suspicion of the theft of Aisha's bank card.'

Like a Bonfire Night rocket the aggression was back, as was the volume.

'On what grounds?!'

Sam knew the best way to hold the upper hand with someone shouting the odds was to keep her own voice normal and conversational.

'Just tell her.'

Bhandal spoke quickly. Ed listened.

'We are being arrested,' Bhandal told his wife in Punjabi. 'It's ridiculous. Say nothing until I get Jill Carver to see you. They will have to get an interpreter. Don't speak until Carver is there. Have you got the bank card?'

Her eyes were still fixed on the floor. She shook her head.

CHAPTER THIRTY-THREE

SAM HUNG back as they all walked to the car and rang Bev Summers.

'Get round to the house and arrest the son for theft of a motor vehicle. Take Paul with you. Get the sister to a Place of Safety. See what Social Services can do but good luck with that on a Saturday. We're bringing the mother and father down. Son dropped father off so you'll probably have to park up and wait for him.'

Ed was leaning against the driver's wing, head turned, watching his rear-seat passengers who were both staring straight ahead, saying nothing.

'You keep an eye on them while I talk to you,' he told Sam, 'I don't want them seeing my lips move.'

Sam nodded.

'He asked if she had the bank card. She shook her head.'

'Really?'

'Really,' Ed said. 'So it's either in London, on the train, or in this station.'

'There's nothing we can do about the train or London

at the minute. Let me go back into the station. You sit with them.'

Sam walked back into the British Transport Police office, closing the door behind her. She contacted Technical Support and told them what she wanted, that it had to be done as soon as Bev had the son in custody and the younger daughter out of the way.

On the platform, she went to the information centre, obtained authority to get through the ticket barriers and walked to Platform 1.

She stood there, looking up to the bridge. Could Parkash Bhandal have seen her and Ed? Possibly, but she didn't recall the woman looking up. She walked the route Parkash had walked towards the ticket barrier, kept her eyes on the ground. Nothing.

She walked to the coffee stall and replayed the fall, the bag sliding across the floor, Bhandal retrieving it for his wife. She remembered Mrs Bhandal had her purse in her hand. Sam closed her eyes and saw her falling, feet nearest her and Ed, her head further away, her hands six feet from the coffee store.

Sam dropped to lie flat on her stomach, ignoring the stares she was attracting, and switched on the torch in her phone. The beam shot like a laser underneath the stall.

Bev had her head against the side window staring out of the windscreen. Sitting around was always boring, often futile. People weren't robots; they had their own thoughts, didn't always go where you thought they would.

They'd been there 40 minutes and were now attracting the curtain-twitchers. Another 10 minutes and they'd have to move. Someone was bound to call the police and there was nothing better at drawing attention than a marked police car pulling up alongside.

'Here he comes,' Paul said, shuffling in his seat, using the steering wheel to haul himself upright.

Baljit drove into the street and stopped outside the family home.

Bev and Paul were out of the car before he had switched off the engine off and by his open door before he put a foot on the pavement.

'Baljit Bhandal,' Bev said, 'I am arresting you for theft of a motor vehicle.'

'What you on about?' he said, climbing out of the car.

She cautioned him. 'Right, let's go.'

Bev took his arm but he jerked it away, 'Get your hands off me, bitch!'

Bev looked at him and smiled.

'Don't like being told what to do by a woman, is that it? An affront to your manhood?' She grabbed his arm again, tighter this time. 'Your sort doesn't frighten me. The car's over there. Let's go.'

He yanked his arm away again but walked towards their car, hands in pockets, silent. Once he was in the back seat, Bev walked to the house and knocked on the door.

'Hi, are you Mia?'

A nod.

'My name is DC Bev Summers.'

Bev knew the girl was 15 but she was tiny and looked about 12.

'Your parents and brother have been arrested.'

'Why? What have they done?' She put her index finger to her lip.

'I can't tell you that, but we'll look after you.' Bev didn't want to sound too official, talking about duty of care and places of safety. 'We can't leave you alone. We don't know how long your parents and brother will be, so we'll take you to the police station and take it from there. Don't worry. You're not in any trouble.'

'Can't I just stay here?' She looked like she might cry.

'No. Really, don't worry. We'll look after you.'

'Is it about Aisha?'

Bev was silent.

'It is, isn't it?' Mia said in a rush. 'Do you know where she is? Do they?'

Bev saw Mia's eyes fill.

'It'll be okay sweetheart.'

Bev looked away, rang the HOLMES room, and asked for someone to come and collect Mia.

'You'll be fine,' Bev said. 'Let's get a cold drink while we wait for my colleague. Where's the kitchen?'

Every member of the family who'd been arrested requested Jill Carver when the custody sergeant asked if they wanted legal advice.

Sam was in the CID office having a cup of coffee when the solicitor's call came through.

'Fifteen minutes,' Sam said to Ed. 'Not bad.'

Forget the pleasantries. Carver, no surprise, was straight down to business.

'You have my clients in custody. They will not be interviewed unless I am present. You will need an interpreter for Mrs Bhandal.'

'Clients,' Sam repeated. 'Am I to take it you will be representing all three?'

'Correct.' The voice glacial.

'Clearly that won't allow us to deal with them expeditiously,' Sam said smoothly. 'We can only interview them one at a time.'

'They understand that,' Carver replied. 'It's not a problem.'

'What about a conflict of interest? You're representing all three.'

Sam heard a long, scornful sigh.

'Inspector Parker, let me remind you it is a matter for me to decide whether there's a conflict of interest, not you. And besides, I understand that my clients have all been arrested for different matters, so how can there possibly be a conflict of interest? Unless, of course, you're suggesting that everything is linked.'

'Time will tell,' Sam said, side-stepping the trap. *You're not daft. You know they're all linked.* 'I'll look forward to seeing you in the interviews.'

'I'll be there within the hour. You decide who is first.'

Sam replaced the receiver and met Ed's questioning look.

'Right,' she told him. 'We've got an hour.'

Sam and Ed showed their ID at the gatehouse. The guy who should have been living on his state pension looked at their warrant cards, checked their names against a list on his clipboard, made a quick phone call and directed them to an allocated parking space. This was not a police-owned building. It was a secure site, manned 24 hours, and certain branches of the police rented office space: surveillance teams, source-handling teams, and technical support. All covert policing was housed here but even the vast majority of police officers had no idea of its existence.

Sam and Ed spoke with Detective Sergeant Gary Ross.

'We'll provide the majority of the officers for the listening post,' Sam said. 'I'll be guided by your staff, but my thoughts were a probe in the living room and kitchen.'

The DS nodded. 'When do you want them putting in?'

'Tonight,' Sam told him. 'Three suspects are in custody. The daughter is the only member of the household who will be at liberty. We'll find a place for her to stay, but that's not to say she won't return to the house.'

Ross was making notes.

'The surveillance team will provide an outer cordon,' he said. 'They'll notify those in the house if she's coming back, give them time to get out. We'll need a photograph of her.'

Sam said that was no problem, she would have one emailed across.

'I'll leave the entry to you and your people,' she told Ross.

He stood and studied the blown-up street map of the area where the Bhandal family lived.

'We'll go in after dark,' he said, breaking the short silence. 'Put a surveillance cordon around here.'

His index figure drew an imaginary circle on the map.

'There are only so many ways on to that street. You go 'live' whenever you're ready. We can talk about a strategy around removing them as and when.'

'That's great, thanks,' Sam said.

Outside, she and Ed stood by the car, enjoying the relatively warm weather.

'What do you want to do about the girls?' Ed asked. 'We were going to get them in tomorrow.'

Sam acknowledged their hands had been forced with the Bhandals, who would still be in custody the following day.

'We'll have to put the girls on the back burner,' she

said. 'We're spread thin as it is. We can only do what we can do.'

She fumbled in her pockets for her cigarettes.

'We've already got three in custody,' she went on. 'They'll need interviewing and we'll need bodies to complete any actions that come out of the interviews. We'll also use a boat-load of staff in the listening post.'

She lit a cigarette, guilt fighting a losing battle with gratitude, and continued: 'Granted we'll not have anything to listen to until they're released, but it needs covering 24 hours a day, so whoever is doing the night shift Sunday can't work days as well…nightmare this. Maybe I should ring Westminster, see if they can spare some bodies from the Home Office.'

Ed leaned against the bonnet, stretched out his legs, and mimed a pair of moving scales.

'Politicians? Real life? Not what you'd call comfortable bedfellows. Best just crack on.'

Sam smiled. 'You're right, and you know what… that's the bloody tragedy. Policing on the cheap and the only loser is Joe Public.'

Ed shrugged and watched Sam take another deep draw on the cigarette.

'We can only do what we can do,' he said. 'Don't worry about things that are beyond your control. Now I don't know about you, but I'm looking forward to getting in an interview room. I just need to see how Bev got on, then I'm off to see Fatty Sanderson. Tell you what, drop me off. His place is only round the corner from the nick.'

Sam found the CID office at Seaton St George empty. She sat down in the DI's office, pulled the swivel chair close to the desk, and began doodling with a biro on the desktop blotting pad.

If Aisha and Sukhi were dead, where were the bodies? Her family weren't gangsters, they hadn't fed them to the pigs. Where would they dump two bodies?

Her phone snapped her out of the trance.

'They've done the checks you asked for on the drowners,' she heard Bev begin. 'Looks like they all knew each other to varying extents, a decent bet with them all going to university, but during freshers' week last year every one of them wore one of those hashtag T-shirts. Apparently there were loads of the student lads wearing them, not just the group we've been looking at.'

CHAPTER THIRTY-FOUR

Ed negotiated the creased and discarded lager tins in the overgrown front garden, stepped over the rusty trike and hammered on the front door. The music was blaring, but he still heard Joey 'Fatty' Sanderson shout 'door!'.

The greasy-haired brunette who appeared was holding a child against her left hip. Ed couldn't tell whether it was a boy or a girl... the infant was naked save for a disposable nappy and two lines of bright green snot were running from its nose to lip.

'Give him a shout, Lizzie,' Ed grinned.

Lizzie Makepiece, mid-20s and about the same in stones, turned away. 'Joey!' she screamed. The child started to howl; perforated eardrum, Ed imagined.

He heard Sanderson before he saw him.

'Will you shut that fucking kid up and wipe his fucking nose.' Sanderson appeared at the doorway. 'Now what?'

'Just a quick one,' Ed said. 'Well, two quick ones. Firstly, Karan Singh no longer wants to employ your security company and neither do any of his business associates on that street.'

'Says who?' Sanderson growled.

'Says me, Fatty,' Ed grinned again. 'Which brings me nicely on to the second thing? If I hear that your security company is still doing business with Mr Singh, I'll tell Billy Wilson if he wants to pay you a visit, he can feel free.'

'He's paid me a visit,' Sanderson snapped back. 'I've had to buy him a new fucking settee. You know when I told you people in my world called you a twat but it was a sign of respect. Forget it. You're just a twat.'

'I love you too.' Ed pursed his lips, blew him a kiss, and lowered his voice. 'Remember you were the one providing information to the police to save your skin. Now that wouldn't go down too well if it got out. So leave Mr Singh alone, understood?'

Sanderson stood there, eyes wild, glaring.

'And don't go in there and take it out on Lizzie,' Ed hissed. 'If she calls the cops because you've beaten her up, I'll let it slip you're a grass.'

Ed pulled away from Sanderson's bloated face.

'You want to sort this garden out, give the bairn somewhere nice to play.'

He walked, almost skipped, down the scruffy path, smiling so wide his cheeks burned.

Sanderson remained at the door, watching, silent.

'Carver's downstairs,' Sam said, as Ed walked into the office.

'Let's crack on. Who we doing first?'

'The brother,' Sam told him. 'Bit aggressive when he got locked up. Looks like he has a problem with women.'

'But represented by one,' Ed said.

'That'll be his dad,' Sam reasoned. 'Let's see if I can rattle his cage.'

Jill Carver was sitting at the front desk, Paul Smith 'Kennington' glasses, a £500 touch with ultra-thin vari-focal lenses, perched on top of her head, a loose-fitting blouse fastened to her neck, and shapeless trousers.

'No tight, revealing gear today,' Ed whispered in Sam's ear. 'She must have got changed. Doesn't want to offend her clients.'

'Ms Carver, if you'd like to come through,' Sam said when they were close. 'We'll interview Baljit first.'

'On suspicion of theft of a motor vehicle?' Carver was walking behind them.

'That's right,' Sam said.

Sam led Carver into an empty interview room in the cell block and put two tapes into the machine.

'I am now handing Ms Carver a piece of paper on which is written the pre-interview disclosure.'

Carver snatched it and read.

Pre Interview disclosure

A Ford Fiesta motor vehicle was found in a lock-up garage in Plymouth. It had been stripped down. The car was owned by Sukhvinder Sahota. The police wish to interview Baljit Bhandal with regard to his knowledge of the vehicle, to which he is forensically linked.'

'What is the forensic evidence?' Carver demanded.

'He is forensically linked to the vehicle,' Sam told her. 'As for what the forensic evidence is, I'm not prepared to tell you at this stage.'

Carver shook her head and started tutting, a stroppy

teenager who'd just been told she couldn't go to the all-night party.

'Let me speak with my client.'

Twenty minutes later, the private consultation between Carver and Baljit finished, Sam and Ed walked into the interview room.

Sam turned on the tapes, completed the introductions and reminded him that he was still under caution.

'I want to ask you about your knowledge of a Ford Fiesta motor vehicle owned by Sukhvinder Sahota.'

'Have you spoken to Sukhi?' Baljit asked. 'Where is he? Top lad.'

'You know him?'

'Course I do. He's my sister's bloke.'

'How long have you known him?' Sam asked.

'Since my sister started going out with him,' Baljit was almost cocky. 'She asked me to meet him. Check he was alright. She couldn't ask my parents… You know what it's like.'

He smirked.

'No I don't,' Sam said. 'Tell me.'

Baljit looked from Sam to Ed as if they were beyond stupid.

'My parents believe in the old ways,' he said. 'There's no way they'd let Aisha go out with a lad she'd chosen. She asked me to check him out. I met him. Decent guy. I gave my sister my approval.'

'Your approval?' Sam snapped. 'What gives you the right to...'

Baljit shot forward in his seat.

'I'm her brother!' he barked. 'She's my responsibility.'

Sam leaned in to him, their noses almost touching.

'Your responsibility? Can't she choose for herself?'

Baljit sat back and looked at Ed.

'Perhaps you'll understand better,' he said, holding Ed's stare. 'Perhaps if your girls were kept in check, had to seek approval, there wouldn't be so many unwanted pregnancies. Does nobody in this country want to marry a virgin?'

Carver, silent so far, took her eyes off the pad on her knee and looked up.

'Perhaps we could stick to the matter in hand, i.e. my client's knowledge of a stolen motor vehicle.'

'Yeah that.' Baljit was enjoying himself, lapping up the attention. 'As I said, Sukhi was sound. We got on. I don't know how many times I've been in his car, I've lost count, so you'll definitely find forensics off me. I don't know anything about Plymouth, though. Is that where you think he and my sister ran away to?'

Sam and Ed stood whispering outside the interview room, their conversation inaudible to others above the ringing telephones and prisoners shouting from their cells.

'Convenient, wasn't it?' Sam said.

'Of course,' Ed agreed. 'Carver's told him about the forensic. He's put himself in the car. But, and this is the big but, he knows Sukhi's not going to contradict him. He knows that because Sukhi's dead. They're both dead, Sam, trust me.'

The custody sergeant looked up from his computer screen and shouted across to them: 'Interpreter's here boss.'

'This pre-interview disclosure is a joke,' Carver said. 'You want to ask my client about a trip to London and the use of her daughter's bank card. Have you got the bank card?'

'Let's just leave it for the interview, shall we?' Sam said. 'I have given you what I consider to be sufficient information with which to advise your client.'

'So you keep saying,' Carver glowered. 'I'll advise her to go no reply.'

'A matter for you. Now shall we get started?'

Ed took them into a different interview room, one where he could dictate the seating arrangements. The interpreter was next to Parkash, leaving Carver to sit in the only remaining seat, slightly behind and to the left of her client.

Ed turned on the tape, Sam again explained the procedure, everyone introduced themselves and the interview began.

'What was the purpose of your visit to London today?' asked Sam.

'Tell her not to answer that,' Carver ordered the interpreter.

'Which train did you catch?'

'Tell her not to answer any questions,' Carver said.

Sam looked at the interpreter.

'Please tell Mrs Bhandal that she doesn't have to follow the legal advice offered by Ms Carver. It is advice, not instructions, and it will be her, not her solicitor, who may have to explain her no replies at court.'

Sam turned to Carver. 'You've given your client your advice. Now I suggest you stop interrupting the interview.'

Imaginary daggers were flying from Carver's eyes.

The interview would last longer than normal; each question translated into Punjabi, any answer then translated into English.

'During the course of the morning a withdrawal was

attempted from your daughter's bank account at a machine in London. Was that you?'

Silence.

'Do you have possession of your daughter's bank card?'

Silence.

'Do you know her pin number?'

Silence.

Carver spoke.

'Did my client have possession of the bank card when she was arrested? When you searched her?'

Sam looked at Aisha's mother.

'As you are aware, we did not find a bank card on your person when we searched you.'

A smug smile appeared on Carver's face.

'But what you are unaware of is that I went back on to the platform and searched where you fell... '

Carver jumped in, the smile history.

'I have not been informed of this.'

'I'm informing you now,' Sam told her.

Carver was barely holding back her fury.

'You're trying to hijack this interview.'

'No,' Sam answered. 'I am trying to get the truth.'

Ed covered his mouth with his hand, thinking it best to hide his smirk as Sam continued, her voice calm.

'Your client has, on your advice, gone no reply. Now I wish to ask her about her fall in the station.'

Carver slumped against the chair.

'Do you remember falling over?'

Bhandal glanced at Carver who shook her head.

Silence.

'Well, let me remind you. It's all captured on the station CCTV. You fell near a coffee stand. I went back there while you were in our car. Underneath the stand I found this.'

Sam pulled out a plastic bag from her pocket.

'I am now showing Mrs Bhandal a plastic bag, marked Witness Reference SP1.'

Nobody moved as Sam held it up.

Aisha's HSBC debit card slipped to the bottom of the bag and nestled in the corner, the embossed details catching the light.

Carver broke the silence, her voice flat.

'I need to speak with my client.'

CHAPTER THIRTY-FIVE

Ten minutes later, Sam and Ed were back in the interview room.

'Before you had a private consultation with your solicitor I showed you a debit card in your daughter's name that I found on the station platform where you fell. Do you know how it got there?'

Parkash's hands were clasped together on her knees, her eyes staring at the floor. Her words were slow, measured, barely audible and translated into English by the interpreter.

'It must have fallen out of my purse, when I fell...you saw me fall.'

'Mrs Bhandal, can you speak up please?' Sam said.

'I did use it this morning in London, by accident. At the tube station. Embankment. I was meeting a friend. I withdrew £30. I always looked after Aisha's card and we both had the same PIN number. It was a horrible mistake. I'd forgotten I had it.'

'Which friend?'

'I'd rather not say.'

'You can't have spent much time with them?' Sam pressed her.

'As soon as I realised I'd used Aisha's card, I broke down,' Parkash said. 'I just wanted to get home to my husband…'

She started to cry.

'These last few months have been awful. You won't know what it's like to lose a child.'

Ed and Sam stood outside, drawing in the evening air, doing their best to rid their nostrils and clothes of the stink of the custody office; a windowless space regularly sprayed with a giant aerosol of human sweat.

Sam was the first to speak. 'How the hell people work down there day in, day out, never seeing the light of day, the noise, prisoners shouting for solicitors, cigarettes, their freedom… it's beyond me. And the stink.'

'Some of them enjoy it,' Ed told her. 'Keeps them off the streets.'

Sam was pulling a cigarette from the packet. 'Like HG Wells's Warlocks in the Time Machine, living underground.'

'Warlocks?' Ed smiled. 'Now there's a good name for the custody office vitamin D dodgers.'

Sam lit a cigarette.

'Two down, one to go. All very neat and tidy so far.'

'Yep, the Butcher's doing her thing,' Ed said. 'Let her think she's winning.'

Ed glanced at his watch – 8.25pm.

'Interview the father then call it a night?'

'Absolutely.'

Carver had finished her private consultation.

Sam led the interview.

'Mr Bhandal. I want to ask you about a settee you bought from Karan Singh in December.' Her nose twitched. The stench-thermometer in the interview room had risen.

Sam and Ed believed Bhandal's attitude towards women, his sense of superiority, would make it difficult for him to sit there and go no reply. They hoped he would disregard Jill Carver if that had been her advice.

If the son had a problem with women, it was likely he had learned those beliefs and behaviours from somewhere... or someone.

So they weren't surprised when Bhandal, unlike his wife, spoke loudly and clearly.

'We've all heard of the fashion police, but none of us have heard of the furniture police,' he sneered. 'Is it an offence to buy a settee in England now?' He smirked and relaxed back in his chair, in control and confident.

'How many settees did you buy in December?'

Carver coughed. Bhandal looked at her, theatrically raising his hand, pushing his palm towards her face.

'Two.' He turned back to Sam and Ed. 'I bought one which my wife didn't like, so I bought another one.'

'And what did you do with the first one?' Sam asked.

He raised both hands, palms facing the ceiling. 'My old one, or the one I bought and my wife didn't like?'

'The one your wife didn't like.'

'I sold it.'

'Who to?' Sam asked, the exchange gathering speed.

'I don't know his name. Just a man I met in a pub.'

'Which pub?'

'I don't remember.'

'So you sold it to the proverbial unknown man in a pub you cannot remember.'

'I'm a busy man,' Bhandal protested. 'I cannot remember everything.'

He stretched his legs out in front of him.

'How long did you have the settee before you sold it?' Sam asked.

'Not long. My wife didn't want it in the house. She thought I'd made a bad choice. And as you know, Inspector... '

He paused and flashed a smile.

'... if you've upset the wife, you rectify it as quickly as possible.'

To Sam, the smile was one of utter disregard for her and the circumstances surrounding their conversation.

'And how long was it before you got another one?' she asked, masking her contempt.

'Oh, just a couple of days. Mr Singh was very good.'

'Can you remember the exact date?'

'The exact date?' Another smile. 'I don't know about you, Inspector... ' each syllable was pronounced for maximum effect, reminding her he'd deliberately got her rank wrong, '... but I couldn't begin to remember the exact date when I bought something in December.'

The interview was turning into a game of chess, a head to head that Sam always somehow enjoyed.

'Okay, let's see if we can whittle it down,' she said now. 'Was it before Christmas?'

'Most definitely.' Bhandal shuffled forward, rested his elbows on the table, and steepled his fingers in what Sam saw as a mocking sign of concentration and sincerity.

Sam wanted to pull him across the table and punch him. 'What day was it delivered?'

'Monday,' Bhandal said after a pause. 'The second one was delivered on a Monday.'

'And the first one?'

'Umm, I believe it was a Saturday. Yes, a Saturday.'

'Okay,' Sam said, trying to shape the game her way. 'Did they arrive before Aisha went missing.'

Bhandal dropped his head at the mention of his daughter's name.

'No. I think that's why my wife didn't like the first one. It came the day after Aisha disappeared.'

'So the first one was delivered on Saturday 14th December.'

Bhandal sat back, looked up, scratched his cheek, and looked back at Sam. When he spoke it was quiet, slow. 'Yes, I suppose it was now you put it like that.'

'Well, Mr Singh agrees. So Saturday it is.'

Carver looked up and pushed her glasses from her eyes to her head. 'Is there any purpose to this line of questioning?'

'Indeed there is,' Sam told her, turning her gaze again to Bhandal. 'The first settee, the one you gave to a man in the pub.'

Bhandal and Carver both stared at her.

'That man is Joey Sanderson,' Sam continued. 'We have a statement from him saying you paid him to burn that settee.'

Bhandal was rigid. This time his words were neither quiet nor slow.

'Who? I've never heard of him. He's lying.' The knuckles on his right hand were white, his grip on the desk tighter now than his grip on the interview.

Sam seemed almost serene. 'He says he and another collected the settee from your house, but here's the thing. He didn't burn it. He sold it.'

When Bhandal glared at Sam, she saw defiance not surrender. Neither looked away.

Sam blinked first, the involuntary movement a trigger to speak.

'And now we have it,' she paused, allowing the significance of her words to register with Bhandal and Carver. 'I presume you want a word with your solicitor. Interview terminated at... ' she glanced at her watch '... 8.53pm.'

Sam turned off the tapes and took her time packaging them, enjoying the moment, savouring a trap well sprung.

She pushed the chair back, the legs screeching across the floor. She nodded at Bhandal, turned and walked out. Ed followed, fighting the urge to smile. He didn't want the cameras recording his glee.

He didn't hide it once they stepped through the custody door into the corridor. 'Marvellous, bloody marvellous!' Ed said. 'Couldn't have gone better... I knew the little shit would ignore the Butcher's advice.'

Sam was also feeling elated.

'He was so arrogant, it played right into our hands,' she said. 'He had to show who was boss. I want his balls on a plate. If that poor girl is dead, I want him to rot.'

She glanced at her watch. 'I need to ring Bev, check on Mia.'

She made the call on speaker phone, Ed listening at her side.

'How did you get on?' Sam asked.

'Nightmare.' Bev's voice was weary. 'Social Services are bad enough Monday to Friday but on a Saturday? More life in a tramp's vest. When they eventually got their arses in gear, they wanted to put her somewhere culturally appropriate... '

Sam dived in. 'She hasn't gone to Asians has she?'

'No,' Bev reassured her. 'I remembered what Ed said.'

Ed nodded.

Bev went on. 'I argued for Mia go to a white family,

somewhere where she wouldn't be asked all sorts of awkward questions. They weren't happy, but I pointed out if they chose a so-called culturally acceptable placement and something happened to her, we... well, you... would crucify them in the media. She's with a white family.'

Relieved, Sam thanked her, ended the call and slipped the phone in her trouser pocket.

'It's about time we called it a day,' she told Ed, rubbing at the tiredness in her eyes. 'We'll leave Technical Support to get on with their bit.'

They walked towards the underground car park.

'The three in the traps can be bedded down for the night,' Sam said. 'We'll re-interview tomorrow. I'm minded not to mention the blood on the settee yet and we can't use the ID evidence against the son from the UC in Devon and Cornwall until we get their go-ahead, so there's not a lot we can put to Baljit. We can ask if he's ever been to Plymouth etcetera. We'll go through the train times with the mother and push her for who she was supposed to meet. The father… I'll sleep on it. He might come up with some cock-and-bull. If he knows we've got the settee, he'll know we found the blood.'

Sam looked at her watch. It was gone 10.

She got into her car, her head a food mixer again. No point going straight home, the mixer would continue stirring for some time. She detoured and drove into the town centre to watch the revellers walking about, the noise and colour of a vibrant town hopefully providing a distraction, a handbrake to slow down her thoughts.

Neon lights flashed, doormen policed queues, staff in empty takeaways prepped food. Young people were staggering, yelling, laughing, or a combination of all three, the streets alive.

Sam pressed two switches and the Audi's front windows

opened. Corona's 1993 disco hit came into her head – 'The Rhythm of the Night'. Music, shouting, and sirens: the Saturday night soundtrack of every town centre in the country. Paramedics and police working flat out, the paramedics stitching up the individual wounds, the police stitching up the fabric of a broken society.

The pedestrian lights turned to red. Sam stopped and left a gap between her and the car in front. The Green Man was beeping. *Is this a Pelican, Puffin or Toucan? Who cares?*

She closed her eyes; saw her teen self dancing around her bedroom to that Corona song.

She opened her eyes.

What the hell?!

She shot upright, reached for the visor, and flicked it down. They were oblivious to her as they crossed. Just another young couple out for a good time.

Elliott Prince linking arms with Amber Dalton.

CHAPTER THIRTY-SIX

Sam called Ed the minute she walked into her kitchen. The fluorescents under the wall units shone dully on to the granite worktops, the subdued lighting a complete contrast to the excitement in her voice. She told him what she'd seen.

'There's a link between the self-help group and maybe the cause of the women needing help in the first place,' Sam said in a rush. 'Forget the Sisters of Macavity for now. Amber facilitates a self-help group. Elliott is the alleged leader of Mortimers. There's got to be a connection.'

Then she heard Sue shouting in the background, catching the words 'just bloody left her' and what sounded like 'joined at the hip'.

Shit, I didn't mean to cause him grief.

'Look, sorry, we'll talk about it tomorrow.' Sam ended the call before Ed could speak.

She'd considered getting fish and chips on the way home but reasoned the lunchtime Chinese takeaway was more than enough fast food for one day.

The light from the fridge was as bright as a UFO in a Hollywood movie. *There must be a way to dull it.*

She took the last slice of Wiltshire ham, pulled out the plastic salad drawer and found half a tomato. The brown paper bag on the bench contained just enough uncut wholemeal, although it was probably out of date. The knife battled through the organic bread, the bruised skin of the soggy tomato failing to soften the two slices it ended up between. Another couple of days and the loaf would have been croutons, but tonight it was just the wrong side of fresh.

She sat on a high stool in the kitchen.

Memo to self... apologise to Ed.

Why had Prince not mentioned Amber Dalton? Why had Amber not mentioned Elliott? She would never have put them in a relationship, if that's what it was.

She bit into the unforgiving sandwich, jaws getting a gym workout.

Was there any significance between TS Eliot's Cats, and Prince's first name? Two names, spelled differently but pronounced the same.

Her teeth fought the sandwich.

Get a grip Sam! Stop being ridiculous.

The power shower failed to clear her head. Amber Dalton and Elliott Prince were still banging around in there when she went to bed.

Stephen King was waiting and willing on the bedside table, but Sam gave him a pass. She turned off the light and tried to sleep.

Sunday 20th April 2014

Pounding water bounced off her skin and hit the gloss tiles. 6.30am and Sam was back in the shower. She couldn't remember if Dalton and Prince had been the last thing on her mind before she fell asleep, but they were certainly bang there when she woke up. Their relationship needed closer examination. Had they been communicating on social media?

She was out of the house before eight, the drive to Headquarters so uneventful she couldn't remember it. Ed was walking across the car park and when she shouted, he stopped to wait for her as she ran.

'I'm really sorry about last night.'

'Don't be daft,' Ed said, forcing a smile. 'Forget about it.'

'No I should have realised. Saturday and you'd been at work all day. It was thoughtless of me. I just couldn't get the two of them out of my head.'

Sitting in Sam's office, they'd barely sipped their coffees when the Custody Sergeant at Seaton nick rang. Sam listened as he told her Jill Carver had been there since 8am talking with Davinder Bhandal, who now wanted to speak to the investigating officers as soon as possible.

'Jill Carver's already there and Bhandal wants to be interviewed again,' Sam said, putting the phone back in her pocket. 'No doubt ready with his next defence statement.'

Ed worked on his coffee.

'No doubt but we won't rush, eh?' he said mildly. 'The Butcher can wait. At least until I've had my caffeine hit and a bacon sandwich. Bilton's is open on a Sunday.'

Sam stood up as Ed rubbed his hands together.

'The day's off to a flier,' he grinned. 'Bacon sarnie from one butcher, ear-ache pie from the other.'

Jill Carver theatrically checked her watch as they were admitted into the custody office.

'Morning,' Sam said. 'Sorry, had a briefing to do.'

The detention officer brought Bhandal from his cell. He may have looked dishevelled, but the smug look was back on his face.

Once the tapes were running, introductions made and caution given, Jill Carver spoke.

'My client wishes to make a verbal statement that will hopefully clear up this misunderstanding.' She nodded to Bhandal.

'Chief Inspector, I apologise if my answers were not clear last night. It was not my intention to mislead you or Detective Sergeant Whelan.'

Sam and Ed said nothing. They both knew a load of bollocks was about to be served up.

'I was upset last night, disorientated, stressed. The loss of our daughter is still raw. We just want her found, want her to come home. I did buy a new settee, a family Christmas present. It was delivered on the Thursday before Aisha went missing, not the Saturday as Mr Singh states. An easy mistake for an old man to make. None of us are getting any younger, and with age the memory fades.'

Sam and Ed remained silent, staring at him. Carver, motionless, kept her eyes on the A4 pad on her knee.

'That night Aisha got a nosebleed.' He shook his head, smiled. 'She was always getting them, had done since she was a child. They'd come on without warning. Sometimes there was such a lot of blood. She was laid down watching TV, testing out the new settee, then whoosh!'

His hand went up to his nose. 'It was so sudden. By the time she got up there was blood everywhere.'

Sam watched him. He was good; Oscar statue good.

'My wife was heartbroken. I told everybody not to worry. I would get another settee. You were, of course, correct. I sold that one to a man, and having slept on it, yes, perhaps his name is Sanderson. I did not tell him to burn it although I did explain that there was human blood on it. I think I saw him in the pub on the Sunday. On Monday I saw Mr Singh, chose another settee and he delivered it that day. Mr Sanderson picked up the ruined one on Monday morning. Came with a big trailer. He said the blood would wash out.'

Bhandal paused and looked at Carver, who nodded.

'Mr Sanderson bought it off me. To suggest I paid him to take it is ridiculous, but as everyone knows he is a common criminal. Nobody in this room has a single conviction between them, whereas Mr Sanderson has them going back years. Surely you don't take the word of a man like that? No court in the land would believe him.'

'Mr Singh keeps records,' Sam said.

'Which he writes himself, often days later,' Bhandal countered smoothly. 'Ask his family. He's always behind on the paperwork. He always gave me my receipts late and there'll be plenty of people who'll say the same thing. He's a lovely man, a fair man, respected in the community, but he is forgetful. I would not want you to go to court on the say-so of someone who could be discredited.'

Jill Carver jumped in, clearly not wanting her boy to over-egg the dish.

'I hope that clears up the misunderstanding,' she said, a statement, not a question. 'Mr Bhandal has apologised, but given his mental state yesterday, what with the shock of his and his wife's arrest at the station, it's not surprising he was confused.'

Ed spoke. 'Why did you say last night that the first new settee, if I can put it like that, was delivered on the Saturday after your daughter went missing, the same day Mr Singh said he delivered it to you?'

'I was upset.' Bhandal opened his palms again. 'I didn't want you thinking that Aisha had run away because she had bled on the settee. Once I knew you had the settee then it was incumbent upon me to tell the truth.'

Sam glanced at Ed, saw his fist clench and knew that at that moment, he wanted to punch Bhandal. She nodded at him as she reached across to the tape machine.

'Interview terminated 9.45am.' She pressed stop and packaged the tapes in silence.

'Will you be conducting more interviews with my other clients?' Carver asked, packing her A4 pad into a Radley bag that looked very new.

'Not me personally, but they will be interviewed,' Sam said.

Outside the custody office she spoke to Ed. 'Well how nice and tidy was that little lot?'

'Very, but all the better when we prove he's lying,' Ed said. 'Christ, I wished we'd done it on video, got the smarmy bastard on film.'

Like Ed, Sam knew their time hadn't been wasted.

'He's lying,' she said. 'We can put the son in Plymouth once we can use the UC to identify him, and nobody's going to believe the mother's story of a day trip to London to see people she won't name, where she just happens to accidentally use Aisha's bank card the day after our door to door.'

'Yeah, all rubbish,' Ed agreed. 'We just a need a bit more.'

Sam looked around, stopped walking, and dropped her voice to a whisper.

'The probes are in, one in the kitchen, one in the living room. Let's see what they have to say to each other when they get home.'

'Everything sorted in the listening post?' Ed asked.

He hoped the bugs would deliver and that they would remain safely hidden, despite Sam's reassurance.

Sam telephoned Bev and told her what she wanted doing in the final round of interviews.

She turned to Ed. 'I'll meet you back at the office… we need to find out the connection between Amber and Elliott?'

'Tell you what, I'll go and see Glen Jones on the way back. Speak in vague terms. Might drop in on Billy Wilson as well. Doormen know all sorts.'

Glen Jones, wearing nothing but a pair of red-spotted boxers, was sitting in a plastic chair in the back garden. One of his flatmates had let Ed in.

'I need a word.' Ed was speaking before he was through the kitchen door. 'Get dressed.'

Jones looked around. 'What's up?'

'Just get dressed. Me and you are going for a walk. Hurry up. I haven't got all day.'

Jones pushed himself out of the chair, sloped past Ed with his head down. He looked like he was walking to his execution.

Ed waited in the garden and wondered who cut the

lawn. It wasn't Wembley, but it wasn't bad. A bird chirped away in one of the mature trees by the fence.

Jones returned, grey joggers and a plain white T-shirt added to the boxers.

'Bit boring isn't it?' Ed nodded towards him. 'Your T-shirt. No witty messages today?'

Jones kept his head down, a young child being rebuked by a parent. 'Where we going?'

'Let's have a nice walk along the pier,' Ed told him. 'I can get a coffee with our Sunday stroll.'

Twenty minutes later they were walking out to sea along the Victorian pier. Ed had a flat white in his hand. The local yacht club was staging some sort of race, boats of various sizes on different tacks approaching marker buoys. The boats made Ed think of Sam but he pushed her out of his head.

'I'm pleased I haven't got a hangover,' he said, looking at Jones. 'Your trainers are dazzling me and that's with a clear head.'

Ed remembered the trainers of his teens, Adidas Sambas, the only non-black part being the three white stripes. Nobody would have dreamt of day-glo orange, a shade so bright they could probably spot them from space.

'Mortimers,' Ed said, back to business. 'How many of the members have girlfriends?'

'What, like a steady relationship?' Jones asked.

'Yeah.' Ed stopped, raising the disposal cup to his lips.

Glen Jones gave that some thought.

'None,' he said finally. 'It's not about being tied down.'

He looked away, out to sea.

'It's about, you know, as much sex as you can get with as many different girls as possible. It's all about the numbers.'

'What about Jack?' Ed asked him. 'Did he have a steady girlfriend?'

'No.'

'Jamie?'

A shake of the head.

'Elliott?'

'None of us did,' Jones told him. 'It wasn't like that. Out drinking, chat them up, have sex, move on.'

'One of my colleague's saw Elliott last night with a girl,' Ed said. 'Linking arms. He looked pretty close to her, as in relationship close.'

Jones gave that some time, too.

'Don't know who that could be,' he said after the thinking was done. 'He was out last night, but with a girl? He never said anything. You sure it wasn't his sister?'

CHAPTER THIRTY-SEVEN

'SISTER?' Sam said, looking up from the witness statements she was reading.

'That's what he said.' Ed pulled out a chair.

'But she was an only child.'

'Was she?' Ed said. 'After the attack she said she couldn't talk to her mother and she had no sisters? Did we ever ask her about a brother?'

Sam realised they hadn't. There had been no reason.

Ed was speaking again. 'So let's just work on the premise for the minute that she has a brother, it's Elliott Prince, and he knows his sister was attacked in her own home by a man who is now in prison, a man he can't get reach. Would that make him attack students who were arseholes around women?'

Sam put her pen down. Was that too much of a stretch? Or might Prince let his rage go on the ones who were just a step back from rapists in his eyes?

'Who knows what goes through your mind if a female relative gets sexually assaulted, or worse,' she said.

Ed bit his bottom lip, clenched his right fist.

'Sorry, Ed, that was insensitive of me.'

Ed had told her last year his niece had been dragged into an alley and only saved from rape by two sharp-eyed doormen; she was badly beaten in an ordeal that changed her whole personality,

'It's fine,' Ed said. 'Don't worry about it...I tell you what it does, though: it makes you want to rip their heads off, terrorise them as they terrorised your family. You want revenge. If I'm honest, I still don't know how I'll feel when he gets out. Will I go after him? I'll be retired then.'

He looked away, lost in thought, then returned his eyes to Sam. 'Sorry.'

She shook her head, raising her right palm.

'But would I use what happened to my niece to launch attacks on sexual predators in general? I'm not sure I would.'

'Could give you some serious motivation, though,' Sam said.

'It could,' Ed agreed. 'But Elliott Prince? Really?'

'Keyser Söze,' Sam told him.

'Sorry?'

Sam explained.

'And don't forget,' she went on. 'Luke Wylam and Glen Jones said Prince was the leader. Maybe what you see isn't what you get. I know everybody's snowed under, but can you get somebody to look at the relationship between him and Amber? Starting with why they've got different surnames. Amber said she'd never been married. I did ask her that.'

Progress was slow. Bev re-interviewed the Bhandal family; the mother and brother went 'no reply' to every question about the settee. Davinder Bhandal himself, smile a permanent fixture, said he could be of no further assistance.

The intelligence cell started to look at Elliott Prince's social media and his mobile history. They had completed their content checks of Amber's phone but found nothing of significance other than the texts on the night of Jack Goddard's murder. It was the same story with her social media.

Paul Adams began to look at the relationship between Amber and Elliott, but getting answers on a Sunday was often impossible. He started researching Amber's family tree online. The Internet never took a day off.

Sam and Ed were a couple of miles from the office, sitting with Karan Singh and his two grandsons. Sam had called him. He told her where he was.

Ed accepted Karan's offer of a pint. Sam had a pineapple juice. The youngest boy fetched the drinks.

The mid-afternoon sunshine meant the bar was quiet, one of the less attractive Premier League fixtures playing out on the only TV, the sound muted.

'Mr Bhandal is of the opinion that you made a mistake, that the first settee was delivered on the Thursday, not the Saturday,' Sam said.

Karan shook his head. 'Impossible. The receipt books.'

'Mr Singh...' Sam leaned across the copper-topped round table and spoke quietly, '...do you fill those receipts in at the time or later.'

He looked at her. Everyone at the table waited for his answer. Silence.

Karan drank a mouthful of beer, put the half-pint glass down, and moved on to the tumbler keeping it company. He raised the tumbler to his mouth and drained the remains of the whisky.

'I can't say that I wrote them out at the time,' he said

slowly. 'Probably didn't, but I would have written them out within a couple of days.'

Sam kept her disappointment off her face.

'Could you have been mistaken, Mr Singh?'

He picked up the beer.

'I would be lying if I said I never made a mistake,' Karan said. 'But I wasn't wrong this time. Our van was in for service. Goes in the same time every year. It went in on the Wednesday and we got it back on the Friday afternoon. The garage's receipts are computerised. I paid by card so there'll be records.' He took another mouthful of beer, froth clinging to his beard.

'So we couldn't have delivered anything to Mr Bhandal on Thursday. We only have the one van. I am afraid it's him who's mistaken.'

Sam could have kissed him.

Back in the car, it was Ed who spoke first. 'Do you want to have another interview with Bhandal?'

Sam said no, what would it achieve?

'We have him lying about the settee,' she said. 'We'll tie that up nicely in statements from Mr Singh – isn't he lovely, by the way? – and the statements from the garage where his van was serviced. We've started to build up a nice case but we're a long way short yet.'

They would release them on police bail with the usual 'while we conduct further enquiries' send off. Carver would have a little rant, demanding to know why they weren't being released unconditionally. Then the listening probes would come into play.

'What about the daughter, Mia?' Ed asked.

'She'll go back to them,' Sam said. 'There's no way we can suggest she's at risk.'

Ed's face became tight with concern.

'But she's going to be, Sam. She's 15. Aisha's gone.

There's a promise to be fulfilled to a family in India. Mia will have to take Aisha's place.'

Sam had never thought about that. Why would she?

'We have a duty of care to her,' Ed went on. 'She's at risk.'

'When's that new law coming in?'

'The Forced Marriage Act?' Ed said. 'June this year. Potentially too late for Mia.'

Sam looked for another solution.

'The civil courts,' she suggested. 'Forced Marriage Protection Orders.'

Ed was all cold water.

'You know the difficulties with them,' his voice trailing away. 'Police getting mixed up in civil law.'

Not for the first time, Sam was struck by Ed's passion.

'Okay,' she told him. 'We've got the probes in the house. If her level of risk increases from anything we hear, we'll go in and get her. She'll be fine Ed.'

He said nothing but his grim face spoke for him.

Sam's hand ached, the pen so fast it barely touched the paper, the handwriting more illegible with every word. Notes on both investigations, separate sheets for the different investigations: lines of enquiry that needed to be completed or developed further; witnesses that needed further interviews; Persons of Interest who may become suspects; identified suspects that needed interviewing; inquiries into people's backgrounds; technical examinations, as well as the covert operation which would start as soon as the Bhandals were released.

Logistically, it wasn't possible today, but first thing

tomorrow Charlotte, Tracey, Alex and Amber would be arrested and brought in.

Ed came into Sam's office and talked through the arrest strategies... which officers would go to which address... what time... which stations the suspects would be taken to... who would interview them... who would co-ordinate the searches of their houses... what the search teams would be looking for.

The pre-arrest briefing would take place at 6am, everybody at the respective addresses no later than 7am.

Sam called Paul into her office and agreed the interview strategies. He had made little progress with Amber's family tree but would get on to the various agencies tomorrow.

It was 8pm. Sam had survived the day on a bacon sandwich and a pineapple juice. She was tired, hungry, and her head was pounding. She needed home, food and bed. Tomorrow was going to be a long day.

She ate yet another ready meal in front of the TV, poached breast of Scottish salmon, king prawns, cream cheese and asparagus. *I'm spoiling myself tonight,* Sam thought as the microwave sang its siren song. Sid James's laugh filled the room, a camping field the setting for the 'Carry On' film she'd seen countless times before.

Twenty-five minutes after walking through the front door she dragged herself upstairs, undressed and dropped on to the bed. Her legs ached; her head felt like the big, green watermelon from 'The Day of the Jackal', Edward Fox already having done his worst. Still sleep wouldn't come. Each time she looked at the bedside clock another 15 minutes had passed. 11.50 were the last numbers she saw on the red display.

Monday 21st April 2014

Disorientated, she stretched for the phone and glanced at the clock – 4.03am.

'Sorry to bother you, boss.'

She pushed herself up, rolled on to her side, and reached for the pad and paper that were always on the bedside table. 'What is it?'

'There's a Body. On the tow path.'

Fuck.

'Male. Early 20s. Looks like a head injury. Found by a passing student. Uniform are in attendance. SOCO en route.'

CHAPTER THIRTY-EIGHT

While Eastern Police, like every other force across the country, had failed miserably in its target to recruit, and then retain, more officers from minority ethnic groups, the surveillance team had one Asian officer who spoke Punjabi fluently.

Yesterday, Sam made sure that Sonia Mitchell was attached to the 'listening team' on the Aisha Bhandal investigation. Another three Punjabi speaking officers from uniform had also been drafted on to the investigation, having first been warned of the consequences of disclosing the true nature of their duties.

Two officers were required to work each shift. Ideally it should have been four, two to each device, but cuts had every department straining at the seams. The four Asian officers would work different shifts so there would always be one Punjabi speaking officer on duty.

Any officer removed from normal duties drives the rumour mill into overtime, colleagues asking where they've gone. If they're fobbed off – 'nothing to do with you' or, even worse, 'it's on a need to know' – they started speculating.

Sam was only too well aware that educated guesswork could sometimes hit the mark and if the officers with big mouths started speculating, the investigation could be compromised.

Three uniform officers from the same ethnic background would only be petrol to the curiosity flame... and a flame could become an inferno.

Sam had brought this up with Assistant Chief Constable Monica Teal in a phone call yesterday. The ACC contacted various superintendents, informing them the three officers were required to work under the supervision of DCI Parker for the foreseeable future. She told them the officers were to form a headquarters working party, responsible for developing Eastern Police's response to forced marriages in view of the impending legislation.

Hopefully the only comments would be sarcastic – the words 'working party' and 'headquarters' laughable bedfellows to plenty.

Working the night shift, two officers were sitting, headphones on and machines recording, in an office in the secure compound which Sam and Ed had visited on Saturday.

The Bhandals' house came alive shortly after the family's release from custody.

Doors slammed, the father shouted in a mixture of Punjabi and English, the son shouted predominantly in English. The mother was inaudible.

Then it was over. Ten minutes of activity. Then nothing. Only silence.

Had everybody gone to bed?

In a warm office, no matter how bright, silence equates to boredom for the listeners and a subsequent struggle to stay awake. There is only so much tea, so many quiz questions. Sleep goes to war and becomes a sly, merciless enemy. Many a cop has fallen on the unforgiving fields of 'The Battle of Stay Awake'.

Just after 4am, Davinder Bhandal spoke, in English.

The cops, hearts jump-started by the surge of activity, bolted upright and rubbed their eyes.

Bhandal was in the kitchen. Water was running. A kettle being filled? 'Where've you been?'

The son spoke. 'Out. Clear my head. Get rid of the smell of that stinking place. What are you doing up?'

'Couldn't sleep,' Bhandal answered. 'I will go and see old man Singh today, put him right.'

The sound of a clicking switch. The kettle?

'Do you think that's a good idea?'

'He needs to be reminded of the dates, make sure he gives the police the correct information,' Bhandal told his son. 'That the settee was delivered on Thursday.'

'And what if he goes to the police? Tells them you've been round?'

'He won't.'

'Why?' Baljit's voice rose. 'Because those from the mother country don't talk to the police? They close ranks, protect their own community? I've got news for you – he's already talked to them. And have you thought the police might be watching us, watching this house?'

The two officers smiled, gave each other the thumbs-up.

'So what do you suggest?' Bhandal was asking now. 'You seem to have all the answers.'

'I don't, but I say do nothing. Let the dust settle. The

police haven't got anything. If they had, we wouldn't have been let out.'

Footsteps. Flowing water. A cup being filled?

PC Ranjit Singh was writing as fast as he could. It was true what they said. If you lost one of your senses, the others compensated. If you lost four out of five, the survivor was bordering on extra-terrestrial.

A spoon bashed against the sides of a cup. Sugar?

'And what if they come for us again?' It was Bhandal's voice.

'I think they will,' Baljit answered. 'So what? What have they got? Just tell mum to keep saying nothing.'

'What if they find her?'

The officers pulled their chairs closer, sat up, and clocked the time.

'Aisha?' Baljit said. 'Don't be stupid. How will they do that?'

'What are you two talking about?' A new voice, a woman speaking Punjabi. Baljit answered in the same.

'Dad wants to go round to see old man Singh.'

'What for?' the woman demanded. 'What can the police do? They'll never find Aisha. It will all just go away.'

Silence.

Ranjit Singh, three years into the job, desperately wanted to be a detective. He would never get another opportunity like this. Sam Parker's opinion carried a lot of weight. Impress her and he was on his way. Drop a bollock and the chances of getting *Detective Constable* on his warrant card would vanish quicker than the setting Indian sun.

He brought DC Ian Wilson up to speed.

'That can be taken more ways than one,' said the older, shorter, fatter detective with the cheap trainers and a sweatshirt Ranjit wouldn't wear to wash his beloved black Golf GTi.

The tall young cop with expensive taste in shoes and clothes could never envisage a day, no matter how old he got, when he would be seen in crap sportswear. Ian Wilson had obviously never heard of Adidas or Nike. Did detectives have a style transplant when they hit 50? In fairness, Ed Whelan had dodged it. He was still a sharp dresser.

The DC continued. 'They'll never find her because we've hidden her, or hidden her body, or if we can't find her, the police have no chance.'

He pushed his chair back away from his desk, allowed its wheels to glide across the floor until they lost momentum. He reached sideways for the bag of toffees.

'By the way, do these families use bounty hunters to track them down?'

'Yes,' Ranjit told him. 'There are people who make it their living. In your culture you'd call them private investigators, searching for missing persons. This is slightly different. These are looking for people they know are going to be punished, perhaps even killed, once they are found. Often they'd be distributing photographs among the community in the area the family thinks they've gone to.'

Wilson propelled himself forward and passed his colleague a sweet.

Ranjit took a liquorice toffee, talking again as he struggled with the rapper.

'That's bothered me about this case,' he said. 'Not the distribution of photos but the fact the family hasn't hired any bounty hunters.'

'Would you know if they did?'

Ranjit raised his eyebrows. 'Me, probably. My wife? One hundred per cent. No bounty hunters are looking for Aisha. What does that tell you?'

He looked at Wilson.

'You tell me.'

'They're not bothered,' Ranjit said. 'They know she's dead.'

'Haven't even put him in the water this time,' Sam said, walking along the tow path with Ed. 'You get any grief for getting called out?'

'Nothing that I'm not used to,' Ed shrugged.

They had already crossed the outer cordon, a lone young police officer, clip-board in-hand, writing the names down of every officer who passed through. The instructions had been simple – nobody passes unless it's DCI Sam Parker. Sam knew there would be another police officer at the other end of the tow path doing exactly the same.

Aware it was always the youngest officers on duty who copped for the Scene Log, Sam unfailingly made time to explain the importance of their task; how, for example, any allegations of cross-contamination could be refuted by the scene log. When a job was boring, it was vital that those performing it realised how much it mattered. Sam knew as far as those officers were concerned nothing got the circulation flowing better than being told you were important by a senior officer.

She didn't make time for the young cop today. She managed a cursory nod, no more. She knew she was walking towards a disaster zone, had known that since the call. Her own professional disaster zone.

There was a slight drizzle – 'wet rain' Sam called it – and only their footsteps disturbed the early morning silence.

Although the body had not been identified, Sam knew it was a young male. She didn't doubt for a second he would be a student.

'The press will have a field day,' she muttered.

Ed didn't respond.

She kicked a small stone, which skimmed across the ground and rolled down the bank, dropping into the water.

'How long can we say they're not linked, deny a serial killer's on the loose?' Sam wondered aloud.

She knew there'd be recriminations from the young man's family. Christ, she had organised extra patrols along the tow path for Friday and Saturday night. The original plan had been to arrest the girls – the suspected Sisters of Macavity – yesterday. Aisha's bank card had changed all that and she'd forgotten to organise extra tow path patrols for last night. She'd taken her eye off the ball.

'You could have saved my son, you incompetent bitch.' Sam could already hear the grief-stricken voice.

Professional Standards would have a field day with her. The force might even involve the Independent Police Complaints Commission, although Ed always maintained they were next to useless.

Trying to get extra officers to patrol the tow path at such short notice would have been a nightmare, but that wasn't the issue. She should have got them anyway, or at least tried. She hadn't... end of.

Sam launched the next stone with her right foot, watched it land in the water with a plop and sink without a trace. The arc of the stone replicated her career – rapid rise, dive to the depths.

The path followed the meanderings of the river and as they rounded a bend, ducking under a wet, overhanging hawthorn bush, the white tent and the people scurrying around in white paper suits with cameras and other equipment came into view.

'We're on candid camera,' Ed said.

Sam looked across the river, seeing Darius Simpson and a photographer from the Seaton Post.

'At times I think he's got my bloody phone bugged,' Sam muttered.

Julie Trescothick, the Senior Scenes of Crime Officer, came to greet them, a paper suit in each hand.

'What we got, Julie?' Sam asked as she reached the inner cordon, waist-high tape running around the exterior of the tent.

'Young male, head injury, looks like he was hit from behind. Plenty of blood. We've put the plates down.'

Sam could see the metal plates, the size of small patio paving stones around the tent.

She noticed a couple of plastic bags tied around two branches of a bush.

Julie followed her look. 'There's blood on the branches. Best we could do for now. Better to preserve with a couple of Tesco carriers than not preserve at all.'

Sam nodded. She managed a smile. All the high-tech equipment they had at their disposal and they were using supermarket carrier bags.

'All the photographs are taken,' Julie told her. 'We've done the video. There's a plate in the tent, but you can get in.'

'To be fair, Julie, we'll just look in through the tent door,' Sam said. 'We can see what we need to from there. Jim Melia's on his way.'

'Right on cue,' Ed said, looking over his shoulder, the pathologist striding towards them, bright green moleskins tucked into his black Hunter Wellingtons.

'What we got then?' Jim said, hands in the pockets of his waterproof, looking like he'd been awake for hours.

'Head injury by the sounds of it,' Sam said.

'Best have a look then.'

The three of them put on the white suits and over-shoes. As ever, Ed, 6'4", and broad shouldered, struggled to turn himself into a Teletubby lookalike.

Julie pulled the tent flap back. They all couched down and peered inside. The body was laid on its side, facing away from them, hair matted with blood, a gaping wound in the back of the skull just above the neckline.

His clothing – jeans and a T-shirt – suggested he'd been on a night out.

Jim stepped inside on to the metal plate and knelt down by the body, looking at the head but touching nothing. Sam was still at the entrance to the tent and he spoke to her without looking up or turning around.

'I was at a body the other night, different force, not naming names,' Jim Melia said. 'New SIO asked me about time of death. I told him I could stick as many thermometers into as many holes as he wanted, but it's still a guess. He looked devastated. Really thought I was going to say time of death between X and Y, to the second almost. I told him this was real life, not TV. No voodoo mumbo jumbo.'

Jim shot back on his haunches. 'Jesus, Ed, you made me jump.'

Ed had walked around the tent, removed a metal peg and thrust his head under the canvas. 'Thought so. Sorry Jim.'

'Thought what?' Sam said.

Ed walked back around the tent, hands in pockets, head down.

'Luminous orange trainers,' he told her. 'It's Glen Jones.'

CHAPTER THIRTY-NINE

'THERE's a big rock over here, covered in blood,' a white-suited SOCO shouted, emerging from the long grass. He was 20 metres away, 20 metres closer to the student accommodation block.

Sam and Ed walked over to him.

They remained on the path, the SOCO, back in the grass, photographing the stone in situ. It needed to be recovered before the drizzle washed it clean.

'Good spot that,' Sam said.

She remembered the discovery of Yorkshire Ripper Peter Sutcliffe's hammer. *Thorough search or another search officer taking a leak?*

Jim exited the tent and walked to Sam and Ed.

'Skull crushed, probably one solid blow but I'll know better when we get him to the mortuary.'

Sam pointed to the orange plastic box crate covered in brown paper, which the SOCO was now carrying towards them. Sam marvelled at the odds and sods SOCO carried in their vans.

'What about what's in this crate?' she asked Jim Melia.

He glanced under the paper.

The large stone looked like it belonged in a garden rockery, something of a size not many would be able to carry in one hand. The small, dark brown stain was a dirty blemish on the smooth pale grey surface, a couple of strands of matted hair moving in the cool breeze. Anything more than a drop was 'covered' as far as SOCOs were concerned.

'That would fit the bill,' Jim said, bending forwards for a closer look. 'You'll know for certain when you do your tests on the blood and hair.'

He straightened his back. 'Nothing more for me here.'

He strode off and didn't look back when he shouted: 'See you at the mortuary.'

'Not a hammer then,' Ed said, as he and Sam walked back towards their cars.

'Maybe more spontaneous, maybe the killer didn't have another hammer, but it's another Mortimer, another link.

The dampness magnified the smell of the grass and bushes, but the cold and wet were hindering her thought processes. She hated being cold, hated being wet. Fine on a yacht, not at work. The two together were a nightmare as far as she was concerned.

'Why carry the rock, what, 20 metres? What was that all about?' Ed said.

'Who knows?' She kicked another stone, sunk her hands deeper into her North Face jacket. 'We're missing something here. I know we are, but what?' She pulled her hood up, bowing her head as the drizzle turned to rain. 'I feel we're one piece short. Find the last piece and we can start to put the jigsaw together. How are we doing with Amber and Elliott?'

'They need a bit more time,' Ed told her.

'That's one thing we're pretty short of.'

She answered her phone. 'Morning Darius. How are you?' She tapped Ed's arm and pointed to a large oak tree.

'Give me a minute.' They sheltered under the huge tree. Sam put the phone on speaker.

'Hi Sam. Fine thanks. Listen, just to give you the heads up: the editor's going to slate you in his editorial.'

'Just what we need,' Sam said, heart rate increasing, thoughts racing.

'Knobhead,' Ed mouthed.

'Incompetent investigation, serial killer on the loose, you know the drill,' Darius was saying. 'He's not particularly well liked and everybody knows he has a beef with the police... goes back to his leftie student days when he was locked up at some rally, but he'll run with it Sam. He sees it as his civic duty.'

Ed mouthed 'Tosser'.

'Okay, thanks for the heads up,' Sam said into the phone. 'I'll let you know if we get anything. No doubt we'll have a press conference later.'

'Bound to happen,' Ed said, as they started walking.

Sam's pounding heart and clammy forehead were a reaction to the self-doubt racing like river rapids through her veins. Pilloried in the press would be just the beginning. Soon it would be police officers whispering in corners, stealing glances as Sam walked past.

'Yeah, suppose so.' She stopped again, took a deep breath, spoke slowly. 'Would cops walking along here last night have made any difference?'

'Look at it,' Ed told her. 'Two miles of path, two miles on each side that is, four miles to cover in total. If we had a cop every 100 metres maybe, but what would that be? Something like 60 cops? We had four on mountain bikes and a couple on horses, and getting that many was a bloody miracle.'

Sam knew even those resources were really an exercise in trying to reassure a nervous public.

'The media will still say we could have caught him,' she said.

Ed wiped rain of his shaved head.

'Years ago, when everybody was clamouring for more cops on the streets, I read somewhere that a bobby on the beat would catch a burglar red-handed once in their career, so once in 30 years in other words… Come on, I'm getting soaked.'

They went to their cars.

Ed turned the key in the ignition and adjusted the climate control to high. His trousers clung to his thighs as he depressed the clutch, his leather-soled shoe slipping on the rubber pedal.

What had Sam said? A piece missing from the jigsaw?

He pulled away, the noise of the blown air fading as he lost himself in the mental search going on through the fog of his brain. The piece he was after was floating around, a fuzzy shape he couldn't quite grab.

His wasn't concentrating on the road; he was a child again, running around, trying to catch the bubbles his mother was blowing through a red plastic circle on the end of a red plastic stick.

He saw the teenager sprint, zigzagging across the road, dodging puddles, a cigarette clasped between his teeth.

'Fucking idiot,' Ed muttered, the palm of his right hand slapping the top of his forehead. He didn't mean the teenager.

His eyes darted between the rear-view mirror and both wing mirrors before he swerved into a junction, spun the wheel and re-emerged back on the main road, now travelling in the opposite direction. The surveillance team called a 180-degree turn a reciprocal.

His reciprocal was nothing to do with a surveillance target; he'd caught the bubble.

His finger jabbed the screen of his phone.

'Sam, it's me. Meet me back on the tow path. I want to check something out whilst SOCO are still there.'

'What is it?' Sam said, hurrying towards him.

Ed was standing next to the same oak tree.

'A young lad ran across the road, dodging puddles but still smoking,' he told her. 'Smokers smoke whatever the weather.'

'Okay, let's skip the lecture,' Sam said, more sharply than she intended.

Ed held out his hands. 'I'm not having a go. We stood under this tree for shelter. What if somebody stood under here to conceal themselves?'

'Go on.'

'If they were waiting, they'd be tense,' Ed continued. 'They might chew gum, maybe smoke. I looked at the ground when you were on the phone but it didn't register. They've gone now but there was six cigarettes butts on the ground. I had SOCO photograph and recover them. It's been raining but they haven't been there long. They can't have been. The brown filters were still intact. They weren't like soggy cotton wool.'

'So maybe the killer was waiting?' Sam said, letting Ed's theory play out.

Ed's eyes were alive, shining.

'And if you were chewing gum and about to attack someone, would you spit it out, risk making a noise or would you quietly take it out of your mouth and stick it on the bark?'

'Tell me there was chewing gum on this tree?' Sam almost held her breath.

'Just there.' Ed pointed at the bark. 'Also photographed and recovered.'

If Ed was right, the hidden killer must have known Jones was going to be on the path.

'What are we, a hundred metres from the body, 120 from the weapon deposition site?' Sam said now. 'If he was killed where he fell, why let him get 100 metres in front? Why let him get that far away?'

She walked away, lit a cigarette and inhaled.

'Did the killer carry that rock 100 metres?' she went on. 'Can't see it. Did it just happen to be there on the path? It doesn't fit. Wait to intercept him, but not have a weapon to hand.'

'What if it was put there beforehand?' Ed asked.

'I suppose, but why?' Sam looked up, the grey sky a reflection of the investigation. 'Clear as bloody mud.'

They decided to eat before the post mortem – Sam reasoning if she was going to have a shit day it may as well be with on full stomach – and Ed suggested the Ocean View, a long-established spot by the promenade.

'It won't be open, will it?' Sam said.

Ed smirked and spread out his arms, palms turned up.

'Samantha.' He paused to add to the sarcasm. 'When I first joined back in 1978, I was told even when it was pouring with rain a good copper never gets wet. Why? Because he's always got a tea spot to visit. It's 6.45. Of course it's not open, but Richie, the chef, will be there. We go way back. He'll knock something up.'

Sam smiled and shook her head. Was there anyone Ed didn't know in this town?

Within an hour they were in Ed's car heading to the mortuary, Sam's Audi left in the Ocean View car park.

'Feel better for that?' Ed asked.

'Just what the doctor ordered,' Sam told him, thinking... *it would have tasted even better if I wasn't waiting for that bloody editorial.*

It was a myth that dead bodies affected the appetites of the investigators; they still needed to function. Ed recalled a post-mortem years ago in the early hours where the pathologist suggested a break halfway through for bacon sandwiches.

Ed turned into the hospital grounds, drove to the mortuary, and pulled alongside the SOCO van. They were still in the car when Coolio's 'Gangsters in Paradise' started in his pocket.

Sam made a face and Ed gave her a 'what? I like it!' look in return

'Alright Paul,' he said into the mobile. 'Hang on. Sam's here. I'll put you on speaker.'

'The blood on the hammer is Jack Goddard's, and there's DNA on the handle,' Paul told them. 'No hits on the database but it's a full profile.'

CHAPTER FORTY

THE CONCRETE FLOOR of the large examination room was soaking wet, steam still rising, the smell of disinfectant so strong Sam had to rub her eyes. Glen Jones, naked, was on the metal table unaffected by the ammonia, his Chucky-like eyes wide open, staring at the ceiling, sink hole between his ankles. A SOCO stood on top of a pair of wooden stepladders photographing him from above.

'Ready to begin?' Jim Melia said, standing in a green gown and white Wellington boots, his clothing a much better fit than the white paper suits and overshoes the police were wearing.

Sam looked around: SOCOs and the female mortuary attendant, poised, sprinters under starter's orders, watching her and Jim, waiting for the signal to start. What a place. No dignity in death. She shuddered. *I hope I die from a diagnosed illness. I don't want to end up here, naked, cold, surrounded by strangers and disinfectant.*

'Yeah, let's make a start,' she said.

Jim began his external examination, beginning with the head. The first incision would wait.

Two hours later they were out of the paper suits and back in Ed's car. Jim's findings were as his scene observations – one crushing blow with a smooth object, but an object with a wide surface area. The rock found in the long grass would fit.

'I'll sort the Press out,' Sam said. 'You prioritise the rock. I need to know if that's the weapon and let's see if it's Glen's blood. Authorise the premium service. I want to know ASAP.'

Ed nodded. 'No problem.'

'We need to give some thought to the Persons of Interest in this investigation,' Sam went on. 'Tracey, Charlotte, Alex, Amber, and Elliott. None of them have any previous so they're not on the DNA database. We need to get samples from them.'

'How do you want to do that?' Ed asked her.

'Let me think about it,' Sam's mind was in investigation overdrive. 'And get the cigarettes and the gum fast-tracked.'

Sam did the maths. Six cigarettes, one piece of gum, one rock. Eight items, each to be fast-tracked. *Bang goes the budget.*

Coolio's voice filled the car.

'Hi Ranjit.' Ed answered the call. 'I'm on hands-free. The boss is in the car with me.'

'I just wanted to touch base before I went to bed,' Ranjit's voice sounded thin and tinny through the speaker. 'All the tapes are logged and there's written summaries of what's been said. But my overall feeling, which I haven't put down on paper, is that she's dead. No bounty hunters involved. Why aren't they looking for her?'

Ed agreed but they all knew gut feeling wasn't enough.

'They say anything interesting?' he asked.

'They all got up about four and there was a conversation about how we wouldn't find her but nothing that'll take us very far at the minute,' Ranjit told them. 'The father spoke about going back to see old man Singh. Then at breakfast time there was a bit of a domestic. Daughter can't find her suitcase. Accused the brother of stealing it. I hope you don't think I'm speaking out of turn.'

Sam jumped in. 'Ranjit, absolutely not. We welcome your input. Now do yourself a favour, go to bed and get some sleep. And thanks for the call.'

'He's right about the bounty hunters,' Ed said after Ranjit had gone.

Sam gazed out of the side window. April, and people were still hunched under grey skies and drizzle, collars upturned, umbrellas held aloft.

I need a holiday. Somewhere warm.

'Let's see how we get on this week with the monitoring,' she said after a pause. 'If there's nothing, we may have to think of a way to spark a reaction in that household.'

Ed pulled into the Ocean View car park.

Sam jumped out. 'See you later.'

Before Ed had time to reply, she was opening her car door.

Sam saw the waiting Press pack as she approached HQ.

'Bloody marvellous,' she muttered to herself. It never ceased to amaze her how quickly the media mobilised, the satellite vans already in the lay-by. They were all there – BBC, ITV, Sky, reporters sipping hot drinks, milling around, swapping gossip.

The first person she saw inside the building was

Assistant Chief Constable Monica Teal. Teal was walking towards her, deep in conversation with the Police and Crime Commissioner. As she neared Sam, she spoke without altering her stride.

'Looks like your audience awaits, Sam. Anything you need, let me know.'

She was past Sam when she raised her voice. 'You have our full support as always. Pop into my office today, give me a full update.'

Following the ACC was Inspector Mick 'Never' Wright. He slowed noticeably. 'Be careful, though.' Wright was gloating. 'Don't want them writing your obituary.'

Peter Hunt, the Press Officer, was waiting for her.

'We've been bombarded this morning,' he said in greeting. 'Everyone wants to know if we've got a serial killer, whether we're linking some or all the attacks. Nothing you can't handle.'

Sam looked up at the clock. 10.50am.

'How about noon?' she suggested. 'It can go out on the lunchtime news.'

Peter Hunt thought that would be perfect.

'Give me an idea what you want to say and I'll write up your statement,' he said. 'Then we can go through the likely questions.'

It took Sam less than five minutes to give him the information he needed.

The two officers in the LP – the Listening Post – were still unsure of the identification of the third man. Two voices clearly belonged to Bhandal and Baljit but the third was unknown. They referred to him as 'male 3' in their log.

The plan to identify him, like all the best plans, was

simple. Ed went to the house. Sam was preparing for the press conference so he had an hour.

He pulled up outside, called the officers in the LP to confirm 'male 3' was still inside, and knocked on the door.

Baljit appeared. 'What the fuck do you want?'

'A word with your father.' Ed pushed past.

'Here, you can't just go barging in, not unless you got a warrant.'

Ed spun around, bent down and whispered in his ear. It was becoming a theme of their meetings.

'Listen, little boy, you want to come and play in the big boys' playground, you let me know, until then…'

Ed spun back around and walked into what he presumed was the sitting room. The room was empty.

'CID!' Baljit shouted.

Ed stepped into the adjoining room and saw Davinder Bhandal standing next to the fireplace, the brother-in-law, Gurmej, stretched out in an armchair.

'Mr Whelan,' Bhandal said. 'Come in.'

Baljit followed, closing what had once been a white door, but was now off-yellow, behind him.

Gurmej pushed himself out of the chair and spoke quickly in Punjabi. 'What does this piece of shit want?'

'This piece of shit wants a word,' Ed said.

The three Asians, standing by the fireplace, were wide-eyed and open-mouthed.

Ed began speaking in Punjabi.

'This piece of shit, as you so politely put it,' he pointed at Gurmej, 'wants to know if any of the family…'

He reverted to English and put his hands in his trouser pockets. 'Tell you what, we'll leave it. Maybe speak again in the not too distant future at the police station.'

He walked out, leaving silence behind him.

Back in the car, he called the LP. 'It's Gurmej, the wife's brother.'

'We heard every word,' said the Punjabi speaking officer. 'Quality, you switching to Punjabi. You've started a shit storm in there.'

'Good,' Ed grinned.

'Yeah, they're trying to remember what they said in Punjabi when you could hear,' the officer was telling him. 'The wife's joined in, remembers the husband asking her... hang on, let me read it verbatim... When they said I was arrested, you asked me if I still had the card. She sounded scared shitless.'

'Anything else?' Ed asked.

'No, but they're not sure what's going on,' the cop told him. 'Can't work out what you and the boss are playing at.'

'Anything from the brother-in-law?' Ed wanted to know. 'Looks a nasty piece of work. He's got bully written all over him.'

'He's not said much really.'

'Okay, keep at it,' Ed finished. 'Cheers lads.'

The buzz at the press conference reflected the interest the tow path deaths had stirred. Sam found herself sitting in front of TV cameras streaming live feeds to their respective news channels, a phenomenon her predecessors of not so long ago had been spared. Going out live was not the time for slip-ups, not the time for careless answers that would come back to bite you.

Bright white lights exploded in her face as she made her witness appeal, photographers moving around for the best shot.

Then came the questions, the cat-and-mouse dance. Sam needed to be foot perfect.

'Two murders on the same tow path in just over a week. Are they linked?' The guy from Sky went straight to it.

'The two investigations are being run side by side, and while there are similarities, there are also differences,' Sam answered smoothly. 'The victims are both single, both young men at university, and the location is the same. The times are also similar in that both attacks happened after the young men had been on a night out.'

The woman from ITV raised an arm. 'Were they both drunk?'

'We are awaiting the results of toxicology reports,' Sam dead-batted. 'They had both been drinking but that's not to say they were drunk.'

The BBC was up next, Sam recognising the face of the middle-aged hack from national broadcasts.

'The first four who died on this tow path in the last six months were believed to have fallen in drunk. Is that early conclusion now under review?'

The reporters were bouncing off each other.

Sam blinked as another white flash lit up her face.

'There was nothing to suggest those earlier deaths were anything other than tragic accidents,' she said cautiously. 'But it is only right and proper that we revisit those conclusions. Everything is under review.'

'Including the possibility that a serial killer is stalking the town's students?' Sky man was back.

Sam felt the ice beneath her get thinner.

'While everything is under review, there is no necessity to jump to unsubstantiated conclusions and theories. It is important that we follow the evidence.'

'But will more people die while you review everything?'

The Daily Mirror was now in play, the media knife beginning to twist. 'What steps are you taking to prevent more deaths? Have you put extra police officers along the tow path at night?'

Sam looked directly at the reporter. There was a potential trap here. She knew him, knew his reputation: a dog with a bone. She had to answer on the premise that he knew there had been extra patrols but they'd ceased on the Sunday.

'Extra patrols often provide public reassurance but more often than not they actually fail to catch the offender or offenders,' Sam held his gaze. 'While we will endeavour to have officers on the tow path, you will all know that it runs for two miles on either side of the river and we only have a finite amount of resources.'

She paused, all eyes still on her.

'I would urge people not to walk along the path alone, to consider other routes home, perhaps to use taxis.'

'Isn't that admitting defeat?' the Daily Mirror demanded.

Sam let her face register surprise.

'Two people have been murdered on the path in little over a week,' she answered. 'Suggesting people consider how they go safely home is not an admission of defeat. It's common sense.'

'Do you have a message for the killer?' someone shouted from the back.

Even the hacks at the front turned towards the voice.

Sam couldn't have come up with a better question if she had rigged the whole thing.

'Yes,' she answered with careful conviction. 'We will find you. Walk up our path before we walk up yours.'

Press conference over, Sam did one-to-ones with the TVs and radio. She could feel her phone, in vibrate mode, dancing around in her pocket. Interviews finished, she checked the screen. Four missed calls from Ed.

She walked into a secure area in HQ.

'It's me,' she said into her mobile.

'Another spanner,' Ed told her. 'Someone's just switched on Aisha's phone.'

CHAPTER FORTY-ONE

'THEY'RE PANICKING HERE,' Sam said. 'Where's the phone?'

'Geo locator put it in Battersea,' Ed answered. 'Then nothing.'

South London, Sam was thinking. Not Plymouth. Probably at the bottom of the Thames by now.

'They're well and truly spooked,' she said. 'We're barking up the right tree here. I'll meet you in the canteen for a cuppa and a catch-up.'

Ed's rant was a five-star full burner.

'Don't bother,' he grumbled. 'It's full of civvies eating nut cutlets and quinoa salad. No wonder there's never any cops in there... overpriced shite that wouldn't keep a gerbil going.'

'Do you want to try and breathe,' Sam interrupted, but Ed was in full flow.

'Sorry, but how the hell did it ever get to this? My old sergeants would be spinning. There's even some woman with a make-up stall in the corridor! Supposed to be a bloody police headquarters, not some hippie commune hosting a make-up convention. I'll meet you in the car park. We'll go and get some proper food and I'll bring you up to speed. I need to get out of here.'

She heard him breathe deeply, wondered if Ed's blood pressure would survive the rage.

'Hell, what's rattled your cage?' Sam said.

'The lunatics,' Ed snapped. 'They've finally taken over the asylum. They'll be dancing in circles on the grass next, bollock naked with daisy chains on their heads.'

The wooden planks of the pier were soaking. They were standing at the end, leaning against the railings, land behind them, looking out across the grey North Sea, tankers on the horizon heading in and out of Teesport.

They'd agreed to come here as often as they could, an acknowledgement that Sam needed to get over Tristram's death, needed to enjoy the sea again, not fear it.

Ed opened the white paper bag containing his mayo-free sandwich. The wrapper informed him a 'sandwich artist' called Craig had created it with his own hands. Ed knew that already. He had watched Craig make the bloody thing.

Sandwich artist? He was definitely getting too old. He examined his prawn and tomato offering as he chewed the first mouthful. Not exactly a Rembrandt but nice enough, he had to admit.

Sam spoke in between mouthfuls of Tuna savoury.

'You finished whinging for the day?'

Ed nodded, mouth full.

'Good,' Sam said. 'So let me get this straight. Amber Dalton is Elliott Prince's step-sister.'

'Yeah, that's the size of it,' Ed told her. 'He was the

result of an affair his mother had with a merchant seaman. Hubbie had already gone for the snip after they had Amber. Mother tried to explain it away... the operation mustn't have worked properly... but when he threatened DNA tests, she coughed. Elliott was put up for adoption as soon as he was born.'

'And they got in touch how?' Sam asked.

Ed told her he didn't know but it could be done easily enough through the wonders of social media, especially if you had a name

'Seems like Elliott's adoptive parents told him everything,' he said.

'And once he finds her,' Sam said, taking it up, 'if she confides what happened to her, you've got a decent motive for attacking the creeps photographing the girls.'

Ed said that would fit.

'Could explain why he never received a retribution photograph of himself,' Ed reasoned. 'Potentially he's infiltrating. He's another Gatekeeper, this time avenging his sister's honour, as opposed to enforcing honour in Aisha's case.'

Sam knew the theory was still a stretch. Killing the person who raped his sister would have serious weight but killing people who hadn't raped anybody, even if they were taking those pictures?

She watched Ed roll the paper bag into a ball and put it in his coat pocket. 'Remind me not to leave it there.'

They decided to head to Surf Shack for coffee, Ed telling Sam on the way the Bhandals now knew he could speak Punjabi

'Give them something to think about,' she said.

They placed their take-out cups on the wooden table, the rich aroma of the dark, strong Colombian coffee drifting upwards, their noses twitching in anticipation. Sam lit a Marlboro Gold, the smoke ruining the smell of fresh coffee for Ed as he stepped back from the table.

'Quarter to two,' Sam said, studying her watch. 'Do we go for the girls now, or leave it until tomorrow? We're not getting any more from the phones?'

'What about the chewing gum and the cigarettes?' Ed asked.

Sam shook her head.

'Even if we wait to see if we get a profile, we'll have to get their DNA. None of them are on the database.'

Ed took the cup from the table.

'So it's either today or tomorrow,' he said after a mouthful. 'Early doors tomorrow and we should definitely get them... can't think any self-respecting student will already be out of bed by then. Go now and we might not get all of them. Your call.'

Sam was reluctant to keep delaying but doing it now would mean working late and the overtime budget taking a hit.

She worked on her cigarette.

'Say we get them this afternoon, we'll probably only get one interview with each of them today by the time they get briefed up. 8am start tomorrow and we've got them until 3pm before we need a Superintendent's extension. If we go for that option, we'll waste time because we can't interview them in the early hours. Then we'll be at court Wednesday morning going for a Warrant of Further Detention.'

She inhaled again.

'But if we leave it for tomorrow morning, we've got them all day before they need their eight hours rest. Then if needs be, get a Superintendent's extension Thursday morning until 8pm Thursday.'

Sam was saying out loud what she would later write in

her Policy File, explaining her decision-making thought processes.

Ed waited. 'What's it to be then?'

Sam stubbed her cigarette out in the ashtray.

'Tomorrow morning. Logistically, from an interviewing perspective it makes more sense. Some of their phones are down by the tow path, so they've potentially lied. Tracey and Charlotte go into the club with Jack and Glen, both dead now. Alex rings in Jack's death. They've got plenty to answer so let's lock them up for his murder.'

'Okay,' Ed agreed. 'What about Amber?'

Sam found herself tempted by another cigarette but resisted.

'I've been thinking about Amber,' she said. 'She runs a support group that may or may not be the Sisters Of Macavity, but even if it is, so what? We can put her phone in the town centre at the relevant time, but unlike the others, there's nothing to link her to the victims, other than they may have cropped up in her support sessions. Not a lot really. Let's leave her for now. See what the others have to say.'

'And Elliott?' Ed asked.

Sam thought about it, searching for a solid reason to bring him in as well.

She realised it wouldn't work. Yes he might be raging to learn his new found step-sister had been raped – who wouldn't? – but after that?

She paused, took a slurp of coffee and gave up the fight against another cigarette.

'What if Elliott buddies up with Goddard and Jones and the likes after he meets up with Amber?' Sam said. 'Expands on your theory of the Gatekeeper of Honour, just more like the vengeful angel.'

She gripped the cigarette in her teeth as she fumbled for her ringing phone. 'Sam Parker…Hi Bev.'

Sam listened for a few seconds.

'Really? See you soon. We're on our way back.'

She inhaled and blew out smoke.

'I asked Bev to check out Elliott Prince's phone,' Sam paused, Ed waiting. 'On the nights Jack Goddard and Glen Jones were murdered, it was on the tow path.'

Ed's eyes went wide.

'Jackpot!'

CHAPTER FORTY-TWO

By the time Ed was driving home his head felt like a balloon a jab from exploding. The Op Order spelling out which cops were going to which address, who was interviewing who, had taken time and a methodical brain, and while most of it had been done yesterday, the additions, staff changes and what those entailed, needed covering. Every officer's role and responsibility had to be spelled out to avoid major cock-ups.

He'd spent time with Paul Adams, the Level 5 Interview adviser, discussing and preparing the interview strategies for all suspects.

Everything was in place for tomorrow's 6am briefing. All Ed wanted to do now was sit in front of the TV, watch the second half of the match on Sky's Monday Night Football, and eat. Other than the prawn sandwich, he'd had nothing since Richie's fry-up more than 14 hours ago.

He groaned when he saw Eric and Leela's car parked outside, considering turning around and driving away.

Sue had the front door open before he was out of the car. She walked towards him, her voice quiet but urgent.

'Eric needs to speak to you. He looks really worried. Leela's here, but he hasn't told her what the problem is.'

'Okay, okay. I'll have a word.'

He followed Sue inside, whispering to her back. 'I'm sure it can be sorted, whatever it is. Unless he's got another speeding ticket, in which case he'll have to take the points and the ban that will come with it.'

They stepped inside, Sue pointed Ed towards the sitting room and Eric jumped up. Sue was right. He looked terrified.

'Eric, what's up?'

The man was visibly trembling.

'Ed, I overheard something this afternoon in the Gurdwara, something really bad,' he began. 'I'm scared.'

Ed's voice was soothing, hypnotic almost, years of dealing with stressed victims allowing him to drop automatically into 'concerned' mode.

'Okay Eric, sit down. I'll fix us a drink.'

The bottle of whisky was on top of the drinks cabinet. He poured two large ones, handed a crystal tumbler to Eric and sat down. Ed had flown through turbulence where glasses hadn't shaken as much as the one Eric was holding.

'Do you want to tell me what's bothering you, Eric?'

Eric stared into the glass. 'Today, this afternoon, I was looking for something in the kitchen cupboard of the Gurdwara, the walk-in cupboard. Davinder Bhandal and that brother-in-law of his came in. Never liked the look of him. Anyway, they shut the kitchen door.'

He hesitated. Ed shuffled forward on his seat, but said nothing, waiting for Eric.

'They didn't know I was in the cupboard,' he went on. 'I just froze on the spot. They said they're frightened the house is bugged. Davinder said that.'

They'd be right there.

'They can't believe you speak Punjabi. Davinder now knows you are the Gora married to Sue. The brother-in-law, I don't even know his name... '

'Gurmej,' Ed said.

'Well, he was outraged a Sikh woman was with a white man, kept saying it was shameful, that Sue should have married within her own community and that this was what happened when you let girls get Western ideas. They had no respect, no shame and that women like Sue should have been whipped off to India and married.'

He downed the whisky in one.

'Did they say what happened to Aisha?' Ed asked, taking the glass from Eric's hand.

Eric shook his head. 'Not in so many words, no.' He took the refilled glass Ed held out. 'But she's dead. I just know she is. Davinder said they should move the body but the brother-in-law said you'd never find the suitcase.'

Shit! Ranjit at the LP said there was a domestic. Mia couldn't find her suitcase.

'Did they see you?'

'No. The more I heard, the further I backed into the cupboard.'

'Did they say where the body was?'

Eric shook his head.

Ed poured him another drink. 'Eric, tomorrow I'm going to need you to make a statement.'

He nodded.

'We'll do it on video. That way it'll just be like a conversation. Is that okay?'

Another nod.

Where the hell am I going to find a Level 3 Interviewer tomorrow?

After an hour of reassurance, Eric went home with Leela.

Ed immediately made a phone call.

'Sam, it's me. I've had another visit from Eric, my Sikh mate. He overheard a conversation today between Aisha's father and uncle. We'll get a video interview off him tomorrow. He's terrified. Thinks Aisha's dead and so do I. They've buried her in a suitcase.'

Saturday 14th December 2013

It was dark again. I was lying on the bed; my head still hurt and my throat felt like it had closed up. I needed a drink of water. For some reason I remember Bethany telling me how some girl she knew had her own en-suite bathroom. How cool is that? I started to giggle, thinking about getting a drink of water from my own bathroom.

The whisky bottle was still on top of the drawers. It wasn't full now. I'd drunk about quarter of it, hoped it would help. It hadn't.

I had thought about running and jumping into the window, hoped the whisky would help me do it, but even with the drink I knew I wouldn't survive, or if I did, I'd be in a wheelchair. Marrying off a cripple is not easy. I'd end up with someone older than my father.

I thought about agreeing to the marriage. It was better than being a prisoner, or so it seemed until I realised I'd only be swapping one prison for another, and the thought of being imprisoned with Quasimodo as my gaoler...

I could pretend to agree to the marriage. Hopefully that might get some of my freedoms back. Then I would escape again. Go to the police. I'd heard of those Forced

Marriage Protection Orders, read about them in some magazine left in the school, but I just wanted to be away. I knew things would never be the same with my family now.

If I could just convince them into thinking that I'd go along with it.

Maybe it was the sound of my giggling. Whatever it was, I heard the thumping of heavy feet on the stairs. More than one set of feet.

The noise of the bolts being flung back sounded like rifle shots.

I scrambled up, forced myself into the corner, put my knees up to my chest, and covered my nakedness as best as I could. The room was spinning. Maybe the whisky hadn't been such a good idea.

I thought the door was going to come off its hinges. My father filled the frame, his face as red as the Indian sun at dusk, my mother right behind him.

'Look at the drunken slut,' shouted my mother and she pushed past my father, rushed into the room, grabbed my hair, pulled me towards her, swung her arm right back and slapped my face. If the window had been open, you'd have heard the slap across the street.

She bent down, screamed at me. Her face was so close to mine I could feel her spit hitting my cheek. 'We have raised a drunken whore, no better than the white trash she goes to school with.'

My brother and uncle appeared at the doorway.

My cheek was on fire. I covered my face with my hands, screamed as my mother grabbed my hair again. She yanked me up. My shoulder cracked as it hit the floor. Before I could move, hands grabbed my arms. My mother still had hold of my hair and she banged my forehead against the floor, three, maybe four times. I thought my head would crack like an eggshell.

My arms were yanked above my head and I was spun on to my back. I blinked, focussed, and saw that my uncle had one of my arms, my father the other. I was trying to scream 'get off me' but my parched throat wouldn't let the words out.

My back was in agony, on fire again, as they dragged me across the bedroom and on to the landing. I could see my mother at the bottom of the stairs.

They forced me to my feet. A hand shoved me forward. I tumbled, cried out, rolled, and somersaulted. I hit the hallway floor and whimpered. Instinctively I curled myself into a ball.

I couldn't breathe. Were my ribs shattered or was it just because I had never been so frightened? How many people would ever be this scared?

My mother had stood above me as other footsteps descended. The steps were loud, but they weren't hurried. They didn't have to be. I doubted I could have stood up, never mind run.

I squealed when the tops of my arms were gripped again and I was pulled to my feet. I could taste the salt from my tears. My cheek was numb. I felt battered.

I had tried to scream 'help' but still nothing came out.

The uppercut punch flew into my stomach. I doubled up, only the grip on my arms stopped me collapsing. I don't know who hit me, but my mother couldn't punch like that.

My head was swimming. I lolled forward. I wanted to crash to the floor. That old band from the 80s flashed into my mind – Tears for Fears and that song 'Everybody Wants to Rule the World'. I didn't want to rule anything, just my own destiny, just a say in my own life, a life I wanted to fight for... but my fight had gone. I had nothing left.

My dad and uncle hauled me into the sitting room, my legs dragging behind me, my toes burning against the carpet. They threw me on to the settee. The new settee. I landed on my stomach.

Somebody punched me in the back of the head. I was spun on to my back, my eyes blinked repeatedly trying to focus. The blurred outline of my mother, the only sound her rapid breathing.

'Soon it will be you who has to protect the family honour,' she gasped.

I tried to sit-up but a fist smashed into my nose: a massive crack, a blinding white light, gushing blood.

My father put one knee on my chest. Both his hands gripped my throat. I think I peed myself. I focussed on his eyes but they were blank, nothing behind them. He started to squeeze. Blood was trapped in my throat and I retched. The vomit couldn't get past my windpipe, couldn't escape my throat.

The hazy shapes of my brother and uncle had come into view. They were standing behind the settee looking down, just watching. I was past caring about my nakedness. Then fingers had grabbed my nose.

What had I done wrong?

Wanted to go to university.

Wanted to choose my own husband.

Wanted to have my own life.

Was that so wrong?

Was I so bad?

Was that such a crime?

I couldn't move my legs, couldn't breathe. My back arched and again my eyes felt they were going to pop out of my skull.

Where was Mia? Was she okay?

'Get Mia's suitcase.' The shouted, breathless, order had come from my father.

Why did they want Mia's suitcase?

Mia came into my head. Mia and her smile. The last thing I would remember as my light went out.

CHAPTER FORTY-THREE

Tuesday 22nd April 2014

Ed did the 6am briefing, allowing Sam another hour in bed, but neither the extra sleep nor the early morning sun did anything to lighten her mood. She'd tossed and turned all night, wondering what the editor was going to say in print.

She walked into the HOLMES room. 'Morning. Everybody okay? How did the swoops go?'

'All in the traps.' Ed got out of his seat and flicked the kettle the on. 'Elliott and Tracey want a brief. Charlotte's weighing up her options and Alex had daddy notified of her arrest. He's had a solicitor from down south instruct one from up here. Never heard of him.'

'Any of them said anything?' Sam asked.

'No. Alex and Charlotte were crying. Tracey apparently looked like she was going to batter the arresting officer, and Elliott seemed non-plussed.'

He handed a mug of tea to Sam.

'Okay then,' she said, pausing to take a sip. 'What about that other thing, what you called about last night?'

'Bev's going to see Eric in about an hour,' Ed answered. 'He's off work today.'

The HOLMES staff had their heads down, looking at computer screens, reading written documents, but all clearly had their ears tuned into the conversation; they were detectives after all.

Sam walked out, Ed following. She closed her office door behind them. 'Anything from the Listeners?'

'Nothing worth mentioning. Eric was terrified.'

A DC knocked on the door. Sam beckoned him in.

'Thought you'd want to see the Post, boss.'

'Anything in?'

'Page 5,' the detective told her. 'Seen better.'

She took the newspaper and waited until he'd shut the door behind him.

The front page, written by Darius, was a factual account of yesterday's press conference. The editorial was on page 5. She pushed her chair out of the way and bent her head towards the page, Ed alongside her.

Keystone Cops – How many more have to die?

Eastern Police, like the bumblers from a silent movie, are running around clueless, while a predator preys on the young men of our university community. For months the police have said they died as a result of being drunk and falling into the river. Even after the discovery of a second young man on the tow path yesterday morning with fatal head injuries, DCI Samantha Parker announced 'there is no necessity to jump to unsubstantiated conclusions and theories'. Her answer – go home via a different route.

Our response is that we pay the police to ensure our safety, not to suggest no-go areas. Seaton St George is not a war zone, nor is it a repeated target of terrorist activity. If the local police cannot protect us, then I suggest the Chief Constable, his Executive Team, and his Senior Investigating Officers step aside and let someone who knows what they are doing assume command.

Perhaps it is time we all write to our local MP and suggest the Home Secretary looks at police force mergers again.

Would anybody really lament the loss of Eastern Police?

'I'd love to have that bastard,' Sam said, grabbing the paper and flinging it to the floor. 'Slinging shit from the sidelines.'

'Today's shit but wrapping tomorrow's fish and chips,' Ed pulled a chair from the desk.

Sam turned and stared out of the window. *Deep breaths, count to 10.*

'Nothing we can do about it now,' she turned to Ed as he leaned against the wall. 'Best way to stick two fingers up is to box this off but come the moment, I'll have my day with him.'

Ed had been holding in his smile but now he let it go, not just his mouth but his eyes and his whole face.

'That may come quicker than expected.'

'Brighten my day,' Sam said.

'He only got locked up last night by traffic,' Ed grinned. 'Drink-driving.'

Her brow concertinaed like an accordion under the deft fingers of a maestro. 'You're joking?'

'No,' Ed went on. 'Went through a red light. Almost fell out of the car and blew over a hundred on the CAMIC. He's at court this morning.'

She raised her arms above her head, looked up at the

ceiling. 'There is a God!'

'Course he's claiming victimisation,' Ed said. 'But it's not going to get him very far when he's about three times over the limit. He'd been speaking at some black-tie do... and it gets better.'

Ed was enjoying himself, grinning so hard it hurt.

'His boss is a tee-totaller high up in the Salvation Army, family tree back to the Temperance League, and our pissed-up editor also had some female company in the car.'

Sam almost held her breath. 'Please tell me it wasn't his wife?'

"Chantelle Bellvedaire!' Ed delivered the name like a stand-up comic hitting the punch line.

Sam's eyes were as wide as a kid on Christmas Day. 'You're kidding me?'

'The one and only,' Ed laughed. 'Crack addict and street prostitute. He's hours off getting the sack.'

Sam was shaking her head and reaching for her Marlboros.

'This calls for a celebratory cigarette,' she said, making a mental note to have the editor's court appearance flagged up by the press office. 'Come on then.'

Ed asked where they were going.

'I told you, a smoke to celebrate,' Sam waited for his quizzical look. 'And I want to revisit Jamie Telford.'

'The reason being?' Ed asked.

'I want to tell him Elliott Prince's in custody. Ask him if he thinks Elliott could have been the one who sent him the photograph.'

Sam glanced at the silver intercom, found the button for

23, and pressed. The buzzer sounded three times. Nothing. She pressed again.

'Yeah.'

She recognised Jamie's voice, albeit it had taken on the deep Darth Vader version that spoke of too many cigarettes and too much booze.

'DCI Parker. I need a word. Buzz us in.' It wasn't a request.

The door clicked and Sam pushed it open, walking into a communal hall that was surprisingly tidy considering the three-storey block was populated by students.

Jamie was at the door to his flat, barefoot, rubbing sleep from his eyes, the rumpled T-shirt and joggers probably hastily dragged on. 'What's up?'

'We'll tell you inside.'

The small square sitting room had two undersized leather armchairs, the type you'd find in one of those stuffy London gentlemen's clubs, and a blue beanbag. The huge wall-mounted flat screen TV dominated the room.

The detectives didn't bother sitting down.

It was Sam who spoke. 'Elliott Prince is in custody on suspicion of murder.'

'What?!' Jamie flopped into one of the chairs. His hands started to shake.

'Now what I'm interested in is this,' Sam said. 'Could he be behind the photograph that was sent to you?'

'Murder?' Jamie had closed his eyes, fingers running through his hair. 'What are you on about?'

'It's a simple question, Jamie. Do you think he had anything to do with the photograph?'

Jamie rubbed his face. 'No. No, of course not. Why would he?'

'The photographs of the girls, was he up for that?' Sam asked.

'Well he never said he wasn't. Look what's this about? How come you're asking me if Elliott's sent the photographs? Who's he supposed to have murdered?'

Ed sat on the arm of Jamie's chair. 'It's like this, young man. We're wondering whether in fact it was Elliott who got you to pose for the photos. When did he join your little group, Mortimers?'

'When he moved in with Jack and Glen,' Jamie answered slowly. 'I still can't believe they're dead.'

He covered his face with his hands. 'Are you saying Elliott killed them? I'm leaving after this term, try to finish the course somewhere else. Either that or start again. I've never had a night out since Glen died. Why would Elliott want to get photos of us?'

Sam glanced at Ed. 'It is just something we're exploring. Maybe he wasn't into the banter like you all were.'

Jamie reached for the packet of cigarettes on the floor, took one out, and managed to hold the shaking flame of the lighter close enough and long enough for the tobacco to catch. He inhaled. He looked as if he was contemplating an exam question.

When he spoke, it was slow, deliberate. 'You know, I've never considered it before, but now you come to mention it, when he laughed at the photos of the girls it seemed a bit contrived, a bit put on. Maybe he was testing us? You know, see who enjoyed it the most. He never tried to put us off taking photographs, but he always tried to find out who wanted to do it the most. And…' he looked at the floor, his voice dropping in time with his gaze. 'Jack did have some Rohypnol.'

Ed walked away from the chair.

Sam's spoke with thinly veiled contempt. 'Jack had Rohypnol?'

Jamie ran his hands through his hair again. 'Yeah.' Tears fell from his eyes. 'I don't think he used them.'

'Did Elliott know about them?'

'We all did. Jack was just playing the big man.'

'I thought you said Elliott was the leader?' Sam pushed him.

'He was. Jack thought he was, but we always went where Elliott said, always drank what Elliott said. But he never ordered us. He was more subtle than that. He'd plant the seed; by the time we'd decided to do it, we would be convinced it was someone else's idea. It was only afterwards you realised it was down to Elliott. Manipulative, that's what he was.'

Macavity, thought Sam.

The ash hung perilously from the end of his cigarette. Jamie tapped it into the glass ashtray just before gravity did its work. 'Why didn't Elliott get a photo? He was always with us…maybe it was him?'

'Do you remember anything about the night you had the photo taken?' Sam asked.

'Nothing. I can't even remember which night it was, except sometimes, in my dreams, I see bright colours, shapes, and the feeling someone was stood looking down at me.'

CHAPTER FORTY-FOUR

'Move it where?' the voice belonged to Davinder Bhandal. 'It's fine where it is.'

'But what if they find it?' Aisha's mother said.

'They haven't found it up to now have they?' Bhandal said.

'But what if they're watching us? What if they follow us?'

The uncle spoke. 'They've found the car. I said we should have burned it.'

'But they don't know who drove it there, do they?' Bhandal's tone a mix of aggression and defence in equal measure. 'They had Baljit's fingerprints from it but he's explained those away. If they had a witness who could identify him, they wouldn't have let him go. It's the same with the bank card. They accepted it was a mistake.'

'What about the phone?' his wife asked.

'Used once and lost in the River Thames.'

'You hope,' the wife told him. 'You said the settee was burned. I told you not to trust that fat man. Burn the settee, you told him.'

Both officers winced when they heard the slap and the woman's anguished yelp.

'Shut up, woman,' Bhandal shouted. 'If you had brought your daughter up to have less love of Western ideas and more respect for our ways, this wouldn't have happened. I didn't bring you over so you could raise a whore.'

'You let her go to college,' the mother shouted. 'I told you to get her married before she left school. Nobody would have asked where she was.'

The two LP cops nodded. One whispered. 'She's right. They'd have played the racist card and we'd have run a mile.'

The mother was on a defiant roll, red cheek or not. 'You said let her finish college. Why? That's where she met the boy. That's where it all started. I kept her in. College was where it went wrong, and you let her stay.'

This time the sound was a full-blown scream of pain followed by sobs.

'Shut up, woman. Can a man get no respect in his own house.'

The officers looked at each other.

'What do you think?' the younger one asked.

'If we send the cops round to a domestic, they'll wonder who called it in,' the other reasoned, torn between instinct and the integrity of their operation. 'When the neighbours deny it, they'll start wondering… He's hit her twice, though.'

They listened to silence.

'It's quiet now. Give it a few minutes. If it starts again, we call it in via Ed Whelan. We can't sit here worrying about blowing the job when she's getting a hiding or worse.'

When the empty space was filled, it was the uncle who spoke.

'In this country, do they need a body to prosecute?'

'I don't know,' Bhandal told him before the silence returned.

A no-body prosecution was possible but rare and never easy. The prosecution team needed to prove beyond all reasonable doubt that the victim was dead before they even began the task of proving murder.

The older cop explained it when he saw the unspoken question flash across young colleague's face.

'What about the boy?' It was the uncle again.

'What about him?' Bhandal's voice was pitiless. 'Just a worthless piece of humanity. Fox food.'

'Fox food?' the younger cop murmured.

The other whispered. 'Could mean anything, but foxes tend to operate in the open countryside and above ground.'

Perhaps the boy was dead and dumped somewhere, providing they weren't being led up a blind alley.

'We'll mention it to Ed,' the older said. 'Wouldn't be the first time people have found probes and just given us the run-around.'

'Hi Bev.' Sam shuffled in the passenger seat, pressed the phone to her ear, and listened. 'Spot on. Cheers.'

She turned to Ed. 'Everybody's provided a swab. We've got something to compare now. They'll have the profiles off the cigarettes and gum tomorrow.'

Now it was Ed's turn to answer his mobile. 'Tom, how's it going?'

He turned to Sam and quickly mouthed 'Tom King'.

'What, now? We're snowed under today, Tom. How about tomorrow?'

He slowed down and depressed the clutch, one hand on the wheel, the other around the phone. Sam changed gear for him with her right hand. 'Look I'm driving… okay, I'll come now, but we've only got 10 minutes… Where?'

He stopped at the lights. 'Yeah, I know it.'

Ed rang off and dropped the phone into the centre console.

'He says it's urgent,' Ed glanced at Sam. 'We're meeting him on the marina, near Giorgio's pizzeria. He's already there.'

The tall figure of the young doorman stood out, hands in his jean's pockets, staring at each approaching car. He walked over when he saw Ed parking up.

'You remember DCI Parker?' Ed said, as he and Sam got out.

They all leaned against the railings, Tom in the middle, each watching people on the decks of their boats, all busy with ropes and fenders in the way boat people always seem to be busy with something. The fishy smell of the sea was strong but the screeching gulls seemed to be flying higher than usual, the collateral benefit a drop in their decibel level.

'I saw my mother last week.' Tom's eyes never strayed from the marina, his voice flat, without emotion. 'She said you were sound, knew you from the old days as she put it, remembered you were one of the ones who did try to help her.'

Ed spoke. 'I've always tried to be fair, treat people right.

A decent woman your mother, just mixed up with the wrong bloke.'

Tom still stared straight ahead when he spoke again.

'Sunday,' he said quietly. 'I was on the tow path.'

Sam and Ed's heads whipped around to look at Tom. He looked at neither, kept his eyes on the boats.

'I saw one of the dickheads from the pub with a ginger lass, standing under a tree. Certain it was him, although I was on the opposite side. They had their backs to me, but turned around when they heard me. That's when I saw their faces. I know it was dark, but it wasn't too bad, and they used a Zippo to light their cigarettes, lit up part of the faces. Then a lad walked past them, pissed. He was all over the shop. That's it, but my mam said I should tell you, that it might be important. I've given you the benefit of the doubt.'

Ed nodded once. 'When you saw them, were you standing still?'

Tom finally turned his face from the water and shook his head,

'I was walking towards them,' he said. 'I was past them when I saw the pissed lad. By then I had my back to the two under the tree.'

'What time was this?' Ed asked him.

'Half three.'

'Did you see anybody else?'

Tom turned his eyes back to the marina and the slow-churning water, silent for a moment.

'I did see a lass walking towards me,' he said. 'She was on the same side of the tow path as me but I never took any notice of her. I was too busy watching what was going on over the other side.'

Ed shot a glance at Sam.

'Would you recognise any of the people again,' he looked back at Tom.

The doorman looked up to the gulls falling and soaring above them.

'Probably the two under the tree but not the drunk lad,' Tom told them. 'He was bent over, face down at the floor. I remember he was wearing jeans, a T-shirt, and bright orange trainers.'

Sam pushed herself away from the railings.

R v Turnbull spelled out the guidance for identification evidence and she knew any identification by Tom would be open to challenge.

ADVOKATE was the pneumonic thousands of police officers used to remember the rules of identification: A - amount of time suspect under observation; D - distance from the witness; V –visibility... and so on, everything that should be covered in a witness statement when identification was an issue.

Fleeting glimpses, at night and across a river, would be closely scrutinised.

But if Tom's ID evidence was corroborated by DNA profiles on the discarded cigarettes and chewing gum, the case became a little tighter. It still didn't prove Prince and Davies were the killers, but putting them on the tow path when a person wearing the same trainers as Glen Jones was walking towards them less than 150 metres from where his body was found would start to build a case.

'Tom, we might need you to look at some CCTV footage from the club,' Sam spoke for the first time. 'See if you can identify the two under the tree.'

Tom King, tall and brushed with sadness, held her eyes.

'Fair enough, but I'll only do it with Ed.'

CHAPTER FORTY-FIVE

Sam's phone rang. 10.33am.

'Slow down, Bethany. What's wrong? Wait a minute.'

Sam waved the phone at Ed, indicating that he pull over, then dropped her hand to dangle the mobile near her ankle.

'She's really upset,' she whispered.

Her finger tapped the icon for speakerphone. 'What is it, Bethany? Try and speak slowly.'

The voice was ragged and quick, Sam's words lost in the girl's tumult.

'What if Aisha's ran away and it's all my fault because I sent her a photograph on Messenger when she was drunk on a bed wearing hardly any clothes and everybody saw it.'

Racking sobs replaced the anguished torrent, sobs as loud and as quick as the words they silenced.

'Bethany, where are you?'

'Victoria Park.'

'Wait there. We'll be there in 10 minutes. Can you do that for me?'

Bethany was sitting underneath a huge sycamore tree like a child upset or sulking, knees under her chin, head down, and arms wrapped tightly around her legs.

The detectives walked across to her. She looked up, cheeks wet and glistening.

Sam bent down and ran her hand across the last of the dew hiding under the tree, resisting the sun. She sat down beside the frightened teenager. Her trousers would dry. Ed moved a few steps away.

Sam put her arm on the girl's. 'Bethany, the photograph? Where was it taken? How was Aisha drunk?'

The girl looked at Sam, eyes damp. 'We'd been to the Jolly Roger.'

'Aisha?!' Sam didn't mean to interrupt but even as a cop some things still shocked. 'Everybody we've talked to said she wasn't even allowed out.'

Bethany sniffed and rubbed her nose.

'She wasn't, but this one time, maybe a week before her mother told her she would have to marry that guy, we went out. An Asian doctor was having a house party. He saw Aisha's dad and asked if she could come.'

Aisha's dad had been pleased, Bethany told them. The doctor had a son a year older than Mia and Aisha's dad had been happy she was socialising with a doctor, even agreed she could sleep over.

Bethany heaved in some air and looked back down.

'We went with a couple of lads we met in the pub,' she spoke again. 'Ended up in their house. Aisha came over all funny and crashed for a couple of hours on their bed. I was downstairs. I had to give her loads of coffee just to get her back to the doctor's house. I didn't know they'd taken a photograph of her until I saw it on Facebook. I sent it to her on the Saturday, the day after she went missing. I forgot about her family taking her phone. I just never thought.'

Bethany's slender shoulders shook as the sobs returned.

Sam looked up at Ed. Words weren't needed. The photograph, not Aisha's stolen kiss, may have been the final straw.

'So you sent it on the Saturday,' Sam said. 'Okay. Let's go back. It all happened maybe a week before, but it wasn't until the Saturday you sent Aisha the photograph. Why?'

'I only just got it that day,' Bethany answered quietly. 'I'm not Facebook friends with the lads. Elle sent it to me. Elle's from college. It was her older sister who showed her the photo. Her sister didn't know we knew Aisha.'

Sam felt a surge, a snap that zigzagged through her brain.

'What's Elle's sister called?'

'Tracey,' Bethany said. 'Tracey Davies. She had been raging, had messaged me to say Aisha wasn't the only one they'd photographed. She told me not to worry,' Bethany's voice was breaking. 'She told me they'd get what was coming to them. She didn't know Aisha, but she said it wasn't right. I wish I'd never sent it.'

Sam waited for the tears to slow.

'Did you know the lads' names Bethany?'

Bethany's eyes were red, a little swollen even.

'The two who are dead,' Bethany said, so quietly Sam had to strain to hear. 'Jack and Glen.'

Sam and Ed were in Sam's office at Seaton St George police station. Bethany had declined a lift to college saying she'd walk, that she needed the fresh air.

Sam was pacing.

'Tracey Davies just keeps coming more and more into the frame,' she said.

'Let's see if we can find her and Elliott on CCTV on Sunday night, see what they were wearing and go and recover their clothes. Get their shoes.'

Ed looked up from his A4 pad, another scenario taking shape in his mind.

'What if Aisha's family saw the photo? The shame. The anger. What if they identified Glen and Jack, identified the others?'

Sam had been running the same thought but still wasn't convinced the others were linked. They might well have been pushed in, but they could just as easily have fallen. While they had all been on the tow path, only Jack and Glen had head injuries and didn't die by drowning.

She kicked off her black shoes with the sensible heels and continued her pacing barefoot.

'The media, students and stupid editors driving around pissed with prostitutes next to them might think we have a serial killer on the loose, but we're the ones who run the job, decide whether they form part of a series,' she said. 'Jack and Glen almost certainly do. Sneak up behind and hit them with a blunt instrument, albeit different weapons. The blow killed Glen outright. Jack gets finished off with a carrier bag. Both ways their deaths were much more certain than just pushing someone in the river.'

Sam paused and sat down.

Students sadly did drown in rivers. It happened. And if they were tragic but accidental drownings, what better location for a cold-blooded killer than a place where there had already been four deaths.

She had been thinking out loud, Ed listening.

'So if Aisha's family found out about Glen and Jack,

about what they had done, they beat the shit out of them, maybe kill them,' he said when Sam fell silent. 'Even if the family's already killed Aisha, what Glen and Jack were part of would still be seen as an insult to the family, a dishonourable act that would have to be avenged.'

Sam had another moment, struggling to see such a brutal code in play in a small English seaside town in the 21st century.

'Jesus, we're not living 500 years ago,' she said.

'Try telling them that,' Ed snorted.

'Reality is it's just as likely Aisha ran and that the Sisters of Macavity decided to dish out the punishments,' Sam was back on her feet, back on the move.

The ringing phone brought her back to her desk.

'Boss, it's Sharon Gaskarth, down in custody.'

Sam didn't really know the Custody Sergeant. Sharon had not long been promoted.

'Hi Sharon. What can I do for you? I know we've made your morning a bit busier than normal.'

'That's no problem,' the Sergeant said, appreciating Sam's words. 'It's Elliott Prince. He wants to speak to you and Ed Whelan, nobody else. Says he'll tell you everything you need to know.'

'You lot took your time,' Prince said, already rising as the interview door opened.

Ed pulled out a chair from underneath the table, its back legs screeching along the floor. 'Sit back down.'

Sam spoke in a quiet and measured voice. 'You wanted to see us?'

'You might find Glen's blood on my trainers.'

Sam pulled her chair closer to the desk. 'Let me

remind you that you are still under caution. We need to put the tapes on.'

Ed stretched out his legs, put his hands behind his neck, and looked up at the ceiling. Years ago it hadn't mattered what colour they were painted, within months they were nicotine yellow.

The red light went out and the recorder stopped beeping.

'I am DCI Parker. Also present is... '

'Detective Sergeant Whelan.'

'And... '

'Elliott Prince.'

Sam cautioned him. 'Do you wish a legal adviser present?'

'No.'

'Sgt Whelan and myself are here because you asked to see us, and us specifically. Is that correct?'

'Yes.'

'And when we entered the room, without any prompting from us, you said, we might find Glen's blood on your trainers. Is that correct?'

'Yes.'

'Why might we find Glen's blood on your trainers?'

Elliott Prince's eyes shot upwards and to the left, a sure sign of a liar according to body language experts, although they weren't allowed to be experts in the Criminal Justice system of England and Wales, no more than polygraph tests were allowed. Body language could still prove a useful indicator to interviewing detectives, though.

'I stood in his blood…'

Neither Sam nor Ed responded but waited for Prince to carry on.

'... on the tow path. When he was lying there.'

'I think you'd better start at the beginning,' Sam said. 'Take your time.'

Elliott Prince looked from Sam to Ed.

'I was on the tow path. So was Glen. We wanted to catch the killer.'

'What?' Sam needed all her experience not to laugh.

'That night I hid under a tree,' Prince went on. 'Glen walked past me, pretending to be drunk, like we knew Jack was the night he got killed.'

The plan had been simple, Prince told them. Glen was the bait that would flush out the attacker and they would overpower him. Like avenging heroes, they would hand the killer to police.

'But it all went wrong,' Prince said.

'Why choose Sunday?' Sam found it difficult to accept they chose any day.

Prince shuffled in his seat. 'We were going to do it on Saturday but your lot were everywhere.'

Jesus, I hope this is all bull.

'And if nothing happened, what... you'd just keep going back?'

'Something like that,' Prince answered, eyes down.

Sam looked at Ed. If he'd been stretched out on a sun lounger in Kefalonia he couldn't have looked any more relaxed. His face was expressionless, not like a poker sharp's exactly, more a '*what makes you think I give a fuck*' look. It came with years of practice.

'So if that was the plan, what went wrong?' Sam asked now.

'Like I said, I waited under a tree. Glen walked past. We wanted to see who would follow him, but no one did.'

Prince dropped his head, stroked his thighs. 'I need a cigarette.'

'I'm sure the Custody Sergeant will let you in the exercise yard later,' Sam told him, an image of her own cigarettes suddenly flashing.

Prince didn't look up. 'I heard something, you know, like a thud, and I ran from the tree. The further I ran, the more Glen came into view.'

Sam watched his hands move to the table, watched his fingers tighten around the table, watched the blood drain from them. His eyes closed. He was back on the tow path.

'I screamed his name. Got to him. But his head... '

Sam jumped as the edge of his fisted hand banged the table.

Prince looked up. His shoulders started to shake and a sob more like a hunted animal's howl came from somewhere deep inside.

'His head,' he cried. 'You should have seen his head.'

Sam had seen it.

Prince was almost shouting above his tears. 'I knew he was dead. I checked for a pulse. Nothing. I couldn't believe it.'

Neither do I. Sam sat, silent, watching.

'So while you're talking to me in here, the real killer's out there taking the piss.'

Sam winked at Ed, who pushed himself up.

'Anyone with you under the tree?' his first words since the tapes went on.

'No.'

Ed spoke again. 'Under that tree are what I consider to be recently discarded cigarette butts. DNA testing may very well tell us who had them between their lips. You've already given a DNA swab. Now if you're lying,' Ed dropped his voice, 'and believe me, I'm far from convinced that you're telling the truth, but if you're lying about being alone under the tree, then as far as I'm concerned your whole story begins to fall apart.'

Prince for the first time flashed defiance. 'What do you mean?'

Ed shuffled his seat closer towards Prince. 'What I mean is that everything you've said could be nothing more than answering in advance why we've been able to link you with the scene of a murder.'

Prince opened his mouth. Ed raised his hand, pointed the palm at Prince.

'So you see, from where I'm sitting, it's like this: we don't have any forensic evidence yet, but that's not to say we won't get any. You asked us down here to tell us Glen's blood may be on your trainers. So maybe you're getting your defence statement in first, explaining why we've got that forensics on you.'

Prince was motionless, his face still. 'It's not like that.'

Ed stood up and took hold of the door handle

'We'll know soon enough,' he said, turning.

'Tracey Davies!'

Two words that sounded like an exclamation of shock.

'What about her?' Ed said, turning back.

'She was under the tree with me.'

CHAPTER FORTY-SIX

The monotony of everyday life is magnified when you're sitting, headphones over your ears, hearing someone else's daily domestic routine.

Sonia Mitchell found herself listening to Parkash tell her husband about the local gossip at the Gurdwara, and what she wanted him to pick up at Akbars Mini-Market.

The shop, in an area many whites referred to as Little India, had been there since Sonia was a child and it hadn't changed: bunch after bunch of coriander producing the sweet smell she adored, tins of chickpeas, spinach, okra neatly stacked on the shelves; bags of flour the size of builders' cement sacks piled on the floor; kilo bags of turmeric, each cheaper than a little glass jar of the same in the supermarket.

'Baljit!' the mother shouted. 'Time to get up.'

Get up? It was noon. She would never have been allowed to lie in bed that long. Her family were very British in their outlook, she'd married a white, but she was still expected to look after the men in the house. You've got things to do young lady, her mother used to say.

Sonia stood up, stretching and yawning as the headphone leads pulled against their jack-point.

Listening into others' lives was invariably boring, even if gaining vital evidence was a possibility. How people watched reality TV shows for entertainment was beyond her. A recipe for brain death. Shock value, that's all they had going, each becoming more outrageous than the last. At least The Truman Show, one of her favourite films, made her emotional.

Sonia jumped when the front door slammed, lifted the earphones.

'Parkash! Parkash!' It was her brother, Gurmej.

Sonia knew the mother was in the kitchen; she could still hear pots being washed. The plan on the wall, courtesy of the council planning department, indicated how long it would take Gurmej to walk along the hall into the kitchen. Not long, especially when you took into consideration the urgency in his voice.

Sonia dropped into the chair, pen poised, ready for whatever he was about to say.

'Look! Look! Page 7.'

A newspaper? Sonia scribbled 'get today's Post' on a sheet of paper and held it up to her colleague in the LP.

'What's happening?' she heard Parkash speak.

'They're holding a book festival next week,' Gurmej told her. 'The marquees are going up today.'

In the LP, Sonia's colleague was already on the phone to the Intelligence Cell.

'But it's not in there,' Parkash said.

'But it's close!' Gurmej shouted, voice raw with panic.

'What's all the noise about?' It was Bhandal.

'Read this,' Gurmej told him.

Through the headphones, Sonia heard a newspaper rustling.

'Sam and Ed remained in the interview room after Elliott Prince was taken back to his cell. The door was open.

Tracey Davies, accompanied by the Custody Assistant, walked towards them, back ramrod straight, a *don't fuck with me* look etched on to her face.

A young uniform cop walked into the cell area, his instinctive reaction to stare. Tracey Davies was not your typical prisoner... healthy skin, smart and freshly cleaned clothes, and head-turning attractive – a glamour model mistakenly dropped on to the ugly catwalk of incarceration.

She caught the young cop's eyes.

'What the fuck are you looking at?' her own eyes blazing.

He hurried red-faced behind the custody desk, the Custody Sergeant grinning at the put-down.

'Take a seat, Tracey,' Sam said.

'I'm not saying anything. I don't need a brief, but I'm saying nothing.'

Sam raised her eyebrows. 'For someone not used to this kind of situation you seem to know the sketch.'

'I know plenty who've been done over by your lot,' her voice harsh, hostile.

Ed put the two cassette tapes into the machine.

'It's 1.15pm. I'm DCI Parker. Also present is... '

'Detective Sergeant Whelan.'

'And... '

Silence.

'For the benefit of the tape, please state your name.'

Davies folded her arms, turned to face the wall.

'Tracey, for the benefit of the tape, state your name.'

She spun in her chair. 'Fuck sake. Tracey Davies. Satisfied?' She spun back.

'Thank you.' Sam cautioned her and asked if she wanted a legal adviser to be present.

More silence.

'For the benefit of the tape, Tracey Davies is now shaking her head.'

'Oh my God.' She spun to face Sam. 'No, I don't want anybody here. Alright?'

Sam ignored the attitude. 'I want to ask you about your whereabouts last Sunday night. Where were you after 10pm?'

Davies stared at the ceiling.

'We intend to ask you a series of questions,' Sam told her. 'It is your right not to answer, but as I said when I cautioned you, failing to answer now... '

'Yeah, yeah.'

Sam relaxed back into her chair.

Ed hadn't moved. He was back in his reclining position, legs outstretched and hands behind his head. He stayed that way as he spoke.

'Tracey, we have interviewed Elliott Prince,' Ed said. 'He has given us certain information... '

'Don't think I'm falling for that,' she snarled. 'Is that the best you've got? Keeping me in here for sod all, that's what this is about.'

The anger was sweeping off her like heat from a wildfire.

'I can assure you there is nothing to fall for,' Ed told her, his tone patient, unhurried, almost gentle. 'Your friend, Elliott Prince, has given us certain information. As we speak, scientific tests are being conducted and an examination of your phone has already been completed.

Amazing what information can be retrieved. Why any criminal uses them is beyond me.'

Davies slouched forward, leaning across the desk towards him.

'Did you get off on the bits where we were talking about you, saying what we'd do to you,' her laugh dark, humourless. 'I've got news for you. We just wondered what it would be like with a father figure, somebody old.'

She ran her tongue around her lips.

Ed had let the hate wash over him like dead air but now he sat up and moved to the edge of his seat, much closer to her. When he spoke, his voice was quiet.

'Phones, cigarettes, things people take for granted,' his eyes never left her. 'They can yield so many forensic opportunities.'

He paused and saw the flame in Tracey Davies' eyes flicker.

'We will be able to put you on the tow path on Sunday.'

Ed sat back.

Geronimo and his Apaches believed that after death the spirit left the body. Ed and Sam saw Davies' arrogance float out of her. They'd seen it in interviews all their careers – resignation followed by admission.

'You don't get it do you?' she said, her voice changed.

Sam and Ed waited.

'Yes, I was on the path. Yes, I was with Elliott. Glen was pretending to be drunk. We weren't trying to kill anybody. We were trying to stop someone killing.'

Sam already knew the answer to her next question.

'Who, Tracey? Who were you were trying to stop?'

She looked at the floor, closed and opened her eyes in a slow heartbeat, and whispered. 'Amber.'

They had restarted the interview after a 30-minute break, Sam and Ed grabbing coffees and regrouping.

By the time Ed set the tapes rolling again, some of Davies' anger had been rebooted.

'What that sick bastard did to Amber... ' She was spitting out the words, the veins in her neck bulging. 'Raped in your home by some masked arsehole who sticks a knife at your throat and then rings you up afterwards.'

Sam had been the first person Amber had told about the attack, a memory of that day shooting into her mind.

'I know how hard it was for her,' Sam said, meaning it. 'She went through something unthinkable and came out the other side. She even told me she was going to start a self-help group.'

Tracey slid down the chair.

'That's what Amber did and it was good,' she said. 'She understood. None of us had been through what she had but she got it. We'd talk about sexual harassment, the online bullying, and those fucking photographs. 21st century yet it's worse than it's ever been, even at uni and that's supposed to be full of the educated.'

She shook her head and glanced at the ceiling before her eyes settled on Sam again. 'Actually, half of them are thick as pig shit. The place is full of immature lads who can't see past what's in their pants. It's why lots of us go out with older men.'

She glanced at Ed, no lip-licking this time.

'Did nobody think of reporting it to the university authorities?' Sam asked.

'What, for nothing to be done?' Her bone-cold laugh again. 'What would be the point? Anyway, things changed when Amber got back in touch with Elliott. She told him and that's when the photographs of the lads started. Tit-for-tat, Amber called it. Elliott did the photo shop trick.'

'What trick?' Sam asked her.

'They were on their hands and knees but the dildos were photo shopped,' Tracey said. 'The camera never lies and all that.'

When she asked for water, Sam paused the interview, recording that Ed was leaving the room. A minute later he was back and gave Tracey a plastic cup filled with cold, filtered water. She gulped it down in a rush.

'Detective Sergeant Whelan is back in the room,' Sam said for the tape. 'You were telling us how things changed when Elliott came on the scene.'

Tracey took a deep breath, remembering, laying out the path that had led her here.

'Amber wanted to do more,' she said. 'Talking never achieved anything and she wanted to be, what she called, pro-active. Her favourite phrase from then on was 'nothing was ever resolved over a cup of tea and a biscuit'. We thought that was funny at the time. Amber told us we needed action. Elliott volunteered to set them up. Rohypnol and us girls did the rest. Next thing, the photographs.'

Tracey fell silent but her face stayed fixed on Sam, defiance glowing deep in her eyes.

'Amber reckoned you had to fight fire with fire, and I agreed with her,' she said. 'Sending those photographs was liberating, 'girl power' and all that.'

Sam asked another question she had already answered herself.

'Was the group called Sisters of Macavity?'

'Yeah, that was just a laugh,' Tracey said. 'I can't remember who came up with the name. It might even have been me.'

Sam knew it was still a leap to turn Amber from a victim spreading photo-shopped revenge to a ruthless killer, no matter how much fire she had been ready to light.

'Why do you think Amber was responsible for the murders?' she asked now.

Tracey looked surprised, and said: 'Who else could it be?'

'Amber always said posting the photographs wasn't enough for Jack and Glen. They needed worse. Me and Elliott both thought she'd killed Jack. It just fit.'

'And if she'd turned up the night you were all on the tow-path?' Sam asked.

Tracey said they wouldn't have gone to the police.

'We weren't going to grass. She needed help so we would have tried to get her to a psychiatric hospital. If that got us into trouble further down the line, so be it. Amber never admitted any murder but we thought she needed re-wiring. Now there's two dead.'

When Sam asked about the others who had died, Tracey said the Sisters of Macavity were just a 'talking shop' then, that Elliott wasn't yet on the scene.

Sam steered the interview back to the photographs of the sleeping girls, aware that Tracey had slipped into a comfort zone, everything about her now radiating control.

'Amber was furious with Glen and Jack for sending out those photographs, I mean, fucking furious, and when she found out about the young Asian girl running away because of them, she was even worse.'

'When did she find about the Asian girl?' Sam asked.

'A couple of days before Jack got killed.'

Sam glanced at Ed. 'But when we spoke to Bethany Stevens, that's your younger sister's friend, she said she sent the photo to Aisha on Saturday 14th December.'

Tracey's defences began to trigger on reflex.

'That might be right, but I'm not talking about, what was her name, Bethany,' the voice edged. 'I'm talking about Amber.'

Sam pushed. 'But Bethany says you told her not to worry, that, and I quote, 'they'd get what's coming to them'. Do you recall saying that?'

'Hey, I might have done,' Tracey said. 'Sounds like the type of thing I'd say when I'm pissed off, but you're talking about December. Elliott and Amber hadn't even met up then. Nothing had happened.'

Sam smiled, watched Tracey fold that comfort zone back around her. It was time.

'You see, Tracey, the problem I have, I'm not sure I believe anything you say.'

Tracey jumped up, sudden fear powering an adrenaline surge and panic masquerading as outrage.

'Are you calling me a liar?' Her voice was too loud, too forced.

'Sit down, Tracey,' Ed said, his voice slow, as if she'd just disturbed him from an afternoon nap.

'It's her, calling me a liar!'

'Sit down, you're giving me a bad neck looking up at you.'

Tracey theatrically dropped on to the seat, her outstretched arms and open mouth resembling the footballer who can't believe the referee thinks he took a dive.

'I happen to agree with her,' Ed said.

Tracey glared at him.

'What night do you have your Macavity meetings?' Sam said.

'You know, you saw us. Tuesdays.'

'So every Tuesday you meet, and yet you only mention the Asian girl to Amber a couple of days before Jack gets killed, even though you told Bethany not to worry back in December.'

'Yeah.'

'This all sounds a bit convenient.'

Tracey pushed against the desk, the chair legs screeching against the floor.

'Don't move,' Ed said.

Tracey relaxed her arms but her voice was still tense and loud. 'She's calling me a liar again.'

'Going back to Sunday,' Sam said, unmoved. 'You tipped Amber off that Glen was out. Then what?'

Tracey took a breath. 'We hid under that tree and then Glen staggered past, pretending to be drunk. Nobody followed but then we heard something, like somebody running. Glen never shouted or anything but I just knew something had happened, I just knew.' She wiped her left eye. 'When we got there it was horrible. Glen dead. Amber vanished.'

CHAPTER FORTY-SEVEN

It would be another 40 minutes before the Intelligence Manager could get hold of Sam and Ed for a face-to-face meeting. While Tracey was in the mood to talk, they had wanted to get as much information as possible.

The story was on page 7 and written by a reporter whose name Ed didn't recognise. The story told how Lord and Lady Farquarharson opened the land at Highmounde Hall, their ancestral home, for many events, among them classical music concerts, charity garden parties, and an annual book festival now in its fifth year. Ed read and made notes on an A4 pad.

'If we start searching just hours after they were talking about it, they're bound to get suspicious,' Sam sipped a black coffee; the milk in the CID office was so far gone, it was cheese. 'We need a way of doing a covert search. I don't want a media frenzy, I don't want anybody being tipped off, and I certainly don't want to be sent on a wild goose chase by people who've sussed we're listening to their conversations.' She sat on the edge of a desk.

'I might be able to help.' Ed blew across the top of his coffee and delayed saying anything else just long enough to make sure he had her attention. 'Brian Banks is doing the security for the literary festival and... '

'Jesus, he gets where a draught won't,' Sam butted in. 'I thought he was scrap metal and property?

She bit on her bottom lip and shook her head slowly from side to side.

'Diversification.' Ed slurped his coffee, black and bitter. 'Look, whatever he is or isn't, I've known him for years.'

'What you suggesting then?' Sam asked.

'Get a couple of security uniforms off him and send a couple of our search team in to have a look around. Better than going in all guns blazing.'

Sam's brow creased with concern, wary of getting a helping hand from someone like Banks.

'It'll be fine,' Ed reassured. 'I always keep him at a safe distance. We'll make something up about what we're doing, counter terrorism maybe. He'll love that. Leave it with me. And you know, if there is a body close to the marquees nobody will try to move it for fear of being spotted. We've got as long as the literary thing is on to find it.'

Sam squeezed shut her eyes, a headache ticking like a time bomb at her temples.

'I can't drink that.' She stood and placed the mug on the desk.

'Okay, work up a plan, the usual stuff, including a risk assessment. Let me see it before we put people at the hall. Did you find out how we're doing with your mate Eric?'

Ed told her Eric had done a video interview that gave up nothing they didn't already know.

'Bev Summers has found Elliott and Tracey on CCTV,' he went on. 'Listed their clothing. She's gone to recover it.'

Sam felt like her head was bursting.

'Excellent,' she said, trying to ignore the pain. 'Next steps, you sort Banks and I'll go for Amber. I know her. No need to make a big show. In and out.'

Ed told her to be careful, that if she'd already killed two...

'What, she'll kill me?' Sam said. 'I doubt it.'

'Well take a radio with you just in case.'

'Yes Dad.'

Ed sat in the car, enjoying 10 minutes solitude, his jaw barely moving as he worked on a steak and kidney pie. His hand reached for the ice-cold Pepsi in the drinks holder. Pity it wasn't in a glass bottle; much nicer, or was he just harking back to his childhood?

He swirled the fizzy drink around his mouth, the pie gone too soon even though he'd chewed slowly. He was still regretting not asking the butcher for two when he drove into Brian Banks' scrap yard. Banks was expecting him.

'Ed Whelan, as I live and breathe. Long time no see. What's this favour you're after then?'

His huge hand enveloped Ed's, the cordial handshake a sign of mutual respect.

They walked to Banks' cluttered office, both standing as Ed laid out what he needed.

'So let me get this right,' Banks said. 'You want to put two cops in my uniforms to, what was that phrase, sweep the area for devices? Like bombs you mean?'

Ed nodded, sipping the Glenfiddich and water.

'Pardon my ignorance but does Health and Safety allow that?' Banks demanded. 'Are my staff going to be in danger?'

Ed said to let him worry about health and safety and risk assessments.

'It's a precaution, Brian, belt and braces job,' he said easily. 'There are a couple of high-profile international authors attending. Bomb sweeps are becoming standard practice.'

Banks's face darkened, his mouth a scowl.

'Fucking world we live in. Who do you blame? Bush? Blair? Muslims?'

He downed his drink and set the crystal tumbler on one of the dust-surrounded circles on the silver tray.

'Enoch was right,' Banks grumbled. 'If they'd listened to him, we wouldn't be in the sticky stuff. Jesus, the garbage they've allowed into this country. Left-wing do-gooders. Shoot the lot of them.'

Ed was familiar with the invective, always amazed Banks in his ingrained hatred could swat aside Ed's own domestic situation.

'So I take it that's a yes then?' he asked lightly.

'Always happy to be of service.' Banks raised his refilled glass. 'Just do me a favour and keep some of those enthusiastic young detectives off my back.'

Ed raised his eyebrows.

'Since the powers that be stopped us buying with cash, they're in the yard twice a week,' Banks told him. 'Half of the lads who come in here selling stuff have never had a bank account.'

Ed knew the law had been changed because too many dealers – Banks maybe among them – were conveniently forgetting to ask where the so-called scrap had last resided.

'My heart bleeds,' he said with a grin. 'Now where do the lads pick up the uniforms?'

Sam knocked on the black door. It had been painted since her last visit and the garden was well kept.

'Amber.'

'Sam.'

'Can I come in?'

She was across the threshold and walking into the sitting room before Amber had time to answer.

'What is it, Sam?' Amber questioned, perplexed as she followed.

Sam stayed standing, legs apart and hands on hips.

'I need you to come to the police station with me, Amber, to answer some questions about the murders of Jack Goddard and Glen Jones.'

Amber sat on the arm of the chair. Her voice was shaky and quiet. 'Am I being arrested?'

'Not at the moment.'

'What does that mean Sam?'

'It means not at the moment,' the voice clipped, commanding. 'Now get your coat. Let's go.'

They walked in silence down the path and got into Sam's car.

Amber pulled the passenger door; it was heavier than she expected. 'What's this all about, Sam?'

Sam turned to look at her.

'Let's cut the shit, shall we?' She turned the ignition. 'Put your belt on.'

Sam pulled the Audi from the kerb, the sound of the engine a symphony to power and German engineering.

'You've not been totally honest, Amber. You knew about the photographs of the girls, knew the name of the group, your group. I've cut you some slack. I've come for you. I didn't send anyone else to arrest you and search your house.'

She flicked one of the stalks on the steering column and turned left at the junction, Amber silent and still in the passenger seat.

'I'm giving you a chance here. Elliott and Tracey are under arrest.'

Amber jolted. 'Elliott? What for?'

'Murder.'

'No way.' The response was instant. 'Not Elliott, not Tracey. They're all talk.'

Sam slowed for a roundabout ahead, glancing at Amber who had swivelled in the seat to stare her way.

'They've come up with a good reason why they were on the tow path the night Glen was killed, but it all sounds a bit convenient to me,' Sam said. 'And what do you mean, they're all talk?'

'They wouldn't hurt anyone.'

She clasped her hands together and pushed her head into the headrest.

'Amber, any more lies from you and nobody will be able to help you,' Sam said, stealing another glance.

'Look, I haven't done anything,' Amber's face had drained, white tension lines around her mouth. 'They haven't done anything.'

'How do you know? Were you with them on the tow path?'

Amber turned and looked at Sam. 'Of course not, but I know my own brother.'

'Something else you conveniently forgot to mention.'

Sam's phone rang, Ed's name and number lit up on the screen.

She pulled to the kerb and picked up the mobile.

'I'll not be long, Amber,' Sam said, opening the driver's door. 'Stay put.'

She closed the door and leaned against the bonnet, back to her passenger. 'Go ahead, Ed.'

'I'm back in the Incident Room,' Ed's voice sounded far away, the signal not strong but good enough. 'The DNA's come through on the hammer handle. The one used to kill Jack. It's Elliott Prince's.'

CHAPTER FORTY-EIGHT

SERGEANT IAN ROBINSON, a Police Search adviser, was wearing a Banks Security jacket with his police issue trousers. He approached two of Banks's men who were stood by a large marquee. 'Alright lads, what's the craic?'

The elder of the two, greasy, wavy brown hair, jacket unzipped and vast stomach hanging below his crotch, spat gum at his feet.

'Just look busy and draw your wages. Piece of piss.'

'We've been told just to wander around the perimeter,' Ian said.

A grunt and a shrug before Ian and his colleague moved away.

'Nailed on for the after-dinner speaking circuit if he ever gets sick of security,' Ian said, glancing back as the man tried and failed to hitch his pants over his stomach.

They had reached the middle of the field furthest from the house and adjoining a public road, a 12-feet-high brick wall marking the boundary of Highmounde, open moorland rising in the distance.

Shooting probably made more money than a literary

festival, but from what Ian had read, James Farquarharson enjoyed wandering among authors, agents, and publishers.

Ian studied the perimeter wall, barely visible behind mature shrubs, trees and undergrowth, no doubt as old as the house.

He was mindful of the CATCHEM database, initially kept by Derbyshire Police, but now housed at the Police College Bramshill in Hampshire. The database held the details of every child murder in the UK since 1960. In those cases where the bodies had been dumped, the deposition site was rarely more than 50 metres from the road. While a child had not been murdered in this case, the 50-metre rule still applied.

His other thought revolved around the Winthrop search method, initially developed by the British Army and used in Northern Ireland to locate caches of arms. In its most basic guise, it required the searcher to put themselves in the shoes of the secretors: a dark game of hide and seek.

Ian knew the roads outside the walls. If a body was hidden near the wall, and on this particular field that was the only place it could be hidden, then those responsible had two choices: come on to the field to dump the body, or throw it over the wall. There was a wooden gate accessing the field and two lay-bys adjacent to the wall a few hundred yards apart. To throw a body over would require a pair of ladders and someone with enough strength to perform a 'fireman's lift'.

Ian opted for the wooden gate first and walked the 200 metres to it. 'This looks a good bet,' he said to his colleague. 'Access to the road and a lot lower than the wall. We've got one shot at this and if we blow it, if we miss something, we'll be doing school crossing patrols until we retire.'

His younger colleague licked his lips and nodded nervously.

'We'll stick together and only move when we're both satisfied we've seen nothing,' Ian told him. 'We've got plenty of daylight so there's no rush. If we have to come back tomorrow, we have to come back, although I feel a right twat in this uniform.'

His colleague smiled, still nervous. 'They might let us keep them as a souvenir.'

The plan was to search 75 metres in each direction from the gate. Ian had noticed when he checked a map before they arrived that a river ran by the wall.

'Right, let's crack on,' he said. 'And be careful when we're near the water.'

Sam was pulling into the station car park, silently thanking the God of rank and privilege that a bay would be waiting.

They had talked about Elliott, how Amber had felt when she found out she had a brother, how shock had given way to excitement and discovery, and how they never stopped talking.

Sam had listened but now she had a question.

'I want you to think very carefully,' Sam said. 'Did you tell Elliott about your attack?'

They opened their doors and got out, staring at each other across the Audi's roof.

Amber's words were slow and hesitant when she answered.

'I did... not straight away, but I did,' she told Sam. 'But please don't think that sent Elliott off on some kind of crazy revenge, sent him hunting down the men he thought could do to another woman what was done to me.'

They walked across the car park.

'Were they?' Sam asked. 'Were Jack Goddard and Glen Jones those kinds of men?'

Amber stopped and turned to face her, Sam letting the question hang between them.

'If you're asking do I feel any sadness for Jack Goddard and Glen Jones, I'm sorry but I don't,' Amber said. 'They were vile and arrogant and thought it was funny to publish the photos of those girls. To me they got what they deserved. They're no loss to society.'

The words were stark and matter-of-fact unemotional, the hatred in them ice cold. Sam felt like she was suddenly watching a glacial bird of prey, pitiless and unforgiving.

'I agree it was vile, but are you telling me their punishment fitted their crime?' she asked, as they began walking again.

'Any retribution should be considered a possibility.' Amber stopped again. 'Who knows what they would have become, how many women they would have hurt? Their deaths may have spared more victims like me and if that's true, I can't be sorry they're dead.'

They walked on in silence and when they reached the station, Sam opened the door.

'When we get inside I'll have an officer sit with you for 10 minutes,' Sam said. 'I've got to see someone first.'

'I've driven up there,' they heard Baljit say. 'There's no police. Just marquees and some private security.'

He was speaking English so the LP team assumed he wasn't talking to his mother.

When the answer came, they had been right.

'Even private security can find things, report them to the police,' Bhandal told his son.

The officers heard a snort then Baljit again.

'Come on, Dad,' he said. 'Private security? They're not interested in anything apart from doing as little as possible, and to find it they'd have to be really looking or very, very lucky.'

'I shouldn't have listened to you and Gurmej.' Bhandal's voice was edgy and angry. 'Burying is much better than just hiding and hoping for the best.'

Baljit response came rich with the confidence and certainty of spoilt youth.

'You were going to burn the car!' It was almost a taunt. 'Then the police would have looked for the owner, much more suspicious than people running away from home. Yeah, they might have found the car now, but they're months behind. The trail's gone cold. They've got my fingerprints but no witnesses. Even if they find a body, so what? What's it got to do with us?'

The LP officers heard a door open and close then Bhandal saying: 'I don't like it.'

'Look, we had little time,' Baljit said. 'We did the best we could. It'll be alright.'

Bhandal started speaking Punjabi, explaining that Baljit had been to the 'big house', as he called it.

'No police there,' Bhandal said. 'But I'm just worried it's found.'

Aisha's mother was the next voice, sharp and spiteful and betraying no fear.

'If it's found, what has it to do with us?' Parkash said. 'If they drag us to the police station, we'll make complaint of racial harassment. The solicitor, what's her name?'

'Jill Carver,' Baljit said.

'She'll make complaint for us.'

The sound of a door again, more distant, and then Mia.

'Hi everyone,' she shouted.

The LP officers were missing nothing, even when Parkash whispered: 'Change the subject.'

The tape was running. Ed cautioned Elliott Prince and held up an open-topped box covered in clear plastic. Inside was a yellow-handled hammer.

'I am showing Elliott Prince a yellow-handled hammer, witness reference JT4. Do you recognise this?'

'No, should I?'

'The blood you can see on the metal ball is Jack's, the handle is forensically linked to you,' Ed told him. 'We can show you have had possession of it'

Elliott Prince was still staring wide-eyed at the weapon.

'That's not possible,' his voice hoarse, strung out. 'I've never owned a hammer in my life. If it's got my fingerprints or whatever, it's a mistake or a set-up.'

'So you've never owned a hammer?' Ed said.

'Never,' the response as fast as a rifle recoil. 'Why would I want a hammer?'

'Protection.' Ed leaned back. 'Or to use it for what it was intended, you know, putting nails in a wall.'

He had put the box behind him but when Elliott asked to see it again, Ed reached back, picked the box off the floor, and held it up.

Elliott stared at it again while the seconds became a minute on the red timer of the tape machine.

When he spoke, it was quietly. 'I used one like it once, a few months back, to put up a picture.'

'In your house?' Ed asked him.

Elliott shook his head, his eyes never leaving the hammer.

'I put a picture up for her in her bedroom,' he said. 'I bought it for her, the picture, a pencil sketch of two ballerinas.'

'Who?'

Elliott finally moved his eyes from the weapon and put them on Ed.

'Amber,' he said softly, almost sadly. 'She got the hammer from a toolbox in her downstairs loo. The box was always open.'

'And when you finished putting the picture up?' Ed asked him.

'Went downstairs and Amber put the kettle on.'

'And the hammer?'

Elliott looked like a man emerging from a mist.

'I put in on top of the toolbox.'

Ian Robinson was bent down, hands on knees, looking into the dark undergrowth. The ground dropped away from them down towards the narrow, shallow river, its flow speeding as it rushed between the protruding rocks. Upstream, Ian could see a waterfall about 10 metres in height, the falling water dropping into a deep plunge pool, moss and foliage covering the nearby rocks and stones.

They were about 30 metres from the gate. Progress was slow, their eyes having to continually re-adjust from the bright sunshine to the dappled shade of the deep green foliage. He didn't have his police issue Public Order leather gauntlets, a loss that had left his hands and wrists a reddened mix of nettle stings and hawthorn scratches.

Ian blinked, focussed, rubbed his eyes, and focussed

again. He bent further forwards to pull a couple of stubborn, knotted branches apart.

Standing up straight, he told his colleague to stay where was. He fumbled in his pocket for the mobile and rang Ed Whelan.

'Perfect timing mate, I've just walked out of an interview,' Ed said in answer.

'I'm at Highmounde,' Ian told him. 'We've found a body.'

CHAPTER FORTY-NINE

'Ed, where are you?' Sam asked, speaking into the phone.

'CID office upstairs.'

'Meet me in the DCI's office. He's off today.' She put the phone back in her pocket.

Ed walked along the corridor, the bare walls harbouring decades of stories and secrets. *More whispered meetings than in any office.*

Sam was sitting on the desk. 'How did you get on with Prince?'

'Before I update you on that, there's something else. Ian Robinson found a... '

'Body!?' she interrupted, jumping down. 'Aisha?'

'Don't think so,' Ed said. 'Looks male, although it's difficult to tell. SOCO en route. They'll need to cut back some of the bushes and undergrowth to get at it. Looks like it's been carried over a gate and rolled down. Might have been thrown over the wall but there's no lay-by at that point and they'd have needed a ladder. Probably too dodgy.

Easier to pull into the lay-by next to the gate, get it over and roll it down.'

'How far from the gate?'

'Within the Catchem limits,' Ed said.

'Okay.' Sam was forcing her mind to slow down. 'Before we shoot up there, what about Prince?'

'Says he used the hammer to put up a picture at Amber's,' Ed said. 'According to him, it's her hammer and I believe him.'

Sam leaned against the desk as Ed carried on.

'I believe him about the blood on his trainers, I believe him about the hammer, I believe him doctoring the photographs and I believe he believes Amber's the killer.'

Sam shuffled back so she was once more sitting on the desk.

'Pretty convenient, all his excuses for the forensics.'

'That's why I believe him,' Ed said. 'It's too well thought out.'

'Are you still thinking it's got something to do with Aisha?'

'Can't get it out of mind,' Ed told her.

Sam stood and walked towards the windows, dismissing the idea of sneaking a forbidden cigarette.

'If it is Amber's hammer, how did Aisha's family get it?'

Ed had been expecting that, the Achilles heel that left his nagging hunch a hobbling wreck.

'That's where my hypotheses falls down.'

'I'll get Bev to interview Amber,' Sam said. 'She took the statement from her for the rape so she knows her. You'll need to give Bev a quick update about Prince's interview. Then we'll go and see what Ian's found at Highmounde.'

'Have you seen this hammer before, Amber?' Bev asked. 'For the benefit of the tape, I am now showing Amber Dalton a cardboard box with a plastic see-through lid, referred to as Witness Reference JT 4, containing a yellow-handled hammer.'

Amber looked.

'It's similar to one I have in my toolbox at home. Not that I use it.'

'We believe this hammer was used to kill Jack Goddard,' Bev said.

The 'Oh my God' seemed genuine, the apparent shock that flooded Amber's eyes was harder to judge.

'Mine's at home,' she said after a pause, 'Go and check. The toolbox is in my downstairs toilet.'

'I intend to,' Bev told her.

Sam phoned Ian Robinson from the car.

'Ian, make sure someone's got a camera. Photograph any onlookers.'

They both knew what the stats had to say about offenders returning to the scene, albeit in this case the scene was more likely a deposition site.

The line was faint and scratchy. Ed could just make out Ian's voice on speakerphone, but not what he was saying.

'Okay, me and Ed are on our way.' She disconnected the call.

'Ever had any success with that, the offender returning?' Ed asked her.

'Not yet. You?'

'Not personally, but I've known it to happen.'

Ed told Sam he would need to ring Brian Banks, to tell

him before he heard it from the media and realised Ed had been playing him.

'He's useful at times so I'll keep him sweet,' Ed said. 'You see his lordship to tell him what's happening on his turf and I'll ring Brian.'

Ed turned into the driveway of Highmounde. In the distance they could see the marquees, the SOCO van and a high-top Ford Transit.

Ed pulled up outside the stately home and Sam walked up the sweep of immaculate stone steps. A beanpole butler opened the huge oak doors and Sam stepped inside, her wide-eyed gaze taking in the Gone With The Wind staircase and galleried landing.

She was shown into a heavily furnished study where beanpole asked her if she would please wait. James Farquarharson joined her within a minute, hand outstretched as he strode into the sunlit room.

Sam took the hand but not the offer of a seat that came with it.

'I'm here to tell you we have found a body in your field, near to the marquee.'

'Good God,' Farquarharson spluttered. 'How long has it been there?'

Sam could never quite predict the first thing people asked once they heard about a body. Farquarharson's was another odd one.

'No idea yet,' Sam told him. 'But we'll obviously keep you abreast of all developments.'

'Yes, yes. Thank you.' Farquarharson was reaching for the right air and expression.

'Will it, err, affect the Literary Festival?' he asked, at least dusting a little embarrassment over his words. 'I don't wish to sound insensitive but the organisers have done a fantastic job and we have authors coming from around the country.'

Amazing, Sam was thinking. *We wouldn't want something as inconvenient as a body to put the good and great off their bedtime reading, would we?*

'I'm sure we will be off-site by the time the festival starts,' Sam said, giving Farquarharson what she hoped was an understanding smile.

Ed was perched on the wing of the car when Sam rejoined him.

'Some people and their priorities,' she said. 'Unbelievable…you sorted with Banks?'

'Yeah.'

'Let's walk across the fields then. I could do with the exercise. And I need to get some food. I can't remember the last time I ate.'

They walked until they came to a stile and dropped into the field where the festival was to be held.

'We need to go through the transcripts from the Bhandal house with a fine tooth comb,' Sam said. 'If this body is anything to do with them, we need to start building a case.'

'The transcripts are already there. It's just a case of what you want doing with them.'

'I want every mention of the body putting into a summary,' Sam said, strategy taking rapid shape. 'Time, date, who said it, what was said, the works. I remember 'fox food' being mentioned, which is interesting given where we are.'

Julie Trescothick walked across to meet them. They were 20 metres from her van.

'Body is a male,' Julie said after a brief greeting. 'Decomposition has set in and no doubt a few animals have had a nibble, but it's only the top half of him that's decomposed. The bottom part's been jammed in the stream, so with the cold running water, it's been pretty well preserved. Trousers and trainers are intact, upper clothing looks like it's been torn... animals probably.'

'Age and ethnicity?' Sam asked, as always liking Julie's work.

'Not sure about age, but he's Asian. His legs may be freezing, but his skin tone's still obvious.'

Ed recalled Sue's conversation with Mrs Maan, glad he drilled her to get a description of the young lad who'd been attacked, what clothes he was wearing.

Now he repeated what Sue had been told... white T-shirt, dark blue jeans with zips in them, and lime green trainers.

'Could be,' Julie said. 'He's certainly wearing lime green trainers.'

Thank God it was no longer a world full of Adidas Sambas, Ed thought. Made things so much easier.

'I'll get on to control room,' Sam said. 'Get them to give Jim Melia a call. He'll enjoy this one, poking around a body that offers something different. He can hold the floor next time he's swapping stories with his pathologist chums.'

Call made, she turned to Julie.

'Come on then,' she said. 'May as well have a look.'

The interview door opened.

'Let's put another set of tapes in the machine,' Bev said.

'Did you find it?' Amber rushed.

Bev waited until the beeping of the machine stopped before she began talking, reminding Amber of the caution.

'A search of your house has been undertaken.'

'And?'

'There's no hammer in the toolbox.'

Amber's face sagged, her open mouth a disbelieving oval.

'There must be. Where else could it be?'

'You tell me,' Bev said, watching as closely as she was listening. 'Or perhaps you already know?'

Amber had drawn into herself, knees tight and shoulders hunched.

'That one you showed me. That's not it. It can't be.'

'Then how is Elliott's DNA all over it,' Bev turned the screw.

'I don't know? Ask him.'

'We have,' Bev said. 'He said it's the one he used to put a picture up in your house. He says he's never touched another hammer even remotely like it.'

Bev thought she saw a shadow of desperation cross Amber's face, her eyes searching.

'He must have. That can't be mine.'

'Why not, Amber?'

'Because I haven't hurt anyone.'

Bev looked at her notepad, reminded Amber how she had reacted to Jack Goddard and Glen Jones's deaths.

'So you see the predicament I'm faced with here, Amber?' Bev said. 'We have a hammer we believe is a murder weapon, a hammer Elliott says belongs to you. You accept you own a hammer like it but can't tell us where it is. You can see where I'm going with this.'

Amber had put her palms flat and hard on the table, her whole body drawn tight with tension.

'I can but you're wrong.' Her tone was so strong it took Bev by surprise. 'You've got to believe me, Bev. It's nothing to do with me. I trusted you last time. You have to trust me now.'

'Are you saying that Elliott stole it?'

'No, I'm not saying that at all.' Bev saw the tension ebb away like a blood pressure cuff deflating. 'I know he didn't.'

'Could somebody else have stolen it?'

'No, of course not. No…unless.'

Her chin rested on her chest.

'Amber, can you remember one of the other victims attacked by the same person as you? She was called Danielle Banks.'

'Vaguely.'

'She was the one who found a broken window but presumed that it was caused by her ex-boyfriend. That presumption caused her not to get the window fixed that night.'

'I think I can remember.'

'Well humour me,' Bev said. 'Here's a pen. Write down everybody who has been in your house since that hammer was last used.'

'Elliott was the last to use it.'

'Okay then. Write down the names of the people who've been in your house since then. Are there many?'

'Not really.'

She took the pen and started to write.

Bev was watching her. The names were upside down as she was looking but upside down or not, she bit her lip when she saw the fifth name. She didn't want Amber to know.

By the time Amber had finished the list – five minutes that felt more like five hours – Bev was buzzing.

She needed to get out the interview room quickly and call Sam.

CHAPTER FIFTY

'I NEED A BEER.'

It was Baljit, only just returned. The listeners already knew his mother and father were in the kitchen. They heard the 'whoosh' escape from the can and imagined the foam spewing out. Baljit reverted to Punjabi. 'They've found him.'

'How?' Parkash demanded.

'I don't know,' Baljit said. 'But there's police everywhere... blue tape, people in white suits. It's like something off the TV.'

'There's nothing to link it to us,' his mother said, almost dismissive, arrogant. 'Keep calm.'

Sonia Mitchell was scribbling down the salient points. *She's a cool one.*

'Your mother's right,' Bhandal said. 'They cannot link him to us. If they try, remember to ask for Carver.'

In the LP, Sonia could hear Baljit slurp again then crush the empty can.

'They'll try to link him with us, though,' he said. 'They've already linked him with her.'

His mother broke the short silence.

'They need more than links,' she said, 'They haven't got any and they haven't got her.'

'They will never get her.' Bhandal's voice was ice. 'She's gone for good.'

'Who's gone for good?' It was Mia.

Sonia hadn't heard her come down the stairs. *She was very quiet. I wonder.*

'A girl on my course,' Baljit said quickly. 'Her family has moved down south. She was in my group. Now we have to do her work as well, otherwise it won't get marked.'

This lot can lie without breaking step. It'll need a good interviewer to sort them.

'Any food?' Mia asked.

'I'll make Dahl,' her mother said. 'I'll call you when it's ready.'

Sonia heard the door open and close.

'Do you think she heard?' It was Bhandal.

'I don't think so,' his wife answered. 'Keep an eye on her, though.'

I heard. I heard everything. Who have they found? If it's the police it must be a body. Who else wears white suits and puts tape up. But what did Baljit mean about them making links? Were they talking about Aisha and that lad she was seen with in the shopping centre? He can't be dead! Where is he, though?

And who's gone for good? Not some lass from uni that's for sure.

Why can't we ever talk about Aisha? Why did we have to play happy families and get that photo of us all on the settee, the night Aisha was locked in her room? Why did I have to go to my auntie's that night? Why did the papers all say Aisha went missing on the Friday? Why is Aisha's name banned in the house? Why is she dishonourable? So she didn't want to marry some 'Freshie'. Big deal. Who would? Freshies... on their way to England or just arrived, bringing their stupid rules of expected behaviour with them.

I'm scared now. I've been scared since Aisha ran away. What if my family has done something to that lad? I've overheard my parents talking, talking about the shame. I think I'm going to have to step into Aisha's shoes. I'm going to have to marry the bloke she ran away from marrying. I don't blame her for running. She told me he was ugly. But what if I have to marry him?

Things were bad before Aisha ran away, the two of us being monitored all the time. But it's a million times worse now. My mother walks me to school, can you believe that, and meets me at the gate on an afternoon. I'm 15 and I'm getting walked to school.

We have a Diversity Officer in the school. She's Punjabi, keeps asking me if I'm alright since Aisha ran away. I just keep saying I'm fine; like I'd tell her any different. She'd be straight round to my parents if I said anything out of turn.

Why do they keep giving these diversity jobs to Asians? Give them to white people. I've heard the arguments... 'Oh they don't understand our culture.' Guess what? Asians say that so whites can't infiltrate. It lets them keep control while they smile sweetly at English society, the same society where that social worker wanted to put me in a 'culturally appropriate' placement. Put them where they'll be looked after, not just where the carers have the same colour skin.

I'd like to tell Mrs Leadbitter at school that I think I'm going to be forced to marry. She's really nice, but what would she do? I'm scared she won't believe me, or worse, she goes and talks to the Diversity Officer for advice.

I've decided I'm going to run. I don't know where yet, but I have to run. Aisha was scared she was going to be married when we went to India to see our grandparents. Me? I'm scared I'll be married and left there.

I can't run from here. They all watch me like a hawk, especially Baljit. He's the worst. I can understand my mother. She came here to marry my dad and never integrated. If you ask her, she probably hates it here. My dad just wants a quiet life so he does what my mother tells him, even if he has to look like he's always in charge. But Baljit? He was born here but goes on like he's a Freshie, talking about Izzat. Him and Uncle Gurmej. He's horrible. Aisha was always saying how he gave her the creeps. I think I know what she meant. I've started to notice him watching me, like a dirty old man perving over young lasses.

So I know I have to run from school. We get an hour for lunch. That's when I have to go. Get a head start, before anyone knows I've gone, before my mother and the whole neighbourhood come looking for me.

I know if I get caught it will be big trouble. I'll never see England again. To have one daughter run away is shameful, but two? My mother would never get over it.

So I have one chance. I cannot waste it and I cannot take anything with me. I have to go in the clothes I'm wearing. I know I have to run. I just don't know where.

'Bloody hell,' Sam said as she and Ed bent down. 'Gone six already.' A mounting pile of discarded foliage and branches were stacked up near them, Julie Trescothick making it grow ever higher.

'A little early for Bonfire Night,' Ed said.

'Thought I'd take some cuttings for the garden,' Julie didn't miss a beat.

Ed smiled. 'Touche.'

'You'll get a better view of the body now,' Julie told them as Sam and Ed took a couple of steps forward. It was impossible to tell whether the body had been thrown or rolled into the stream, impossible because the undergrowth had grown back. What was obvious was that the water had preserved the lower part of the body. The corpse was laid on its back, but from the waist down it was completely submerged in flowing water, not a torrent, but not a trickle either.

'I don't know how full this stream gets,' Julie said. 'But the slope of the land and those floods in January won't have seen it dry up.'

The face had almost vanished.

Ed, hands on knees, started to hum an Elton John song from the Lion King movie.

Sam swivelled her head, scrunching her brow. 'Any reason why that song?'

'Circle of life,' Ed said. 'He's dead but he's fed others.'

Sam shook her head. 'Bloody hell, Ed, only you could bring Walt Disney to a rotting corpse.'

She turned to the SOCO chief. 'Julie, do what you need to do here, photos, and we'll do the rest at the mortuary. We'll search his clothing there as well. I'll arrange a fingertip search once you've finished but I'm not hopeful. Jim's on his way, so we'll wait for him.'

'Have you considered anybody else Sam?' Julie said.

'Forensic Anthropologist?' Sam understood. 'I'll speak with Jim. We might need to involve one at some stage.'

'What a job,' Ed joined in. 'Trying to work out how

long somebody's been dead from the state of maggots in the body.'

Sam dismissed Ed's throwaway line, well aware of the skills the scientists could bring to the table, even when they were faced with nothing more than a skeleton.

'I've known them be spectacularly wrong,' Sam said. 'But they can get it right and they can aid in identification.'

She straightened up. 'And you know my maxim.'

'Surround yourself with experts,' Ed said.

Sam nodded. 'Too right... scientific, search, interviewers... whoever. If it progresses the job, I'm all for them.'

She stopped and answered her ringing phone. It was the DI from Devon. Sam listened.

'Great. Thanks. Look, I'll speak later. I'm just about to go into a meeting.'

She ended the call.

'Their undercover op in Plymouth has finished,' Sam said. 'The UC will provide a statement identifying Baljit as taking Sukhi's car into the garage.'

Sam and Ed both turned as Jim Melia walked towards them.

'This should at least provide the literary festival with a start for any creative writers' workshop,' Jim said.

He then imitated the clipped tones of an aristocratic thespian. 'The decomposing body of a man was found in the grounds of a stately home, continue.'

He had a paper and pencil in his hand, ready to make a rough sketch. 'So where is he?'

Sam, still holding her phone, realised she had an answer-phone message.

Seconds later she was listening to Bev's urgent voice, then moved away and made a call.

'I've been trying to get hold of you,' Bev told her. 'Amber said her hammer was in a toolbox in her downstairs loo but I've searched and it's not there. She's not had a break-in so I got her to write down everyone who's been in her house in the last couple of months. It's not a long list but her study group, four of them, met there on the day Glen was murdered. One name jumped out.'

Sam felt an adrenaline kick. 'Who?'

'Baljit Bhandal.'

CHAPTER FIFTY-ONE

Where've they all gone? What was their rush?

'Wait here,' my mother shouted to me. 'Do not leave the house.'

Typical. The only time I'm left where I can pack a few clothes and I'm not ready yet. Will I ever be ready?

I turn on the TV, open the sour cream and onion Pringles, stretch out on the settee, and channel hop through boring news and quiz shows.

I miss Aisha. I hope she's happy. I wonder whether she's somewhere with that lad. I don't know him but I hope he's okay.

I'm outside now, sat on top of Dad's new garden shed. Why did he want a shed? He doesn't do gardening. Not that we've got much garden anyway. It's all paved over now, same as Uncle Gurmej's. He's got a new shed as well. They both got them the same day, thinking about it, not long after Aisha ran away. Maybe they're going to make some of that illegal booze. What do they call it? Desi. Indian firewater.

But something's definitely happening today. They're all

panicking. No, it's more than that. They're shitting it. I love that phrase. Nobody's ever heard me say it, though. I wouldn't dare. That would have me whisked off to India on the next flight. Punjabi Airways: speedy passage for overly Western girls.

Here's the rain. Typical. I've not been left alone since Aisha went. As soon as I get the chance to do something I would never be allowed to do, climb on to the shed roof, it rains.

I spoon the Dahl out of the pan. It's good. My mother's a good cook. So am I. That was her mission in her life. Make sure her girls can cook.

There's still nothing on the TV, just people you've never heard of interviewing people you've heard of even less.

The house is so quiet.

I know where the squeaks on the stairs are. I can get up and down in total silence. Aisha could as well. I know Baljit can. He sneaks in when he's been clubbing. Hypocrite. Tells me not to look at men, look at the floor, only speak when I'm spoken to, do what he says all the time, and there's him clubbing, ogling all the white girls.

He always gets his own way. Do you think I'll get a car like he did? No chance. I didn't even get a bike when we were kids. He did. Golden child. I had to count myself lucky I got a pair of roller skates. Lucky me.

I try one of the doors upstairs. I cannot remember the last time it was unlocked.

That multi-coloured spread on my mother's bed is so tacky. And so heavy. She must sweat like a pig. Probably stops my dad trying to have sex with her. *Oh that's gross.*

She keeps the passports in her bedside drawer.

There they are. I grab them. All there except for Aisha's. Did she take it with her?

Now I can see the plane tickets. Heathrow to New Delhi. Four tickets. Must be the trip to see our grandparents. Here's mine. I quickly compare it to the ones for Mam, Dad and Baljit.

My hands are shaking.

I read them again. Check them again.

Mine's one way.

Why?

I don't want to answer. There's only one reason.

I run out of the room, slam my bedroom door behind me and sit on the edge of my bed. I'd chew my fingernails if my hands weren't shaking as much.

Then the front door slams shut.

Sonia Mitchell heard Parkash shout. 'Mia! Mia!'

Footsteps on the stairs.

A heavy silence.

Whatever was happening, Sonia couldn't hear.

More shouting from Parkash. 'Davinder! Davinder! Come here!'

'What is it?'

Footsteps running up the stairs.

Silence again.

Sonia breathed deeply, held her breath. What was happening in that house? Every possible scenario flew through her head and almost all of them ended badly.

Wait or act? Sit back or send someone in?

The silent seconds felt like hours. Sonia was in NASA control centre, that nail-biting period of radio silence waiting for the astronauts to re-enter the earth's atmosphere.

Give it a few more seconds. How many?

Her ears were straining that hard she felt they would start to bleed.

Footsteps.

Sonia stiffened. Took another slow, huge lungful of air.

Running water; a pan or a kettle being filled?

Someone was downstairs.

'Sit down, sweetheart.' It was Parkash again. 'What were you doing in our bedroom?'

Sonia exhaled, bowed her head. *Thank God for that.*

She had 'ears again'.

'You're not in trouble,' said Parkash. 'But I see you've seen our surprise.' Her voice was full of compassion, no anger.

'What surprise?' Mia shuffled on the seat. She'd left the passports on the bed.

'That we're letting you stay with your grandparents all summer. We can only go there for three weeks but we thought you might want to spend all the holidays with Papa-ji.'

Silence.

'You always said you wanted to, didn't you? Stay with grandad?'

'Yes but…'

'But what, darling?' More soothing tones.

'My ticket is only one way.'

'And you thought… Well, I don't know what you thought.' Parkash started to laugh. 'Come here, little one. You thought we were going to leave you? Is that it?'

Silence. Maybe a nod from Mia, thought Sonia.

'Don't get upset, little one. Of course we weren't going to leave you.'

'We would never do that, Mia.' It was Bhandal. 'You can only book tickets so far in advance. We couldn't get you a return. Nearer the time we'll get you one and send it.'

'I thought you were going to leave me there because of Aisha.'

'Aisha has shamed us.' It was the mother, voice full of scorn. 'She has run away and now I cannot look at anybody in the Gurdwara. She has betrayed us. But you... ' her tone changed, quiet, melodic. 'You have done nothing wrong. You're a good girl. We just want you to be happy.'

Sonia Mitchell had heard enough.

'Get the boss on the phone,' she told her colleague. 'She needs to know about this.'

I'm back upstairs now. I don't know what to believe. I want to believe them. You don't want to think your parents are going to leave you in a dusty village in the middle of nowhere where running water is a luxury, to marry a bloke old enough to be your dad, do you?

But I never thought they'd force Aisha to run away.

That guy was coming here to marry Aisha. Once he'd done that, his parents would come over and Aisha would be running the house surrounded by Freshies. And when I say 'running', I mean waiting on them hand and foot. Who could blame her for not wanting that life?

But it could be even worse for me. I might be left there. My ticket was one way, and I know Bethany's grandma goes to Benidorm for six weeks in January and she must get a return ticket because she hasn't got a computer. She can't remember it's called the Internet, never mind use it.

At least here Aisha could have had the TV or radio on in the background. Over there? You must be joking. I'm not talking Delhi or Mumbai or Goa. I'm talking a small village in the Punjab.

Drive down to the supermarket? We've done the Tudors at school. It would be like Henry VIII asking one of his courtiers to pop into Tesco for a couple of wild boar steaks for tonight's banquet.

Grandad's rich by their standards – he has a tractor, even if it's old. Loads of them still use an ox and plough.

Car? You're doing well if you have a moped.

The people all seem happy, but they don't know any different. My mother yearns to go back because she never settled here, never integrated. But me? Aisha? We're different. We know nothing other than this... England, and all the technology and convenience that go with it.

Honestly, if you went there, you'd feel like a time traveller. Going backwards obviously.

Would they really leave me there?

CHAPTER FIFTY-TWO

SAM WIPED egg mayo from the side of her mouth and reached down into the foot well of the car for a tissue.

'Wonder how Jim's getting on at that other job in Newcastle? Kiddie murders. Never good.'

She wiped her fingers. 'Our body can wait for his PM until tomorrow. Gives us a bit more time to concentrate on the Bhandal family.'

Ed, sitting behind the wheel, gulped from the plastic bottle of Fanta – no Pepsi in the shop - before answering. 'We'll need it.'

'Yeah, but don't you just love it when a plan comes together? ' Sam said. 'The whole bloody family captured on a digital photograph behind the blue tape. Even the uncle.'

'Uh huh,' Ed said.

'I want to get Mia to a Place of Safety tonight,' Sam went on. 'I know they'll not take her on a plane tonight, but I don't want to give Carver or anyone else the opportunity to say there was no risk otherwise we'd have acted sooner.'

She dropped the tissue. 'Then tomorrow I want to start on the application for a Forced Marriage Protection Order. Bev and Paul Adams can meet us after Bev's bailed Elliott and Tracey. Amber's never been arrested so she can just be allowed to go. If we need to get them back in, so be it.'

'What do you want to do about the rest of Aisha's family?'

Sam paused, thinking it through.

'Baljit can be arrested tonight. He's hidden the car. The UC will identify him. Lock Baljit up on suspicion of theft of a motor vehicle. Recover his shoes. Every pair. Leave the parents and the uncle to stew. See what tomorrow brings. There'll be the PM, a press conference and no doubt a bit of grief from Jill Carver.'

Ed told Sam to make her calls while he drove.

'Tell Bev we'll rendezvous at Morrisons, the big one on Newcastle Road. Get some uniform back-up there. We'll need transport for Baljit and Mia. And tell them in the LP to keep their ears open.'

Ed knocked on the Bhandals' front door. Sam, Bev and Paul stood behind.

Baljit opened the door. 'What the fuck do you lot want now?'

Ed stepped towards the door and took hold of Baljit's arm just above the elbow. 'You're under arrest for theft of a motor vehicle... '

'What? Get off me.'

He tried to pull away but Ed yanked him on to the street. The marked Ford Focus moved from its position further up the street.

'Stop pulling,' Ed said. 'You're going nowhere.'

A uniform cop jumped out of the front passenger seat, slapped the quick-cuffs on Baljit, and walked him to the car.

He was being driven away before Bhandal came to the door.

'What is going on here?' he demanded.

'Is Mia home Mr. Bhandal?' Sam said.

'What have you done with Baljit?'

Parkash appeared at the doorway, followed by Mia.

A heated exchange in Punjabi took place between the couple.

'Your son has been arrested for theft of a motor vehicle,' Ed said, the voice of authority. 'Sukhvinder's vehicle.'

'That's ridiculous,' Bhandal shouted.

'And now,' Sam said, stepping forward. 'I'm taking Mia to a place of safety. I'm making an Emergency Protection Order.'

Bhandal's hatred and rage were boiling over.

'You're not taking her anywhere,' he shouted, spit flying from his lips.

He turned to his wife and spoke quickly. Her aggression echoed her husband's.

Ed switched to Punjabi. 'We have every right to arrest Baljit and to remove Mia.' He leaned closely in towards them. 'This is not rural India. The laws of the Elders hold no sway here. The only law is the law of the land, this land, England. I am coming inside with my colleagues to search your house. If you try and stop us you will be arrested for obstruction.' He looked over his shoulder. 'Let's go.'

'You come with me Mia.' It was Sam.

'What's happening? Why do I have to come with you?'

'I'll explain in the car.'

'Stay where you are,' her father barked. 'Don't you dare move Mia.' He stared defiantly at Ed.

'I don't intend having a tug-of-war with your daughter's arms, but she is coming with us.'

Parkash had moved away from the doorway.

'She stays here!' Bhandal pushed Mia back into the hallway.

Ed stepped forward, shoved him out of the way, and put his arm around Mia's shoulders.

'Come on sweetheart.' He ushered her towards the door, towards Sam.

Sam felt her phone vibrate against her leg, a text that would have to wait.

Later she would learn it was from Sonia in the LP.

Kitchen drawer slammed. Knife?

Sam took hold of Mia's arm. 'Come with us now.'

Ed watched them walk to the car then turned around ready to start the search. Bhandal, eyes full of hate, looked towards the kitchen at the same time as Ed.

Parkash was running towards them, a long piercing scream escaping from her lungs and a steel cook's knife above her head.

Paul moved fast, grabbed Bhandal around the neck from behind and dragged him out of the house. Bhandal flayed his arms and kicked his legs as his heels scraped along the floor.

Parkash launched herself at Ed, who never took his eyes off the knife. He tried to side-step her like a rugby fly-half but the hallway was narrow and she was on him as he grabbed for her wrist, both of them falling to the floor. Ed rolled on top of her and punched her hard on the temple as her eyes fired wild fury.

He heard the breath rush out of her and watched those burning eyes cloud into unconsciousness as he slowly struggled to his feet. He felt no pain, even as he saw the blood stain spreading like a rip tide from the collar of his shirt. When his knees buckled and the shadows closed to blackout darkness, Ed let himself drift to an ocean deep and starless.

CHAPTER FIFTY-THREE

OUTSIDE, Bhandal was laid on the pavement on his stomach, arms cuffed behind his back. Neighbours were starting to come out of the houses. Youths began to gather, menace on their faces, ready for confrontation.

Sam had run from the car when she saw Paul grappling with Bhandal.

She saw Ed where he had fallen and her stomach lurched as she rushed to his side, dropping to her knees and ignoring the blood pooling around her. Parkash was still motionless a few feet away.

Sam saw the knife close by and rose to kick it away before kneeling beside Ed again, her voice high and tight as she repeated his name.

Sam grabbed the radio from her coat pocket.

'Ambulance required. Officer stabbed. Repeat officer stabbed.'

She shouted for Paul, pulled off her coat, and pushed it hard against Ed's neck, whispering 'no, no, no' in fear and disbelief.

'Paul!' Sam shouted again. 'Get a towel...anything.... Ed's been stabbed.'

Paul sprinted into the kitchen and had pulled open three drawers before he saw a tea-towel hanging over the back of a chair.

He grabbed it and ran back into the hall.

Sam snatched it off him.

'Stay with me Ed,' she said, as she pushed the tea-towel against his wound with one hand, throwing her blood sodden coat to one side with the other.

She cradled his head and applied more pressure to his neck.

'Where's the fucking ambulance?' Sam barked. 'Paul don't just stand there. Go outside. Keep hold of the husband. And keep an eye on Bev and Mia. Make sure they're alright.'

'Stay with me Ed,' Sam said again. She kept the pressure applied with her left hand and held the radio with the other.

'DCI Parker…ETA ambulance?'

'En route. ETA five minutes.'

'Roger.'

She bent down and spoke softly into Ed's ear, tears dripping onto his face.

'Five minutes and we'll have you out of here, Ed. Five Minutes. Don't you dare leave me. Don't you dare...'

Outside Bev watched the ever-increasing crowd. There were probably about 20 now, but social media would allow a call to arms to spread quickly.

'I'm scared,' Mia said.

'Don't worry,' Bev told her. 'Do you know those lads over there? Not the parents, the lads?

'Most of them.'

Bev grabbed a pen and a piece of paper from the glove-box, handing them to Mia. 'Write down their names for me.'

From the hallway, Sam glanced outside and spoke into her radio again.

'Further assistance required: two prisoners need transportation, one already en route; angry crowd gathering, request Public Order Unit ASAP. Ian Robinson is up at Highmounde. Divert him.'

'Stand-by…Public Order Unit en route. ETA two minutes. Serial comprising sergeant and six.'

'Roger.'

A few feet away, Parkash had begun to come round, slowly pushing herself into a seated position against the wall.

'Don't you fucking move,' Sam shouted.

Parkash, eyes locking on Ed and the blood turning sticky on Sam's hands, stayed where she was. You didn't need English to understand what Sam was ordering.

On the street, Bev got out of the car and took half a dozen photos of the mob on her iPhone. She bent down and spoke through the car door.

'Stay there Mia. I'll not be long.'

She walked over to the crowd. She could make out Bhandal, now on his feet, standing in the middle of the youths, the position of his arms, pinned behind his back, signalling he was still cuffed.

Bev shouted. 'You need to clear this area. Move away or you will face the possibility of arrest.'

'By you darling? I don't think so.' Young Mr. Gobshite clasped his teeth together and made a clacking sound.

Bev stared at him; twenty, thin, hair bouncing over his eyes, skinny jeans tight over feminine legs. All mouth and no action.

'Not just me arsehole,' Bev said. 'You might want to take a peak over your shoulder, you little piece of shit.'

She flicked her head to the left. The agitator and his group followed with their eyes and saw seven officers piling out of a van.

'Pity,' skinny said. 'I'd have liked sorting you.'

Bev smiled. 'In your dreams.'

A forearm Popeye would have been proud of grabbed him and dragged him out of the crowd. The shaven headed, brick-outhouse-sized owner of the forearm glared. 'You're locked up. Section 5 Public Order. Threatening words and behaviour.'

Skinny's bravado melted as the forearm squeezed tighter. If eyes could shit themselves Skinny's suddenly had a bad case of diarrohea.

'I suggest you all take a wander,' Bev shouted.

The group parted when they saw the paramedics run from their ambulance as two more police vehicles driven by members of the Major Incident Team screeched to a halt.

Bhandal was put into the back of the first one.

'In here,' Sam called.

Ed's body suddenly jerked upwards, a movement quick and contorted and uncontrolled.

Sam had seen enough trauma injuries to know what that meant.

So had the paramedics.

Heart attack.

Sam bolted to the front door, slammed it shut and watched Ed jump like some emergency-ward actor beneath the defibrillator.

Three times he bounced before the female paramedic said they needed to move him.

Sam sniffed back her tears. 'I don't know if it's connected to his heart but he passed out a few days ago.'

'We'll get him checked out love, but right now we need to go.'

Sam quick-marched alongside the trolley squeezing Ed's hand, oblivious to the gawping bystanders and their mobile phones.

Paul Adams pulled Parkash Bhandal to her feet. Unsteady, she wobbled like a boxer recovering from a knockout and glanced at the bloodied knife on the floor.

'Don't even think about it,' Paul said.

She spat once in his face.

Paul had never hit a woman in his life but at that moment he seriously considered an exception.

'May as well add assault to your ever growing list,' he said instead, wiping his cheek before grabbing her wrist.

Ed was carried into the ambulance and Sam put one foot on the step.

'You sure you should be going Sam?' Bev had walked across the road. 'There's loads need sorting here.'

'I'm going,' Sam's voice told Bev the decision was made and cast in stone. 'Take Mia to my office. Tell Paul to oversee the arrests.'

'We need to go now ladies,' the paramedic in the back of the ambulance said.

Sam climbed inside and shut the door.

Bev watched as it pulled away, all sirens and flashing lights.

The only female member of the search team walked over to Bev.

'Will Ed be okay?' she asked.

Bev's eyes never left the ambulance. 'Hope so.'

'The boss seemed upset.'

'What do you expect?'

'More partner upset than boss upset.'

Bev's turn was snappier than anything she had ever managed on the parade square at training school all those years ago. Her tone was acid.

'Watch your mouth. You haven't earned the right to speak like that. Now fuck off and keep your mind on the job and your stupid thoughts to yourself.'

Mia looked relieved when Bev reached the car and slid back behind the wheel.

'Is everything alright?' she asked.

'Hope so,' Bev told her, the image of Ed unconscious still hanging like dark art in a gallery in her mind. 'Come on, let's find somewhere for you to stay tonight.'

'What will happen to my parents...my brother?'

Bev said they would be interviewed, asked some questions.

'About Aisha?'

'About many things.'

'Do you think Aisha is dead?' Mia asked now, her voice small, frightened.

'Do you?'

Mia waited long seconds before she answered.

'I didn't, but I'm not so sure now. There've been funny things going on since she left. They all rushed somewhere this afternoon. I don't know where. We've got a new shed, never had one of them before, and a new patio and I don't know why. And my suitcase has gone missing and I know Aisha didn't take it. She would have taken her own.'

Bev was trying to process what she was hearing, trying not to make reflex conclusions. *You should be here Sam.*

'Let's go to the office. We can talk there.'

Bhandal was shouting into the custody office telephone - his legal advice call.

'They've taken Mia! My wife and son have been arrested! My wife was beaten up. I was thrown to the pavement and handcuffed like a common criminal.'

Jill Carver listened.

'Don't allow them to interview you,' she said. 'I'll speak with the custody sergeant. You all need to be medically examined before anything else. I will make sure that happens. Who were the arresting officers?'

'Parker, Whelan and some other man and woman,' Bhandal said. 'It was that man who threw me to the ground. Kicked me as well.'

'Well just sit tight,' Carver sounding calm. 'Put me onto the custody sergeant.'

Sam jogged alongside the trolley, the small, squeaky wheels turning faster and faster as it gained speed along the straight corridor before crashing through the double doors.

A small, squat nurse appeared from behind them and stepped in front of Sam.

'Now love,' she said, placing a hand on Sam's shoulder. 'There's nothing you can do for him here.'

She combined a small smile with a look of concern in the way only nurses seem able to do and gently closed the doors.

Sam stood and watched them slowly come together, acknowledging what her feelings had left at stake.

Head reeling, stomach churning, she turned and walked rapidly through the hospital and down the pedestrian ramp away from A and E. At least twice she thought she would collapse.

In the cold air she bent over and put her hands on her knees. Ed's dried blood was on her hands and her trousers. Her tears splattered onto the concrete.

There had been a hospital on this site for generations, its elevated position overlooking the sea once considered a health benefit for those suffering from tuberculosis; patients wheeled out onto the lawns to breathe in the clean coastal air.

How many tears have been shed here, Sam wondered.

She stood up and shivered and reached for a Marlboro. Thank God they weren't in her blood sodden coat still lying like a voiceless extra at the Bhandals. She saw a security guard wandering around the car park, making his way towards her. She shivered again.

You'll need balls of steel to tell me this is a non-smoking site.

Sam inhaled and launched into a coughing fit, the reason she never heard the high heels clip-clopping behind her.

'I should have guessed you'd be here.'

Sam didn't turn around but the security guard made a hasty about turn, not prepared to referee a female fight on minimum wage and a zero hours contract.

Sam took a deep breath and at last turned slowly to face Sue Whelan.

'Sue.'

'Where is he?'

An origami master couldn't have put as many folds in Sue's twisted, contorted face.

'Surgery.'

'Well there's no need for you to hang around is there? His wife's here now, and she doesn't want you around when our daughter comes. And if anything happens to him…'

She saw the blood on Sam's hands and ran up the ramp.

'Tell me about your suitcase?' Bev said.

Mia was in Sam's office, a bottle of Pepsi on the desk, a bag of cheese and onion crisps in her lap, salt already on her fingertips.

'It just vanished,' Mia said. 'Aisha was locked in her bedroom when that settee came on the Saturday. I don't know how she escaped, but it wasn't on the Friday like my dad told the police and TV. My suitcase was there the day the settee came. I know that because I keep old clothes in there and I was looking for a headscarf when the settee came. My mother said I could go in the room and look for it. My uncle let me in. He was guarding Aisha. Aisha was on the bed. She was naked.'

Mia stared at the wall and put a handful of crisps into her mouth without moving her eyes. The crunch was loud, aggressive.

The crunching stopped. Mia was thinking of something.

'Aisha's little case…the pink one. I've just remembered. It wasn't there. They were next to each other, under the bed…I can't remember seeing it when I was looking for the scarf. Maybe Aisha did take mine. Maybe she did get away.'

Bev needed to be careful. Interviewing a juvenile

without the presence of an appropriate adult, even though Mia was a witness, was not best practice. That said, she could justify it if she needed some vital information and she needed it quickly.

'What does your suitcase look like Mia?'

'Red with brass buckles,' she told Bev. 'Hard…and it had a leather label holder attached to the handle and my name and address written on the paper inside.'

'What size?'

Mia held her arms wide.

'Oh it's big. One of the big ones we take when we go to India.'

'And the shed and patio you told me about,' Bev asked now. 'When did they appear?'

Mia thought for a moment.

'The Sunday afternoon after the settee was delivered,' she answered. 'My dad, brother and uncle put it up and laid the patio. I'd never seen them work so hard, especially Baljit. Lucky for me it wasn't considered women's work. Where will I go tonight? Can I go back to the family I stayed with the other night?'

Mia put the last of the crisps in her mouth, scrunched up the bag and reached for the Pepsi.

'I'm sure we can arrange that with social services.'

Mia drank, giving something some thought.

'Okay, but whatever happens please tell them I don't want to go with an Asian family.'

'Any reason?' Bev asked, thinking of Ed's words.

'They'll ask me loads of questions about my family,' Mia said. 'And when they realise I'm from the family on the TV with the missing daughter they'll tell me how important it is to do what my parents say. They'll say I have to show my loyalty to them, not to Aisha and certainly not the police. I've heard it all before. From my own family, from people at the Gurdwara.'

Bev said she would make the arrangements and offered Mia more crisps.

'I know I'm setting a bad example, but one more bag won't hurt, as long as you don't make a habit of it.'

Mia nodded.

Wednesday 23rd April 2014

Sam was onto her third cigarette when Monica Teal strode past the hospital Pay and Display machine. As the on-call Chief Officer she had been notified about Ed.

'You okay Sam?' Monica said.

'I'm fine thanks, just a bit shaken. Ed's not great.'

'Why don't you go home? Get some rest. There's nothing you can do here.'

Sam shook her head, told her she still had staff working, that Bev was with the Bhandal's youngest daughter, Paul Adams was sorting the arrests, and the search team was at the house.

'In that case, go back to the office,' Monica told her. 'Freshen up. Get a cup of tea. Wash your hands. Change your trousers if you can. I'll take care of everything here. If there's any change in Ed you'll be the first to know. And it goes without saying Sam, any officer affected by this, and that includes you, Welfare are ready.'

The Welfare Department and Police Federation did a great job in looking after traumatised officers. Few talked about using counselling services - the *I-can-cope* syndrome keeping their struggles hidden behind a stubborn wall of bravado - but many did reach out for professional help.

Sam parked outside HQ, got out of the car and lit another cigarette; she seemed to have one permanently attached to her lips. She couldn't stop thinking about Ed, emotionally shattered and sickened that she couldn't stay at the hospital waiting for news.

She inhaled deeply, tears pooling on her top lip before falling to the floor.

Bev suddenly burst out of the building.

'Jesus Sam. How's Ed?'

'Surgery.' Sam's cigarette shook as her hand tried to find her mouth. 'He didn't look good Bev.'

When Sam started to sob Bev threw her arms around her.

'I know,' she said. 'I know.'

Sam trudged into her office and turned on the computer. The room was freezing and emanated the only light on that wing of the building. She had sent Bev home after getting her update on Mia, satisfied she was safely settled with an older couple on the edge of town. She thought she could answer a few emails while she waited to hear from Ian Robinson and the search team's progress at the Bhandals.

But all she could think about was Ed.

She rang the hospital at 1am and was told he was still in surgery.

It was gone 2am when the search team requested her attendance at the uncle's house.

Later, Sam would struggle to remember the journey there. The rest would never leave her.

She was standing inside a tent in Gurmej's back garden, suited up, hands in pockets, under bright white lights powered by a generator. Ian Robinson had already apologised to the neighbours. The press had started arriving soon after, a story born and gathering wings. They would be there for the duration.

Cold and starved of sleep, Sam looked into a newly dug hole in the patio.

She stared at the writing. The name was clearly visible, printed on the paper inside the leather label. *Mia Bhandal.*

'Open it,' Sam said.

One of the SOCO's unfastened the suitcase's brass catches but it remained shut, the two bungee ropes and their end fastenings holding firm. Once they were simultaneously released the suitcase flew open, under pressure like a cork shooting from a champagne bottle.

The arms and legs were bent at unnatural angles beneath the torso; long black hair was trapped in the sides of the case. The eyes were open but held no light.

Aisha's unmarked grave was below her uncle's shed; Mia's suitcase was her coffin.

Sam wiped her eyes. She said a short prayer and then telephoned the control room to request a Forensic Pathologist.

Jim Melia's counterpart attended.

CHAPTER FIFTY-FOUR

SAM ARRANGED for a transit van to come into the alleyway. Screens were placed at either end to block out the telephoto lenses. Aisha was placed in the back of the van.

Under Sam's instructions she was still in the suitcase. The van floor was covered in layers of new brown paper to avoid cross contamination with particles of debris on the floor. Aisha would be removed from the suitcase at the mortuary; the clinical environment ensuring not one scrap of forensic evidence was lost. Once she had supervised the removal and arranged for the post mortem later that morning Sam drove home and collapsed in the armchair. There was no point in going to bed.

Less than three hours after she walked through her door, the shower was again pounding her body.

With a towel wrapped around her she looked in the mirror. Did the sunken eyes in the gaunt face staring back really belong to her?

Nothing a couple of days at a spa won't sort, she told herself.

Who was she kidding? She needed to get away properly. No phones, no emails, no dead bodies, no human grief, just food and drink, preferably alcoholic.

She had called the hospital almost before her eyes were fully open.

Ed was in an induced coma. The official press statement would give his condition as 'critical but stable.'

No one needed to tell Sam he had lost a lot of blood.

Dressed but still only half awake, she grabbed a couple of chocolate biscuits out of the fridge and snatched her car keys.

Her head was spinning again, her forehead clammy. She had a job to do, but she couldn't think beyond Ed.

Induced coma. No guarantees he would come through.

Come on Sam, she said it out loud. What would Ed say? Sort this mess out.

Who killed Aisha? Who killed Jack and Glen? How was she going to prove it?

Those thoughts consumed her until she reached HQ. The sight of the black Porsche was her snapping point.

Sam felt like the water-skier no longer able to grip the towrope, tumbling and skimming across the surface before eventually going under. Snatching up breaths and consumed by raw anger, she leapt out of her car and quick-marched towards Jill Carver who was striding towards her.

'My clients will be making complaints of assault,' Carver was saying even as she moved closer, her index finger wagging. 'Their treatment has been appalling and...'

Sam walked into the wagging finger: the fight in her snarling face, eyes wide-open, matched the venom of her words.

'Before you go any further, Ed Whelan's in a coma, stabbed by one of your clients last night and Aisha's body has been discovered in a family suitcase under her uncle's shed. I suggest you consider your words and your next course of action very carefully.'

Sam glanced around and saw no one. She bent down and put her mouth to Carver's ear, lips almost touching the Pandora pearl and silver earring that was firing off chards of watery sunlight.

'Now fuck off, I've got work to do.'

Friday 25th April 2014

Sam turned off the ignition, lifted the button that applied the handbrake and stepped onto the car park. The bonnet shimmered in the sun.

It was just after 10.30am; less than fifty-seven hours since she'd been asked to go the uncle's garden.

She'd been told to keep away. Ed's family didn't want to speak with anybody from the Murder Team. All family liaison had to be done via Monica Teal.

Sam strode towards the entrance.

As far as she was concerned some instructions were there to be ignored. This was one of them.

What did her father used to say? 'Rules are there for the obedience of fools and the guidance of wise men.'

Exactly.

Ed was a colleague, a friend, and whatever Sue Whelan thought of her, she was going to see him. Sleep deprivation always made her belligerent.

He was in a private room, laid on his back, eyes sunken and shut. She smiled at him; she'd never seen him with stubble.

There were tubes everywhere, the bleeping and hissing

machines and monitors doing the work some of Ed's organs used to do.

Sam sat in the brown leather armchair next to the bed. A portable TV was plugged into a DVD player on the small table; her knowledge of football wasn't great but the commentary and the tinny sound of the crowd told her someone had left Ed with Alan Shearer's greatest hits. Sam smiled. Ed would like that. She wished she'd thought of doing that for him.

Sam had no idea if he could hear her, but talking made it seem less real, less threatening, less final.

'I know, I know, you're right,' she said, taking hold of his hand. 'I do look like shit but I didn't get to bed the night you were attacked and I still haven't caught up on my sleep. Me and Bev are supposed to be going to a spa this weekend and while we're away we're going to sort out a holiday somewhere warm.'

She stroked the back of his hand.

'They've all been to court this morning. Mother, father, uncle and son all coughed their roles in Aisha's murder.'

She dipped a tiny sponge on a stick into a plastic jug of water and gently rubbed it across Ed's lips.

'Mother was the last, evil bitch. Only coughed it after Carver advised her all the others had coughed.'

Sam poured herself a glass of water and sipped. It was hospital warm.

'Carver represented them all,' she said. 'Bhandal, Baljit and Gurmej coughed killing Sukhi.'

She let her fingers trace a gentle circuit around Ed's, dropping instinctively into the rhythm of the machines around him.

'You were right of course,' Sam said. 'No remorse. Honour was more important than any white man's law. Izzat before Gora's law.'

She leaned forwards, put her ear next to his mouth and imagined he was speaking.

'What did you say? You're always right? If you insist, sweetheart.'

She kissed his forehead.

'Sue was pissed off when she saw me the other night,' she began speaking again. 'Bev hit the nail on the head. She thinks Sue's pissed off because another woman got to stab you before she did.'

Sam imagined Ed laughing. He'd have liked that line.

'We got Aisha and Sukhi ID'd by their dental records and got hair samples from their brushes,' she told him. 'We'll get a DNA comparison through next week.'

She began stroking his fingers again.

'Baljit drove the car to Plymouth. He also coughed the murders of Jack and Glen. His motive...'

Sam heard a commotion nearby, voices raised and doors banging.

'...You've guessed it. The photos. And the good news, if there's any to come out of all this, is that our favourite editor has been suspended pending his court case and reading between the lines, he'll then be sacked.'

She dipped a new sponge into the water and let the droplets fall onto Ed's lips.

'Anyway, the temporary editor is under strict instructions to write a powerful editorial all about the dangers of students and heavy drinking, so that should put the serial killer theory to bed.'

Sam stood, walked to the window, and watched noiseless waves rolling towards high tide.

'No bail applications,' she said to the distant water. 'Even Carver knew she'd never get round the risk of them all running. The mother's been charged with your attempted murder.'

She shook her head, disbelief etched on her face.

'All of this because of some skewed view of honour. '

She sat back down, took hold of his hand.

'Anyway, I best be off. I'm not even supposed to be here. Long story. I'll tell you later.'

Sam pushed herself out of the chair and kissed his forehead again.

'I'll see you tomorrow if I can.'

Her eyes glassed over.

'The Spa will have to wait. I can get plenty of carrot juice down my neck and cucumbers on my eyes at home for a loss less cash.'

Sam was reaching for Ed's hand again when the door burst open and Sue stormed in.

Two flustered nurses were behind her, apologies written all over their faces.

'Out!' Sue shouted. 'Get out! We don't need you here. You're not welcome.'

She held the door open and pointed with an outstretched arm and rigid finger.

'Go on, get out!' Her voice was a taunting sneer. 'Go and find someone single you shameless whore.'

Sam dropped her head, stared at the floor and walked into the corridor.

Outside she let the tears come and when they had gone, she stared at the rolling sea and the hypnotic movement of the breaking waves.

Why is it that something that once gave me so much joy, seems to do nothing now but cause so much pain?

The tide edged up the beach, cold and remorseless and as likely to turn early as a world without murder.

ACKNOWLEDGMENTS

As ever I am indebted to the team of people around me.

Thanks go to Cheshire Cat Books Head of Publishing Paul Jones and my editor Garry Willey. Without you guys, as always, this book would not be what it is.

As ever, my photographer son Ben and designer Laura Swaddle have come up with a great cover.

And thanks to you, the reader. A book that is not read is just words on a page.

In 2007 I set up the first dedicated helpline for victims of Honour Based Violence and Forced Marriage. In its first month that line took over 100 calls from across the country.

I had tremendous help and support with the set-up from all spectrums of the Asian community, the vast majority of whom are peaceful, law-abiding people who want no part of this practice.

Public awareness of Honour Based Violence and Forced Marriage is much greater now but tragically they haven't gone away; so-called honour killings are still reported in the press. I whole-heartedly agree that there is no honour in murder, but those who worry about the label miss the point: it is the 'honour code' that drives the behaviour.

The law has changed since I retired and I am pleased to see that forcing someone to marry is now a criminal offence.

I was privileged to meet survivors of forced marriages; young people who ran away from their families to live the life they wanted even though that meant leaving everything behind. I shared platforms with some of them at conferences and their stories never failed to bring a lump to my throat. Their bravery is a source of inspiration to us all.

There are many organisations out there offering help and support and I would actively encourage anyone who feels the need to contact them. Please remember, you are not alone.

32553401R00251

Printed in Poland
by Amazon Fulfillment
Poland Sp. z o.o., Wrocław